What readers are saying about Love Heals:

'A superb ending' - Robert Nisbet, *Western Mail*

'An insight into human relationships' - Suzanne Oakley, *Llanelli Star*

'Gill's characters feel like real people - complex, thoughtful, and with believable histories and motivations… she unwinds her tales with the deftness of a born storyteller. I look forward to more of her offerings.' Leslie M Ficcaglio, *visual artist*

'I read 'No Bed of Roses' in one go without being able to put the book down. Written with brilliant observations into the way people feel and think. A book to relate to, a story we all carry with us.' Fiona McClean, *From Under the Bed*

From the author of The Troubadours Quartet
Winner of the Global Ebooks Award for Best Historical Fiction

'Believable, page-turning and memorable.' Lela Michael, *S.P.Review*

'Historical Fiction at its best.' Karen Charlton, *the Detective Lavender Mysteries*

'Wonderful! If you love historical romance and adventure, you must pick up this series!' Autumn Birt, *The Rise of The Fifth Order*

'A stunning masterpiece of tangled alliances, conflicting loyalties and tested love.' Kristin Gleeson, *the Celtic Knot Series*

'As soon as I finished this novel, I longed for the next in the series and can't wait to read more from this extremely talented author.' Deb McEwan, *Beyond Death*

'Jean Gill is the master of historical intrigue.' C.M.T. Stibbe, *Chasing Pharoahs*

'One of the best historical novels I've read in a long time.' Paul Trembling, *Dragonslayer*

'Fascinating history - the plot was terrific.' Brian Wilkerson, *Trickster Eric Novels blogger*

'A walk through time! That is what it was like to read this fine novel. It drew me into the pages and would not let go of me until done! Bravo for a wonderful read!' Arwin Blue, *By Quill Ink and Parchment Historical Fiction blogger*

More than One Kind

Love Heals Book 2

Jean Gill

ISBN 9791096459001

Cover design and artwork by Jessica Bell
using images from Adobestock.com

Jean Gill's previous publications
Novels
Someone to Look Up To *(The 13th Sign)* 2016
A dog's search for love and understanding
The Troubadours Quartet
Book 3 Plaint for Provence *(The 13th Sign)* 2015
Book 2 Bladesong *(The 13th Sign)* 2012
Book 1 Song at Dawn *(The 13th Sign)* 2011
Love Heals
Book 2 More than One Kind *(The 13th Sign)* 2016
(first printed as San Fairy Anne *(lulu)* 2010
Book 1 No Bed of Roses *(The 13th Sign)* 2016
(first printed as Snake on Saturdays *(Gomer)* 2001

Jamie and Ryan Books (middle grade)
Book 2 Crystal Balls *(lulu)* 2010
Book 1 On the Other Hand *(Dinas)* 2005

Non-fiction/Memoir/Travel
How Blue is my Valley (*The 13th Sign)* 2011
A Small Cheese in Provence *(The 13th Sign)* 2009
Faithful through Hard Times *(lulu)* 2008
4.5 Years - war memoir by David Taylor *(lulu)* 2008

Short Stories and Poetry
One Sixth of a Gill *(The 13th Sign)* 2014
From Bed-time On *(National Poetry Foundation)* 1996
With Double Blade *(National Poetry Foundation)* 1988

Translation (from French)
The Last Love of Edith Piaf - Christie Laume *(Archipel)* 2014
A Pup in Your Life - Michel Hasbrouck 2008
Gentle Dog Training - Michel Hasbrouck *(Souvenir Press)* 2007

for Dave, who doesn't like (other) lady writers

Acknowledgements

Lyrics by Francis Cabrel on pp18 and p21 courtesy of Sony Music, France, translated by Jean Gill

Quotation from 'Shema' by Primo Levi on p187, courtesy of Faber and Faber

'Thannenkirch' first published in Envoi

Thanks to my special vet for his professional input; any errors are mine not his.

A big thank you to Sian for introducing me to another of the great loves of my life, and to the usual one for taking me there.

Thannenkirch (Alsace)

Meet me at the crossroads of
the black cherry tree in the pines.
Walk by the way-marked path
that winds from blossom to dark firs.
Look back before the bend;
the church tower points Germanic
to the village roofs of slate,
still shining from late snow.

Two storks migrating northwards
circle, searching out a twiggy crown.
Diminished log-piles, stacked
methodically by homesteads
feed the fires I'll hold you by.
Of mountain water turned to wine
in long-stemmed flutes, green-rimmed,
hand-etched with graven flowers,
we'll sip the future dry.

Chapter 1

If you thought you might die tomorrow, who would share your today? The question, and its answer, beat in Vernon's blood as he shouldered the wireless pack. He zigzagged along forest paths in his automatic safety precaution to avoid being tracked. He flicked wet hair out of his eyes, nostalgic for the rain of his Welsh home instead of this lethal game of hide and seek in the high Vosges.

Sometimes, he couldn't even find his Alsacien comrades, and voices through the trees would whisper mud and trench rats, ghosts from the last war. He'd stumble into a clearing and despite the pre-arranged signal, there would always be a heart-stop when he'd wonder if these were the enemy, these French-German allies of German-French no-man's land, whose very language was border territory, neither one thing nor the other. Alsace had been tossed from one country to the other for centuries and at what cost!

Some days, Vernon too doubted his own nationality or wondered what exactly he was fighting for, or against, but he had been dropped - quite literally - here in Alsace, and orders were orders. From the moment he untangled himself from his parachute, he was in enemy territory, reliant on hard-eyed men who risked their families' lives, not just their own, to reclaim their mountains.

Vernon worried about the risks more each week, longing for the visits of Elsë, his sixteen-year-old comrade, and nervous on her behalf. Today, he met her by the old stone of the Pagan wall, on the long ridge known as the Taenchel, high enough to give them a vantage point and awkward enough as a climb to ensure privacy. Elsë contributed to the quiet disappearance of bread, saucissons and beer, and its reappearance, through a chain of equally quiet glances, among the men of the mountains who resisted the occupation.

By her very existence, Elsë sustained a man's sense of what he was fighting for, but it was more than that for Vernon. She seemed the very spirit of the forest in the way she silently appeared, startling even the birds, with that sudden scent of lily-of-the-valley, which announced her presence. She showed him where the ancient stones made natural hideouts, and where the tree line stopped and the snow fell first, at a thousand metres up the mountains.

Today, she was there before him, waiting, as still and patient as the forest itself. Drizzle spotted her face and dress through the canopy of the trees and he kissed the freezing raindrops from her cheeks, her skin warm underneath the tingle of pure water on his tongue.

'We go tomorrow.'

'I know. I heard.' They both avoided names and knew the risks they took. She asked him once if he knew what happened at Le Struthof, some kind of prison camp the Germans had established in the mountains further north. He didn't, but he'd heard the rumours too, crazy rumours. Perhaps it was better not to know.

He held her away from him, cupped her face between his hands, and held her gaze until she flushed and looked away.

'Let's make today special,' she whispered.

He knew what she meant. His blood insisted on a young man's dues to life itself. He said gently, 'No.'

Because he'd said no, she insisted and, because he loved her, he took the gift she offered. He kissed her closed eyes and held her hand against his heart, then lost his sense of self in his body's flow.

In his returning awareness of small sounds, rustling leaves and water on stone, he watched her eyes open like butterfly wings flashing blue on the forest floor. She sat up, shook the sparkling raindrops from her hair and held his gaze.

'I'll come back and we'll be married,' he promised, knowing the risk of death but believing in his own immunity.

She smiled, trusting, and wiped the spots of blood from her thigh with some wet grass.

The next day, 23rd November 1944, Vernon 'the Hand', was among the French troops mobilised by General Leclerc to try and retake Strasbourg. The bilingual Alsacien/English nickname had been earned by the young British wireless operator, or 'pianiste', for putting isolated resistance groups, such as those known as 'the Alliance', in touch with each other and with their military leaders.

This time, he was part of a concerted military operation, which drew his comrades out of the woods and into the army ranks, to win Strasbourg and advance across the vine plains of Alsace as far as Colmar. There, on 1st January 1945, the Germans regrouped and launched such a strong counter-attack that the Allied Commander, Eisenhower, ordered that Strasbourg and the Vosges be abandoned. General de Gaulle argued against this decision and was granted the concession that the 1st French Battalion could defend Strasbourg.

The orders from de Gaulle were transmitted by a young Welsh wireless operator, now attached to the 1st French, and it was 'the Hand' who made the vital contacts from his mountain hideout. Against all odds, Strasbourg held and was saved while Alsace once more counted the cost.

'You're old and cold,' he flung at her.

Anne noticed that the Agenda for the departmental meeting was on the Staffroom and it was crooked, pinned carelessly - shoddy work, like everything else Marianne did.

'What do you think you are?' Anton still hurled words at her, 'some kind of ice-maiden? Only ice-maiden are twenty-three not forty-three, blonde not grey and when the ice melts they get out into the world open-mouthed and open-legged not -'

'Not here,' she spoke over him. 'This is not the place.'

'Your choice,' he challenged, 'You chose to end it here.' The

Staffroom door opened, some papers fell on the floor as the incomer tried to balance books and nudge the door closed. Neither Anne nor Anton moved to help their colleague as he gathered his documents, talking to himself in the sudden silence. 'Now where did I put that... oh yes...' he muttered as he grabbed something out of a locker and jammed his work-pile into it. He nodded a token bonjour to his motionless colleagues and left.

'You're right,' Anton said, 'Let's go somewhere else.' He didn't have to ask when she was teaching; they had known each others' timetables for three years.

'I'll drive.' Three years going nowhere. Had it ever been going somewhere? Perhaps, she acknowledged, they had both enjoyed the debates about language and the education system. Perhaps she had even enjoyed the skin against skin contact... perhaps, sometimes.

She glanced at the tic throbbing below a hairline just starting to thin. She didn't have to look to visualise the 'grande marque', designer label jacket, trousers, pristine shirt and co-ordinating tie, all classic and understated. No shabby schoolteacher clothes for Anton. Once, she had thought him attractive, thought them so compatible, thought his neatness of mind and body, a virtue.

She had been here before and she had rules; no answering back if you were the one to call quits. No name-calling, no grudge-counting and most of all, no wavering, nothing to let them think you might change your mind. Once, worn down by pleading, she'd made the mistake of trying again. It only prolonged the death throes. Not that it was always Anne who said when. On balance, she thought that it was easier being on the receiving end - she could at least guarantee that her own behaviour would be civilised and afterwards - she admitted it - she had felt relieved. She sighed and followed Anton to a quiet corner of the Winstüb, the local bier-keller where they had known better days. Of course he would jerk a string or two, just in case, but at least he seemed calmer now.

'I suppose I saw this coming,' he surprised her by saying, 'but it is a waste... we have so much in common. Neither of us is getting younger, you're well past having children and I don't want any...'

'You have no idea what I want,' she couldn't help interrupting him, knowing that she should nod, glaze over and endure.

He focused on her, as if really looking at her for once. 'Don't be ridiculous - you're far too old.'

She could feel the flush. A hot flush? That would be good timing. 'I'm talking about feelings.'

He patted the hand she had left lying on the table 'I understand," he soothed. 'Let's leave it there for a while. Perhaps after a few months... we can talk again. Perhaps start again with a concert in Strasbourg?' He gave the smile she had once considered charming, and the invitation, like the bier-keller, was supposed to be a reminder of warmer moments between them.

'I don't think so.' Anne rescued her hand and stood up, 'I won't change my mind.'

'We'll wait and see,' he smiled again, showing perfectly even white teeth. She steeled herself for the kiss goodbye that she felt was owed but she couldn't do it. What was the point anyway, when he steadfastly assumed that this was a minor hiccup in their to-be-continued apology for a relationship. She drove carefully back to school in awkward silence, desperate for home and a long, long shower.

Anton had at least the courtesy - or smugness? - to leave her alone in the Staffroom where she passed a restless hour before her next class, starting to mark and losing concentration. So, this time, she was just dregs, so desperate herself that she should be grateful for this last chance being offered her by this man who knew nothing, nothing about her private longings and regrets.

Her stomach heaved with anger but when she imagined lashing out, hitting him or even shouting, all she could see were her colleagues' faces, pitying, disapproving, making it more difficult to go about a day's work. The anger converted to bile, lying sour and poisonous. The weeks to the end of term loomed long... passing Anton in corridors, avoiding and evading, smiling back - and then, after a summer off, another year of the same.

No, that Agenda was really too much. She stamped across the empty Staffroom and re-pinned the offending document in neat alignment with its neighbours and, as she did so, a notice caught her eye and she read it, disbelieving. Strange, the way she had grown used to ignoring most of the notices on the board, whether the old 'Fire Regulations' or this new one, labelled 'Fate' not only in what it offered but where. What if?

She almost took the advert from the board, thought no, Anne Grüber does not make rash spur-of-the-moment life-changing decisions. She turned her back and felt the notices smiling behind her back, a smug white-toothed smile that leered, 'Too old'. She turned again, unpinned the advert, photocopied it, then neatly pinned it up again before gathering her thoughts on 'school vocabulary' for an English lesson with thirty twelve year-olds.

Elsë read her daughter's face when Anne arrived home from school but she asked her anyway, 'Anton?'

'I've finished it.'

'Then that was the right thing to do.'

'And if he had finished it?'

Elsë didn't hesitate. 'Then he would be a stupid man who doesn't appreciate a beautiful, talented woman who takes the whole world on her shoulders every day and teaches it English.'

'Maman, I'm forty not fourteen to believe such rubbish,' was the reproach but Anne smiled. 'And you forget, I teach German too.'

'But that it is simple.' Elsë dismissed the German language with a wave. '*I* can speak German, there's nothing to it. But English...' she shook her head. 'It's impossible.'

Anne laughed, 'I keep telling you, you could learn.'

Elsë was emphatic, 'No, never. Not even if... Vernon... had come back, I would never have learnt his English.' She could not follow that thought through, into the life that hadn't been. 'But never mind that, what about you? How do you feel?'

'How did you feel, with Vernon?'

Anne had earned the right to ask, this daughter of hers who had so much to give, and Elsë tried to answer. 'The sweetness of the moment, a belief in forever, young, so young...'

'You still think of him?'

This was old, painful ground but Elsë was patient. 'Yes.'

'And with Papa?'

'You know the answer to that... you were there... you know there was nothing missing with your father.'

Anne's mouth twisted. 'You find it twice and I find nothing with anyone.'

'I paid for that first time,' Elsë said softly,' and I think you are better off without this Anton if that's how he makes you feel, this 'nothing'. There are many ways of being yourself...'

'... and none of them include Anton. I agree.' Anne brought a sheet of paper out of her bag and passed the advert across to her mother.

Elsë read it twice, tried to get past the word 'Llanelli' in her thoughts. 'You want to go?'

'It's for a year.' Elsë waited, watching her daughter's face, the new shadows under her eyes. 'I don't know. It would mean so much new, so much work... but I would bring my English up to date, learn from different teaching techniques. It would... stop me getting old and stale.'

'Old? You?' Elsë queried. 'Don't be ridiculous - I am old.'

'Ridiculous seems to be my word of the day.' Anne's mouth twisted then she continued, answering the real, unspoken question. 'It is too much of a coincidence, it being your Llanelli,' she corrected herself, 'Vernon's Llanelli. If I go, I will try to find out what you want to know.'

'But do you want to know?'

'I'm not sure,' she admitted, 'but I'll do it anyway. We've talked about it often enough - this,' she pointed at the advert, 'makes it practical.'

Elsë struggled to find the words. 'My heart goes with you.'

'I might find nothing,' Anne warned.

'My heart comes back with you, regardless...' and Elsë held her daughter long enough to need no more words.

Neil Phillips drove along the region of the Rhine Valley recovered by the French army over fifty years ago, retaken by the Germans and finally declared French once again. In accepting the challenge of a teacher exchange, Neil was most worried about the domestic arrangements.

In taking on Anne Grüber's teaching commitment, he also stepped into her life. He and Anne had met briefly in Llanelli in September, as the French School Year started later than the Welsh one. Like him, she was single, and like him, she lived with her mother. Although she spoke freely, in excellent English, of her home and her school, he gained an impression of deep reserve and there was no mention of her friends or her social life. Her affection for her mother was evident, lighting her eyes with warmth and worry over her own absence.

Neil's own reservations about leaving his own mother, also widowed, were allayed by his conversations with this capable middle-aged woman. He also knew how insulted his mother would have been at the very existence of those reservations. She was clear in her instructions to him to 'Live your life' but also enjoyed the closeness the two of them had shared since the death of Neil's father.

His reservations about leaving the pupils, for whom he felt responsible, also faded after meeting Anne. He felt he was growing stale as a teacher and it would be good for both him and his school to get fresh ideas, whatever culture clashes that might mean. He knew enough about the French education system to think that clashes there would be.

He could not imagine being without his car so he drove to his exchange home, following the autoroute east along the Rhine Valley, past Strasbourg. The vineyards coloured the plain with dusty end-of-summer greenery; on his right the folds and peaks of the Vosges shifted in the sunshine; on his left, in the distance, the misty slopes of the Black Forest bordered Germany.

When he left the valley to follow a small road meandering up into the mountains, he entered a different world. The wooden-beamed medieval architecture of the houses in picturesque Bergheim gave way to vineyards, then small orchards and roadside homesteads, nestling in the great forests which dominated the upper slopes. A hairpin bend brought Neil to Anne's home village of Thannenkirch.

The floral window boxes faced whichever direction was frontal for the mountain lodges perched at angles on steep streets branching off the main road. Neil parked by the church in the Central Square and checked directions while the chime of the hourly bells rang out, floating over the trees and down into the valley.

Neil adjusted to the change of scale; halfway up a mountain in the Vosges would have been the top of a mountain in South Wales. On the other hand, Neil was used to sloping streets and hill starts, and cheerfully took two right turns to find the wooden, three-story chalet-style house that was to be his home.

Madame Elsë Grüber put down the watering can, left the geraniums and lobelia, and from the moment she took his hand and smiled, she created space for them to get to know each other, in talk or in silence. Neil felt the same reserve in her as in her daughter and was relieved not to be grilled over aspects of his private life, which he preferred to keep very firmly private.

They gradually established a routine for meals, she having made it clear that she would happily cook for him and he being unused to any domestic chores; a routine for conversations, centring on his teaching, his weekend activities at the Stork Centre and on her knowledge of local customs and language; and a routine for occasional trips in which Neil drove Madame Grüber on a shopping trip down to Bergheim, or to visit a friend.

Although she said he could call her Elsë, somehow this lady in her seventies called for a degree of respect which kept her as Madame Grüber. Perhaps the Alsacien tendency to shake hands rather than kiss cheeks helped to create that sense of distance. The most personal conversations were her reminiscences of her daughter's childhood and her speculations on what Anne's life would be like in Neil's shoes.

She couldn't get enough detail of the Llanelli home her daughter was sharing. Neil waited for memories of further in the past but they never came. He was told the bare facts that Monsieur Grüber was a cooper and had died ten years earlier, of a heart attack, but stories of her youth never came. Neil knew enough about local tensions not to ask what his new acquaintances did in the war but many of them told him, however selective their stories might be; not Madame Grüber.

Most of these new acquaintances were formed over the months working at Hunawihr's Stork Sanctuary, where Neil spent his weekends. The far greater freedom of French teachers to come and go when they were not actually teaching meant that he rarely saw his colleagues, so it was his fellow-conservationists that formed his social life, such as it was.

On this particular February Sunday, Neil was concentrating fully on the large white bird struggling in his arms, and in particular on its thrashing red legs. In his early days at the Centre, he discovered the brutal impact of a stork-kick between the legs, much to the amusement of his co-workers.

That, delete expletive, bird challenged Neil's conservation theories to the limit, receiving clear instructions to go fly to Africa, electrocute himself and get shot, for all Neil cared. The two fatal options were the consequence of migration for so many storks in past decades that Alsace nearly lost its lucky mascot forever. In 1982, only two pairs returned in the spring. Now there were one hundred and fifty in the centre and an estimated two hundred nesting in the wild.

Given his love of the herons that lived on the estuary marshes near his Llanelli home, Neil could imagine nothing better than this opportunity to work at weekends with the stork experts at the Sanctuary. His weeks were committed to the school timetable of his Alsacien exchange partner and to his professional aim of improving his French and German.

It was very strange to be teaching English as a foreign language but Neil's first language, Welsh, gave him some insights into the quirkiness of English. It also helped him to understand some of the passionate disagreements which raged over the old language (according to some) or dialect (according to others) of Alsace. Attempts to encourage the younger generation to use their 'inheritance' was livened up by television adverts which showed the native storks speaking their native Alsacien.

Perhaps, Neil thought, the birds would be more co-operative if he could speak to them in their own language. He was careful in closing and locking the wire door behind him, with the prisoners safely at a distance. Some of the older ones were capable of plotting the great escape and he was wary if one stayed near the door as he was trying to leave.

One good shove with that solid body, or even those feet he shuddered to remember, and he'd be a road to be trampled by a penful of storks. That was not how he wanted to be remembered at the Sanctuary. He noted which birds he had tagged or checked, completed the record sheet and let himself out.

'What's new, Michel?' he greeted the Centre Manager, who was checking data on the Internet in the small wooden office.

'The Czechs are tracking their black storks. So far, so good. Keep your fingers crossed for September.'

Neil looked puzzled. 'September?'

Michel mimed a rifle shot. 'Hunting season, especially in the south. You didn't hear about Hynek? It was a big Czech research project. The African Odyssey Project tagged a black stork family and Hynek was one of the babies. You know how many we lose when they cross Africa - through trigger-happy natives.'

Michel shook his head. 'Hynek was everyone's favourite, people all round the world watched him every day on the Internet from his birth onwards. They followed his daily flights starting migration. Every detail of co-ordinates was plotted so the whole world knew when - and where - Hynek's data stopped. It was a massive scandal.' Michel's guttural accent slurred the French word 'scandal' harshly. 'He was shot down near Dondas, a village near Agen.'

Neil was starting to understand the Frenchman's reluctance to tell the story. 'Agen's the twin-town of Llanelli - south-west France, isn't it?'

'Yes,' Michel sighed heavily. 'There we were at the forefront of conservation, taking the high moral ground over these ignorant Africans, and where did Hynek die? In France, in total contravention of the laws protecting species. Pah! Southerners! There were protests at the French Embassy in Prague and Czech Radio is still crusading. If you listen to the Czechs, the Dutch and the Belgians,' he shook his head again as if this was the worst possible consequence, to be looked down on by the Belgians. 'The Belgians!' he repeated, 'If you listen to them, the most dangerous place for endangered species is France.'

Neil carefully said absolutely nothing.

Michel's grin was disarming. 'I know. You're right. There is a difficulty of attitude, especially in the south. But look what we have achieved.' His gesture embraced the whole Centre. 'Storks and otters in the wild again. We have so much to tell the world, including the Czechs, the Dutch and,' he gritted his teeth, 'the Belgians. We must use this,' he patted the computer with the flat of his hand,' and people like you will go back to your country with understanding.'

'Do you ever get black storks here?' The Centre bred Alsace's indigenous white storks.

'One has been know to drop in, en route, but they've not been known to stay or nest here. You'll find any sightings noted in the books.' He pointed casually at some shelves.

Neil had quickly realised that the voluminous records of the Centre were not so much filed as gathered and that it was a lot quicker to ask the relevant enthusiast for some information than to explore 'the system'. 'I have to get back now but I'll look through some time.' Michel returned to the Internet.

The Sanctuary was still closed to the public for the winter and the huge car park was empty bar Neil's own Megane and a couple of transit vans. The huge wood-stack with its 'Beware vipers' sign seemed hardly reduced by its regular use for fuel in the freezing Alsace winter. The white trails of wood-smoke hung over the houses of Hunawihr clustered behind the stork centre and winding up to the distinctive one-spire church which figured on the local wine labels.

At this time of year, the pruned stumps of vines hung on wires, marching in rows from field to vineyards to the horizon, beyond which lay Strasbourg. Above the small church and vineyards on the lower slopes, loomed the forested sides of the mountains. A footpath was clearly visible, passing strange rock formations which proved, on closer inspection, to be man-made and ruined. Higher again, a bald peak of the high Vosges defied all greenery, glinting white in the weak February sunshine.

Neil's route home followed the meandering lanes along the valley until he reached the road that would take him up through Bergheim, past the pink and purple houses, through the medieval archway and up into the mists of the lower mountains.

Madame Grüber was waiting for him with strong black herbal tea and some solid 'küchen', the marzipaned cake which was one of the Sunday treats that she laid on for her guest.

'Anne phoned,' she told him. 'It's raining.'

'That's not news,' he smiled.

'Your friend Helen has been taking her out and about. I think she liked shopping in Cardiff better than looking at birds through binoculars. It's not very French to talk about what a bird is called.' How like Helen to take a visitor to the Wildfowl and Wetland Centre, the place where she and Neil met and became friends. He had asked her to keep an eye on his mother and Helen was obviously looking after his exchange partner too.

'But you do know what all the birds are called, don't you.'

'Of course. We live together. But I don't chase them with little glasses,' she mimicked the bird watcher with binoculars, 'I use my eyes and my ears. You need to know what is good to eat and what is not; that's what your mother teaches you.'

Neil could not imagine his mother pointing out a lark and saying, 'You can eat that, casseroled in red wine,' or even picking field mushrooms. He envied Madame Grüber her apparently instinctive knowledge of her environment but he could only learn it through study. It was frustrating that the people who seemed to have some kind of natural lore by birthright were the very ones who were most difficult to convince of the importance of conservation. Like Madame Grüber, they found the Stork Centre slightly ridiculous, at best an academic hobby to be tolerated.

Neil's allies were people like Helen, another 'townie' who had discovered the countryside with the enthusiasm of the convert, or intellectuals like Michel for whom conservation was a scientific field. If everyone was a Madame Grüber and just left everything be, there would be no storks left in Alsace.

As if reading his mind, she said, 'Some people watch the river; some build dams. Who knows what is best for the river?'

'The otters are doing well.' The Centre also had a programme for breeding and re-introducing otters to the wild. 'They seem to like eels and frogs best, which should please the local fishermen.'

'I'm glad. You and your friends at the Centre work hard. I'm glad that you care so much about our storks and otters.' Neil felt absurdly pleased, as if he had been given both praise and permission. She did not ask him why he cared so much, a question that sometimes worried him with its implication of something lacking, or out of proportion in his life. He had been away from his closest friends for six months now.

'It was the storks that attracted me. But there is so much here to explore. '

Madame Grüber considered her words carefully. 'Easter is coming. It is very important here in Alsace, a time for remembering things that are... difficult. There is a place in the mountains further north. It was a concentration camp in the war and it has become a place of pilgrimage, especially at Easter. Le Struthof,' she nodded, 'you should go there at Easter if you want to understand a little more about Alsace.'

'I will. Can you tell me more about it?' He held his breath, sensing something important.

'Nearer the time.' Her tone was final and changed, lightening. 'There are so many places you should see, be a good tourist while you are here. Why don't you go to see the monkeys?'

'I get enough of those during the week - I'm a teacher!'

'No, you should go. People tell me that the monkeys make you smile. And it is also one of your wildlife sanctuaries, another endangered species - you would be in your element *and* having fun.'

'You think I should smile more?'

'Too young to be so serious. And so thin! Have some more küchen.'

Neil helped himself to more küchen, having one of those physiques which enabled him to eat and eat without ever putting on weight. This was just as well, given the solidity of the Alsacien diet, saucisson, sauerkraut and tarte flambé (a type of creamy, cheesy pizza), all laced with 'lardons' (cubes of bacon fat). In his experience, all mothers cooked, persuaded him to eat more and were reassured about his happiness when he complied.

In the bedroom which had become his - not Anne's but a slightly musty, rarely used guest room - he faced his laptop and typed up the lines of poetry he'd scribbled during the day. Cabrel's songs played in the background and again he thought of Helen, who loved the music as soon as he'd introduced it to her in the weekly French lessons that they shared. There was one particular song that reminded him of how she struck him when they first knew each other. She was so brittle, so cagey over her past. He'd often wondered why. He repeated the song and started playing with a translation of the first lines.

Winter
She said that she had walked too long
Unbalanced by the weight of words unsaid
Of too much pain.

That was exactly what Helen had been like, full of secrets, unable to carry on but never talking about it, whatever 'it' was. Although Helen told him, 'Friends are for keeps; lover are for fun' it was her lover, Dai, who reached her and brought about a change. Perhaps Neil would never know what had been wrong, or what had made it right, but he could see and enjoy the difference.

C'était l'hiver
Elle disait:'j'ai déjà trop marché,
Mon coeur est déjà trop lourd de secrets,
Trop lourd de peine.

Difficult to capture the lyric qualities of the original, the internal rhyme of 'disait' and 'marchait', then chiming again with 'secrets' and then the jarring third line, 'peine.' He looked back at his attempt in English. If he kept the mood, the bitter tail to the verse and set up his own rhymes, out of step and irregular as in the Cabrel but not necessarily in the same place, perhaps it would work. He set to work. Late that night he went online and mailed the final version to Helen.

Chapter 2

...*reminded me of how you used to be before your vet,*' read Helen, having just kissed her vet goodbye as he headed off to morning surgery. It was one of those days where there was a real danger of him changing his mind and reversing the day's progress from bed to clothes to breakfast and the door to work. 'Go,' she pushed him, 'save a puppy.'

'Bugger the puppies, 'he responded, encouraging her backwards towards the bedroom.

'I think that might be professional misconduct and anyway, you didn't used to say 'bugger'.'

'Good Yorkshire expression.'

She closed the door behind her before he could guide her through it. 'No, I've got work to do. So've you. I don't want those dragons who work with you glaring at me because I make you late.'

'Bugger the dragons,' he said, but he'd accepted the inevitable and dutifully brushed her cheek, then headed for his range rover. He whistled up the Jack Russell, Janie, to join him on his rounds. 'Bugger, bugger, bugger.' She smiled as she heard his attempt at a Yorkshire accent vanishing into the car. After six years in south Wales, she still retained the northern accent which entertained her Welsh-speaking lover.

Her routine mailbox check to start the day revealed Neil's email and a message from her business partner Amélie Voudoir. Helen read Neil's poem first, hearing Cabrel's music in her head as she read the familiar contents, translated.

Winter
She said that she had walked too long
Unbalanced by the weight of words unsaid
Of too much pain.
She said that she could not go on;
The future was just more
Of what had gone before
More pain again.

She said that living on was just too hard -
She'd lost all faith in sunshine
And the silent depths of churches,
Flinching at each smile of mine
Ice to her core, wintered too sore.

Never wind colder,
Never rain wilder
than the night - her twentieth -
When she stilled the fire
Behind her inward-looking sight
In one last blinding light.

Although my heart says she's above,
A sparkling sun,
A new church gleaming love.
At times still since that night I cry,
Ice at my core and winter once more.

She blinked away the memories of how right her friend was, and remembered how much of a friend he had been in the days when no one came close to her. How much had changed. She would mail him later; she had to settle to work. She opened the mail from France and translated in her head.

The birds were wonderful. You would have loved the window display but they have all sold. We have some new nubbled cottons in pastels, very fresh. I'm sending you samples to give you some ideas. There are some possibilities for

summer markets, good for tourists. We should talk.
Amélie

It seemed that Helen's idea of a series of knitwear designs, each with a different bird motif flowing into her signature to raise her couture status, had worked. Marketing her designs through the shop run by Amélie and her mother in St-Geniez d'Olt in the Lot Valley, was a gamble based on a chance encounter. So was her partnership with Dai and both - she quickly crossed her fingers - had paid off.

The Voudoirs had good business acumen and knowledge of their market; they also had a market which was expanded by thousands of tourists in holiday spending mode. Their own knitting however was competent and limited to mass-produced patterns, pedestrian in impact. Helen's experience of running her own shop in Llanelli had taught her respect for and understanding of the market place but what she did best was design and create the product itself.

Unable to sustain the shop, she transferred her design skills from paper to computer and was able to mail these to the Voudoirs at the flick of a switch. The partnership was so productive that Helen was even able to sub-contract piece-work once more to the two workers she had 'let go' - the employer's term for 'sacked' - the previous year. To pay off her debts, both literally to the bank, and emotionally, to her loyal ex-workers, was going to give her enormous satisfaction and she was nearly there. In fact she felt confident enough in her earnings that she would seriously consider a moneymaking scheme that Gwen, Dai's mother, had mentioned. She must find out more details.

She must also think about a visit to the Voudoirs and take that into account in her costs. 'Markets' sounded very attractive, both as a business proposition and as a visit. Would it be feasible for her to spend some time working a stall herself? Just the thought of France made her itch to go there, taking Dai with her. Their fortnight together in the Lot sealed their relationship at a stage she had nearly finished it; what a fool she had been!

Neil was so perceptive - 'Inward-looking' and 'ice to the core' indeed. She wondered how he was really getting on in Alsace.

Although they made frequent email contact, his messages were all of storks, otters, school and Alsace, and she was wary of asking him any personal questions where there was a chance they might be seen by others. He must miss his visits to London but she didn't dare ask about that through emails.

She wasn't sure how private his system was and even though she shared her life with Dai, even she preferred a little privacy in her conversations with her closest friends. Taking Anne under her wing was not totally generous. It gave Helen conversation in French, about France, and a chance to imagine the life Neil was living. Nostalgic for France, she reached for a Cabrel CD and played the songs in the background while she worked on a new design.

Mair Phillips brushed her hair, applied some deep pink lipstick and fastened all the buttons on her coat. Even though it was just a walk to the library, she ensured that she looked her best to go out into the world. Her son would have opened the door for her and held her arm along the path, and she missed the old-fashioned courtesies now that Neil was in France for a year.

Still, it was good to talk to Anne, who seemed genuinely curious about Llanelli and its past, as if Llanelli were a place of interest and as if the people here were any different to people anywhere else. Mair supposed that it was being French that made the ordinary seem interesting to Anne. They were supposed to be more excitable, weren't they. Although Mair couldn't say that Anne seemed very excitable as such. In fact, the idea of going to the Library had seemed the most exciting possibility Llanelli had yet offered Anne. Most odd.

Opening her front door on a view of Parc Howard's fencing and lawns, Mair automatically checked that the brass knocker was shiny and the step clean, then left the large semi-detached Edwardian house to walk with Anne into town. They took a short cut by the big church, isolated in the town centre by a moat of traffic, and entered the newly refurbished library.

'You can use the computers here now. The Internet too,' Mair said the word 'Internet' as if holding it with pincers in case it was contagious.

'That might be useful. I would like to spend some time in the reference library. There are things I am trying to find out. I know my way back now, thank you.'

'What are you trying to find out? Anything I can help with?'

There was a pause. 'No, thank you. It will all be very boring and I probably won't find what I'm looking for.'

Mair was still curious as to what exactly Anne was trying to find out but she didn't pry further. Instead, she checked that Anne had a key and headed for the section where she could find the most gruesome murder stories in the library. She had discovered the modern variant of the 'who dunnit', the female forensic pathologist investigating 'how dunnit' and getting threatened, chased and half-killed - but always surviving. It whiled away a grey evening when there was nothing on the television. She browsed amongst the lurid paperback covers, unaware of a man her own age glancing at her more often than at the books.

Anne looked at the flickering letters on the screen. Vernon Davies. Why did her mother still feel so much? Anne considered her own feelings for her first love. Who had been Anne's first love? She probably felt more for the fourteen-year-old who had held hands with her for an hour in the woods than for the man with whom she had disposed efficiently of her virginity. She shrugged. At least she'd tried. Meanwhile, there was the matter of Vernon Davies. How could her mother still feel all this and yet have loved Anne's father so? And Anne knew this deeply, could not contradict her mother's simple, absolute statement that her marriage was complete.

Her father's workshop was Anne's childhood playground and the smell of wood shavings would always evoke her father supervising the steaming of a barrel frame to bend the staves into a ring, ready for binding with metal hoops for a new barrel. His men made new barrels for the Edelzwicker wine, which was meant to be drunk young, but what Ernst loved was to recondition an old barrel to age and flavour the noble wines. More rarely, but best of all, he would carve his traditional figures on a decorative specimen, while she sat on discarded planks, whittling on her own little piece of wood with the bone-handled knife, which was a present from her father.

It was strange how, when someone died, your memories of them could skip the most recent images, particularly those of ill health, and return to much earlier times. It was as Papa, in his prime, that her father lived in Anne's heart, and she could still see him routinely coming home from work and holding her mother to him in brief acknowledgement of their physical relationship. Slight as the contact seemed to the watching child, if her mother was not immediately present, or was out, her father's first question was always, 'Where is your mother?' and he was not at home until he pressed her against him.

The image of her parents' quiet contact filled her with regrets, with self-pity. Biological clock, she supposed. You reached an age where you could no longer fool yourself that all the options were open. There was certainly no shortage of children in her life, she always reminded herself, knowing that she could walk through the streets of Colmar and be greeted in English by some man with his family who still thought of her as his teacher. There were however no children in her own family, no nieces or nephews to cuddle for a bedtime story on an auntie's visit.

She had always been fiercely glad of being an only child, knowing that a brother would have taken her place among the craftsmen in the workshop, diminished her father's aspirations for her education and career, and as for a sister - she couldn't even begin to imagine coping with the competition.

Her teenage disapproval of her mother matured into respect for her strength and patience. During her father's illness, mother and daughter shared the nursing and confidences in the heightened closeness which is often a consequence of waiting for death. Although they became more distant again as life gradually returned to an ordinary plane - more quickly for Anne, she suspected, than for her widowed mother - there was a deepened underlying mutual understanding.

In the weeks leading to her father's death, her mother only spoke of him, of their courtship and their special moments. After Ernst's death, her mother said nothing at all. Then, so gradually Anne could not have said there was a particular day when it happened, Elsë would again tell a story from her past, but now these included her history from the time before Ernst. It was as if, as time went by, Elsë felt she could share with Anne a chapter she had left closed during her marriage. At first, Anne felt an instinctive outrage at what seemed a betrayal of her father, even though she knew this reaction did not make sense. Later, listening, she ached for the sixteen-year-old in trouble, and it was her mother's face she saw as Anne finally settled to her search for Vernon Davies, his sister Ffion and all that the results might lead to. If she was successful, it would turn her own life upside down, as well as her mother's.

Chapter 3

The robin's tail feathers swirled into the letters 'en'. Helen sighed, keyed the eraser and redrew the tail feathers, wondering whether isolated purl stitches in brown would look more like scales than feathers. Perhaps if she used a textured brown yarn that would fluff round the stitches... What about letting the claw trail into 'Helen' so that her signature seemed almost part of the small branch on which the robin perched?

She experimented, using the freehand drawing tools on the computer to try different lines. She still used the computer package like electronic graph paper, usually drawing freehand with her new graphic tablet, although she knew that the technology could calculate and repeat patterns, draw from a bank of shapes, rescaling and copying according to her instructions. It frightened her just how much potential was in the machine, or rather in its software packages. Was all her craft for nothing?

No, indeed. She looked with satisfaction at the little robin, which captured all the cocky chirpiness she intended, and she imagined some small Sophie or François wearing the hooded jumper. The robin decorated a kangaroo pocket where small hands could hide a winter handkerchief or just keep warm.

She couldn't wait to show the Voudoirs her children's collection for the winter but was also nervous in case she had misjudged the tastes of a market apparently dominated by cartoon characters and pop stars. She flicked again through her design file, looking with particular approval at an acrobatic bluetit whose primary yellow and blue was echoed in splashes across the whole jumper. People would buy them; she just knew they would. If they bought the Lion King as well, she didn't mind at all. She returned to the robin.

'Where's the mouse?' Helen smiled at the sound of his voice and the feel of his hand and mouth on the back of her hair. He was home.

'You sneaked in quietly.'

'I wanted to check you're working. I've heard you can get anything you like 'virtually' these days.'

She just laughed. 'Well 'virtual' working feels very much like any other kind of working so I'm not sure I'll experiment beyond that, as yet. I'll keep my options open though, just in case...'

He held her close, his tone serious. 'I love coming home to you.'

She pointed at the screen. 'The mouse, as you call it, is in the claw and trailing onto the branch.' She had told him about Mousey Thompson, the Yorkshire carpenter who carved a mouse onto every piece of furniture he made. Half the pleasure of looking at a Thompson piece was finding the mouse, which could be running up a table leg or along a strut of a ladder back on a chair. 'What do you think?'

He studied the robin. 'Too small for a matchstick splint, you could bind each toe but the shock would probably kill the bird - budgies can die of shock from the treatment, not the injury itself, so wild birds have little chance, especially small ones.' He shook his head. 'No, with a deformed foot like that, I'm really sorry Miss Tanner but it would be best for your little robin if we sent him to the happy pecking grounds in the sky.' He mimed a garrotting action. 'Gave him the chop. Leave it with me.'

'You're impossible.'

'I'm a vet.' He smiled broadly. 'I'm a good vet.'

'Had a good day then?'

'The usual mix but it finished with puppies. The last client at surgery brought in a litter of six German Shepherd puppies for vaccinations. There's just something about puppies can cheer you up... and that wonderful smell of clean straw and dried faeces, it's just so earthy.' He was happily oblivious to her grimace as he headed to the kitchen. 'Makes you hungry. What's to eat?' He'd already opened the fridge and she knew better than to answer or to comment as he created a concoction of bread, cheese, chicken and peanut butter accompanied by a can of beer. Some bits of lettuce dropped out the sandwich as he headed back towards her and she was aware that the ring-pull had gone nowhere near the bin, but she still felt that the trail of culinary chaos he left behind was a small price to pay for all that Dai gave her. Perhaps the honeymoon period would end but not yet.

He was looking through the day's mail, some bank statements and a circular for Helen that she had left out for him to read.

'You going to go for it?' he asked, through a mouthful of sandwich.

'I think so but I don't know what I'm going to do yet. It's very different from anything I've ever done before, and I'm not Welsh - that will stand against me.'

He brushed her objections aside with a gesture that sprayed crumbs over the surrounding polished wood floor. 'You're marrying me. You'll be Welsh soon. And anyway, you're good - they'd be mad not to choose you.'

'Don't you think you could be just a bit biased?' Although it gave her a shiver of pleasure to hear his repeated enthusiasm for them marrying, she was still a little wary of the commitment. 'And you didn't tell me I'd have to join Cymdeithas yr Aith and fight for Welsh Independence if I married you. Are you trying to put me off or what?'

'I've been thinking.' He gave her one of those disarming grins. 'You can keep dual nationality - Welsh and Yorkshire. We'll show them all that a mixed marriage works.' He spoke a few words in Welsh to her, passionate and loving.

'Dafydd', she managed, unable to say more. She looked back at the circular, changing the subject to something safer. 'The bid's due in by 1st April so I've some time to get my ideas together.' The circular was an invitation to artists to bid for grants available to create works for the various display areas at the new National Botanical Gardens. Helen had read over the examples, which included a variety of media, and she was interested in the idea of wall hangings.

She only ever produced knitwear and the thought of using her design talents for pure decoration was both exciting and daunting. The huge scale required was in itself a challenge and it would be highly unusual to use knitted yarns for such a purpose. They would tend to stretch and lose shape, particularly over such a large area. She would need a backing of some kind, canvas perhaps. If, by some outside chance, she were lucky in her bid.

While she was musing, Dai settled into a comfy chair by the television. 'Quay Largo,' he called, which could be translated as 'Come and watch this Humphrey Bogart film with me.' Dai loved any film which starred one of his favourites and Bogart their donkey was grazing outside their cottage, as dour and stubborn as ever.

Dai was again watching television, this time with his father, when Helen first had the chance to follow up her mother-in-law's suggestion for making money. The two women were in the farmhouse kitchen, taking the opportunity for a private chat.

'They were talking about it in the Post Office,' Gwen began, 'and I'm sure you know how things are with us for money, so I thought if I could make a little it would be a help.'

Helen was well aware of the problems suffered by the farm during the BSE crisis and she knew that Dai had invested heavily in a venture to turn the farm around, which involved buying in a special breed of cows from France. 'I am looking to put some money into savings but I don't really understand this hearts scheme. Tell me again.'

'Well as I understand it, there's a club for women only, and you put your money in - up to £3,000 - and then when enough people join the club you get your winnings. There's women saying they had carrier bags of cash. One of them spent it all on a holiday.' Gwen looked wistful. 'Farmers like us don't have holidays.' With a firmer expression, she went on, 'It's for the farm I want it, to make sure Will can keep going. He's put his life into these cows and I thought he'd give up what with BSE and the Charolais not paying, after all that pride he took in them. Then his Dad died - I really thought that was the end of us. But Dai getting him to start again with these Salars - pretty cows they are - it's made him hope that Dai will take over one day, and it's given him something to live for. If I can get a bit of cash to pay the bills, we'll get by.'

'And it's just women you say.'

'It's this 'Women Empowering Women' that started it. You can trust other women, see.'

'So if you put £3,000 into this club, what would you get back?'

'That's the best part; £24,000.'

Helen looked sceptical. 'There must be a catch. If it was as easy as that, everyone would be doing it.'

'Everyone is doing it. You just listen round Llanelli. And you might have to wait a bit, until others join the club.'

Helen shook her head. 'No, I don't get it. Where does all the money come from?'

'From the club, from the new women joining. It's all simple really.'

'I don't know. It all sounds a bit too good to be true. What does Will think?' Although she'd been told to call him 'Dad', Helen found it too hard to call Dai's father a name that reminded her of her own parents.

'I'm not telling him,' replied Gwen. 'I do all the bills and I don't want him to know how much things are going up. He has enough to worry about. Besides, I can make a decision on my own, you know.'

'I'm sure,' Helen responded quickly. 'I certainly wasn't suggesting we couldn't think for ourselves.'

The 'we' soothed Gwen a little but not completely. 'So will you be talking to Dai about it?'

Helen's pale skin flushed. She was only too conscious that Dai earned far more than she could and that living with him gave her comforts she could never have afforded alone even when business was buoyant in her shop. She was well aware that working from home meant that premises and utilities were provided from Dai's income. Although she contributed and claimed a percentage back in tax relief on her income, the reality was that she was always cushioned by Dai's money. Dai's generosity just made it worse; he thought nothing of paying for a crazily expensive meal out, or an impulsive gift of perfume, when she could not afford to reciprocate. She felt beholden.

'No,' she said shortly, 'I won't be discussing my savings with Dai.'

Gwen picked up on the slight emphasis on 'my' and smiled. 'And I shan't be discussing my savings with Will.'

There was a shout from the sitting room. 'Woman, where's that cup of tea?'

'Speak of the devil,' Gwen acknowledged to Helen and then called back, 'with you in a minute.'

Helen watched Dai's mother following the familiar routines in the heart of the house. The kitchen looked exactly as it had done on Helen's first visit to meet Dai's parents. She was sitting at the scrubbed table, facing the traditional dresser displaying old crockery. What looked like the same pair of wellies stood on a newspaper by a range stove.

Even Gweneira, the fat black cat named 'Snow-white' in jest, was curled up on her favourite cushions, exactly as she had been - was it already over a year ago? She felt a familiar ache looking around Dai's childhood home that he took so much for granted. He had taught her the Welsh word 'hiraeth' and told her it was impossible to translate, that it was like 'soul' but with a sense of Welshness and family and feeling... She felt that the family kitchen was full of hiraeth and, for all her love for Dai, there was still something missing in her own life.

Gwen was still thinking about money. 'There's a special bus laid on to take women to a hearts meeting in Llanelli on Tuesday. Will you come with me?'

'Yes. I'm interested enough to find out more. Can anyone go?'

'I don't see why not - the more the better.'

'I was thinking a couple of friends might like to go, and maybe Neil's' Mum, and Anne, the French teacher who's staying with her - Neil's swap partner.'

Gwen pulled a face. 'Don't like the sound of 'swap partner.' Sounds like they've been throwing their keys in.'

Helen laughed. Gwen could still surprise her. 'You know what I mean. Anyway, I'll need an address to give them.' It might be of interest to Anne just to see the different people likely to be at the meeting. It would do Anne good to get about a bit and talk to people. She was spending far too much time on some kind of personal research, digging up old Llanelli history and trying to find out about registers of births, deaths and marriages. Some kind of history project Helen supposed. Helen was no help at all. She was the last person to know or want to know anything to do with people's past history. It had taken her long enough to come to terms with her own.

'Let's join the men, then. Would you take the biscuits.'

Helen opened the door to find the television switched off and the two men plunged in total silence.

'Surely you aren't that depressed over the tea being a bit slow coming?' she asked brightly but there was no lifting of the atmosphere. Helen sat down quietly and waited. This was nothing she had ever dealt with before.

Gwen passed the teas around, saying nothing, then sat down too, quietly waiting.

It was Dai who broke the silence. 'There's a case of foot and mouth. In Cumbria. On a pig farm.'

'Oh, Dai.' The words were wrung from Gwen. Helen was still bemused. She knew that foot and mouth was a contagious animal disease but that was all she knew. She understood that a farmer would feel for another farmer with problems but surely after all they'd been through with BSE, this was just something for the Cumbrian farmer to sort out with his vet.

'That's forty years we've been clear. I can't believe it's back.' Gwen clearly understood implications that Helen could only try and follow. 'Does anyone know how it happened?'

'On the news they said the pigs were given meat in their swill, restaurant left-overs, probably imported meat.' It was Dai who replied. His father still sat, silent. Dai's tone was bitter. 'Our meat's expensive because we follow the regulations and then some idiot imports cheap meat with foot and mouth.'

Gwen was still thinking. 'They'll be tracking contacts now.'

'Yes, but do you know how long since the foot and mouth was known to be on this pig- farm?' Dai's voice rose with anger and his mother shook her head at the rhetorical question. 'Two weeks at least. Two weeks! Somebody's cocked up in a big way this time.'

'Cumbria's a long way away. I know you're sorry for the farmer but surely the disease can't reach here,' Helen offered.

Will flared up. 'This is the first case of foot and mouth, only the first. For two weeks there've been pigs travelling the country, spreading the worst disease there is. Sorry for the farmer? I'd like to shoot the bastard.'

He rose and left the room, leaving Helen shaken and looking to Dai for explanation.

'Animals are sold on, all over. In two weeks those infected animals will have contact all over the UK, and the newly infected animals will be sold on, and so on. It could be anywhere. It could be carried by air, it could be carried by water, no-one seems to bloody know how it's passed on - black magic for all we know. There's going to be a load of animals killed in Cumbria and that's just the start.'

'Let's just hope they've got it in time,' Gwen put in quietly. 'We can ride it out. We might need to take precautions, with disinfectant and such, like in the sixties, but we'll probably be all right living where we do. Let's not write the headstone when the man's caught a cold.'

'I hope you're right.' Dai stood up, touched Helen's shoulder reassuringly. 'I'll see Dad and then we'll be going.'

He knew exactly where to look. Will was in the cowshed, giving a pretty brown heifer with doleful eyes an unexpected treat of linseed. Dai stroked the cow's broad nose.

'A lot of your money in here, boy.' Will's tone was gruff with the underlying tears.

Dai carried on stroking the cow, clearing his throat. 'Exactly what I'm thinking and there's no way I'm losing my investment.' There was a gulp in the silence and a throat cleared.

'What is the point?' Will's tone was one of total defeat. 'You pick yourself up and wham - down again.'

'We're not down again yet Dad, though we both know there's a hard time coming.'

'Again.'

'We'll get through.' Dai punched his father lightly on the back. 'And you stop feeding that damned cow or you'll be phoning the vet in the middle of the night.'

'Can't afford the sodding vet,' grumbled Will, both of them knowing full well that Dai did all the veterinary work for the farm without payment. 'Vets these days start the meter running if they pick up a bloody phone.'

'I'll ring you - no meter - from the practice tomorrow after I've found out a bit more of what's really going on.'

'Thanks. I'm sorry I snapped at Helen. It's not her fault. Nice girl she is.'

'She'll understand.'

Dai found a peppermint in his pocket and let the heifer nuzzle the treat off his palm. When he had gone to shows as a little boy with his father, Will taught him to lure a cow into following sweetly - for the peppermints.

'Typical woman - always wants more,' was his Dad's comment.

Dai turned back at the door. In the half-light across the yard, he could see his father, sitting on a hay bale, his shoulders drooping with despair, staring at his prized new starter herd of Salars as if he could keep them safe by watching them.

It was Thursday the 22nd February and the first case of foot and mouth had been announced. What Dai would always remember was his father, keeping vigil over his cows.

'I still don't believe it - Ceri Griffiths! After all these years.' Mair Phillips was staring in amazement at a man her own age, trying to recognize the sixteen-year-old she'd abandoned so she could date Neil's father. 'How on earth did you recognize me?'

When she was approached in the library by a strange man with thinning white hair and a curiously hopeful expression, who ventured 'Mair Thomas?', her first instinct was to report him to a librarian for pestering her. When she realized that this was the reincarnation of her first boyfriend, from the time they held hands at nine-years-old to the stormy teenage parting, she was lost for words, repeating, 'Well, Ceri Griffiths.'

It was such a shock that she needed to sit down and Ceri kept asking her if she was all right and whether she needed a glass of water. When she regained her composure, she accepted his invitation to join him for a cup of tea and took the arm he offered. She would have walked out of the library without checking out the books still clutched firmly in one hand, if the librarian had not called after her.

He answered her question, 'You haven't changed a bit.' He wasn't going to tell her that he had guessed that if she were still in Llanelli, she might be a library-goer and he asked the librarian, explaining that he was trying to track down an old school-friend.

Since his wife died he had been thinking more and more about the past and had wondered whatever had happened to his first love, curious to see her again. He was prepared for failure, worse still for news of her death, but nothing prepared him for this embarrassing adolescent thump of his heart and knots in his tongue. In truth, she had not changed, in any way that mattered.

'You certainly have,' Mair replied tartly. 'A bit of flattery would have been beyond the Ceri I knew.'

'So you do remember.' He didn't dare to ask her yet the question that mattered the most. He had never wanted to be 'just friends' with Mair Phillips.

'I remember when we were at school together. Do you remember Mrs Richards in juniors? That time I was talking and you said it was you, to take the blame. Vicious she was. They'd lock her up nowadays. My son's a teacher and it's more likely the children would hit him than the other way around. Although they're not children any more, are they, not like we were.'

Son. So she has a son, as well as the wedding ring.

'I heard you'd gone away, to university in England, and then to work there.'

So she was interested enough to ask after him.

'There were worse than Mrs Richards. Do you remember that woman who stood the little ones in cold water till they were blue, if they were naughty. Hard to believe now. Yes, I went away. There wasn't anything here for me any more.' He gave her a straight look.

'After you dumped me. I don't think I ever got over it.'

'Get off with you, you were only sixteen and that was years ago - no, decades ago. I bet,' she said shrewdly, 'you're married with ten children.'

He laughed, acknowledging a partial hit. 'I did marry but no children, not like you.'

'Did?'

'My wife died last year, cancer.'

She was serious immediately. 'I'm sorry. I wasn't meaning to be hurtful.'

'You didn't used to mind hurting me now and again as I remember, Tinkerbell,' he teased using the nickname for which started with a school Christmas production of 'Peter Pan', when he was backstage and she had a starring role.

The small café above a Llanelli bakery was starting to fill up with lunch-time customers and they lost track of time reminiscing, nursing empty tea-cups, until they started to become aware of frosty glances from both the staff and those in the queue.

Mair was flushed, her eyes sparkling and Ceri hoped it wasn't just from the oppressive warmth rising from the busy ovens in the shop below. He was reluctant to part from her but didn't know what to say to keep her and they both paused awkwardly at the door.

Mair pointed to the right, 'I go this way.'

'So do I,' he lied. Arm in arm, they reached the edge of the shopping precinct, halting at the zebra crossing which would take Mair on her route home but which was quite clearly not on Ceri's route anywhere. They both started to speak at once and then laughed.

'Ladies first,' Ceri offered gallantly.

'This is silly. We have so much to catch up on. Would you like to come to my house and have lunch with me. Unless of course you have to...?'

'No, no, I'd like that. In fact, I'd like that very much.' '*My*', he wondered, hoping.

'Well then, that's settled. It's not far, just by Parc Howard.' She took his arm again and he thought that anyone watching might have thought they had been together forever. His heart had not sung like this for so many many years, perhaps not really since he was sixteen.

When Anne returned from school to her host home, there was no sign of a visitor, and if Mair's eyes were brighter than usual, Anne was too pre-occupied with her own thoughts to notice. She excused herself early and in the privacy of her bedroom, she looked over the details she had accumulated.

It was easy enough to trace Vernon Davies' birth details and she even saw his name on the school roll of Llanelli Boys' Grammar School. It was also easy to find the birth registration of his sister, Ffion, but finding Ffion's marriage details had proved too difficult. The whole notion of tracking every 'Davies' over several years was too slow.

Anne gave up for the night and picked up a volume of Trollope from the bedside table. She had been assured by colleagues in France that this was a great English classic which would improve her language skills, but she was disappointed that few teachers in Neil's school had even heard of Trollope and no-one she had met read any. This business of foreign culture was very misleading. It might have cheered her up if she had known that Neil was getting exactly the same response when he mentioned the celebrated French poet Jules Laforgues, in Anne's collège.

Chapter 4

His room was as dark when Neil woke as when he'd fallen asleep, the heavy wooden shutters keeping out any daylight that might have alerted him as to the time, encouraging the Saturday morning luxury of a lie-in. Deep brown shadows and the smell of camphor suffocated him and he padded across the cold tiles to throw back the shutters and look out.

He had indeed slept in and the view down the mountain to the plain, where morning mists still hung in patches, was as bracing as icy water over his face. He missed the shimmering silver of the Loughor estuary, which would be welcoming its winter visitors of redshank, dunlin and lapwing in their hundreds.

He imagined his mother putting on her lipstick and her blue wool coat, tucking her shopping basket over her arm and walking into the town, missing his father with that quiet stoicism she had shown ever since his death. Neil's closeness to his mother was a solace to both of them and although she would never again know a husband's love, Neil thought that her life had been reshaped in companionship and the comfort of home. He hoped she was finding company in Anne to compensate for his own absence and that she was not too lonely. He looked again at the distant sparkle of river in the plain and shivered. Definitely a day for an outing.

The mists were lifting as Neil drove the lanes between the vineyards on the lower slopes and the villages of the 'Route du Vin' which huddled behind closed shutters and plumes of woodsmoke. Thick greyness gloomed from chimneys, as if all the dragons of Wales were breathing out their fury from cellars right along the

Rhine plain, then drifted to wisps in the vast skies.

Turning a corner, Neil noticed a wayside shrine to la Vierge, a Mary with brown hair and a broad Teutonic face, considering a little grimly the little posy of fresh flowers laid even in February. It was easy to see how people found her more approachable than the gruesome Calvary further along the road, a suffering Christ six feet high, his crown of thorns silhouetted against a field of bare, twisted vines tied to their wires.

Even in its religions, Alsace stood apart from both France and Germany, with a separate charter of unprecedented Christian tolerance that enabled churches to be used for both Protestant and Catholic services, at different times. Neil's chapel childhood left him uneasy before both the grandeur and the morbidity of the ways in which Alsace had worshipped its God for centuries. Even the smallest village had a church dripping with gold and an altarpiece the like of which could be seen nowhere in Wales where poverty perfectly matched the puritanical.

Musing uncomfortably, Neil braked only just in time as a man in a blue Renault cheerfully sped in from a small track on his right, carved him up and gave him the full treatment of horn, verbal abuse and universally recognized - though unofficial - French hand signals.

The Renault was out of sight before Neil even thought of a response and the half-hearted beep of his horn as he hit it in bemused frustration and swore softly, sounded pathetic even to him. In theory, the old law which gave priority to the right in any situation, had long been rescinded. In practice, there was always a chance of someone taking advantage of tradition and, even on a major road, the sudden appearance of a tractor entering from the right and assuming priority, was a hazard quite likely to win any ensuing legal dispute.

The homesickness which had been threatening all morning, suddenly engulfed Neil. He felt a terrible nostalgia for the courtesy of his home roads, the unofficial code of lights where you flashed to say 'Come on in,' where a left flash meant 'All clear, overtake me now,' left/right flash meant 'Thank you' and some thoughtful prediction earned you a flash, a smile and a wave from some grateful lorry driver. He truly, desperately missed the lorry drivers on the M4. Catching himself in this ridiculous line of thought, he grinned ruefully and shook his head. Definitely a man needing distraction.

He pulled into his destination. Following Madame Grüber's suggestion, he was visiting some monkeys. Barbary Macaques, or Maggots, to be precise, which lived in troops on 'Monkey Mountain' near Kintzheim, another Alsace nature reserve with conservation and research at its heart.

The reserve was not open to visitors on an off-peak Saturday but a phone call from Michel at the Stork Sanctuary arranged a rendez-vous with a 'Monkey Man' to let the 'English visitor' see work at the Reserve. Neil was still not making any inroads in convincing Michel that Wales was not part of England and that he was most definitely a Welsh-speaking Welshman, not English.

Michel just made huffing noises, shrugged, accused him of being as touchy as an Alsacien, said no-one in France would know where or what Wales was, and attempted to be reconciliatory by saying, 'What's in a name, huh?'. He then continued, with no compunction whatsoever, to introduce Neil as English, from England. Sometimes Neil made it an issue, sometimes he didn't. Life was too short.

The gate was open for him and Neil went through, then hesitated outside the ticket office. Perhaps this was not such a good idea. He did not feel very sociable and he could summon up little interest in a lot of monkeys.

'Monsieur Phillips?' Neil jumped at the voice behind him and turned to face the Monkey Man, who was holding out an elbow in greeting. Neil laid a hand on the proffered forearm, flushing a little at the odd intimacy of the contact with hardened muscle.

'Neil, call me Neil.'

'Luc,' responded the Monkey Man. He was a couple of inches shorter than Neil's lanky height, his dark brown hair very straight and shoulder length, in what Neil thought of as French intellectual cut, or of course 'Gibbon cut'. Good for mutual grooming. There was a sense of restrained power about Luc's physique, emphasized by a dark curl of chest-hair escaping above the crew neck of his jumper, as if he had difficulty staying completely inside his clothing.

'Michel told me all about you,' *Great*, thought Neil, 'so I'm sure you will ask me impossible questions about the international research. First I will give you a tour so you can meet the family. 'Luc's voice was unexpectedly cultured, precise and authoritative. Neil wondered how long it would take him to look at some monkeys, think up a few intelligent questions and politely beat a retreat.

'We have been looking after the macaques for over thirty years now. As with your storks, there is a danger of extinction, and we have tried to learn as much as possible to facilitate their re-introduction into their native habitat of Morocco.'

Luc threw Neil a sideways glance. 'After you meet some of the troop, I will show you the other buildings, the isolation cages, the animal hospital and the pet food production area.'

Without any change in tone, he continued, 'Inevitably macaques die and we butcher them on the spot to keep the meat as fresh as possible. Old ones have so little meat on them that it is hardly worth the effort but if young ones die they make very good pet mince.'

Neil's gave an involuntary grimace of disgust as he burst out, 'You're joking. I don't believe you French! All you think about is how to turn everything into food!'

Luc's calm tones replied, 'Yes, I am joking,' and he turned towards Neil so that he could catch his eye and smile.

When Luc smiled, you had to smile back. His wide, expressive mouth quivered and a devilish light sparkled in the black depths of his eyes. Neil could not use English - or Welsh - to describe such eyes, as neither language allowed for 'black eyes' as anything other than the consequence of accident or fight. Other languages, including French, celebrated the passion which could hide in such depths. 'I was told you were a serious young Englishman and I made it my aim to make you smile. I did not think I was quite getting your full attention and I like that, full attention.' Again Neil was held by the other man's intensity.

'I'm homesick and lonely,' Neil surprised himself by saying, only realizing that it was true as he spoke the words. He was not sure

Luc heard him as Luc was opening a gate through low fencing, past a public information board and into a copse of small trees where the chattering noises of the inhabitants could be heard before they were seen.

Luc was turning away as he spoke and Neil half-caught what he thought was, 'I too, I am homesick and lonely.' The moment passed in a bombardment of macaques, which invaded every inch of personal space that Neil allowed them. He couldn't help laughing as he was professionally pick-pocketed and had to rescue his car keys while a small macaque clung to his back and blinded him with its pink old-man's fingers pressed firmly over his eyes. When he'd peeled the fingers back he could see Luc similarly besieged, but, armed with food, he was organizing an apple here, a potato there and freeing himself. He sat on his haunches, looking down at the ground but facing what was clearly a large male.

He spoke softly, conscious of his simian audience. 'They don't usually like too close a contact with people but they're hungry and they don't have the visitors for entertainment. We tell people not to touch them - they are wild animals and they bite - but when the visitors are gone, sometimes I make a little cross-species contact. Purely for research you understand.

This is Beni. It doesn't do to challenge the alpha male, or indeed any of them, so I try to keep my body language conciliatory.' Again that flash of lightning laughter in his eyes as he glanced at Neil. 'Although you don't want to be too submissive. I wouldn't want this one mounting me by mistake in the silly season.' He reached out, every movement open and slow, and ran his fingers through Beni's body fur, combing through a tangle and mimicking the search for fleas.

After a couple of minutes, Beni reached out, chattered at the inadequacy of human hair but found Luc's head and returned the favour. Neil watched the deft hands sorting strands from crown to tip, scratching, picking a pine needle out of the gleaming brown mane. Beni moved closer, sniffed and sneezed, then backed off to take his share of the booty. The men were surrounded by chewing, broken only by an occasional squabble over whose apple was bigger and better.

'Always, you must establish and maintain your position. To be thrown out the troop is the end for a macaque. And there are vicious rivalries and jealousies. See Thea there?' Luc pointed to a medium size macaque sitting near Beni. 'She is pregnant, should give birth any day now, and we must keep an eye on her. She is not strong in herself and there are two females challenging her status - they might try to get her baby and her too if they can.'

'Get it?' queried Neil.

'Bullying mostly. Conditions here tend to decrease some of the nastier conflicts you can get in the wild. There have been recorded incidents of cannibalism and what we might call wars, between tribes. You get fond of them but they are always animals.'

'Should you be intervening? I mean, what about the research? Do you end up invalidating it?'

Luc shook his head. 'You're talking to the wrong guy. I was put on the planet to make things happen. For me, research is about recording what happens with me right in the middle of it. What about you? I mean taking away a stork's migratory instinct isn't exactly nature's way, is it.'

'No, I didn't mean I thought you were wrong." Words tripped over themselves in Neil's effort to explain. 'I make things happen, too.' It just sounded gauche, coming from him. 'Michel doesn't know me really. I'm not young at all.'

Luc's smile was mischievous. 'Not even so serious perhaps.'

'No, definitely not serious,' Neil said earnestly. He found himself facing a quizzical expression and self-realisation dawned. He laughed.

'There is only one thing for it,' Luc told him, standing and holding out a hand to help the taller man to his feet. Neil took the hand, bigger than his own, warm and firm. He waited. 'I must get to know you better and judge for myself.' Neil's hand was released and he walked beside Luc, expressing an interest in macaques enthusiastic enough to warm any Monkey Man's heart.

'So I was right and the monkeys did you good,' observed Madame

Grüber.

Neil glowed. 'The monkeys were wonderful.'

Madame Grüber just smiled. Still smiling, she answered the telephone and called back, 'Don't go, it's Anne and she'd like a word with you when I say goodbye.' Neil sat, half reading, half musing, aware of the soothing sound of mother-talk eddying, stilling, then rippling again in the background.

He tried to imagine Anne, her daily life as Neil. It was easy to conjure up his study, to remember swivelling idly on the leather chair, looking across his desk to the park or around the room at the shelves of books, some valuable first editions from trawling the myriad bookshops of Haye on Wye. That was something else he missed, the visits to what surely must be the best and most unlikely bibliophile magnet in Britain, no in Europe, if not the world. W

here else than in that little Welsh village would you find such a range of antique books or the crazy international scale of its annual literary festival? It was much harder to bring to mind the cramped office in school which he shared with two colleagues, his reward for taking on all the duties of a Head of Year. He felt removed by more than mileage from the daily social problems which came his way as a by-product of teaching.

It seemed to him that the French system expected teachers to walk in a classroom, teach - preferably teach well - and walk out. In theory, 'problems' were passed on to someone else, a non-teacher whose job it was to worry about absence, abuse or drugs. Anne would surely be finding a culture shock but at least she wouldn't have any of the Head of Year work. Neil smiled as he imagined her trying to cope with the Welsh social services.

'Neil,' Madame Grüber was calling.

'Fine,' he found himself saying as he told Anne of the latest meetings in the collège, where English had to fight for its status in this bilingual French/German area, particularly now the Education Minister had declared a Year of Languages in which languages other than English were to be promoted throughout France. With a name like 'Jack', perhaps he had accounts to settle with the English.

'You just make sure there is a job for me to come back to - I don't want to find they've cut down on English teachers while I'm away.'

'No fear - I'm indispensable. Of course I'm teaching German too...' Neil teased. 'And there are plans for someone to teach Welsh as part of a drive for minority languages and re-introduction of Alsacien, so clearly they're hoping to have someone next year who can teach - let me think now - English, German and Welsh. It could just be that I'll stay on here and eat your mother's wonderful Kugelhopf every weekend.'

'Don't,' moaned Anne. 'Kugelhopf.' There was a reverent sigh. 'Still, if I stayed here, I would have such resources to teach with. I am tired every minute but you have such games! If I can keep up the energy it is so much fun to teach.' She reflected. 'With a lot of the classes.'

'Ah.' Neil understood that thought only too well.

'Pff. We have naughty ones in France too,' Anne dismissed those not interested in learning as not worth her concern. 'But there is one I have a little worry about. I have followed our system and I have talked to the Head of Year but Darren,' she hesitated, 'is very good at tellings-off... and I don't think this is one for going in with boots on. Darren said you knew all about Alex and that unless I have trouble in the class, there is nothing more to be done.'

Alex. Neil knew only too well about Alex. One of many cases where his involvement of police and social workers seemed to have resulted in increasing absence and isolation of the child, although in theory there was 'family support' and as Alex was registered as 'at risk', Neil ought to be reassured that all the checks were in place.

The question was how much he should tell Anne who, after all, was only the French teacher for a year. So he applied the principle of 'need to know', telling only what he thought Anne needed to know. He had learnt early in his dealings with confidential details that cats could not be put back into bags once they were out, and he preferred to err on the side of caution. He was not to know how bitterly he would regret his reticence.

'There are very difficult home circumstances,' Neil began. *Difficult! Understatement of the year.* 'So I would try and make it easy for Alex to catch up and join in as much as possible - I'm sure there are bad absences but I wouldn't shout over that. It's usually whole days not odd lessons, so the registers will show that to the Form Teacher as well as Darren. I don't know how much French Alex will ever get but perhaps there are more important things... If you pass any details on to Darren - bullying, illness in class, anything unusual, I'm sure Darren will be doing all he should behind the scenes, with parents and what have you.' *Like contacting the named social worker. I did remind him of the key ones to check on. Of course, he will.*

Anne sounded relieved. 'Of course, I just felt... worried. There's nothing else I should know?'

There was a pause. 'No.' More firmly, 'No, if you keep an eye on Alex, give what support you can in lessons and pass anything on to Darren, you really can't do any more.'

'Thank you Neil, you've been a big help.'

'But I've done nothing.'

'Just to be told I'm doing the right thing, that helps.' Their conversation finished with some gossip about Neil's mother, who was apparently out with a friend to hear a rendering of Vivaldi's 'Four Seasons' in a local church. Neil was surprised that Anne had not gone with them but perhaps she was tired, or busy, or it might not be her sort of music. Whatever the case, he was glad that his mother had gone out with Eleri or Betty or whoever and was not moping without him. He returned to his pleasant reminiscences over the day, mellowed further by a glass of Schnapps.

'That was marvellous.' Mair joined in the applause as the conductor gave a final bow and the first violin reached out to take her music from the stand. 'But the cold really gets into your bones after a while.'

Ceri was immediately concerned. 'You should've said. You could've had my coat.' Both of them were wearing overcoats and wool scarves but even Mair's additional precaution of a plaid shawl was not proof against the marrow-freezing cold that seeped from the stone surroundings. Mair shivered and stamped her feet to get the circulation going.

'How about a little nightcap?'

Mair blushed. 'I don't think we should, not straight from the church.'

'If we go back home, no-one will see us...' Mair blushed even more but not because she found the prospect unpleasant.

'But it's already nine o'clock. If we go back to Swansea and then you'll have to drive me back again... it'll be so late... and so much trouble for you...'

He knew when she'd given in and he placed his hand over hers as it took what felt like its customary place tucked under his arm. He patted the gloved hand reassuringly. 'No trouble at all. I'm a lucky man if I get to see you for longer.'

Mair felt a little pang of guilt at leaving Anne on her own, after having so conspicuously not even invited her on the outing, but it was only a very little pang. It would be rather nice to see Ceri's home and to be alone with him, quite an adventure. Her heart fluttered. Diw, hadn't the doctor warned her to take things a bit easier. As she smoothed her skirt down over the passenger seat and Ceri shut the door he'd held open for her, she wondered if he'd kiss her goodnight. Her heart definitely fluttered again and she had no intention of seeing the doctor.

Neil couldn't wait to leave the Stork Sanctuary. He threw the records he'd just completed onto the pile on the shelf, hardly pausing in his stride.

Michel didn't look up. 'Hey, you keep those untidy habits for the monkey house where they belong,' he called amicably at Neil's retreating back. Neil made monkey noises in response without stopping.

The watery sunshine of late afternoon backlit the Vosges but Neil only noticed the figure leaning against Neil's red Megane, swinging his own keys impatiently. Neil counted to ten in four languages and was still not cool enough.

'Hey, Luc.' Did he imagine that trace of ironic understanding in Luc's expression?

'Hey, Neil. You should have let them all fly away and got out early.'

'You only get out early for good behaviour.'

'But I am told you are such a good boy.' Again, that mocking undercurrent. Neil looked at him quickly but read nothing in the open smile.

'Today we begin the education of the senses,' announced Luc.

'It's a wine-tasting,' responded Neil pragmatically. 'We do drink wine in Wales you know. Pretty good stuff too.'

'Wales.' Luc had more facial expressions to show contempt than anyone Neil had ever met and he used most of them every time Neil defended the culture of his home country. 'No, I will concede poetry and dragons, but wine? 'Good stuff'? You are in Alsace and must learn respect, no - reverence. You cannot buy a vineyard here. Plenty of people try, especially Americans, but this,' he pointed at the vineyards surrounding them as they walked uphill into the village of Hunawihr, 'is wealth beyond price. Do you know that men will marry to get their hands on an Alsace vineyard?'

Neil shook his head. 'You exaggerate so much, I never know what to believe.'

'So I must show you the horrible depths of your ignorance? What are the seven varieties of Alsace wine?' Neil shook his head after naming three - and getting one of those wrong. 'What is the meaning of 'vendange tardive'? Of 'selection de grains nobles'?' Neil thought he was doing OK with a literal translation of the first term as 'late harvest' and a guess that this was a special, sweeter wine, but the second term stumped him as seeming to mean the same thing. 'I bet you don't even know what you would serve to complement Gewurztraminer!' Neil's face gave away the answer to that and Luc shook his head in disbelief, muttering, 'Foie gras, or even nowadays, spicy cuisine... '

'Like Chinese takeaways,' contributed Neil, fully aware of his heresy and enjoying himself.

'Quite,' was Luc's clipped reply. 'I bet... I bet... you don't even know why Alsace Riesling - with the same grapes - is so much better than the German!'

'Is it?' Neil asked without thinking, adding hastily as he saw Luc gathering thunderclouds, 'I mean, is it something in the soil?' Luc was still waiting. 'Or the aspect, the way the slopes face?' Neil was pleased with that suggestion and waited hopefully.

'No!' Luc's arm scythed the air. 'It is because Alsace is French!'

They reached the entrance to one of Alsace's many wine co-operatives where eighteen producers pooled their harvest to produce the region's finest. The vintners combined the highest modern technology of pristine aluminium cylinders and hypersensitive thermostats with ancient knowledge of weather and timing.

'So educate me,' Neil invited.

'It will be a pleasure. I will enjoy teaching the teacher.'

'I'm usually a bit kinder to my pupils...' Neil commented ruefully.

'That,' Luc was granting no quarter, 'is what is wrong with you English. Too kind to children and animals.'

'Welsh,' said Neil, 'we Welsh,' and followed Luc to begin his 'education of the senses'.

Two hours later, Neil felt he was on intimate terms with seven varieties of grape, six white and one red. Overwhelmed by the seriousness with which each wine was sampled, compared, described and discussed, he let Luc do the talking.

His own contribution was variations on 'I don't know much about wine but I know what I like,' and that seemed to cause no offence. Luc's combination of fire and intellect struck sparks from all around him and Neil was able to observe the range of his passions. One of the vintners joined the tasting, giving his views of government edicts drawn up by 'suits' which prevented workers gathering the harvest beyond fixed working hours.

'As if the frosts will keep to the laws!' spat the vintner. 'When it is time, we all work twenty-four hours a day for the harvest. And to get the noble rot, we must risk some of the harvest, so when it is time, every second counts and we need everyone working flat out. What do they know?' Luc sympathized, explaining how the Monkey Sanctuary was affected by new bureaucratic legislation regarding temporary and part-time workers.

'We are funded on a kiss and a prayer so how are we supposed to pay 'severance' every time we change working hours. And these new laws regarding immigration laws!' Both men shrugged, considering how useful migrant workers were at harvest time. If no-one checked papers too closely, who was the worse for that? 'My little English friend here is an immigrant,' Luc joked, throwing an arm round Neil, who added automatically, 'Welsh,' and been more conscious of the friendly arm than offended by 'little' or 'English'.

Evidently the vintner had known Luc for some time as he said, 'I sometimes wish you and your Anarchist friends had grown up less restrained, huh?'

Luc laughed, 'It happens. Three children and a dog, most of the others. Even suits, some of them. Santé,' he raised his glass and sampled a Gewurztraminer sweetened and strengthened by the fungus known as 'noble rot' which, if the vintner were lucky and timed it right, would affect those grapes deliberately left to risk the frosts and would produce nectar.

'You were an Anarchist?' Neil asked, incredulous.

'As a student in Strasbourg,' Luc dismissed it. 'We all were. It is very French. On the one hand you have the grand institutions, like the Acadèmie française; on the other you have the extreme individualists. It is the tension which creates freedom don't you think. Or has England forgotten the individualism with your right wing socialist government, your parties that all road hog the middle of the road? Or,' his face alight with wicked humour, 'has your Welsh Assembly established Utopia which you will now explain to me?'

Neil realized how calculated were the references to England, and how little he knew about politics outside Britain, by comparison, even when he had drunk less. He took refuge in the tasting. 'I thought this was an education of my palate.'

'Your senses,' corrected Luc, 'and this is a mistake many people make. They do not realize that the brain is a sense too. You feel it don't you, the quality of an idea that lights up your mind. Thinking talk is food for the brain.'

'Well it doesn't complement Gewurztraminer then.'

'I told you to taste but not swallow,' Luc laughed.

'If you think I could spit out something as good as this...'

'Now,' offered the vintner who by now had become Gerhard, 'try the crémant. It is the champagne of Alsace, made by the same methods and twice as good...'

It was just as well that Luc was driving as Neil had 'tasted' more than he would consider acceptable otherwise. Neil's education was to continue in Luc's Strasbourg apartment with some French cuisine. 'Not Alsacien tonight,' Luc explained, 'because I am cosmopolitan and I feel in the mood for butter and cream. I have a fat craving.' Neil tried - and failed - to imagine any of his friends or acquaintance back home expressing a craving for fat. 'So it will be the cuisine of Normandy.'

Neil's alcohol content gradually subsided as he looked through Luc's music collection, noting the Satie with approval but finally selecting Berlioz' 'Nuits d'été'. 'Always a poet,' Luc commented en route to the kitchen as the ethereal strains of the French lyrics worked their magic. 'Do you like jazz?' Neil recognized some of the names, Reinhard and Grapelli, but little more than that. He raised his voice to reach Luc, who could be seen diving into cupboards and grabbing kitchen implements. 'I don't know. Does that mean I'm in for the education of the ears as well?'

'Not tonight. I have to start the rescue operation on your nose as soon as possible.'

'Sounds painful. What's wrong with my nose?'

'Too old.'

'Like the rest of me then. I did tell you I wasn't so young. I'll be thirty this year.'

'So old, I am sorry, I had no idea.'

'And you?'

'Me? I have been thirty. There was nothing to it. I am thirty-five.'

'You look older,' Neil said without thinking.

'When I was nineteen I would have taken that as a compliment,' was the dry response over the noise of the cooker hood fan.

'No, I didn't mean... What I mean is, you seem as if you have... lived...' Neil finished tamely.

'Yes, I have lived, but I hope to have some living to do yet.' Suddenly Luc was beside Neil, waving some herbs at him. 'Sniff this.'

Neil obediently sniffed. 'Rosemary?' he queried.

'Tarragon,' contradicted Luc. 'You see what I mean? The true education of the nose must happen before you are twelve years old. After that, a nose which has not had the range of scents cannot make the fine distinctions which are required.'

'Required for what?'

'To appreciate the world of smell, to cook, to eat, to scent the bouquet on a bottle of wine... How can I talk to you of blackberries if you did not smell a blackberry as a little boy, so you know the exact blackberryness of it. Smell is the most instant of the senses, the least manageable. It will bring back a memory so strongly you will be there again.'

'Like Proust and the Madeleine.'

'Huh, Proust. That's all you English ever read.'

'Welsh. What are you cooking? And don't tell me to sniff and work it out - we've already established that my nose has not been well-educated.'

Luc's choice of menu provoked a heated debate on the respective merits of lamb from the salt marshes of Brittany, awarded the Grèvin label as appellation contrôlé and the best in France, versus lamb from the small Welsh hill farms with 'plenty of lush grass and just as many salt marshes'. As far as Luc was concerned, the award clinched the debate.

'But,' Neil argued, 'I thought you were against these national bureaucratic decrees, and all for the individualists like the Welsh farmers who tend their flocks in traditional ways.' Well, some of them, he thought more truthfully, firmly crossing his fingers.

Luc closed the discussion. 'I see no problem in having my cake and eating it too. Tarte au pomme?' he asked, returning from kitchen to dining table with a superbly glazed pâtisserie presentation.

'What did you think of the wine?' Luc tested him on his afternoon's lessons.

'The best in the world,' Neil answered with more honesty than sophistication but it was the right answer.

The meal was leisurely, the clearing up - with which Neil helped, one aspect of upbringing on which his parents were insistent -

amicable and efficient. Neil was seated, flushed from the heat of the kitchen, knowing it was late but reluctant to bring the evening to a close.

'Shut your eyes.' Neil followed instructions. 'I have two liqueurs and I want you to sniff each one and tell me what it smells of.' Neil felt a little waft of air and could smell alcohol under his nose. He knew the menu was from Normandy so he guessed, 'apples... Calvados.' He opened his eyes. 'I'm right, aren't I?'

Luc said in frustration, 'You couldn't be more wrong. This is almonds, Amoretto...'

'Why did I have to shut my eyes?'

'It should help you concentrate, but with you? I give up.'

'No, let me try the other one.' Neil reached out as Luc moved forward and between them they spilt some of the second liqueur on Luc's arm. Neil laughed, held Luc's arm steady and sniffed the alcoholic perfume. 'This is it,' he said triumphantly, 'apples, Calvados...' He sniffed again to make sure.

'You're right,' murmured Luc, his voice heavier, charged with that electric passion which seemed to have fired him all day. Neil continued to hold Luc's arm and his nose brushed the short dark hairs as he inhaled deeply. 'It's not just apples,' he said, 'there's a woody note, and...' he glanced up, into the unmistakeable desire in the other man's eyes. He turned his attention very deliberately back to Luc's arm and ran his tongue along the trace of alcohol. 'I need to taste more,' he said simply and continued an education of the senses in which, this time, neither was a novice.

Chapter 5

Mair had both received and returned a kiss goodnight, after an evening basking in compliments and nostalgic conversation. There were so many shared memories of childhood and adolescence, and even the years since then seemed to have been similar journeys although undertaken separately.

They were even able to talk about their widowhoods, both deprived of their partners by cancer, robbed of the planned retirement years together. There was an ease in the company of someone her own generation that, however close they were, could not be found with her son. Not just 'someone', for she had women friends, but a man of her own generation.

She realized how much she missed a certain perspective on life, not to mention a man's embrace. She blushed, although no-one could see her, as she prepared to go to bed, turning down the cover on her side of the double bed, too accustomed to the empty half to notice the absences in the room any more. On her bedside table were a clock radio, a box of tissues, a murder story and, once she was in bed, her glasses. Its twin held an ornament - a pottery chaffinch which Neil bought her - and nothing else. Once, it carried her husband Harri's own choice of book for bed-time, his clock, his spectacles case, his watch and, in the last year, an increasing number of pills and potions.

Mair shifted position, trying to get comfortable and aware of an ache down her left side, probably exacerbated by the cold of the church. She was glad that she had encouraged Neil to go to Alsace. They had become so close after Hari died, almost like a married couple in the little routines of domestic life and she was not convinced that this was for the best, long term.

Neil seemed very happy with their arrangement; he never had to learn where the 'on' switch was on a vacuum cleaner, or cook anything beyond an egg, which left him free to play that depressing music or read deep books. She was sure he let his hair down on his occasional weekends in London but generally he seemed so temperate, staid even, for such a young man. Not that she wanted excesses.

She heard friends' tales of their children's divorces and drug habits and who knows what else; she wanted none of that for Neil. Indeed, his father would have been proud of him, a teacher, respected within the community. Oh, Harri.

Neil had matured in the eight years since his father died and she felt it was time for his life to move on. For herself too, she admitted. In telling Neil to live his life and go to Alsace, she was thinking only of him but, as it turned out, she was glad he was not at home. Her feelings were complicated enough without the silent reproach of her son's presence, a reminder of his father in every gesture. She had lived long enough with the cold comfort of her ghost and yet it hurt to even think of letting go.

Could she really be courting again, at the age of fifty-six? But that was so young, these days. How had she forgotten that she was still young, with a possible thirty years ahead of her? Was she so busy watching Neil that she forgot to live her own life? Had she left her own life in a grave?

Ceri made her feel young. Her brain raced round, replaying the conversations with him. She even shared with him her worries about a financial decision. She had gone along with Helen and Mrs Evans to a meeting run by this group 'Women Empowering Women' which was all the talk of Llanelli, to hear about the Hearts scheme, and she had needed to talk it through.

'So tell me again and let me get this clear,' Ceri requested.

'If I put in some money... I can put in anything from £250 to £3,000... then I will get back eight times as much, as soon as enough new members have put their money in.'

'And how long would that take?'

'Well, the lady who talked from the platform - wearing a nice pink two-piece she was - said that it's taking two to three weeks at the moment but it would depend on us all getting lots of friends and family to join and then it could be quicker. She was very honest - she did say it was a gamble with big returns and a bit of a risk like any gamble. '

'So who looks after your money then? Can you trust someone not to scarper with the takings.'

'It goes straight out to the first heart, see, so the woman or women who put that £3,000 in will get their winnings, so there's no money hanging around at all except winnings. There was a woman in the hall with a carrier bag full of cash and she was so happy, she was having a holiday in Benidorm and she'd never been away before. I am tempted...'

'I suppose it can go wrong if there's not enough new people...'

'It's just I've got some savings now because my TESSA has matured and I was thinking...'

'Returns are very low at the moment in the building society, and even with shares...'

'Oh, I don't understand shares and such. I wouldn't like to take those sort of risks.'

'I think it's worth a shot but I tell you, if you're going to go in, you should go in quickly while there's plenty of people joining so you're most likely to get your winnings.'

'Does that mean some people might get nothing?'

'Well, yes, perhaps, but there's more places than Llanelli for them to get more people aren't there? They could just keep it going. And if people who've won put back in, then it can keep going forever. They can put back in, can't they?'

'Yes, I think so.'

'Tell you what, I'll put half in myself. What do you say, I put in £1,500 and you do the same, so if you take my advice we share the risk and share the profit?'

She'd felt warm at the idea of sharing anything, but replied regretfully, 'I'm sorry, fach, but it's women only as members.'

'Well I'll give you the money and you put it in for me then.'

'But you'd have no security.'

'I think I can trust you to pay out if we win. When we win,' he'd corrected.

'It's good to have a man to talk to about money, someone who understands these things.'

And it was. Knowing that she had the approval, even the business partnership, of a man who was a manager of a company until he took early retirement two years ago, gave her the confidence to go ahead and join a heart. So that would be - she calculated - £12,000 for her when the heart paid out. She could do a tidy bit around the house for that and still have some from the TESSA to put safely in the building society, for her to live on the interest and have the capital safe for Neil one day.

Why, if Helen and Mrs Evans went in, the money would be theirs even more quickly. There was no point asking Anne if she wanted in. In fact, Anne had expressed her opinions very forcefully against the scheme, in that French manner which came out sometimes as quite rude. Anne earned black looks from all the women sitting near them in the hall by declaring the scheme to be 'a rip-off' and Mair worked hard to explain quietly that Anne was a 'French visitor', implying that she did not really understand what was going on. Mair was even more sure of that after talking to Ceri; Anne did not really understand what was going on at all. You couldn't expect it from a French person.

Anne's English was so good that Mair sometimes forgot that she was a foreigner. But Mair's judgement was backed by Ceri, so she must be right. Ceri said how pretty she looked. Ceri was always telling her how pretty she looked. She really ought to pay herself a little more beauty attention. Which reminded her... reluctant to leave the warm bed but determined to rescue her face from years of neglect, she heaved herself out from under the covers, put on slippers and dressing gown, and rummaged through the bathroom cabinet until she found the little jar of rejuvenating night cream which she was given as a sample free with some perfume. Dutifully she applied it, extra thick for compensation.

Too sticky to risk her face against the pillow, she lay stiffly on her back. Perhaps she could mention the scheme to some women at chapel. She shifted position again, wondering whether she should put the radio on to sing or talk her to sleep as was sometimes needed. Her last thought before she finally fell asleep was that there was time to find out how she felt about Ceri, before Neil came back, and it would probably all be very good for Neil anyway...

It was not the first time Neil had woken in bed with a stranger. In fact, he preferred strangers. Or had done. He thought of sex as an occasional light physical recreation which had very little to do with his life. Which was why he limited it to odd weekends in London, rather than bring complications to spoil his established pattern of life in Llanelli. Why would he want to face comments behind his back at work? Or bring into the open something he and his mother were content never to discuss or even acknowledge. Something, however, had changed. Overnight.

His mother had always warned him about playing with fire but she had never told him it would leave him burning, burning bright, Blake's tiger in the forest of the night. He put an experimental palm on his lover's back, on the smooth small of the back where the dark hair thinned out, and he could feel the connection sizzling. He did not believe in love, he told himself, just chemicals which could be controlled and adjusted. Luc rolled over and smiled at him. Just chemicals...

Later that morning, Neil traced LUC in huge letters in the condensation on the bedroom window, paused and then added POB before LUC.

'What is POB?' demanded Luc, pulling on a pair of jeans.

'It's Welsh. Luc means the same as 'chance' in French and you say it a bit like its English meaning, 'luck'. So 'pob luc' means 'bonne chance', 'good luck'.'

'Luc le Bon, Good Luc,' Luc grimaced. 'No, I don't think so.'

Neil laughed. 'No, that's too literal. 'Pob' on its own is more like 'toute','all' or 'every'.'

Luc brightened. 'All Luc, everything Luc.'

'Yes,' Neil agreed, 'Everything is Luc.'

Back at Madame Grüber's, Neil finger-wrote on his own

bedroom window,'*Pob Luc. Luc is everything*', then hastily wiped it off with a handkerchief, rubbing in careful circles to make sure that no trace of the letters remained. He thought that if someone took a vertical section through his brain he would find 'Pob Luc' written through his core like in a stick of rock. He wiped the clean window again and gazed for several minutes across the valley to the black mountains that were Germany, before joining Madame Grüber for lunch and a description of how much he enjoyed staying in Strasbourg with his friend, a description which left out everything that mattered.

I have met someone. Too dramatic. Neil deleted the opening words of his email to Helen. *I am now weekending in Strasbourg, a bit like I used to in London.* Helen would know that London meant gay clubs and casual sex - was that what Strasbourg meant? He hit the delete button, angry at the tone. Too trivial. *A friend has been showing me Strasbourg. Said nothing. I feel truly alive for the first time.* Said too much. He opened Helen's email once more and read,

'I don't really understand what's happening with this foot and mouth disease. After the first announcement there were two more, so far apart, Devon and then Anglesey. Now there seem to be more cases so quickly and instead of being shocked at announcements of each new case, we are starting to just pray selfishly 'Not here, please, not here.' Anglesey is so bad and yet I know that each of us is thinking 'Thank God it's North Wales.' Isn't that terrible?

Neil clicked 'reply' and inserted:-
It's just human to want to protect your own. It doesn't mean you don't care about those who are suffering.

Dai is moody.

I don't blame him. He must be facing it every day at work and at home. Anyway, it's not as if he hasn't seen you moody. Remember what you used to be like and think that if your relationship could survive that, it could survive anything. I'd make a good marriage guidance counsellor, don't you think.

He and his father have put straw soaked in disinfectant across the entrance by the lane and there's even a soaked mat in front of Brynglas and our own Brynglas Fach. I've wrecked a pair of shoes because I didn't know it would be there and there's no way I would have faced the wrath of the Evans if I hadn't walked through the stinking stuff. I'm wearing the same grotty shoes all the time now so it doesn't matter what they get like. I can't afford to lose any more good ones.

I know I must sound so trivial at such a time but I can talk to you about the little things that annoy. I certainly have to keep my mouth shut at home. It's like being in a medieval plague. I know they don't really like me going out at all because nobody knows how the infection is passed on and every time I go beyond the farm gate, I'm adding a risk. They seem to accept Dai going out and about. I like being on my own but not when I feel like a prisoner.

I feel much better for having had a little moan. Truly I am heart sorry for Dai and his parents. I know how much those cows mean to them and there is this terrible threat hanging over our heads. I thought it would go away in a week or two but it's getting so much worse and the fears seem to be hanging over the fields across all of Wales. Someone said that if you're told your stock must go because you're in an infected area, then your pets are put down too. I can't bear the thought of losing Bogart and the dogs, and I daren't ask Dai in case it's true and it's something he would have to do as a vet. I'm not sure I want to know. When I watch the news, that's all you seem to get is the latest cull and most of the animals don't even have the disease.

Same on the news here. You can't avoid hearing about it. The French seem to delight in the most gruesome photographs of bonfires with cows' legs sticking out of them. It ought to be some outrageous seventies' comedy programme but it's not. Don't tell Dai but the angle here is that British farmers have such bad habits, what can you expect, almost as if they deserved it. There's a real reaction against British animals and British meat - they haven't really accepted it after BSE but it's got worse again. There is a hysterical note here too because animals - sheep I think - were imported from Britain before the ban - and they're trying to trace them and get the vets out checking for signs of disease.

On a lighter note, I am still working on ideas for the Botanical Gardens. I thought maybe traditional Welsh legend, flowers springing up where Blodeuwedd walked seemed appropriate, but then maybe it's a bit obvious. What do you think?

Sounds good to me but I can see that others might come up with the same idea. Sorry, can't help more.

You asked when we are getting married. You should know better than to tease me over something like that. Dai has even stopped asking, he is so caught up in checking sheep's mouths and reading instructions from the Ministry of Agriculture who don't seem to know their proverbial.

Don't want to miss the wedding, even if we all have to wear scruffy shoes and be dipped on our way into chapel or whatever.

For all that these are hard times, I love him more. I just wish I could lift his spirits more but he has said it helps him knowing I am here. He does try to smile for me. It's the fact that he has to try, that tears at me. It is as if the countryside is at war and we don't know whether we will win. Tell me something entertaining.'

My friend Luc took me to a bar in Strasbourg where there's live music. It was part of my introduction to the blues. He's educating me. People think it's funny that he works with monkeys and I spend my spare time with storks so there are a few witticisms get thrown around. One guy told this joke:-

'There was a Mummy stork, a Daddy stork and a baby stork, all living in a little apartment in Strasbourg. One night, Baby woke up and found his Mummy gone.

'Don't cry,' said Daddy, 'Mummy is working and bringing happiness to Mummies and Daddies all over Strasbourg.'

The next night, Baby woke up and found Daddy gone.

'Don't cry,' said Mummy, 'Daddy is working and brining happiness to Mummies and Daddies all over Strasbourg.'

The next night Mummy and Daddy Stork were worried sick because Baby went out. When he came back, they asked him where he'd been. He grinned and said, 'Scaring the shit out of the university students.'

Well, you asked me to entertain you and it seemed quite funny after a couple of litres of Belgian beer.

Love

Ditto

Helen

Neil

Neil keyed 'Send'. He had named Luc, which in itself ought to tell Helen that this was someone special. To say even that much was to give more away than he wanted to think about. You could shout all you liked that you did not believe in lightning and it would make no difference at all to whether, or where, the lightning struck.

'The nesting place is prepared but so far the storks have not come.' Madame Grüber pointed to the wheel on top of the old Bergheim church of Notre-Dame before they ventured inside to inspect the fifteenth century paintings. 'Perhaps all your work this year will bring the storks back to Bergheim.'

'I hope so. But if not this year, then they will be back another year.'

'They are the luck of Alsace you know, the storks.'

Neil bit back the comment that the university students would not think so. 'I thought they brought babies.'

'Long life, prosperity and yes, babies, are the associations of the stork for us. You don't think babies are lucky?' The sharp eyes regarded him with curiosity.

'They are for me,' he responded flippantly. 'If there were no more babies, I'd be out of a job.' He looked at the church spire with interest. 'I'd love to see storks nesting there.'

'Me too. I've pinned a little hope on the stork coming back this year.' Her voice was suddenly very serious. 'It is often the hope which is too hard to live with, you know, not the ending of it. I will show you when we reach the place in the woods.' She returned to her role of tourist guide.

'Just beside the church was a hospital, in medieval times and right beside that is the ossuary. You can read some stories on those stones, I can tell you. I think it was a very quick journey from the hospital bed to the cold bed next door in those days.'

'We must stop here.' Madame Grüber directed him to a military cemetery just outside Bergheim, one of so many signposted off the Alsace roads. He was surprised that he was being taken to see the graves of German soldiers. In so far as he thought at all, he thought of Madame Grüber as French, and Germans as 'the enemy'. He read the names and dates on the simple crosses marking the graves of young, dead soldiers. Here, as in the church cemetery and at the war memorials they passed this Easter Saturday, were fresh spring flowers. He recognized daffodils and freesias, which he instinctively stooped to sniff. Luc would have been impressed, although perhaps less so if he had realized that freesias were the favourite flowers of Neil's mother and it was the sweet scent of his childhood home which flooded Neil. He was aware that a posy was in the back of his car, biding its time before being placed by Madame Grüber wherever it was they were headed.

Madame Grüber pointed towards the Rhine and the Black Mountains. 'Their graves are facing their homeland.'

They returned to the car in silence, broken after a while by Madame Grüber.

'It will take about half an hour to get to the place in the woods. I wanted to go to the cemetry because I need to tell myself some truths before the Easter Ceremony. My family has always lived in Thannenkirch, for generations, and yet my mother was born German and her mother was born French.

My people have been born French, become German and then become French again in their own lifetimes. Many people of the Rhine Valley are buried in Alsace, sometimes in separate graveyards for those who were on different sides, sometimes together. Who knows how many are still lying together in the high mountains under the soil itself?

If you visit le Linge,' she named somewhere Neil knew to be a World War 1 battlefield, 'you will see ten metres of mud which cost tens of thousands of lives. But if you are me, you look at it and know that it is your people against your people.'

Neil spoke quietly. 'I have always felt that too. Human against human.'

Madame Grüber shook her head. 'No, it is much more than that when it is - or it could be - your actual brother against your actual uncle, when you are French one minute and German the next. This is not understood in Britain because you are an island. Vernon did not understand this. He did not understand what we were doing when we helped him. He did not understand what the Resistance were jumping into, hurting ourselves to help ourselves. The British are always outside, knowing so clearly where they stand and what is right. It is not so easy on the borders as it is on an island.'

Neil listened, letting pieces of information inform his hazy picture of the past, sure that the full answer lay in the place in the woods and that he could ask his questions there. He slowed for each sharp bend that took him ever higher through forests of mainly evergreens until there was a fine sprinkling of snow along the verges. He automatically registered a woodpecker's spotted head and wings, with the flash of red, vanishing between trees, and, with more excitement, two honey buzzards circling over a clearing, then lost them as he took yet another back-tracking turn.

'Here,' Madame Grüber alerted him. 'You can park here.' There was a designated car park of scraped earth, with a notice board at one end. On investigation, Neil found that this displayed information about types of tree, each depicted with an accompanying leaf for identification.

'I always forget the difference between a fir and a pine,' Neil mused aloud, reading the relevant caption, but his companion's thoughts were clearly elsewhere. She was clutching her posy of flowers and although her face was pink with the cold, Neil fancied she was paler than usual, her expression unreadable.

'I will be a minute on my own and then I would like to show you something,' she said. He nodded and studied the tree-board while she walked, favouring one hip as she did when the arthritis played up. He was fond of this old lady, the grandmother he never had, and he knew that whatever was in these woods was of great importance to her. Through the corner of his eye he was aware of her slow progress to a footpath, along which she vanished.

This high up, spring in Alsace wore white, a delicate frosting which would be thick enough, even at Easter, to please the skiers at the station higher up again. The pale, clear blue of the sky hurt his eyes as he looked too long for the honey buzzards and the switch to the gloom through the firs, searching for Madame Grüber to reappear, made him feel dizzy, so that at first his dazzled eyes missed her. He walked quickly towards her, to save her the extra distance, and took her arm as he so often took his mother's. The flowers had gone and there was a trace of tears as she spoke, leaning on him as she re-traced her steps into the darkness of the woods.

'Imagine the Vosges in war-time, these woods a hiding-place for the men who chose - or were driven - to resistance. Perhaps each of us was resisting something different, the dog-jerk response to a uniformed command, the loss of identity... for Jews, for Arabs... the humiliation for so many of being described as non-Germans... perhaps just one time too many for an Alsacien to be told to turn, turn French, turn German, turn French again - enough turning!

You don't have to be old to be cynical if you have watched Alsace go back and forwards on the card table of politics; France says 'We give you Alsace if you leave the rest of France alone,' Germany says, 'Thank you very much but Alsace is ours anyway, was ours before it was yours. We will have it back - and the rest of France too.' I was sixteen, so much older than the sixteen-year-olds now, for all their street-wise talk, but still so much to learn. Here,' she broke off, 'this is what I would like you to see.'

Neil had already seen the four white wooden crosses ahead of them, erected at a crossroads of footpaths, the fresh posy a patch of yellow and lilac among the sombre snow-sprinkled trees. Each cross had the French tricolour diagonally across the upright, a name and a date carved into the wood. While Madame Grüber spoke, Neil deciphered the lettering, weathered to a deeper brown almost black by its half century exposed to the elements.

'Vernon Davies,' she said simply but Neil was newly sensitive to the way a name could be written across your very soul and he guessed something of what she was going to say. 'I was sixteen and I loved him.'

Neil saw the dates underneath the name 1925 - 1945. 'He was from Llanelli and like you he was good at languages so they trained him as a wireless operator and parachuted him into France. That's all I could be told in case they caught me... they caught Golda Bancic and took her to Stuttgart where they guillotined her on the day of her thirtieth birthday.

Her last letter to Dolorès, her daughter, was published recently in the Vosgien... so much to break your heart. And always there were the rumours of tortures and of le Struthof. Some of the Resistance were Jews and they knew of things, they used to start to tell us and we couldn't listen, we didn't want to know. Sometimes I am so ashamed for all of us, of what we chose not to know.'

Neil heard the echoes of Helen's fears. 'A friend has told me she is afraid of asking questions in case she can't handle the answers. I know the situations can't compare but perhaps the feelings...?'

'Maybe. And maybe this was a time the world just watched the river flow and it was wrong because the rivers were flowing with blood. And maybe we were busy, busy, even being brave and risking lives, but not looking the right way when it matters.

Perhaps it is just how evil gets in - you are fighting one evil and another happens because you can't fight them all. I don't know, but if you go to le Struthof, you will see what we all have - even you British on your island - to be ashamed of. All I knew then was the idea of fear... le Struthof was the bogeyman in my adventure and I had to be careful for my mountain men and for myself.

I had two jobs. One was to slip food up to the men in the mountains. It was easy for a girl my age to go between her uncle at the café and her home, and to go for broody walks in the hills. I know the mountain so well no-one could have followed me or found me if they'd tried. But it's been a few years now since I have been able to climb the Taenchel. Even if my old legs were not so stiff, I think my heart would give up. One of the men I took bread to was Vernon.

He would let me listen to the BBC, Radio-Londres as we called it. It was dangerous but how it gave us heart that kept us going. You have heard of Jean-Pierre Rosnay?' Neil confessed his ignorance. 'But you should. He is a poet like you. He was fifteen when he joined the Resistance, he was even captured by Klaus Barbie - you have heard of him?' Again, Neil had to confess his ignorance. 'But he escaped and, at seventeen, Rosnay was writing poems of the Resistance and we, from the Alliance, the Maquis, the resistance all over France, heard them on Radio-Londres.' She sang a few lines of what was clearly a stirring Resistance favourite. He was known as 'Bébé' because he was so young and the Baby spoke for all of us.

Vernon and I loved each other. In war-time, you know, there could be no time, no second chances, and you make your mind up quickly. Whatever problems I put to him, he would say,' It doesn't matter.' I think that was his favourite saying, especially in French.

He promised to marry me when he returned from some final action. I heard among the men that there was a big push planned. That was November 1st 1944, All Souls Day, that I spent high up a mountain with the pagan spirits. If we had known we would never see each other again, we would not have done or said anything differently.' She put out a hand and stroked a spar of the simple cross, lovingly.

'You must understand how confusing it was at the time. The mountain men told us of the landings on the Normandy beaches in June, and there was underground news about allied successes but the truth for us was that Alsace was in German hands. Especially after Vernon left, I only knew what the Germans told us and they were so strong. Colmar was our nearest town south and I knew for a fact that the Germans were as strong there as ever, more so when it came to punishments.

Our nearest town to the north was Strasbourg, and I know now that it was Strasbourg they went to, Vernon and our mountain men, and that on November 23rd they were successful in liberating our city. Then, I knew only that he and the others were gone, that I was a prisoner of my ignorance with no radio, no news and for company only the looks between those of us who knew of each other and of the mountain men. It was such a lonely time. It is the hope which hurts the most you know, when you are waiting.

And especially with what I knew... such a lonely girl, who could do nothing any more but wait. News started coming back, of our victory in Strasbourg, but always we had the German version ringing in our ears that there was a 'temporary setback' and when in January we were told to 'rejoice' because 'Strasbourg was ours again', I thought he must have gone with Strasbourg and that my life was over.

It was not true of course... the Germans tried to retake Strasbourg and Eisenhower would have let them. It was de Gaulle who said Strasbourg was too important to lose again, who said the French 1st should defend it. And they did - defended it, held it and by February 1945 the allies reached us.

None of this made any difference for Vernon but I didn't know that then. Still I hoped he was somewhere and that hope... as well as my situation...I just had to keep going and wait again. Still there was no word. We met in secret and we had no way of communicating so this meant nothing but I always felt I would know, that he was all right or... that he was not. I could tell nothing.

Months turned into a year and I heard nothing. Although the war was over I was... unable to travel and the only news was what all the village heard. Now the name of le Struthof was said loud enough, the only concentration camp on French soil. Every day brought new, sickening details, and I knew in my heart, he ended there.

That was the blackest time of all. Every horror I heard, happened to him. I was afraid to sleep because of the nightmares. I could not hope because so many told me it would have been better to die than leave that camp after what was done - and seen. How I was punished for not wanting to know! You couldn't help but hear. And I could talk to no-one - in those days, how it was for me, I could tell no-one about my Welsh love.

Then God ended my suffering. A man called Tobias Goldberg brought news to my uncle in the café of one of our mountain men, of how he died. Tobias had his own story to tell, of how he fled from Paris to Algeria, tried to join the Free French Forces of North Africa but been told he was too young at sixteen so he lied about his age and joined a parachute battalion of the SAS, along with other Jews and exiles of all races.

He fought in Arnheim and then Alsace, where he met up with a small cadre of Resistance men, hiding out in the mountains. Their radio operator was a Welshman, who - according to Tobias - was the key to the operation with his capacity to give misinformation in fluent German as well as coded information in English, French and German, to the allies. He too died along with Marc, our villager. Tobias had a little token from Marc for his wife, and he came to let her know of her husband's love - and death.

So it was from Bernice, Marc's wife, that I could find the details I needed. I would go to comfort her and get the comfort for myself. The rest is simply told. They were spared le Struthof, thank God, but were found standing around the wireless, by a German patrol who were wild from panic and killing as they ran from Strasbourg, shooting in their own fear at all around them.

Four dead, three wounded, were found as the allies themselves spread from Strasbourg into the surrounding countryside, pursuing German patrols, and these crosses were put up to mark their courage. 'Mort pour la France," she read from the cross, 'like so many. This is not the only little cross in the woods of the Vosges, and I am not the only one who remembers. There will be flowers all over France this Easter. Comme toujours.'

There was a lump in Neil's throat. For all the emotion, he could sense something important not being said but he didn't know the right question or even whether he should ask at all. What he did wonder was, 'You said two jobs. What was the other job you did?'

'It was more dangerous. I was a postman for the leaflets that they printed in Strasbourg, the Resistance poems, news bulletins and propaganda, cartoons making fun of the Germans with big faces and even bigger helmets.

I remember one where two German Officers shot each other over a debate as to whose spike was bigger on whose helmet. Laughter is a very powerful weapon and it aroused very powerful anger and reprisals if anyone was caught. Some of the pamphlets were very crude. I liked the poems. You have heard of Ivan Goll?' A third time, Neil had to confess his ignorance.

'He is a very famous poet from Alsace, born in St-Dié.' Neil had to accept the rebuke. 'He was also a Jew who escaped to America. He is known all over the world. Are you sure you haven't heard of him? You must read 'La Grande Misère de la France', it is a very famous poem.' She quoted softly, '*Nous n'irons plus au bois ma belle...*'

Madame Grüber bent over to adjust the posy at the foot of the cross, scooping a little of the powdery snow over the tied stems to hold the tribute in place. '*Nous n'irons plus au bois ma belle...*' she softly repeated. Neil automatically translated into English, '*We will go no more to the woods, my dear...*' as Madame Grüber placed a kiss on her hand and transferred it to the wooden cross. 'Au revoir.'

She took Neil's arm once more and they made their way out of the forest canopy into the startling brilliance of the spring blue skies. Birds could be heard rehearsing their mating songs, encouraged by the sunshine. The young man and the old lady left the place in the woods behind them.

Over their evening meal together, Neil risked asking Madame Grüber the questions which most bothered him as he reflected on her story. 'You told me you went there every Easter. What about Monsieur Grüber? Didn't he mind?' She hesitated and he said quickly, 'Please, tell me to mind my own business...'

'No,' she said, 'it is good to tell an old story. And there are times... a trace of accent perhaps... you remind me of Vernon. Another Llanelli boy... Monsieur Grüber, Ernst, was a good man and I loved him. I did, truly, love them both.

Ernst was three years younger than me, and he became my friend. I watched him grow into his craft, so skilled in the small details, choosing the soundest wood, the metal bindings, the sealing... But best of all was when he could carve.

A cooper then was not a factory worker, he would make a barrel to last a life-time and carve a little piece of Alsace into it. You know the barrel by the fountain in Bergheim? Ernst made that.' Neil had indeed noticed the huge barrel, as big as a Welsh garden shed, carved with a rustic scene of farm labourers and bunches of grapes and typical of those decorating the Winstübe. Like Llanelli, Alsace was proud of its breweries.

'Ernst knew me you see, heard all the stories in the village, grew from my friend to my husband and married me with open eyes and an open heart. I have been twice lucky in my life and tomorrow I will say a thank you prayer for a long and happy marriage as I put flowers in the churchyard for my Ernst, Anne's father. But my first love is in the place in the woods and Ernst understood that. A day each year for memories is allowed. I had no secrets from him.'

'And Anne, she knows too?'

'Oh yes. Anne knows. She has taken me on my Easter visit many times. It is partly for Anne that I hope we will see the stork again in Bergheim.'

Neil presumed Madame Grüber was alluding to her hopes of a grandchild and was bemused at the suggestion that Anne might oblige. She was after all over forty and with, as far as Neil could tell, no partner. However it was not for him to comment on someone else's wilder hopes.

So much involvement in someone else's family gave him the sudden need to phone his mother that evening. As always, she put such a brave face on his absence that anyone would have thought she was happily enjoying a wild social life.

'Never mind me. Have you made some friends?'

'You make me sound like a twelve-year-old on his first day at school, but yes, I've made a few new friends.' He found himself unable to name Luc to his mother. To name him casually in conversation would be a betrayal of the enormous change in his life.

'That's nice dear. And Anne's mother is a good cook, I think?'

'A great cook. I hope you've got the recipe for kugelhopf from Anne.'

His mother laughed. 'No chance. She's like you. She says if your mother's too good a cook, you don't ever learn yourself. She says my roast dinners are 'superbe'.'

Neil enjoyed the French word in his mother's strong Welsh accent but picked up on the slightly competitive undercurrent. 'And so they are. No-one in France understands how to cook roast dinners, not even Madame Grüber.' He could not tell her, especially over the telephone, of four crosses in the woods and the feelings they left in him.

'It all sounds very exciting dear but that's someone at the door so I'll have to go now. Bye, cariad.' No doubt some door-to-door charity collector, Neil thought, and, knowing his mother, she would fall for every line anyone threw at her.

If anything, he was even more restless after the phone call, and became increasingly convinced that he was doomed to die young. He kept thinking of the dates on the crosses, men who never even reached his age, whose lives were stolen. Thinking he might die the next day for all he knew, he followed unwittingly the same instincts as Vernon over fifty years earlier and he drove through the night to bury his face in Luc's hair.

Chapter 6

Helen replaced the stitches on her knitting chart with sums of money, sometimes clusters of £250 and sometimes one £3,000. The first row of eight stitches represented eight hearts, including 'her' heart. It didn't matter whether she put in a contribution of £250, along with several other women, or whether she paid £3,000 herself to create a heart, her money would be in one of those eight stitches.

Over three rows she increased eight times into each stitch and looked at the pattern she created. It was a huge multiplication that was needed but then that was where the huge profits came from. It certainly would not work as fabric - even a batwing sleeve did not grow as quickly as that - but then, the hearts could develop over time and it would just take longer until people got their money. She looked at the mathematics of the financial knitting pattern and was still not happy. Neil's mother seemed very keen and had already put some savings in, although she did not say how much and Helen was too polite to ask.

Then Helen realized one of the flaws in her thinking; her money would not be in the first row or even the first tier as there had certainly been pay-outs already.

If she thought of it as a repeat pattern and if she assumed that there had been two pay-outs... she moved her row of hearts to Row 6, performing the necessary multiplications and she found that, when you looked at it like that, her heart was among the 512 needed to pay all the second tier and it would take 4096 new hearts to pay all her tier.

If women were putting in smaller amounts than £3,000, that could easily be 10,000, or more, women needed to ensure payment. And for them to get a pay-out, multiply by eight again...

The calculations had gone way off the page and Helen used a zoom to bring her own little square, with her precious £3,000, back into focus. If she only looked at that square it looked reasonable, but she was the sort of person who needed to see the whole garment and that was a mess.

She had no idea what row she was on and at some stage this scheme was going to go off the page, collapse and hurt all those people. No, she couldn't do this. She phoned Dai's mother, hoping that Will was out in the fields so that they could talk freely.

She was in luck but it proved more difficult than Helen had expected to explain to Gwen the way she thought the scheme worked - or rather, didn't.

'But Helen, there's no need to work out the numbers for the women of the world, fach, we only need to look at what happens to our money. You're making it too complicated. When eight new hearts have started, then we win our money, that's all there is to it.'

Helen tried a new tack. 'But suppose that's your friends, in those new hearts, and you're just taking their money.'

'Same as I'm giving my money in the first place, isn't it, and there's plenty of women wanting to join - you saw how many were there in the hall. And like Lisa said, you can always put back in to keep the kettle boiling.'

Lisa had been well-dressed and well-spoken, talking rings round people's questions. Helen had needed to sit down quietly at home and work it all out in her own way, in her own time. Her unhappy schooldays had at least taught her that she could not learn just by listening and repeating, and her development of her own business had taught her that thinking things through for herself might be slow but paid dividends.

Helen made one last attempt. 'Please don't join in. I've learnt a bit through running my business and I have a really bad feeling about this.' It was the wrong thing to say.

'And what would I know? I'm just a farmer's wife. Well, this farmer's wife has kept food on the table and paid the oil and electric through the worst times we've seen. And don't think I haven't thought about the money I'm putting in. I know every teabag, every sack of dog meal that money could buy.'

'I didn't mean to say...,' Helen tried to placate.

'No-one means to but it's what you think, all of you, Dai too. Just a housewife. If I didn't managed the money there wouldn't be even this little bit but it's not enough. I know what we could do with the winnings from hearts and I only wish I could get into town sooner to put the money in.

I can't get out without Will wondering why I'm adding to the risk. He's security mad at the moment - even the fruit and veg man has to stop outside the gate and sound his horn. Will won't let anyone in over the cattle grid but Dai of course - and you.' There was a hint of disapproval to the 'and you'. Helen was only too aware that her rare trips by bus to Llanelli were regarded as irresponsible, if not criminal. 'I thought it might ease a bit with no cases near us but all these cases in Powys give you the jitters.'

Any hope that the disease would stay in Anglesey was been dashed by first one, then several, cases in neighbouring Powys. Helen knew that one of the landfill sites being used to bury corpses from the culls was on the county border and there was concern that the disease would be spread even more quickly by the methods used in the attempt to prevent it. Farmers were afraid of the air, the water and - most of all - of each other. Who knew what lurked in the mud on the soles of shoes or what was picked up from vehicles travelling from the devastation in Cumbria or Devon across the Welsh countryside?

'We can just keep our fingers crossed.' *That it doesn't reach us.* Always that unspoken, shameful plea, *Anyone else, but spare us, not us...*

With no further mention of hearts, Gwen and Helen repaired the links forged initially by their love for Dai but which, over the last year as family and neighbours, had become genuine affection. Helen could only hope that the enforced time lapse before Gwen could pay money into a heart would give her time to change her mind.

Helen wiped the hearts patterns off her screen and pondered

again her bid for the wall-hanging at the National Botanical Gardens. She would have to make a decision soon as the deadline was 1st May. She looked at her previous ideas, which seemed inspired when first conceived and now struck her as stale. Daffodils, dragons and Welsh myths - surely she had lived in Wales long enough to get away from the stereotypes. What would symbolize Wales?

She played with a map of Wales, placing images in key places, a small sheep on the Brecons, the Millenium Stadium in Cardiff, the Botanical Gardens itself in Llanarthney, near Carmarthen. She could create stylised representations through yarns and stitches but she knew better than to aim for photography realism. It was certainly possible... but it looked like something mass-produced for a tourist brochure, about as thought-provoking as a biscuit wrapper.

It would be more realistic if the sheep were on its back and burning, its legs sticking up from a pile of the dead - although, so far, the Brecons were clear. She hit some keys and accidentally brought one of her hearts screens back up, the one which magnified the section with 'her' heart. She brought the map of Wales to the screen again and magnified a section.

It didn't work because she hadn't created any detail to the images but she had the glimmering of an idea. 'Wales' was too big, too varied to capture on one page, one screen or one wall-hanging. What she needed was a detail, something from the life she lived in Wales, that would be Welsh of itself, not through some kind of self-conscious stereotypical nationalism.

That was as far as she could get in her thinking and after playing fruitlessly with various images, she gave up on the brainwork and allowed herself a break. She could go for a walk but knowing that she should not walk beyond the boundaries of Brynglas, for fear of accidentally spreading foot and mouth, diminished the farm's attractions. Also, she would earn disapproving looks if Will saw her even walking about the farm.

She would have to go out somewhere or she would scream. Dai volunteering to fetch shopping, as he had to go out anyway for his job, only increased her feelings of isolation and imprisonment. She had promised Neil that she would befriend his replacement, Anne, and provide his mother with company, and it would be wrong of her to let down her friend, so in fact it was her duty to take Anne out somewhere. What's more, it was the school Easter holidays so Anne must be desperate for company and some activity.

Having convinced herself that it was a necessary and charitable act for her to go to Llanelli, and having phoned Anne to make some arrangements, Helen found herself stuck for somewhere to take Anne. She didn't want to make Anne drive and even if they could have found, and timed, public transport to take them to a tourist attraction, everywhere Helen could think of was closed due to foot and mouth restrictions.

She would have liked to visit the Botanical Gardens, seeking inspiration, but they were closed. The Wildfowl and Wetland Centre was closed. The nine miles of sand-dunes leading to the beaches and Country Park of Cefn Sidan, Helen's favourite haunt when she first came to live in the area, all were closed. Helen could ask Anne to drive as she had brought her own small Renault over to Wales with her, but that would hardly be a relaxed outing for Anne and still wouldn't solve the problem of where to go. Sitting in Neil's house, Anne and Helen looked at each other, stumped. Neil's mother was out, as so often seemed to be the case nowadays.

'I know. If we go for a walk along the seafront in Llanelli, we could visit my friend Charlotte, play with her baby for half an hour. She lives in Seaside.'

'Is there a seafront in Llanelli?'

Helen shook her head. 'That's disgraceful. We've been so busy taking you out and about everywhere else, we haven't shown you the improvements in our own back yard. Grab a coat and let's go - I'll phone Charlotte and let her know we're coming.'

'Shouldn't we have a small dog?' asked Anne as they passed yet another ankle-height fur-ball scampering along the promenade. 'Or should we stay in the car and eat fish and chips?'

'I think the dog's optional,' laughed Helen, picking strands of wind-swept hair out of her eyes. 'I should have put my hair up - I'd forgotten how windy it could be.' She paused, leaning over the sea-wall. She looked back at the cars, occupied by old couples and workers on their lunch breaks, parked in front of the information centre. 'We're too young to sit in a car.' Even from this distance, the women could see the car screens condensing so that the passengers would have seen very little of the sea view through their windscreens. Anne shrugged. 'This is not how we picnic in France.'

Helen pointed to the silvery rivulets running between the estuary sandbanks. The tide was low enough to almost connect Llanelli with the Gower Peninsula, across a maze of treacherous mud beds, sinking soft and quickly stranded as the tide turned. 'Look, by the land rover. They could be digging for lug-worm - bait for fishermen or they could be cockle-pickers.'

Anne noted the cars and small pick-up trucks on the beach. 'Is it safe to drive on the sands?'

'Shouldn't think so but that seems to be part of modern cockle-picking.'

'How do they do it?'

'Dig and shake them through a sieve, I think.' Anne was surprised that Helen was so vague about this local curiosity. Still trying to recall more detail, Helen added, 'I know there are quotas and that there have been wars over people poaching on other people's patches.'

'Wars?'

'The papers called them the cockle wars but I suppose it was more of a scrap, you know, the odd fisticuffs. They said that the cockles were being over-fished, so they limited them, and then the next year they said there was a glut and overpopulation was killing the cockles. I think it depends as much on the weather and the river as on the fishermen. Used to be fisherwomen in the nineteenth century.'

'We had this wonderful dish with cockles at home.' Anne could smell the salty wine sauce as she spoke, 'My mother swears by

Sylvaner for cockles...'

''Giving them a little drink', my grandmother used to say.'

'Your grandmother lives round here?'

'No, my grandmother lived in Yorkshire. Plenty of good fish-markets up that way.' Not for the first time, Helen seemed reluctant to talk about her family. 'What does that remind you of?' She pointed at some railings, jutting out above the path.

Anne squinted at the railings and the two of them walked up to the small alcove created. Helen walked to the point where the railings met and she held out both her arms, pretending to fly. 'Now what does it remind you of?'

Anne was puzzled but amused. 'I don't know'

'Don't you get Hollywood movies in France?' Anne was still stuck so Helen enlightened her.

'It's supposed to be like the prow in 'Titanic', you know where he holds her?'

'Ah.' Light dawned. 'And Celine Dion sings. I have seen the video of the song but not the film.'

'Long, miserable... but good,' was Helen's verdict. She led Anne along the prom, enthusing about the lawns and seating which replaced the waste ground of a disused chemicals factory. 'I know it doesn't help with creating jobs but when you think what was here before, it's a miracle. I'll tell you the biggest miracle - ' They were standing on the red gra of an arched footbridge, with a view back along the prom, out to sea, and over a landscaped park with a central lake. 'Sandy Water Park. I lived near here for a bit and there was nothing like this. It was all scrap metal, unofficial tipping and the earth red or blue with hazardous stuff. There have been mallards, wild swans and cormorants here for a while - see the cormorant on the raft in the middle, drying his wings? - but now they've even got otters.'

Anne tried to respond to this enthusiasm at the rebirth of a landscape. 'I think there is some work with otters at the Stork Park, in Hunawihr.'

'Yes, Neil's told me. Great, isn't it.' Anne shivered, losing interest rapidly in cormorants and otters.

'It is cold after a while. Charlotte's just across the road here -

hope you don't mind babies.'

'I'd be out of a job without them.' Like Neil, Anne too could use a teacher's pat response to hide her feelings.

'Thank God. Reinforcements. Auntie Helen's here,' Charlotte told a large, squirming baby as she passed it straight over to 'Auntie Helen' before Helen even stepped over the threshold. 'Here, you have her.'

'Thanks, 'said Helen, holding the baby against one hip and struggling to remove her fleece at the same time. 'Bad day? This is Anne.'

'It's always a bad day. It's ten bad days in one with ten good days in between and that's all in one normal human day.' She glared at the baby, took coats from Helen and Anne, hooked them at the bottom of the stairs and led the way into the sitting room, talking all the while. 'You have no idea what it's like.'

Helen knew exactly what it was like but only Dai knew that. It was hard for Helen to watch her friend becoming a mother, hard to listen to the innocent patter knifing her wounds and hardest of all to hold Chloe, with her smell of milk and baby shampoo. She cried in Dai's arms after the first time being 'Auntie Helen' but when he told her not to go, not to put herself through it, something in her had determined to win through. Her reward was the baby herself, nestled against Helen's neck, sucking her hair in the perennial search for food that was still Chloe's obsession, even at eight months, when the oral fixation was heightened with teething problems.

Charlotte alternated between hysterical depression and equally hysterical pride, often fluctuating more quickly between the two than Chloe between her alleged mood swings. 'This is so cute, you have to see her,' said Charlotte. 'Put her down beside the coffee table. There, so she can hold on to it.' Helen followed instructions dutifully.

To her mother's delight, Chloe performed. She took toddling steps around the table, clinging on tightly, and was going for a second round tour when one hand slipped, she banged her chin and the room filled with Chloe crying and Charlotte cooing as she cuddled her. Both noises ceased, Chloe was placed standing by

Auntie Helen's knee, where she repeated her manoeuvre along Helen and the settee, a softer landing when her hand slipped.

'There,' declared Charlotte, expecting praise for this child prodigy whom she had produced. Helen and Anne were kind enough to oblige.

'She'll be walking before you know it.'

'Such an expressive face. She looks just like you.' If there is a parent who can resist having a child's resemblance being pointed out, it was not Charlotte. She beamed.

'If I'd known you were out walking, you could have taken Chloe,' she said, her tone making it clear that this would have been a treat and concession for the two women rather than for Chloe.

'Another time...' Helen was politely regretful. 'How's work?' Charlotte worked as a care assistant at the local Prince Phillip Hospital.

'I'm still not sure I did the right thing staying on. I know it's only part-time and I'd probably go crazy if I was with Chloe all the time and Dan wanted a baby but he doesn't get the changes to his life, does he, and all these Malaysian nurses, I can't always understand what they say and I wonder if my job would still be there to go back to if I did take a year or two out...' As Charlotte talked, Helen nodded and listened, but she was watching Anne.

Chloe edged around the couch and reached across to the next chair, where Anne was sitting. She stretched out a tentative hand, un-noticed by her mother, who was taking the chance to talk to the only person over one-year-old whom she had seen that week - according to Charlotte, who talked of her husband Dan as if he were an alien with visiting rights.

Chloe's hand lighted on the stranger's lap and was quickly withdrawn as Chloe weighed up this new woman and her potential as furniture. What struck Helen was the wistful look on Anne's face as she waited patiently for the baby to decide on its next move.

Anne slowly held out a hand to offer support and encouragement. Chloe sucked her thumb meditatively and then took first one hand, then the other, which was held out to support her across the abyss between the couch and the chair. Chuckling, Chloe placed both hands on Anne's lap and bounced enthusiastically until she sat, suddenly. Anne was smiling but with tears in her eyes as she lifted the baby off the floor, onto her lap and into her arms. She picked up a cuddly rabbit and sang a French nursery song softly, catching Helen's eye as both women reached for someone else's baby.

'It's been really good to talk to you and Chloe's always so good with you. You're a natural - you'd be a great mother, Helen - I don't know why you don't go for a baby, yourself.' Charlotte was cheerfully saying goodbye.

'I can always borrow yours - and give her back. The best of both worlds,' Helen said lightly, kissing the fine blonde hair on Chloe's head.

The two women spoke of Llanelli's industrial past, unemployment problems and cockles, all the way back to Neil's house. No-one mentioned babies.

Dai was in heated argument with his senior partner David, trying to control his anger enough to keep the dispute from the veterinary nurses the other side of a thin wall.

'Why should anyone go to Powys? One, we have more than enough work here; two, foot and mouth could reach us and then all hell will break loose here, never mind Powys; three, I have personal commitments, a family and my own stock to check up on - why the hell should I put myself through that sort of strain - and you know the sort of work it will be. As if you don't get enough heartache in the day to day of this job without farmers pointing guns at you and the Ministry for Agriculture and Fisheries on your back.'

David, as always, was the calm voice of reason. 'We've been offered a lot of money and we've been asked for help - the combination is hard to resist. '

'So we say very sorry - no.'

'I don't need to tell you that the money would be useful.' David didn't need to press the point that the routine tuberculosis and brucella checks, funded by the Ministry, had stopped with the onset of foot and mouth, severely depleting the practice income. 'The Ministry desperately needs Temporary Veterinary Inspectors. Also, if we can keep it in Powys, we keep it away.'

David certainly didn't need to spell out the consequences of foot and mouth reaching Carmarthenshire, along with neighbouring Pembrokeshire, the dairy garden of Wales. Even if it reached a neighbour's herd, the honey-brown dual purpose Salar cattle, which he and his father bought in from the French Aubrac with such optimism, would be doomed. To create the 'fire-wall' that they hoped would stop the disease, beautiful healthy animals would be killed in their hundreds. Which was exactly what David committed him to in Powys. Diagnosing and killing, day upon day. And endless paperwork to read, reconcile with the real world as far as was possible, and return to MAF.

'Why me? Why can't you go?' He knew he sounded petulant but he didn't care.

David's grey eyes held his, absolutely on the level. 'Because when I diagnose foot and mouth, I'm going to be right 90% of the time; you'll get 99%.'

'That's bull. Anyone can recognise an epidemic. One cow goes down first thing in the morning, four by lunch-time, ten by tea...' but Dai couldn't help being flattered and he knew that his instincts about animals and his interest in homeopathic veterinary treatments sometimes got results where David's technology couldn't help them. On the other hand, if it was a question of state-of-the-art testing or surgery techniques, David was your man every time. The partnership worked very well but Dai felt he was really drawing the short straw this time. He demurred.

'I don't know how old you think I am but I wasn't around in the sixties. I've never seen a case of foot and mouth in my life, outside a text-book, any more than you have.'

'You can see as many as you like when you get to Powys, get your eye in. Anyway, you'll know what it's not and be able to eliminate.' Both vets knew that it was easy to confuse the symptoms of foot and mouth, particularly in sheep, with the common ailments of watery mouth, which also showed in blisters, or foot rot. The weather did not help during this cold, wet spring, promoting not only foot and mouth but all the diseases that came from over-wintering in boggy fields with diminishing fodder. 'Half the game is being able to work with the farmers and you have the edge there - you can put hand on heart and say you know how they feel.'

'That's why I don't want to go,' but Dai knew when he had lost. 'When have you said I'd be there? And how long for?'

'I said you'd get back to them.' That was something anyway. Dai was feeling the 'Junior' in front of partner rather more than was comfortable. 'I think it would be wise to call it a fortnight but leave it open-ended. If only we did know what this bloody disease would do next.'

'What about the work here?'

David gave a wry smile. 'I've cancelled sleep for a while. I'll do double surgeries and we'll postpone some of the more routine stuff if we can. I might be able to get a Bristol student, especially if I play the national crisis card, but there's high demand and short supply at the moment.'

Dai should have known he would not be alone in taking on extra work.

'Oh,' David added, 'I should have said that the arrangement is 60:40. You get 40% of the payment and 60% comes to the practice.'

'Me personally?' Dai frowned. 'I didn't think we took a personal cut.'

'These are not normal times. I do know what it's going to be like - you might as well get paid for it. Fair bit of money gone on those Salars I should think.' With average costs running at £3,000 a cow, Dai had indeed spent a lot of money on his father's herd. He had also spent heavily on the cottage; he was paying his father monthly for its purchase and the renovation and furnishing cost more than he had expected. It was worth every penny to see Helen's face when she walked into her dream house. Still, he didn't like to think too much about finances at the moment and the extra income would be very welcome.

'Thanks,' he said awkwardly.

'I forgot to mention,' David added as he turned to go, his hand on the door handle,' the Evening Post wants to interview you about the work you'll be doing. Every crisis makes a hero.'

'No,' was the unshakeable response. 'No. I will face all hell in Powys for you, for the money, for whatever, but I will not go through a newspaper interview.'

David too recognized defeat and shrugged. 'OK. I'll take the interview. It's good for business.'

Dai felt no guilt. 'I'm sure that would be better - you can give it the right spin.'

'You might regret that. You do realize you'll be the town's sex symbol once I've built you up?'

'I'll cope. Haven't we got some work to do?'

'Amputation on a terrier, two cat castrations... and a scale and polish on an alsation.'

'Time I was off then.' David was carrying out surgery that day and Dai was doing the farm rounds. He whistled to his black and white sheepdog Demi, who often joined him on his rounds, and headed off down the valley.

Helen was browsing through some leaflet when Dai arrived home.

'Anything interesting?'

'Junk. But look at this.' The leaflet was a mail order catalogue for discount books and Helen showed him the thumbnail picture of a cover with the title 'FOR WOMEN ONLY a revolutionary guide to overcoming...' and the last word covered completely by a red sticker with 'NEW' written over it in yellow lettering. 'I've been trying to work out what the word should be.'

'Fat,' he contributed.

'Boring. How about 'blocked sinks'.'

'And you thought 'fat' was boring. How about 'their fear of spiders''

'Wouldn't fit in the space 'Their fears' isn't bad - it might just be right.'

'I didn't know we were aiming for realism. 'Blocked sinks' wouldn't fit either.'

'But they're very realistic,' she grinned winningly.

'I'm not playing with you any more - you keep changing the

rules.'

'What's wrong?' She always knew. Sometimes he wished she didn't. He needed to know more about his own feelings before he could share them. Sometimes words were difficult and he didn't want to say the wrong thing.

'I've got to go to Powys.' She looked puzzled. 'They haven't got enough vets. There were forty-five cases last time I checked.' Every night, he checked the designated Teletext page which gave an update on the number of cases and every day it was worse. Like so many farmers, he found out more from the television news than he did from the official sources.

The communication problems were exacerbated by the farmers' desire to isolate their properties, preventing even postmen from calling, and by the additional agencies now involved in the crisis. He was not sure what the role of the army was, and what the role of MAF. He was pretty sure that they were no wiser themselves and into this chaos he was expected to bring his professional judgement.

He tried his best to explain to Helen, giving some of the answers that David gave to him, but he knew how inadequate he sounded.

'I don't see why they don't just vaccinate the animals. It's not as if it's contagious to humans anyway. Why kill healthy animals?' Helen too was

clearly following the media debate.

'There's so much we don't know, Helen. If we could go back two months to when this started, if we'd known it would be on this scale, perhaps the Chief Vet would have tackled it differently - who knows? The idea is that we stop it as quickly as possible, with British meat okayed for export again as soon as we can show we're clear. Vaccination would slow the whole process down and the animals would still have to be killed and disposed of at some stage.'
'I just don't understand, 'Helen complained.

'Truth is, neither do I. There are too many different views and they're all based on predictions. You've got the hair for it,' he reached out and stroked the red wires frizzing in a halo around her pale face, 'if you could only use your witching talents on a crystal ball, it would help a lot.'

'I wish I could keep you safe, and your Dad, and even your beloved cows, and end all this... mess'

He stroked her cheek with the back of her hand and she caught it in her own. 'No cow has freckles like yours.' He smiled at her.

'What can I do to help?'

'Just be here.' He kissed the top of her head lightly. 'I need to talk to Dad - I'm going to be away for at least a fortnight and he'll need to carry on checking the cows every day, to see they're clear. I've got some video to show him so he knows what he's looking for. Are you coming up?'

There was a pause and her voice seemed very subdued when she replied. 'No, I'll stay here.' It must all be a strain for her too, thought Dai, and he knew she chafed at the constraints. It was not just the stock that was under movement restrictions. He must talk to his father about that, too.

The top field was getting over-grazed, more mud than grass, and they were not allowed to move livestock across a road or across someone else's land, so Will would have to leave it to the last moment before letting the cows into the other field on this side of the lane. No-one knew how long the restrictions would last, even if - Dai crossed his fingers - they stayed free of the disease.

He knew of farmers who were already having problems from lack of grazing land that they could legally access and who had to watch their sheep or calves fighting for a last blade of grass in the churned mud of their field. He also knew the despair that was caused by the closure of the markets. Farmers, already beaten down by the BSE years, had to feed and house unwanted animals growing too big to keep or sell.

It was small wonder that lambs were being dumped, one of them even found in a telephone kiosk, and that the welfare problems were as much of an issue as the foot and mouth itself. Dai needed a long talk with his father to ensure that he knew all the likely problems - and their solutions - for the coming weeks. With so much on his mind, he was abstracted in his leave-taking, kissing Helen briefly and whistling all three dogs to accompany him to BryngMore.

Helen watched his back disappearing, wondering if he would turn and wave, but he didn't. The long-legged wolfhound bounded around his master while the Jack Russell, Janie, put the 'dogged' in 'determination' with five steps to Dai's every stride. As always, the sheepdog was within inches of his left side, searching his face, checking what he wanted all the way. What sort of a pet was she, Helen, she wondered bitterly. When he was upset, where did he go? His Mam and Dad.

She made a cup of tea and took it into the garden, braving the cold, grey dusk. At least it was dry for once. She sat on the small wooden seat which Dai had placed at the edge of the rose garden they planted in memory of little Rebecca, and she lost herself in her memories.

Chapter 7

It had come as a shock to Anne to find out that she had a half-sister. She had only just grown used to her mother talking about her young love for a man who was not Anne's father, when Elsë dropped the bombshell.

Anne grew up knowing about her mother's annual pilgrimage to the cross in the woods and accepted it, apart from a brief bout of rebellion as a teenager, when she challenged her father over his complaisance.

'Don't you care,' she fired at him, 'that he still means something to her?' and he thought for a long time, in that slow way of his, before answering, 'I owe him. More than you can ever know... and far more than a day a year for Maman's memories.'

Did he mean that he could not have married Elsë if Vernon had not died? He didn't know that. Who knew whether the attachment would have lasted?

Later, she wondered if Ernst was thinking of the war itself, of the part played by Vernon and men like him, of being too young himself to take the risks they took. She still did not understand his answer but her father was not a man to press about his feelings. They existed, solid as the prehistoric stone monuments on the Taenchel, but you would never read the marks of rain or shine on his square-jawed face. His shy boyhood left him with the habit of avoiding people's eyes and when he did make contact, the blue of his gaze was all the more startling. Now it seemed that he had accepted even more about her mother's past than Anne had thought. How had he coped?

Her mother's story was told over the long winter nights, after her father's death, when there were just the two of them. Elsë's love affair with Vernon resulted in a baby girl, born on 6th June 1945. While France was celebrating the anniversary of the Normandy landings, Elsë was in labour, to the horror and distress of her parents.

There was no way of letting Vernon know he was to be a father and Elsë refused to tell her parents 'who was responsible', to protect him from their anger. However, she believed, and believed it still, at seventy-three, that he would have kept his promise and returned to marry her, if he lived. Strong in that belief, she thought he should know about the baby and so, without telling her parents, she wrote to him at the address of his family in Llanelli which he had given her 'in case of emergency.'

They had both known that the 'emergency' was likely to be his death, about which she would get no information, but which might be reported to his family in Wales. Neither of them had considered the possibility of her pregnancy in their innocence and the passion of the moment. How often she wished she had never sent that letter or that it had been lost, like so many others sent across war-torn Europe.

Although, in June, Alsace had been liberated for three months, communications were still erratic and Elsë took her precious letter to one of the contacts for whom she had played postperson and asked him to send it. Whatever its journey, it reached the large house on the Trimsaran Road, behind Stradey Woods, which Vernon described to Elsë as a tiny bit of Taenchel with a sea view. It was opened by Vernon's parents, discussed in a family conference with his married sister and her husband, and resulted in a written response from the Davies family to Elsë's parents. This letter, too, travelled over water and under fire to reach Monsieur and Madame Bikhart in September.

From then on Elsë was no more than the passive recipient of other people's decisions, which were carried out so quickly she could do nothing but plead, unheard, to keep her baby. She was just seventeen and that was an end to the matter.

The Davies family very kindly offered to take this shame off the

Bikhart family and Vernon's sister would bring the baby up as her own. Not only would the child have a father but she would also have the chance to gain a good education and to grow up in a prosperous family in Britain, free of the after-effects of war - or so it seemed to the Bikharts.

Elsë should be grateful that what could be rescued from the situation, would be. Of course she had ruined her own life and could expect only the treatment her reputation deserved. On September 29th, Elsë's mother took baby Marie out of Elsë 's arms and Elsë had not seen her daughter since.

She cried herself out of tears, hoped that Vernon was alive and that he would return home, find his daughter and come to get her too. That dream ended with Tobias Goldberg's news of Vernon's death. If her parents heard the news too and felt for their daughter's loss, they gave no sign.

Even in times of war, the stigma of an illegitimate birth was painful to them, and they wished nothing more than to pretend it had never happened. The only concession her mother made was to tell her that Vernon's sister, Ffion, had seemed very kind, and being childless still after four years' marriage, was happy to call this baby her own. Elsë assumed from this that her mother travelled to meet up with Ffion and passed over her - Elsë 's - baby, like a pair of black market stockings, she told her daughter bitterly.

Elsë avoided the knowing looks of the villagers, particularly those of young men her age, and found comfort in the innocence of Ernst, three years younger than her. It was not that he was unaware of her story - or the embroideries on it picked out by vicious tongues; it was more that he was unaffected by it. He was Ernst and she was Elsë . When he started carving small gifts for her, she realized that the feelings of friendship had become something more. Surprised at herself, she realized that this was not unwelcome and she let the river of her life carry her away from the storm damage to the broad tide of her marriage.

She loved her husband and she dearly loved their daughter - how she stressed this to Anne when telling her this unbelievable story - but she had never forgotten baby Marie. Having survived the first feelings of terrible loss, she thought it for the best to leave things as they were, but now she was not so sure. She could not help wondering - and Anne must not take this as any lack in her - what if she had grandchildren? For Anne too, wouldn't it be wonderful to know the rest of her family, perhaps find children there to brighten their lives the way that children do, to point to the future.

Anne would have loved to disagree, to say that there was no need for others, but how could she when she was feeling the same longing herself? She was torn between jealous rejection of this 'other family' whose existence changed her place, her sense of who she was, and a curiosity to meet these relatives, to look for the familiar faces and habits. She stalled, said she needed time to think, but in the end there had been Anton and an advert for a teacher exchange in Llanelli.

Anne had promised to try and track Marie down and, if she found her, to tell her of her family in Alsace. It was understood between Elsë and Anne that, if Marie could be found, Anne would find a way to reunite her with her birth mother. The detail of this was something Anne had not yet considered - and might not need to.

So far, her hours online had taken her to the Family Record Centre, where all records of births, deaths and marriages were held, and also, as is the way for Internet users, along the occasional sidetrack. Her searches for 'family tree' offered a list of convicts deported to Australia, a copy of the Queen Mother's birth certificate and various genealogy search services - for a price.

Through the Family Record Centre, she tracked down the registration of Vernon's birth easily enough from her mother's information about his age and birthday. Chatting to the librarian led to the bonus of discovering the school records of the Boys' Grammar School, now closed, where Vernon's name and address were neatly recorded and given a roll number. It gave Anne an odd feeling to see this evidence of her mother's lover as an eleven-year-old starting grammar school and to know his future. She photocopied the entry for her mother, remembering her mother saying, 'We didn't even think of love tokens; we didn't need them. But he did leave a love token after all and she was taken from me.'

Anne intended to keep any mementos of Vernon that she found, as keepsakes for her mother. Perhaps, subconsciously, she wanted to present her mother with a little box of memories to her mother instead of another daughter. She followed the librarian's suggestion, looked through the school memorabilia, and found the Roll of Honour which had hung in the School Hall, with Vernon's name recorded among the fallen. Her mother would be glad that he was acknowledged in his home town and Anne took a photograph to add to the precious box.

Vernon's birth certificate gave the parents' Christian names and enabled her to find Ffion's birth registration. Then the trail grew cold as she pondered how to find Ffion's marriage details, and she used Internet searches to try and spark a new line of enquiry. She found it easy to ignore the site offering 'Particularly silly names - not for the easily offended', but she despaired of the time wasted in trying to find the diamonds among the dustbins of the world's web-site and she paid for a firm to search one particular year's birth records.

From her mother's report - taken from *her* mother - that the child would be 'brought up as her own' by Ffion, she thought it possible that Marie's birth was registered in Llanelli. Also, if you considered the attitudes of the time, when adoption was more often hidden from the adopted child and, where possible, the outside world, it was probable that Ffion would do all she could to pass the baby off as her own.

If - and it was a big if - Ffion had kept the name Marie, then there was a chance of finding baby Marie with mother Ffion, registered in September 1945. Anne reasoned that the baby was already getting on for four months old and, given that births were supposed to be registered within six weeks, Ffion would surely register Marie as soon as she possibly could - the beginning of October at the latest. If Anne was right, she could get a copy of the birth certificate, which would tell her Ffion's married name - and the surname under which little Marie had grown up. What to do after that was a bit of a mystery to her but she would take one step at a time.

'I have some news for you too,' her mother said after listening to Anne's findings. Anne waited. 'I don't know how you feel about him now but I think you should know that Anton is getting married.'

'That's nice.' Pity her, then. Didn't take him long. 'Who to?'

'I don't know. I just heard that he was engaged and getting married in the summer.'

Anne could imagine it all too well, her mother buying some groceries, a friendly neighbour asking after her daughter, saying 'Wasn't she going out with Anton Kagel? Have you heard he's getting married? And Anne? Does she have someone? Such a shame to see her alone at her age...' She was a 'vieille fille', an old maid, to her mother's acquaintance.

'I wish them both well,' Anne told her mother, who changed the subject.

Alone in her bedroom, unable to sleep, Anne contemplated what she wasn't. She wasn't Madame Anton Kagel, although she thought she could have been if she'd wanted. She could have had married status, as it said on forms. She imagined her wedding day, frocks, frills and wellwishers, spoilt only by having to share it with Anton.

Even in her fantasy, he was brushing an imaginary hair from his jacket, spreading his smile like neon lighting. Anne knew exactly what sort of woman he'd married, a designer wife to go with the 'grande marque' suits. No, Anton replacing her so quickly only roused the instinctive, superficial dog-in-a manger ownership - I don't want him but I don't see why someone else should have him. How long was it? Under a year anyway.

The real hurt was what else she was not. She was not a mother and never likely to be. Not that marrying Anton would have changed that. She wondered if Madame-Kagel-to-be knew his feelings on the subject but then again, she thought cynically, she'd seen men his age - and older - change their minds. Women didn't have the option. A dull ache in her belly added its own comment to her thoughts and she padded to the bathroom. *It would have to start tonight*, she thought, *one egg less from the few that were left.*

Weeks turned to a month when the search response reached Anne. There were three lists included, with a name highlighted on each list and a note too, saying that as well as babies called Marie, there was one Mair, the Welsh version of Mary or Marie. Anne looked at the three entries, waiting for some sixth sense to help her. In each case, the entry in the 'District' column was 'Llanelli' and the Volume was the same, indicating the Register used in Llanelli Registry Office during late September. The page numbers were the same for two of the babies and the consecutive number for the third Marie.

JONES, Marie
THOMAS, Mair
WATKINS, Marie

There was no moment of revelation. Anne sighed and tried to think logically. Perhaps this was all a stupid paper chase. It was quite likely that none of these babies was her half-sister. Even if one were, what would she gain from a birth certificate? How would this help her find Marie, now a full grown woman some twelve years her senior? With the same dogged determination that drove her father in his craft, Anne decided to keep going, although with no clear idea of what use she could make of the information. She sent for all three birth certificates, so she could check the mother's name on them. If the mother were Ffion, then Anne would work on the assumption that this was baby Marie and would gain the surname she was seeking. If nothing else , the birth certificate would be another small treasure for the box.

While waiting for the certificates to be returned, Anne visited the Trimsaran Road address to which her mother sent the fateful letter, announcing the birth of her - Anne winced - first daughter. The bus took her along a road which quickly left the terraced streets of the town centre, heading west through wooded verges, with occasional glimpses of the estuary visible down steep slopes between the trees. Uncertain how far along the road she would need to go to find the house, Anne chose to alight at the Farrier's Arms, a landmark to which she could return and which would provide a lunch-time pick-me-up which she suspected would be needed.

She was wearing the sturdy walking shoes that tramped the Vosges and a sudden longing for home, mixed with a sudden reluctance to see the very house she came here to visit, made her cross the road from the pub and take a footpath into Stradey Woods. Spring was struggling through weeks of unrelenting cold rain to bring on the blackthorn in the shrubby edging to the woodland.

Anne went deeper in, among the oaks and beeches, which were shorter and stockier than their siblings in the mountain forests of her home. She was used to craning her neck to see the treetops, thirty feet and more above her, so that she could only just spot the needled crown of a Scots pine through the shimmer of birch leaves. At home, the trees touched the sky and dared the lightning. Here, the trees risked less and the sky hung close and heavy.

A watery ray of sunshine escaped the threatening clouds to illuminate the way ahead of her and she followed the light. Familiar scuffles announced the creatures she could not see; the light rustle of leaves and pause and rustle which was probably a bird; the sustained and diminishing scurry of a small rodent; the vanishing bush-tail of a squirrel up a tree. Although she thought she was going deeper into the woods, the path must have taken a turn for she found herself nearing the road again, the sound of traffic clearly audible.

The wood was a pretty little haven but it amused her to think of Vernon likening it to her home forests. Here it was difficult to get far away from people; at home it was more likely you would lose yourself forever. Another shaft of light broke free and there, among the more widely spaced trees at the edge of the woods, a patch of bluebells glowed violet in the sunshine. Behind them in the distance, a glimpse of sparkling silver shone then dulled again to the moody pewter of the Irish Sea.

Glimpses, Anne thought, Llanelli gave her only glimpses, but she felt less tense as she found the road. She ignored the coke cans, plastic carriers and take-away containers which had been thrown out of passing cars and landed along the verges of the road, and she walked from the pub back towards Llanelli until she could identify a house number.

Anne stopped at the double iron gates and looked up the drive at a large white house, grand in the Victorian style. Sloping lawns, impeccably edged and mowed, were uninterrupted by a single flower or tree. The symmetry of the façade, two windows and front door on the ground floor, three windows upstairs and two in the roof gables had the blandness of a child's drawing, even to the curtains neatly edging each window.

To Anne's fancy, it was exactly the sort of place for such a cold decision to be taken. She imagined the Davies family discussing their duty, dismissing her mother as a foreign slut, an irrelevance, but acknowledging a debt to the family genes. A debt to their son. She knew she was being unfair and she had no reason to doubt that they loved their son, that Ffion loved her brother. Perhaps they wondered if he were still alive. Perhaps they already knew he was dead. Unlike her mother they would have had the right to be informed. Her mother, a seventeen-year-old unmarried mother in a small Alsace village, had no rights at all, not even to her own baby.

'Are you looking for something?' Anne jumped, too lost in thought to have noticed a car pulling up at the gates. The woman driving had wound down the window to ask the question but was already opening her door. She opened the gates, looking with curiosity at Anne.

'Yes. I mean no. Well, yes,' Anne admitted. 'I am over from France,' she hoped that would excuse her strange behaviour, 'and a friend of my mother's lived here during the war.' That was close enough to the truth.

'Well, we've lived here for ten years now and the people before us were Geordies if that's any help.'

'Geordies?' queried Anne, wondering if this meant from Georgia, USA, Russia, the Antarctic?

'You know, from Newcastle way, the North of England. Great accent. At one time Trimsaran was all Durham miners you know. They settled here to work the mines, when the mines were working of course.' She caught herself, 'No, I don't suppose you would know if you're French and that.'

Anne wondered if 'and that' was worse or better than being French. In her Llanelli year, she often had to cope with people being astounded at her ignorance, usually of matters so local that it was unlikely people in a neighbouring town would have known them, never mind someone from another country. She even more frequently had to politely hide her amazement at Llanelli people's ignorance of the most basic knowledge about France or the rest of the world. She wondered if Neil was finding a similarly egocentric view in Thannenkirch.

The house-owner continued, 'I don't suppose that's any use to you.'

'Probably not,' Anne agreed politely, watching the driver return to her car and ease it through the gates, 'but thanks anyway. I'll do that for you.' She closed the gates and turned to go.

'Oh there is one thing,' the woman called through her window after Anne. 'If I say it myself, this is a posh house and there aren't many like it in the area. You might find that the Estate Agent can go back a bit further in owners. They remember houses like this and they might keep stuff on file. James Gordon, Llanelli, was the one we used and I'm sure the bloke said he knew the house way back. You know what they're like - they'd say anything to make a sale so I can't say I listened to half of it.'

'Thank you.' It didn't sound likely but you never knew what snippet might fit with what other information.

The next day, the birth certificates arrived. Only one had a Ffion as a mother, Ffion Watkins, so at least that ruled out the other two, and, if this was indeed the right baby, that gave a surname. 'Marie Watkins,' Anne mused aloud, adding the birth certificate to her treasure box. So she was looking for Marie Watkins, legally born on 27th September 1945, to Ffion and Sion Watkins, actually born on 6th June to Elsë Brokhart and Vernon Davies. There was always the possibility that Marie Watkins was married, and, if so, Anne could now find that marriage certificate, which would give Marie's married name and keep the search going. She could also find Ffion's marriage certificate although she had no idea what use that would be to her.

Meanwhile, there was a complete set of French books to mark and she needed to prepare 'sport' as a topic for a group that she had learnt to say 'had special needs'.

There were some days she felt that every class she taught 'had special needs' and gave her a special headache. Still, that went with the job and her English was really coming on. Her moments of glory in the Staffroom came when she announced, 'I'll just sit by here' and 'I think Angela Lewis is on the mitch.' She was fascinated by the use of prepositions in the grammar of Llanelli dialect but she could not find matching enthusiasm in any of her colleagues.

In her collège there would have been at least four professeurs desperate to discuss the language derivation of this use of prepositions, and whether it was the structure of Welsh which influenced the dialect form of English. Things were different here. Still, whatever the stresses of teaching, the least she could say about being Neil was that it was an effective distraction from the frustrations of her detective work.

Helen shook her long mane of hair, shaking out Wales and its foot and mouth restrictions, and she breathed in France. She was working on her designs, feeling increasingly isolated in the empty cottage, and the suggestion from the Voudoirs that she join Amélie on a fortnight's tour of the outdoor markets in the villages along the Lot Valley, came at the right time. Dai was staying in a Bed and Breakfast in Llandrindod Wells, partly for convenience and partly to protect his own stock from the infectious areas he visited daily.

His phone calls were brief and awkward, neither of them having 'good news' to ease the artificial conversation into familiarity. Helen knew that Dai's only news would be of tests, deaths and farmers' anger, so she didn't ask - and he didn't volunteer - the detail of his day and at such a time she found it surreal to talk of jumpers. It was almost a relief to put herself out of reach, suggesting that phone calls would be too expensive so he should not worry about contact while she was away. Throwing herself into her work would stop her wondering if the distance between them was more than geographical.

Amélie did not stop talking from the moment she picked up Helen from the station but Helen was listening to the quick French with only half an ear as they drove past balconies festooned with anemones, lobelia and the first geraniums; slate gables glistening metallic in the sun; cobbled side-streets where houses leaned conversationally across the gap. In the countryside between villages, the towers and dovecotes attached to rambling medieval farmhouses suggested fairytale princesses and spinning-wheel curses. Running through the heart of the valley was the River Lot, rippling clear and swift over stony shallows with darker, stiller depths under trees or pools out of the main current. The sparkle could have been just sunshine on water or it could have been the trout for which the Lot was famous to fishermen throughout France.

Amélie expertly parked the battered Renault with a screech of brakes and an inch to spare between it, two cars and a tree, and picked her heel-clicking way to the shop window. Helen crimsoned, seeing for the first time her designs in the window of the little wool shop on the square where she first met Madame Voudoir, Amélie's mother. She looked behind her, expecting people to be pointing and commenting but the locals went about their business, apparently unconcerned at her presence or at the shop window display. Which was brilliant.

Amélie had displayed the 'Helen designer range for Spring' against cut-outs of spring flowers and garden birds which echoed the colours and motifs on the knitwear. There had definitely been some marketing savvy applied since Helen had first seen the shop. In fact she told Madame Voudoir at the time that the knitted samples in the window were boring, and the old lady had not missed a stitch as she agreed, explained what they did well - they were proficient in knitting techniques and business knowledge - and what was lacking - designer spark. Some partnerships were made in heaven and Helen had recognized the opportunity as exactly that. As she looked at Amélie's placards emphasizing the 'English cachet' of the collection, she realized that, when she ran a shop herself, she could have done more to catch and retain her customers' attention.

'It looks great,' she congratulated Amélie, 'but I suppose the question has got to be - is it selling?'

Amélie screwed up her mouth in thought and Helen's heart sank.

'I am happy,' was the verdict of the company's business brains.

'You don't sound happy.'

'It doesn't do to be complacent and - as you know - this is a slow trade, to be built up carefully, by reputation and personal contact, so customers will come back, but Christmas was good - and that is so important - and many a mother bought a child's jumper for Easter best, so that is all good. I hesitate because the big test is summer, which started with the spring tourists but is getting into full swing now and we must cash in. That's why these markets are so important and we have a problem.'

Again, Helen waited apprehensively.

'It is great that you are English because in France that gives a little cachet.'

Helen smiled and indicated the window, 'I saw the signs.'

Amélie acknowledged the reference and continued, 'But it is bad news in other ways. There are so many local laws around even the ordinary street markets, which must promote French produce. Any market is only allowed a proportion of licenses for 'outsider' stall-holders. Even Senegalese or Algerians who live in France and sell ethnic goods, leatherwear and so on are limited by these laws.'

'But that's racist.'

Amélie shrugged. 'It's a way of ensuring the French identity of the market and protecting the local producers. How would you have liked it if a French designer set up shop beside yours?'

Helen was not going to admit that she would not have liked it at all, particularly as 'French' would have the cachet in Britain that she hoped for in reverse, in France.

'And the cheese makers would kill someone who sold... I don't even know the name of a British cheese...'

'Cheddar.'

'Who sold cheddar at a French market. I don't understand your farmers who allow a French market in their towns. It is business suicide. Especially when someone compares your cheese to ours.' Helen fought the instinct to defend cheddar and concentrated on her business entente.

'But you are French.'

'Just so. We must perform a political sleight of hand for the markets; on the one hand, our English cachet, on the other hand our French workmanship and business location. I have to be very careful in how I complete the forms to apply for a license. The general markets are not so difficult and we will work the villages while you are here so you can add your English accent to our stall, but there is a Wool Festival in August where we must be seen. This is a craft fair and will attract everyone who has a fabric atelier, a workshop - weaving, knitting, even silk painting and so on - it's not just wool - but only people who register as authentic French craftspeople and are quality checked will be allowed to hold a stall license, and even then there will be a limited number.'

'Is it worth it?'

Amélie looked at Helen as if she were mad. 'It is an appellation contrôlé for craft, it opens doors for craft markets and tourist visits to our atelier and it doubles what we can charge at the same time as expanding our customer base. Oh yes, it's worth it.'

'Is there something I need to do.'

Amélie contemplated her thoughtfully, started to speak, then changed her mind. 'No,' she said, 'I will carry on with the paperwork and tell you how it goes.' The subject was closed. What I want from you is your Englishness for front of shop and some hard work shifting stock into and out of the van, from seven in the morning till seven at night seven days a week, with some evening markets thrown in. How does that sound?'

'Like a lot of sevens,' Helen replied cheerfully, 'but that's what I'm here for.'

Amélie had not been exaggerating about the physical work involved in manning - or rather womanning - a stall. Although the market moved from village to village in a weekly pattern, the traders were mostly the same people, organized in the same way, and Helen found herself exchanging longer conversations each day with the neighbouring stall-holders from the second-hand white cotton and lace, and the bath crystals in fancy bottles. Less amicable was the jostling for parking spaces at the beginning and end of the day, dodging trestle tables, when bad timing or politeness could leave you walking half a mile with armfuls of jumpers which grew heavier with every step.

On the Thursday, just when Helen thought she had the hang of it all, folding French notes into the purse belted round her waist and using a pole to hook a jumper down from its place on display, she faced her first thunderstorm. Amélie had taken a coffee break and Helen was standing helplessly watching puddles form into rivulets when her partner rushed back, grabbed the pole and emptied the dangerously sagging canvas roof of its belly of water.

Although swift, the act was harder than it looked and when Helen tried the same fluid gesture at the next sign of a canvas belly, the roof shook and deposited three streams that landed dangerously close to the feet of two customers. Helen made apology but was starting to worry seriously about the safety of their precious stock, when, as suddenly as it began, the rain stopped and the whole market was white with water evaporating in the renewed sunshine.

Helen made a mental note to add a new term to the lexicon of rain which she had been developing since she had moved to Wales but she had to admit that Wales rarely put on a display of explosive, fiery rain like this... rainy fireworks, she thought... that was it, rainworks.

It was deeply satisfying to meet her customers, to hear them telling their friends 'Come and look at this...', to fatten her belt with their money. It was deeply satisfying to share a glass of wine, tired at the end of a hard day, and dream aloud with Amélie of new collections, of expansion of a national chain of shops.

It was even deeply satisfying to say 'au revoir' and head for home, reminded that she did have some talent and that the future was still full of possibilities.

The moment Gwen Evans came out of Lloyds Bank, her shoulders sagged. She was wearing her chapel clothes but they had made no impact on the young man whom she begged for a loan. He looked at her as if she should have been licking the spots off their over-polished counters, not presuming to ask for money.

She made sure she was a bit early for the appointment, to get off on the right foot, and then that receptionist asked her to sit somewhere different to wait, as if she would put off their other customers by sitting at the front. Then there was the appointment itself with young Mr Whatever-his-name-was.

She refused to remember his when he had to keep checking hers from their bank statement. Forty years they'd banked with Lloyds, joking that it was named after Will's father. Her cheeks were still burning at the talk of collateral, at the way he - that man - listed all the assets which were hers jointly and could be considered, with her husband's consent, but which 'quite frankly were mortgaged up to the hilt and this was a bad time for farmers to stretch themselves.' As if she didn't know this was a bad time for farmers. And the whole point of this was to do it without worrying Will and then surprise him. That b...anker - if she weren't a lady, she'd substitute a letter there - she'd heard the word often enough at a rugby match in the past - sneered at her thousand pounds of savings.

He'd wanted to know what she wanted the extra two thousand for - at least she had the good sense to keep that to herself. Women were trying to empower this woman and it was men like that stopping them.She rummaged in her bag for the business card that one of the women at the Hearts meeting had given her.

Want that extension? That holiday abroad?
Been turned down by other companies?
Loans up to £10,000 available within 2 days.
No credit checks needed.
Telephone Stan Walker TODAY!

The card was very professionally laid out and Gwen thought how much more welcoming Stan sounded than the man in the bank. It was a pity he wasn't a woman, but you couldn't have everything. She knew he'd charge interest but then so would a bank. Even if he charged a bit more interest, it could come out of the £24,000 when she won it.

When you thought about it, if she put her thousand in, she'd make seven thousand profit, and if she borrowed two thousand, then she'd make about £20,000, even allowing for a bit of interest. It was an investment, however you looked at it, and Gwen tucked her brown bag more firmly over her arm and walked away from the bank without a backwards glance

Chapter 8

'You seem full of the joys of spring, this morning,' Anne observed. Mrs Phillips stopped singing to herself in Welsh but she couldn't stop smiling as she brought toast to the breakfast table which, as always, was impeccably laid with checked linen placemats and napkins.

'I wasn't going to say...' Mrs Phillips was quite clearly bursting to pass on her good news.

'Something to do with your friend?' Anne prompted mischievously.

'No, no indeed,' Mrs Phillips protested too much, her colour rising. 'Well, that is, yes, in a way. You remember the meeting we went to, the Hearts meeting about the money?' Anne nodded. 'Well, we've had our money and because Ceri came in through me, that means we've both made a tidy profit. It's a lovely feeling to back a winner and I want to take you out for a meal tonight to celebrate.'

'I'm pleased for you - and Ceri of course.' It was clear from Mrs Phillips' face that she was waiting for more and Anne laughed ruefully, then gave in with a good grace. 'I know, I was wrong. I thought it was a rip-off and I would not have put money in; you have and you've made a tidy profit.' Anne quoted the local idiom back at Mrs Phillips.

'I should say so.' Her finger wagging for emphasis as she named the sum, Mrs Phillips said, enunciating every syllable clearly, 'We have made twenty-one thousand pounds profit.'

'And is it 'we' who are taking me out for a meal tonight,' Anne teased, but she was more impressed than she wanted to show. It was a lot of money. It could be a life-changing amount of money; it could furnish a house, it could start a small school of her own... If she won so much, what would she do? Perhaps travel, a year in the USA and she could research English second language teaching... No, that was work. If she won so much, she would spend it on fun. Anne savoured the word 'fun'. It was not a word that came easily to her and she smiled wryly about what that said about her life.

'I thought it would be a more enjoyable evening with a man's company.' Mrs Phillips was looking sheepish and Anne politely rescued her.

'I think it's a lovely idea. Where are the two of you taking me? Something to look forward to during my school day. '

'I'll let you know tonight. Take your coat - it's going to be a wet one.'

After the explosion into her classroom of thirty-one thirteen-year-olds, shaking rain off bags and hair, steaming up the windows and shouting their break-time arrangements, Anne calmed them and took a register. She sighed. Alex was absent, yet again.

Hop! A billion trillion squillion froglets hopped a tiny frog hop towards the pond. Alex tucked one leg up and repeated the experiment. Hop! Again, the long grass was alive with shiny greeny-black leggy specks. Alex scooped up a handful of frog grass and watched the liquid squirm escaping until only green spears were left. However quick the hand fisted, the froglets escaped.

The word frog-march came to mind, a word of war films and discipline. Just as Alex was about to try to walk on frogs and see what sound they made, the world erupted into barking dogs and snarling muzzles. The frog walk became the fastest running start Alex ever attempted. The quickest exit was across a rose bed and

Alex had no qualms about the breaking branches as the tiny thorns caught in skin and clothing. A stone ended the flight and, pinned to the ground by the giant, unforgiving paw of an Irish wolfhound, Alex gave up.

'Meatloaf! Leave! Paid' Helen desperately tried to think of the Welsh command for 'Don't eat that child.' Bilingual dogs always had an option as to which language they would ignore you in, and Helen had not yet established herself as a pack leader with her lover's dogs. However, the three dogs lost interest of their own accord in their fallen victim, who might be a trespasser but who no longer seemed to pose a threat even to this dubious addition to the family of whom their master seemed so unaccountably fond.

'It's all right. They won't hurt you.' Helen looked at the boy's smeared face and grazed legs. 'Come on into the house and let me look at those cuts.' She could see cuts across the midriff which was bared by a too-short T-shirt and instinctively she reached out, lifted the T-shirt a little more to expose the bruised and cut skin and to assess the damage. The boy flinched away from her and was standing in an instant, defiant and afraid.

'You piss off!' he shouted in her face and limped to the hedge, dived through and disappeared, dogs interested once more and barking through their boundary at the escapee. Helen too looked at the hedge, as if it might explain what she had done wrong. Then she noticed the damage to her rose garden and with angry tears she fetched secateurs and carried out surgery the way Dai had shown her, a quarter of an inch above a nodule and sloping. Where possible, she rescued the flowers from the amputated branches, naming each tiny patio rose with affection.

As she arranged the roses, mixing the white blooms of 'Tear Drops' with the 'Robin Redbreasts', she rationalized the odd events of the afternoon. It was a local boy on school holidays, exploring on a warm day. He'd been caught out by a cloudburst and was probably looking for shelter. He probably didn't even realized he was in the cottage garden rather than a corner of the field and most kids thought of fields as their playground or, with an excitable farmer, a challenge.

Occasionally, kids would cycle or even walk out from Llanelli, loud in their laughter and music, but no harm in them. It wasn't as if he'd known how much the rose garden meant to her or as if he'd deliberately spoiled her memorial to little Becky. He'd been so scared when she touched him and the bruises across his midriff looked really nasty. She hoped he didn't have too far to go home so his Mum could put some antiseptic on the damage. The whole incident would be a story to tell Dai when he phoned. Only a week now till he would be home. Meatloaf whacked her arm with one enormous paw. 'You miss him too, don't you boy.' She caressed his massive head but the only response was a restless whine. 'I know,' she soothed him. 'Let's go walkabout, see if we can find Grandad.'

Helen and her three hairy guardians found Will leaning on a gate, looking across the lane.

'Sure you can handle them now?' he asked, bending to cuff the Jack Russell's ear. He preferred dogs which worked for a living and he respected the small terrier's ratting abilities.

'They're good company.' On returning from France, Helen called up at Brynglas to reclaim the dogs. Her request created a short silence but the 'Of course, fach,' acknowledged her as Dai's partner, as his family. There was an awkward moment when she called the dogs to her, ready to go home, and they looked from her to Will and waited, considering their options. She did not want to put them on leads as neither Dai nor Will needed to, and everyone present knew that. Then Meatloaf broke pack ranks and, always a sucker for affection, bounded over to Helen, tail scything anything in its way, and Will smiled. 'I'd like some air - I'll walk you back.' She did not refuse, knowing that Janie and Demi would happily accompany the two of them.

Taking responsibility for Dai's pets was a premeditated gesture; getting those same pets to do what she wanted was quite a different story, but - she told herself - she was getting there. It was simply a matter of establishing a daily routine, showing them who was boss and deciding how much you would tolerate in the way of a stolen packet of ham or a game of chase-and-bounce-on-the-chairs. She certainly was not going to tell Will about running after a furry behind as it disappeared after the postman's van, or about the dog wars caused by her giving them bones as a treat, with each dog being more concerned about hiding its own bone and stealing someone else's, than about chewing on any of them.

No, there was a lot that she had no intention of telling Will. She smiled sweetly. 'Great company.'

'You must be lonely there with Dai away. You know you can come up.'

'Yes, thank you. I know, and I will, but I'm all right on my own.' She knew the invitation was genuine but she also knew that, without Dai, she was still a bit of a visitor. It was more relaxed during the day especially if Gwen were alone, than if she interrupted the quietness of their nights. 'Everything still all right, I mean as all right as it can be?' They were both looking at the Salar herd.

'No sign of any disease with them,' he said with pride. His expression darkened. 'But there's bad news on the Teletext. There's a case in Skewen.' Every night they checked the number of cases and whether there was a new case anywhere near Carmarthenshire. Skewen was near Neath, only twenty miles away, the first case anywhere near south-west Wales although there were a few cases in the Newport area.

'Perhaps it's a one-off. They're acting more quickly now aren't they?'

'So they say. What worries me - and I've told Dai, is that it's so far from any known infected area. Word is, the farmer's brought it back himself from an infected farm.'

'He must be stupid. I mean, everyone knows the risks - even me.' That's why I'm hardly allowed out to shop, never mind near other farms, and always dipping my feet in disinfectant like I'm a cow myself - and not a particularly valuable one.

'Worse than stupid is the word - deliberate.'

'You're joking! What would make someone destroy his own farm?'

'If it's destroyed anyway, through debt, BSE, lack of markets... you know enough about how hard it's been... the compensation if you're ordered to cull is big money, enough to retire.'

'That's sick.'

'Sick it is, but think. We can't move animals anywhere with all these restrictions. I can't even move them to my field across the lane for fresh grazing and you can see what this is getting like.' The ground around the gate was boggier and browner than Helen had ever seen it, from wet weather and over-grazing. 'God help the farmers who can't get their stock back from winter pastures. The fields are grazed bare and the beasts will die of starvation before these welfare orders will kick in. We can't go to market, there's no chance of exports, the bottom has dropped right out and these are worth ten times as much dead of foot and mouth as they are alive.'

Helen looked at Dai's father in horror. 'You wouldn't.'

'No, Helen fach, I wouldn't. But that doesn't mean I don't understand someone who might have. What sticks in my throat is that he's bringing his choice to every farm beside him, and so near to us I don't like to think. There'll be men out to kill him if the word is right. I wouldn't be in his shoes for the world.'

'I must tell Dai,' said Helen, thinking of her lover's investment in the herd, an investment not just of money - although that, she knew, was significant - but of hopes for the future. 'Perhaps he should come back now.'

'I've already talked to Dai and we've agreed another five days will make no difference. It's not as if he can do anything except worry with me.'

Helen again felt peripheral, imagining those conversations between father and son in which Dai could talk about all the detail of his work in Powys and those feelings he certainly wasn't sharing with her in the terse calls that she received. She swallowed. 'Let's hope it's just the one case. At least it seems to be holding in most places.'

'Not in Powys.'

'No,' she agreed quietly, 'not in Powys.' But he was coming home anyway in five days, home to her.

Alex was huddled under a hedge, far enough away to be safe from the snooping woman with the dogs. It had been a good fortnight round the empty cottage but the woman must have been on holiday or something, and she was back now. The last thing Alex needed was some interfering busybody. The social workers were enough of a problem as it was with their stupid questions and Alex wasn't going to help anyone split up the family.

Legs ached, old bruises and new cuts mingled in the sharp tang of pain but nothing seemed to be broken or even sprained. It would be French now with that new teacher, another nosy woman. Most of the teachers had stopped noticing when Alex wasn't there and certainly didn't comment, let alone giving praise for an occasional appearance. The woman had at least done that bit privately but really! Who needed French anyway? What was the use of it? If the teacher only knew, Alex already had the key to survival in France, but that was private. Sharp pains were already subsiding to dull aches and Alex knew from experience that it would be a long walk home with stiff legs and a throbbing head. Eyes closed, Alex sought comfort in the usual way.

The Place in Alex's mind had no name and no people in it; these were only some of its defences. Others included a briar hedge forty feet tall (added in Infant School when a teacher read 'Sleeping Beauty' to open mouthed six year-olds) and cruise missiles (added more recently).

Alex could not remember a time when The Place did not exist and, although it had changed over the years, it was through additions and adaptations so the original heart of the Place could still be recognized. Alex turned left by the statue of Princess Diana and carefully conjured the frog-pond into being, in the corner of a field impossibly stocked with mushrooms and spring flowers.

It required a great deal of concentration to create, recalling every throaty rumble of hopeful males, every slime-slicked back as it disappeared and most of all the early season froglets, leaping to order. The addition of two dolphins, a waterfall and some tropical flowers encouraged Alex to swim in the pond, now a pool, and the imaginary water soothed aching limbs. Rabbits, foxes and a badger shyly came to the bank of the pool and watched the grace of the swimming mammals.

One rabbit was white and fluffy, with a chewed tail and one glass eye hanging on a thread - Alex included friends indiscriminately in The Place and might bump into any of them, walking the overgrown footpaths, running through head-high grass or even sitting in The Cave. Sometimes weeks or whole seasons passed for Alex in The Place, snow and sunshine alternating to suit the mood, but outside time would be hours at most.

Usually, hours were long enough. Hours would take outside time to four o'clock, home from school time, when it would be safe to sneak upstairs and pretend to change out of uniform. Home, where nothing was within Alex's control.

'I'm home!' and then the dash up the stairs. So far, so good. Always throw a school sweatshirt on first, just in case someone comes in, so it looks like you've taken some uniform off, rather than putting some on. Swap anything too badly messed by a day in the fields. Hide it under the bed ready for washing when they're out. They like it that you do some washing - 'doing a bit of housework, and about time'.

'Alex?' *Just in time. Mam, thank God.* Alex's mother was holding two hangers, each draped with clothes, as she came into Alex's bedroom, giggling. 'God you look a mess.' The glance was cursory and her thoughts clearly elsewhere. Alex inwardly heaved a sigh of relief.

That was a bit close. Still, it looked as if it was going to be an up evening rather than a down one - down ones were more dangerous for Alex, so it was important to read their moods and predict what might follow. 'I'm going out tonight and I don't know which of these to wear.' There was a pause and a sudden focus of attention on Alex, who stiffened.

'Look at you. At your age I had a boyfriend... Jamie it must have been... great kisser. I know, try these on and let me see what they look like on you... it'll help me make my mind up.' Lips were pursed critically. 'I'll get my make-up bag and we'll do the works. It's about time you looked like a girl. You were looking all right when you started to dress up a bit... I don't know what made you change back to those scruffy old jeans.' Her voice tailed off as she raced back to her bedroom to get the make-up.

Alex sat on her own bed. It was a year ago that she had tried the short skirts and make-up that made men look at her mother in that way. She remembered only too well why she abandoned the experiment and she hoped her mother would never find out. Still, it wouldn't do any harm to play with her mother this afternoon and if the mood stayed sweet, they might even have some fun together.

A hand appeared around the bedroom door, making sinuous movements with a sparkling velvety scarf. The hand was followed by the rest of Alex's mother, draped in odd items of clothing and full of girlish enthusiasm.

Despite herself, Alex was intrigued, and was gradually drawn into dressing up in the short straight skirts, the high blocked heels and the metallic lycra strappy - or even strapless - tops, which were her favourite items in her mother's wardrobe. Alex looked at the person in the mirror, her hair combed and caught up high above her head, to feather out in a pony-tail; her figure exaggerated into curves by the clinging materials; her mouth scarlet with a purple outline and her eyes large with liner and surprise.

She looked sexy, she looked beautiful and she looked like her mother, the sixteen years between them seeming less. That same mother was behind her in the mirror, beaming, pleased with the effect of her skills.

'Walk about, go on,' and Alex walked about, putting one plodding thirteen-year-old foot in front of the other, made even more awkward by the sore muscles. 'No,' her mother laughed, 'like this,' and slipping heels on, she swung her hips and strutted. 'Pretend you're a fashion model on the catwalk,' and Alex could see it, her beautiful mother tossing her hair and posing, the cameras flashing. Alex shook her head.

'I know.' Her mother was all movement, darting out of the room, returning with a battered ghetto-blaster and a tape, humming to herself first alone and then with the music. Alex allowed herself to be taken by the hand, partnered along the catwalk of the bedroom onto the landing and back, swaying to the music, stopping to pose, laughing all the time amid drifts of her mother's perfume which had been lavished on both of them. Through laughter, high heels and screaming muscles, Alex tripped, pulling her mother with her and tottering as far as the bed.

Her mother's arm was still round her as they sat, recovering. If only it could always be like this. 'Tell me,' Alex risked, 'tell me again about San Fairy Anne.'

Her mother laughed. 'Always that old story. You must know it off by heart. And you're too old for magic stories. Let me get a fag.' Her mother lit up, took a drag and began. 'Your Gran told me when I was little about a bit of magic to keep me safe in France. She said it was like a spell, given to her by a friend of her Dad's who'd been in France in the war and he said wherever you were in France you just said the magic words and everyone would be nice to you and help you. '

'And the magic words are...' Alex prompted.

'San Fairy Anne!' they both pronounced together and mimed a magician's gesture at an apparition.

'Here,' her mother passed over the cigarette and laughed as Alex copied her mother's elegant way of drooping her hand, flashing purple varnish. It didn't work with Alex's rough bitten nails. 'The San Fairy Anne is the most powerful fairy there is because she is a Welsh Saint - that's the 'San' bit, and a fairy too, and Welsh fairies - the Tylwyth Teg - aren't pretty little things with wings - they play tricks in the woods and give people wishes and make people pay more than they thought so nothing quite works out how it should.

And that's why it's such a powerful spell is because saying her name puts her in your power. '

'I don't get why it works in France.'

'He probably just said that because that was where he was in the war. Listen to me - you'll have me as bad as you next - it's just a story, Alex.'

'And I don't see how a Saint could be a fairy - they're like different religions,'Alex persevered.

'So maybe she was like Superman - a Saint in the day and then when a hero was needed she put her fairy knickers on outside her saint's outfit. It's just a bloody stupid children's story, it doesn't mean anything you know. I thought you were growing up a bit.'

Alex read the warning signals and quickly returned to the safer ground of clothes. 'So what are you going to wear tonight?'

'How about this?' Her mother held up a ribbed jersey, black

tubular skirt. 'With that top you're wearing - it looks good on you, so I reckon it'll look pretty good on me.' She preened herself and glanced sideways at her daughter, flirting, recovering her good humour. 'I haven't lost it yet.'

'You're gorgeous,' Alex told her in honest admiration, and earned a hug.

'Shit.' Her mother brushed the ash off the duvet cover but not in time to prevent a couple of pencil-sized holes with singed edges. 'Sorry.'

'It doesn't matter,' Alex shrugged.

'If things go well tonight, I'll buy you a new one.' Her mother winked. Alex said nothing. Any money coming in was already promised fifty times over and she would be lucky if she got new trainers to replace these, which already had holes in them.

More importantly, her mother's remark meant that she was working tonight, not going out with Alex's father. This was not good news.

'Anybody going to bloody notice I'm home then or what?' The comment shouted from downstairs broke into the music. Alex could hear the alcohol in his voice - more bad news. 'How about a cup of tea?'

'Make your own. It's not as if you do anything else.' Despite the defiant response, shouted back down the stairs, Alex's mother picked up the clothing and make-up and left the bedroom.

Alex dived for the grubby clothing under the bed, used it to wipe her face clean of its make-up, then replaced the clothes, shook her hair into its usual mess and scrambled into her jeans. She checked the mirror for any traces of the young woman who so recently appeared there and shook her head at the way the T-shirt, too small for her, was clinging to her breasts. She found a sweatshirt to cover herself up, preferring to be too hot than to feel exposed.

'Hey, get yourself down here.' There was no defying the command so Alex shuffled downstairs to face her father.

Jimmy Wilkinson called in the Golden Lion for just the one, after cashing his weekly giro and calling at the Job Centre. When he'd first been laid off, the walls were covered with white cards advertising situations vacant and if he didn't know better, he would have thought his luck was in. He remembered telling Charmaine not to worry, that he'd look after her and Alex the way he always had.

He followed up on some of those little white cards, he even liked the idea of doing a bit of roofing or concreting or something a man could do, but all they went on about was training and qualifications, as if someone who spent ten years working shifts in a car parts factory had ever had need or time to go back to school.

He was dead keen to leave school in the first place so why would he want to go back, put himself through all that sitting about and humiliation? He wouldn't have minded going out and about with a bunch of the boys, learning on the job, but he didn't have a friendly brother or uncle to take him on, and if it came to applying for a job it seemed to be back to this qualification lark.

Someone had even told him he was too old - at thirty-four! He was also told that there were plenty of men like him about, with twice his skills and experience, and with 'downsizing' in manufacturing, and no money for labouring on farms, he could forget manual jobs. Not that he'd take farm work - it paid worse money than the social so where was the point?

Nowadays, the walls were bare and the jobs were all stored behind the computer screens placed at strategic intervals on the heavy-duty carpet, like barrels in the old spit-and-sawdust pubs. It was embarrassing in the past, the time it took him to work out where the different types of jobs were, reading that difficult handwriting till his eyes hurt.

Now, it was a bit more private and he could find his way around the screen easily enough, but the writing was even harder to read and there was no way he was asking for help. Bad enough he had to listen to that Adviser every two weeks. If he was unemployed another year, perhaps she'd want to see him every day, to check he was doing enough to get 'back on the rails'.

Well his track had rusted up for good. He knew without even

looking that most of the jobs were women's work, cleaning, looking after old people or answering phones all day at those new call centres that seemed to be springing up everywhere, even in the valleys. No way was he sinking to that level. He'd rather manage on social and the extra Charmaine brought home now and again.

His thoughts flicked quickly away from Charmaine's work, instead returning to his own feelings about the work on offer. Surely no man would clean up someone else's muck for a minimum wage, disgusting it was. He'd been getting four times that, double time for anti-social hours and the odd weekend. He and Charmaine had gone out dancing and it was a miracle Alex was an only child, the way they behaved when they got home. Real looker, his wife had been. Still was, but didn't exactly save it for him, did she.

Jimmy gave up after less than five minutes. He could truthfully say he'd been to the Job Centre and there was really no point wasting any more time there. He caught a glimpse of himself in a shop window but it no longer shocked him to see the oil-stained jeans, holes in the faded sweatshirt, the belly straining above his trousers and the lank hair falling over eyes which never settled.

If you could believe anything the bitch said, he'd been a looker too. So sixteen-year old Charmaine said, even when she caught with Alex and had to face her Mam and Dad. She'd stood up for him then, told them he was a good man who'd stand by her and the baby. Well he'd proved her parents wrong.

He'd stood by Charmaine and the kid, hadn't he. He made sure Alex had a bit of respect for her parents, not like the kids he saw around the streets in Llanelli, drinking and smoking. She'd taste the back of his hand if she started any of that nonsense. If he was a bit hard on her sometimes, it was better than the other way. You only had to look around you to see that.

There wasn't much comfort in his life and she was his daughter, he cared about her, it was only natural that it went a bit far sometimes. She loved him, she understood - you could see it in her eyes. Something in her needed it, same as with him, he could tell. He remembered her dressing up that time, little tart like her mother, same long slim legs and all the other bits he liked, just like her mother used to be and only him to see it. He needed a drink.

'Just the one' in the Golden Lion, turned into four, which left Jimmy a little dazzled by the sudden afternoon sunshine appearing between showers, but not visibly the worse for wear. Although he had the discipline to stop at four, the beer had given him a thirst for more and he thought he'd carry on at home. An evening in with Charmaine in a good mood and a beer or two struck him as a pleasant prospect. He'd buy her a bunch of flowers when he bought the beer. That would put her in a good mood and maybe she'd treat him nice, the way she used to, and he'd be well in tonight.

Jimmy's walk to the Golden Lion took him outside the town centre and he couldn't be bothered walking back, so when he saw a corner shop that seemed to have a bit of everything, he thought it would do nicely. He was less pleased with himself when he saw the turbaned shopkeeper. He had nothing really against the Pakkis, but they made you feel out of place, jabbering away in their own language. Self-conscious, he ordered his sixpack and bunch of daffs, loudly.

'I'm sorry, Sir, I think this gentleman was before you.' A man, who had been collecting a can from a shelf to add to the groceries already on the counter, turned back to pay for his goods.

All Jimmy noticed was the man's skin colour, the fact that he was butting in, and the word 'Sir' being used to take the piss. No-one called him 'Sir'; no-one was polite to him, and he wasn't going to put up with being ridiculed. 'No he wasn't.' Jimmy blocked the counter at the point nearest the till and repeated his demand. 'My money's as good as his. You can serve your friend after me.' From nowhere, a woman materialized, placed the beer and the flowers on the counter and served Jimmy as if nothing had been said.

The male shopkeeper totted up prices for the other customer and avoided looking at Jimmy, who stubbornly added, 'And a packet of fags.'

'Taj,' the woman called to a young man behind another stack of shelves, who collected the cigarettes from a top shelf and gave them to the woman, glancing at Jimmy and saying something in Punjabi.

That was all it took, on top of the beer and the imaginary insults which Jimmy had been swallowing all afternoon. He lurched towards the young man. 'Say it in English if you've got the balls, go on then.'

Not so much as flinching, the other spoke in accentless English. 'I told my mother you've been drinking and can't control your legs, never mind your mouth, with what's left of your brain.'

At the same time as the Shopkeeper reprimanded 'Taj!' and moved towards him, Jimmy lunged with a clumsy fist that was easily caught by the young man. Jimmy's incoherent abuse along clichéd lines with frequent references to 'black' 'taking our jobs' and 'all women are fit for' was ended by an efficient jab to his jaw.

Taj was prevented from causing further physical damage by the older Shopkeeper but was still angry enough to shout, 'You touch my father, my mother or this shop and I will kill you.' The Shopkeeper slapped him and gave a clear command in their language, then said, 'You think your mother and I work to the bone, to pay fees for your schooling, to give you the best, so you can shout threats and get into a brawl every time someone behaves like a fool, huh? Go cool your head and when you can show patience you come back.'

'Yes, Dad.' The young man's lowered head didn't hide the flash of his eyes nor his disagreement with his father's passive behaviour.

'And apologise to your mother.'

Again there was an exchange in foreign gibberish, no doubt some more insults about Jimmy, whose head was hurting. He was torn between sorting out the young man, despite the father, and just leaving, but the word 'fool' was rankling, and he needed to have the last word. He saw the shopkeeper's name 'Guptar Singh' written on the counter and he aimed his words at the easiest target, the woman, emphasizing them with his fist. 'You're going to be sorry for this Mrs Singh. You and your Pakki family. It's not over.'

To his surprise and final humiliation, the woman pulled her sari over her mouth and giggled at him. He stumbled out of the shop, heading for home, without his beer, cigarettes or the flowers which were to have made Charmaine love him again. He was not to know that Ana's giggles were from polite embarrassment at his ignorance, at him not knowing the difference between Indians and Pakistani, nor that only a man could be called Singh.

There was no welcome when he came home, just the tinny noise of that garbage that passed for music nowadays, and the sound of female giggling. Was that all women did, giggle and bitch about men? They came quickly enough when he called but they'd been up to something, he could tell. Both of them had a flush in their cheeks he could have enjoyed putting there. He shifted restlessly, adjusting the source of his discomfort, thinking it could still be a good night with Charmaine if only he could get her in the mood. She had her back to him, was fussing to make the cup of tea he'd demanded, and he watched the shuffle of her buttocks in her tight skirt. Nice arse still. Perhaps he wouldn't have to wait till tonight, if he sweetened her up a bit.

'I'm going out tonight.' He knew what that meant. Sod's law, wasn't it. After the day he'd had, too.

He put up a half-hearted protest. 'I've got the social. You don't need to go out.'

'You've spent half of that already - I can see just by looking at you. And I can't pick and choose you, know. There's a do on at the Club and there'll be a few there, which is always when I do best.'

'I don't like it,' he said sullenly.

'I know you don't,' she surprised him by perching on the arm of her chair, swinging across him, kissing him on the cheek and then swinging away from him before he could grab her, 'and I'm glad you don't like it. You're my husband and I always come back, don't I? It's not as if they mean anything...and it's good money.' It always came back to that. It was very good money, well above minimum wage for an hour - and she would often give a man an hour - and better than those jobs cleaning up someone else's muck. She was fair with him too, she always gave him what she earnt and asked him for a bit for herself, or for Alex or for something in the house. That didn't mean he liked it though. Sometimes he thought there was a sparkle in her eyes on the nights she was going out, a sparkle he hadn't put there.

'I suppose so.'

'You've got Alex for company,' she said brightly.

'Yes. I've got Alex.' He caught his daughter's eyes across the room. There was still an attractive flush across her cheeks and even though she was wearing loose layers, he could see the outline of the young body underneath. 'Alex and I will be just fine,' he challenged. 'Won't we?' There was no reply.

Chapter 9

Anne had turned to leave the estate agent when the girl said ,'You could ask Michael. He's due back from lunch now.' They had already established that house details and records of sales had been cleared out so that there was no chance of tracking the history of the Trimsaran Road house, or its owners. Anne didn't have to ask whether the girl herself could be of any help; she looked as if last year's pop tunes would be considered ancient history.

As if on cue, a young man in business suit came through the door and Anne's business was explained to him before she could open her mouth to excuse herself and leave. Michael looked scarcely older than the girl and Anne was resigned to another dead end.

'Trimsaran Road, large detached, very select area...red brick, porticos - mock columns?'Anne shook her head, trying to interrupt and save his breath but he carried on, 'I know the one, white, Victorian, lots of grass?'

'Yes, that sounds like the one,' Anne acknowledged, but even if he recognized the house there was no way his memories would go back as far as she needed. He would have to go back at least ten years just to remember the Geordies mentioned by the current owner and who knows how far back to remember any trace of Marie.

Anne knew that, with Vernon dead, Ffion was the only surviving child, and so she and her husband probably inherited the house. If they'd kept it and lived there, and if they'd had no children themselves, then there was a chance that Marie inherited the house in her turn.

Clearly it had been sold out of the family at some stage but there was the slight chance that the Estate Agent might know where the Vendor had moved to. So many ifs and maybes. If some Estate Agent did know, it wouldn't be this one, not someone so young.

'Valuation two years ago when they were thinking of moving or so they said,' he smiled, sharing his expertise. 'Lots of people say that and what they really want is to know what their house is worth, especially if it's a bit of a one-off, like that one. Now, with a house on an estate, you never get a valuation check for the sake of it - they can look in any paper or agent window and know at any time what their house is worth. That's why I'd always go for an estate house myself, easy to buy, easy to maintain, appreciates well, easy to sell and you know exactly where your investment stands. Are you looking...?'

Anne took her chance. 'No, actually, I think I'm wasting your time but thank you,' and again she turned to go.

'No, wait a minute. The valuation...' he thought back, 'professional couple, said they'd lived in the house eight years, bought it from a Geordie family who moved back home after the work collapsed in Trimsaran...'

This was nothing new and Anne was shaking her head. 'Yes, I'd found out that much, thank you but...'

With a smug expression, Michael continued, 'And I talked to my father about the house! I remember now.'

'That's very nice.'

'No, you don't understand, my father started this business. He knows every old house in a ten mile radius of Llanelli - or so he's always told me. I remember now, he told me to check the stairs carefully - there'd been some rotten boards when he sold it - but they'd obviously replaced them and put brand new brass rods across when I went round.

He said it had gone downhill a bit when he sold it and I'm sure he said he sold it twice. I remember him mentioning the Geordies - he thought their accents were funny, so quick and down to earth in the way they spoke, and there was something else...' There was a pause while the memories were prodded.

'Something about the sale before... when he sold it to the

Geordies, that would be - they came back to him of course, that's why the business is doing so well - people always come back to us. What was it he said now? Something about a waste, leaving that beautiful property for a farm...It's no good, I can't remember any more. He's retired now but if anyone can remember the people you're interested in, it's my father.'

It didn't do to get your hopes up, but surely it was worth a try. 'Would he mind if I contacted him?'

'If you can hang around town for half an hour, he'll be here. He pretends he's shopping and just called in but really he's checking up on us. I'll tell him you want to see him and he'll be only too keen to talk your head off. What shall I say your name is?'

Anne told him. 'Grüber,' Michael repeated. 'German, eh? What do you want with your people then if you find them? War criminals or something?' He laughed at his own joke while Anne winced but it was obvious that 'war' was a word without meaning to him, as to so many of his generation, especially, but not only, in Britain.

'French,' she said shortly, 'from Alsace. They are my relatives and we lost touch many years ago - there is nothing more exciting than that I am afraid.' She forced herself to smile. It was all true and yet it was not at all the trivial matter she wanted to make it sound. She wanted to get out into the fresh air before the shaking of her hands attracted attention, before she started to cry with the tension of not knowing whether she was one step nearer meeting a sister - and not knowing whether that was what she wanted. The doorbell tinkled behind her, she stopped in front of a hardware shop and looked intently into the window for several minutes until her vision cleared and she walked on.

Anne had looked in every one of Llanelli's six shoe-shops in a long half-hour before she returned to the estate agent's.

Michael was in full flow and she caught snatches of his patter '... just come on the market... snapped up... three reception rooms... '. An older man was leaning over a desk where a young girl was trying to sort house brochures and they both looked up as the doorbell tinkled. 'This is the lady,' the girl told him, clearly relieved at getting rid of him.

When the man turned to face her, Anne could see the family

resemblance but the sharp, rodent lines of the younger man's profile had softened in the older man, and his eyes twinkled. He held her hand a moment too long and then suggested that he buy her a drink at the café next door.

Anne could feel the grateful smile from the desk as she preceded Mr Estate Agent through the door he carefully held open and she decided she would keep this conversation public and to the point.

Mr Estate Agent, who turned out to be 'Jones - call me Wyn', lived up to his son's description. He remembered every picture rail and piece of coving, as well as the various buyers and 'vendors' who'd come his way. Anne endured several tangents before he returned to the Stradey house and then it was mostly repetition of what his son had told her already.

Anne heard a lot about the Newcastle buyers but resisted the temptation to ask him why people from Newcastle were known as Geordies - there were enough sidetracks as it was. She needed him to go further back in his memories.

'And before them, before the Geordies?' she prompted him.

'Well of course,' he beamed, 'why didn't you ask that in the first place.' Anne smiled, apologetically, between gritted teeth. 'Twenty years they were there, give or take a year or two, when the mines were still going.

That was why they came down you know - for the work - and that was why they sold up, to go back home when the mines all closed. 'Might as well be unemployed back home in Newcastle where you can gang canny,' was what he said. Sold it on to a local woman, what was her name now...'

'It's before that I'm interested in,' Anne reminded him, fists clenched under the table. 'My relatives are much older.' When she said 'relatives' it felt like a fiction, a lie, and she couldn't take in the fact that there was indeed a relationship. What would Vernon's sister and husband be to her? A sort of aunt and uncle? She gave up trying to work it out and concentrated on 'Wyn'.

'Well, I would remember wouldn't I, posh house like that and one of the first I sold. Not short of a bob or two they weren't. A married couple they were, with a toddler, a little girl.' It could fit, Anne thought cautiously, or it could all be a... what was that English expression?... a house of cards.

'I don't remember the man so much.' *That figures* thought Anne. 'It was the woman making the decisions - often is, you know. Why I remember one time - '

'What did the woman look like?' Anne interrupted. Not that it helped her but she thought it the sort of question that might take him back to what she wanted to know.

'Young and pretty,' he told her, 'with fair, curly hair and kindly blue eyes - just like yours,' he twinkled at her.' Too young, Anne realised, disappointed. He would hardly have described Ffion as young and Marie would have been... how old? A young woman, surely.

Wyn continued to reminisce. 'Saw her a few times, taking the measurements and everything.' He winked at Anne, 'Of the house, I mean. Her little one was a real mischief - our little chats were always interrupted with her shouting at - what was her name now? Sharon... no, Charlotte... something like that. So we'd be talking like you and me and then all the time it would be, 'Sharon (or Charlotte or something), put that down' or 'No, don't do that.' I was right about the sale being up to her and not her husband. The house really was hers - she'd inherited it when her parents died... 'Marie would have been a young woman, Anne thought, calculating, certainly old enough to have married and be mother to a toddler, and the people she thought of as her parents could well have died...

'So I asked her what sort of property she was looking for - not one to miss an opportunity or the business wouldn't be what it is today - you met my boy, didn't you?' Anne nodded. 'Wanted to go into farming, they did. She said she always wanted more of an outdoors life than her parents wanted for her - got the impression her parents didn't think too much of the hubbie, more from what she didn't say than what she did, if you know what I mean. She seemed fond enough of him herself.' Wyn sounded disappointed. 'But I sold them a farm so it was time well spent.'

'Do you remember which farm?' Anne held her breath.'

'Of course...' Ten minutes later, Anne extricated herself from a handshake. In her handbag was a till receipt with the address of a Swiss Valley farm.

Helen didn't know exactly when Dai would be home but she knew that it would be today and she could concentrate on nothing else. She had been flitting from one mindless household task to another in the attempt to find distraction, and was now nursing her fifth coffee of the afternoon, idly running her nail along the silk of a fallen rose petal.

She noted the fine thread of white she had drawn across the pink and tried to continue it to form her initials but she only tore the petal. A few blown roses had shed petals onto the table and she was about to pick up the flower debris, when she was struck by something about the shapes and textures.

It was something to do with that vision of changing scale, the world seen tiny and the tiny seen magnified, that she had almost captured after playing with the hearts diagrams. She moved her head back to get a different perspective, then she arranged five petals in an overlapping pattern, like feathers on a robin's breast, like scales on a red snapper.

'Eureka!' Helen grabbed a sheet of paper, scribbled notes and pencilled shapes, rubbed out and redrafted, so lost to the world that she jumped as two hands covered her eyes and a familiar mouth breathed kisses and mumbled phrases into the back of her neck, through the thick tumble of red hair.

'I'm home...I've missed you... where's my welcome? Just as well I've got dogs...' seemed to be the gist of it.

'You want me to wag my tail?' she murmured, abandoning her papers to bury her face in his chest.

He lifted her chin with one hand and with the other stroked her imaginary tail. 'Docked like a Doberman,' he pronounced sadly, but his hands carried on their exploration. 'And you?' she breathed. 'Just how pleased to see me are you?' He answered by guiding her hand where he wanted it and they followed their mutual hungers along the loved, familiar routes of each other's bodies.

Dai fell from satisfaction to sleep in seconds and Helen watched the boyish innocence of his profile for some time before she tucked the duvet round him and left him in bed.

Perhaps she imagined it but she had felt a desperation in his lovemaking and the traces of tiredness behind the affection in his expression had surely been the cause of their passion being so brief, leaving her restless, wanting more. How different it was from the planned homecoming. She was to have greeted him on the doorstep, asked him all the right questions which would have let him talk to her, unburden himself of all the horror he must have been through in Powys.

Then she would have produced the carefully prepared meal and they could have relaxed into lighter chat, when she could have told him about St Geniez and about the trespassing boy. Finally, after all of these hors-d'oeuvres, she would have touched him in one of those intimate gestures understood by both of them to be an invitation, and they could have consummated physically what they'd re-established in other ways.

Instead, she'd let herself be taken like a pain-killer, and knew she would do exactly the same again and again if that were what he needed. Patience, she told herself. You're reading too much into a tired man, just come home.

There are many ways of escaping, or at least postponing unwelcome thoughts, and Helen returned to her designs. Sometimes an idea which struck her as pure genius at the time, would later seem banal - like the use of the Blodeuwedd myth - but this time her idea still seemed to be pure gold. She didn't want some naïve interpretation of 'Welsh', no leeks or daffodils, she wanted the Welshness to come from the inside, from the fact that she lived here and was the artist, from the fact that the design itself was the detail of something she saw in the landscape.

She contemplated her rough drawing and then, increasingly excited she transferred the design to computer, using its tools to multiply and make subtle changes to shapes and shadings. She lost all track of time until she put the finishing touch to the outline, the final stroke of genius, and was once again startled by a man's touch, this time lightly on her shoulder.

'Helen?' Tentative, his hair tousled and his eyes searching, he waited for her to say something. She didn't speak and he looked away from her, at the computer screen. 'For the Botanical

Gardens?' She nodded. 'Explain it to me.'

She felt suddenly very shy, exposed. 'You might not like it... and anyway, you're tired...'

'I had a sleep. Tell me anyway,' he ordered, 'please...'

'It was the rose petals that gave me the idea... see, the knot starts off as rose petals...' and she showed him the way the rose petals turned into robin feathers, which turned into pink-silver fish scales - 'sewin, I thought' - which turned into tree bark - 'I'm wondering whether to have a browner note to the feathers so they can flow into the bark, or whether to think of a pinky-barked tree' - and which connected in a continuous loop with the rose petals. The whole was outlined in black, forming a Celtic knot.

'So you got your Welshness with the knot,' Dai mused.

'Yes, that's to make the 'wow' impact, the first impression, and I'm really pleased with it but in some ways that bit is superficial. It's the way the natural world is connected, that I'm trying to get at, the ordinary bits of it - flowers, fish, trees and birds, all round us here where we live - that's what I'm trying to get at.'

'You could have daffodil petals?'

'No, definitely, no - I want to make people think, not stop them by giving them a symbol on a plate.'

'Something on a plate would be nice.' Dai's hazel eyes lit up. 'How about a cheese sandwich with peanut butter?' The wary look came back onto Helen's face until she realized he was teasing her. He held her gaze, direct, honest. 'I love it. I don't know how you thought of it and I don't know what someone as talented as you is doing with someone like me.'

'Well, I was looking at rose petals and I suppose it's got a bit of Magritte in the way one material becomes another, like his skin and wood, and a bit of Escher in the continuous knot idea.' She was losing him.

'So you didn't think of any of it then...'

'Do you really like it?'

'Really, really. What are you going to call it?'

'I don't know. Something like 'Stuff of Life''

'Bit slangy.'

'No, it isn't - 'stuff' is an old word for 'material'.'

'Most people will think 'stuff' is slang. Why not just call it 'Material of Life''

'Sounds wooden.'

'So put some wood in it, like that Magritte bloke. Just joking,' he added quickly. 'I don't suppose there's any chance of a sandwich?' he smiled engagingly.

'I'm not putting peanut butter on it - you'll have to do that yourself - it's disgusting, ' she warned him. 'I know - 'The Fabric of Life'.'

'That's good, I like that,' he approved. 'Can you do it, technically I mean. Is it going to be knittable or whatever the word is.'

'Some special yarns, metallic for the fish scales, fluffy bits for feathers - I've done that before on the jumpers - it'll work, I'm sure it will...'

'There we are then. Sandwich?' he prompted.

Trying to avoid the stomach-churning smell of peanut butter and cheese at three in the morning, Helen felt something click back into place in her heart or her brain or wherever lived that knowledge of all being right with the world, however temporarily.

'Dogs?' Dai queried between mouthfuls. 'How come they're here?'

'This is where they live,' replied Helen smugly. 'I brought them back when I came home.' The word 'home' lingered warmly in the rightness of the moment.

'And they haven't played you up.'

'No,' Helen lied.

'You haven't...' Dai frowned, contemplating a thought too horrible to mention, 'allowed Meatloaf onto our bed.'

'Not often,' was Helen's deadpan response.

Dai was seriously concerned, 'It's not funny, Helen, I've told you he's too big to be allowed to get ideas of dominance, he'd be dangerous if he thought for one minute that he was the boss and letting a dog sleep on your bed gives him all the wrong messages.'

Helen widened her eyes. 'It's all right. I was just kidding - Meatloaf hasn't been sleeping on your bed.' She added sweetly, 'Is there anyone else you'd like to check out?'

His frown disappeared and he laughed. 'I'd forgotten, you...' he shook his head and looked at her again, reaching for her. 'I'd forgotten a lot... would you let me get some more practice...please.'

'I can never resist a man who says please...' was all she managed to say before he revisited at her leisure every part of her body which had been insulted earlier by his short stay.

The memory of his return grew cooler through two days in which the sense of barriers around Dai seemed to increase rather than diminish, and still he hadn't talked about Powys, despite the openings Helen gave him. The harder she tried to reach him, the further away he became, until it reached the stage that her designs and their domestic arrangements were the only safe topics of conversation.

At a loss, Helen was sitting in the rose garden, watching the effect of late - and rare - afternoon sunshine gilding the white flowers of 'Teardrops', when Dai came out to join her. He sat beside her, silent, as so often these last three days and she remembered all the stilted phone call while he was away and wondered, once more, what she should do. A broken branch caught her eye and she tutted instinctively, pointing at it. 'I'm still sorting the damage that brat did to the roses.'

Dai jumped to his feet, walked across the flower bed and kicked repeatedly at the top of broken branch, sheering off the top of the bush. He ripped off a branch still hanging and Helen could see the blood drawn in his hands by the thorns. 'It's only a bloody rose bush for Christ's sake. As if it matters. Your daughter's dead, all right? We know that, never bloody forget it. She's dead. And none of it makes any difference. We don't make any difference. And a bloody rose bush certainly doesn't make any difference.' With a last kick, he turned and walked off. 'I'm off to Mam and Dad's.' There was the inevitable whistle to his dogs and, frozen with shock, Helen watched him leave. She started to shake, like a tree caught in a storm that it could not predict, control or finish, but no tears came.

Janie, Demi and Meatloaf raced over the garden, following Dai out of sight and Helen still sat on the garden chair, not thinking and, most of all, not feeling. So this was where they were heading. What could she have done, or not done?

A large smooth tongue on her cheek broke into her stillness and she looked into the puzzled eyes of a giant wolfhound, returned to fetch the rest of his pack. 'Oh Meatloaf!' she cried and then the tears did start as she flung her arms around a huge, grizzled dog of dubious origin, who whined and pawed her in his disapproval of human goings-on.

'What are we going to do?' she asked him, but his ear-splitting bark was a response not to her but to the lower-pitched yaps of Janie and Demi, returning, all three of them confused by their master's behaviour. Forewarned, Helen mopped her eyes, sat up straight like the little girl she felt herself to be, and waited.

Dai made big, angry strides towards his treacherous dog, berating it in Welsh for disobedience. Meatloaf turned on his back, presented an apologetic tummy but maintained his post at Helen's side and she defiantly dangled a hand by the chair to stroke his soft ears.

'What have you done to him?' Dai demanded.

'Loved him,' she said softly and looked down to hide the tears filling her eyes again.

'He went running off and I couldn't be sure he'd come back here. I couldn't carry on with him on the loose. You know what farmers are like, especially at the moment. If he took it into his head to run off, there's no telling...'

She waited. The silence grew. She knew she should be angry. She could throw things and break things. Like a boy, she thought, a boy scared or upset, or running away through her rose garden.

'I'm sorry.' The words seemed to have been dredged up through a sore throat. She waited. 'I had no right. I shouldn't have... desecrated... the memory of Becky. I'm sorry.'

Suddenly, she could see it. Ever since she told him of the tragedy she carried around like an albatross for five years, ever since he put himself second in order to win her trust, he treated her as if she had the word 'FRAGILE' stamped across her forehead. Of course he didn't bring his feelings to her; he didn't think she could cope. 'Desecrated' for God's sake.

Which is what she said. 'Desecrated, for God's sake. It's a bloody rose bush. And if it wasn't for your...' she hesitated over the word but committed to it and carried on, 'for your love, it wouldn't be there.'

She walked to the middle of the flower bed and lashed out at another rose bush, crying and kicking at it till some branches broke. 'I don't want you to go to your Mam and Dad's, I want you to talk to me!' And as she said 'me', she kicked a clod of earth and low branch so hard they both struck Dai on the cheek, scoring a muddy streak. She gasped and ran to him to check the damage, wiping the wound with spit, and declaring, 'You need some antiseptic on it.'

'Before you destroy our garden or kill me, I think we should go inside, to the comfy chairs. What exactly do you want me to talk about?'

Hand in hand, Meatloaf by Helen's side with his eyes on Dai, they took their problems for the first time to the comfy chairs.

'Your Dad told me about the foot and mouth in Skewen,' Helen began, 'and that things are so bad the farmer might have done it deliberately, and I know you've been diagnosing and killing and hearing the farmers in the worst of it. I feel bad that you'd rather talk to your parents about it than to your wife.' The last words were out before she'd registered them and he smiled ruefully at her surprise.

'And wife you are. The sooner we organize that officially, the better. Although I'm not sure how safe the garden will be...I haven't talked to anyone for a month and I'm not sure whether I want to talk much now, my thoughts are too jumbled. But you're wrong, you know, I wasn't going to talk to my parents instead of you.'

'So what would you have done up there for hours?'

'Sat, watched TV, grunted now and again.' Suddenly she knew it was true, that his relationship with his parents was deep, but founded on silences and boundaries, and was no threat to her at all. What a fool she was.

'So tell me what you want to,' she invited, and, to his own surprise, once he started talking, the details he had thought to bury surfaced and brought the muddled misery of the last month into the cosy safety of his own sitting room.

'I don't think it was deliberate,' Dai reflected, 'the Skewen farmer I mean, I listened to his comments on the radio, but I've seen so much that would make you understand why someone would do that.'

'That's what your Dad said.'

'Thousands of animals slaughtered, most of them healthy, and I still don't know that we did the right thing.' Dai told her of the unforgivable delays between farmers contacting him with concern over an animal, his visit and the dreaded Form D served, which isolated the farm and everyone on it.

Then there was the wait for the lab confirmation - or more rarely, denial - of foot and mouth. Sometimes, with overloaded services and communication cock-ups the process took up to a week. As incubation was two to ten days, sometimes more, and the animals were infectious for ten days, that early diagnosis was crucial.

The sheer work-load was crazy, with farmers reaching for the phone at every sign of lessened appetite; fever; diarrhoea in calves; cows or sheep lying down more than usual because of sore feet; dead young; any blisters around feet, mouth or nostrils; saliva dripping from cows' mouths and blisters on their tongues; any and all of these symptoms could indicate foot and mouth - or something completely different.

To make matters worse, more sheep than usual suffered foot rot in the wet weather, a disease easily confused with foot and mouth, especially by a panic-stricken farmer who feared the worst and needed the vet to tell him it wasn't so.

'And I wouldn't even notice the week passing, I was tearing from one farm to another, supervising the slaughter-men one day and ensuring that all the dead bodies in the heap were dead, administering the coup de grace of a rod through the bullet hole if it was needed to ensure brain death, then the next day I'd be telling a farmer the foot and mouth was on his neighbour's farm and he'd have to lose everything himself.

You just become numb... immune to the look on a man's face when the herd he's bred for twenty years is condemned to die on a rubbish heap, immune to the burning corpses and the blood running from the landfill site.

I've inspected slaughter-houses often enough, you get used to it, but never anything like this and what's awful is, you get used to that too. I know I shouldn't say it but it's like I imagine it was for the officers running a concentration camp taking endless, contradictory orders, filling in useless paperwork until the orders to kill and the smell of dead bodies is just a set of numbers to fill in on the useless paperwork, so you have no feelings, no sense of responsibility for carrying out what you ought to know is wrong, only you don't know anything any more - for God' sake don't say any of this to the papers - they're wallowing in emotion as it is. I can't watch or read the news.'

'What do you think I am?' she reassured him. 'And you don't think it's wrong or you wouldn't have done it. You can't judge in the middle of something like that, and you know everyone - Chief Vet, government, farmers' unions - might disagree about how, but they all want an end to this. That doesn't make you evil.'

'You ask the farmer who went berserk with his tractor, hitting a police car and nearly killing the young driver - he'd have turned his shotgun on me soon as look at me. I've had a gun pointed at me and been told to leave the property, that they were going to fight the directive to cull. You ask the farmers who've turned their shotguns on themselves - there are enemies in this war all right and I don't know whose side I'm on. I kept thinking of Dad... if I had to tell him his neighbour's sheep had it so the Salars were condemned, would he stand there with his shotgun and tell me, over his dead body?'

'Foot and mouth's the enemy, you know that, it's just everyone seems so confused about what to do.'

'Confused! You can't trust anyone. What was MAF doing during that three weeks when foot and mouth was out there, and not a word to anyone? Oh they'll say they didn't know but how come they were stock-piling sleepers and coal?'

'Sleepers and coal.'

'Oh yes, basic requirements for funeral pyres - on a large scale. And within forty-eight hours of that first announcement they knew exactly what serotype of foot and mouth it was - something that would take at least 10 days to test. And even if you divide the stories by two, there have been lab results returned positive when the samples didn't reach the labs - and as for some of the people who volunteered to carry out the cull - you can imagine who'd volunteer for jobs with guns. I was told to supervise three culls simultaneously - how the hell could I guarantee they were done right? I took an oath to put animal welfare first and I can't square that with what's going on this summer, with what I've been part of.

If you asked me now, I'd say nothing will stop it, ever. So many things are carriers - it's more likely to be passed on by careless people and their vans, or the meal sacks and feeding troughs, than contact between the animals themselves. If it is between animals, it could be foxes or dogs and cats that pass it on - it's all possible.' A sudden fear struck him. 'You have been careful with disinfecting haven't you?'

'Yes, and your Dad's watched my every move like a hawk, he's following your orders to the letter.'

'Good. I think that's what really happened in Skewen, sheer human carelessness, one little slip. And being careful still doesn't get you off the hook. Even now there are sub-strains developing and it's likely that animals we've missed, which caught foot and mouth and survived the first round, will catch a new strain and pass that on. We might as well live like Argentina and accept foot and mouth as what we live with, give up on exports, give up on keeping beasts healthy. But if you saw a sheep with it bad, its mouth hanging off like a jagged bleeding letter-box, I just don't know and that's the truth. And I'm supposed to know.'

Helen reached out and just held his hand, unable to do more than listen and be there. She had to strain to hear his words, brought into their world from somewhere darker he had been for too long. 'It was the children that were the worst. Watching their pet lambs and goats being taken from them, knowing enough about what was going on to cry with fear and not enough to understand. Seeing their parents helpless while the fields were silenced. It's the emptiness you see and the silence you hear, in the fields and sheds, when the animals have gone.

One man insisted on lining up his family, his wife, his three children and making them watch while the slaughter-men rounded up the cows and shot them. He said he didn't want them to become farmers and he wanted them to witness what happened to him. Did you know that the farmer has to be there, by law, during a cull?'

'I knew some refused to sign, tried to stop it...'

'Oh Helen, you don't know the half of it...' They sat in silence.

Helen stroked the wolfhound's bristly face and wouldn't look at Dai. 'They said, round here, that if you get foot and mouth, all the pets have to be put down too.'

'What, the dogs and cats?' She nodded. 'That's rubbish. No, no-one's sentenced the dogs and cats to death, though they are another way of spreading the disease - like us...How do these rumours get round!'

'I was scared it was true so I didn't dare ask. Everyone's staying on his own farm and we believe anything - especially if it's bad. We only know what's on the TV - or the Internet.'

'Same way we found out in the first place - and it hasn't improved much.'

'Perhaps David will be a help? Professionally?' she ventured.

Dai contemplated the cool analytical thinking of his partner and conceded, 'He'll have a view, and he'll be up to speed with what's going on.' He added bitterly, 'But he sent me there.'

'If it had to be done - ,' she cut off his protest, ' - and that's what the experts seem to think, then no-one could be better than you.'

He gave a weak smile. 'And you're not at all biased.'

'Not at all.'

'Tell you one thing - every penny of that blood money will go on the herd and keeping the farm going, and if the Salars stay clear of foot and mouth, I'll stand barring the way with a shotgun myself before I let some man in a white suit chase them round and take pot shots at healthy animals.'

Helen hoped it wouldn't come to that but said nothing. It was difficult to be optimistic when the threat was so close, and when he knew so much more than she did, she would just sound foolish. Instead, she offered him her silence and her arms around him.

Return to everyday surgery and visits still left Dai feeling that he had returned from the trenches to a two-dimensional world, but he was starting to recover his detachment. It helped to mix with the farmers of Carmarthenshire, free of foot and mouth - so far - but suffering from movement restrictions and lack of markets.

Dai looked up the dusty 1968 Veterinary Encyclopaedia which lived on his shelf from student days, wondering what the expert view was during the time when Britain last experienced a foot and mouth outbreak.

'This disease is of great economic importance. The outbreak which occurred in West Germany in 1951/52 caused a loss of about eighty-seven million pounds.'

Some things did not change. In a masterpiece of understatement, the entry gave the options of treating individual animals or 'immediate slaughter of all animals on the affected premises' and/or 'immediate vaccination in the endangered area'.

Disinfection and movement control were also listed, but it did nothing to dispel Dai's reservations and fears to read 'Slaughter of the entire herd is particularly suitable in an area where foot and mouth has hitherto not occurred.'

That was not the case in Powys - so were they wrong to cull? It was true in Carmarthenshire so if his father's - and his - Salars went down with the disease, his professional decision ought to be clear. He closed the heavy maroon volume and went back to work.

The logistics of processing welfare orders, and the business of animal life and death, which carried on regardless - and for farmers, life and death *were* their business - gradually re-motivated Dai. His professional skills were challenged again, rather than meeting the same insoluble problem day in, day out. Perhaps the hardest truth of all for him to face was that the work in Powys, and it was after all a job, was repetitive and boring.

David read him well and ensured that a variety of cases came his way and that he had a week off evening surgeries and being on call. It was not only the animals which were started on the healing process when Dai recommended drops of lavender and tea tree oil in solution, to soothe a horse's allergic sore patches, and returned a Labrador puppy to its delighted owner after dislodging a plastic toy from its ear. Whereas David loved an opportunity for complex surgery, Dai's favourite practice was to work with nature and to return an animal to good health with the least artificial intrusion.

He was therefore pleasantly surprised when David told him they could afford to spend the Ministry money on something new for the surgery and his suggestion of an ultrasound scan was instantly accepted. God willing, he would be able to use the scan in his own fields to help his own calves in the coming winter and spring.

The routine of disinfecting, working, disinfecting and returning home became second nature to both Dai and Helen. They had both become accustomed to the tension felt by every farmer in Carmarthenshire, checking Teletext daily to see if there were new cases, if it were closer, worrying about six months with no income and the bottom dropped out of already low prices.

They thought Will was digging in with the same spirit, supported this time by his son in a shared venture, unlike his lonely battle against the depression and financial problems caused by BSE. So they had thought, which is why it came as a shock when Gwen hammered on their back door at midnight, wearing wellies and an overcoat thrown over her dressing-gown, to say she'd had a call from the landlord at the local to say that Will had been arrested, with another man that no-one knew, for being in a fight. 'Grievous bodily harm' the landlord had said.

Chapter 10

There was a gloomy silence in Dai's car as he drove Helen and his mother to Llanelli Police Station. They had rushed out without Gwen changing so she waited in the car, and Helen stayed to keep her company, while Dai went to see if he could 'spring Dad', a flippancy that made no-one smile.

'It'll be all right,' Helen put a comforting hand on Gwen's shoulder. The older woman was sitting in the front, straight-backed against the world.

'I don't know what's got into him.' Helen had a mental image of Dai, and herself, kicking roses and she thought she could imagine the sort of mood that might get into a man, but she said nothing. 'As if we didn't have enough trouble without him looking for it. For all I know he'll have a fine, and I don't know where the money will come from, I really don't. And what if it's worse?'

Car headlights flickered and dipped past them, slowing for the left turn past the station into a one-way street. The disused bus shelters around them looked eerily empty and the locked gate of the small People's Park fronted total blackness, from the depths of which came the occasional clink of bottles and loud teenage voice. A newspaper drifted to join the plastic bottles, torn wrappings and an empty syringe in the corner of a bus shelter. Gwen drew her overcoat closer round the pink candlewick dressing gown.

'There's lots of talk of government compensation grants for farmers - and for all the businesses who've lost trade and tourists. Could you apply for something?' Helen asked.

'Nothing. There's money for those who've had foot and mouth, or been neighbours ordered to cull, and there might be something for hotels and such, although I don't see how they're going to organize it and it won't be fair - I'll tell you that. They'll give something to Mr Jones who owns a posh hotel but they won't give it to the people he laid off all summer and they won't give it to the shop in the village or to anyone who would have made a bit on the stalls at the fayres we haven't had. And here will be sweet f.a. for farmers like us.' Helen was shocked to hear Gwen talking this way. 'Don't get me wrong, I know we're lucky not to lose the animals - so far, touch wood - but I've still got to make ends meet. I hope to God they hurry up with the hearts money.'

'You put in, then.' Helen's voice betrayed nothing.

'Yes, two weeks ago now, so it shouldn't be long. I'll make a bit less if it goes more than a month.'

'Why?' Helen asked carefully. 'Why will it be less after a month?'

'I borrowed a bit and there's interest after a month, see.'

'From the bank?'

'Mmm.'

The women sat in silence again. A police car drew up, swerved onto the hard standing in front of the station and its two uniformed occupants laughed and chatted as they got out, were silhouetted in the door's light then vanished into the interior.

Finally, Dai reappeared, accompanied by a slighter figure. Both women sighed. Helen moved over to make room for Will beside her in the back. Gwen turned stiffly to pass her own verdict on her husband. 'You bloody idiot. What the hell were you thinking of?' Although he made no attempt to answer, she carried on, 'Don't tell me - I don't want to know. Look at the state on you!' Indeed, even in the darkness of the car, there was clear evidence of the fight in a swelling around one eye and the left side of Will's face.

'You should have seen the other bloke,' Dai grinned and smoothly changed lane to take them home.

If anything, Gwen was even more incensed by Dai's levity. 'Well?' she demanded. 'Is anyone going to tell me what happened?' No-one pointed out to her that she had just told them that she didn't want to know. 'Will?' No answer. 'Dai?'

Dai threw the question back to his father. 'Dad?' There was still no answer from the back. Will turned a stony face to look out of the window and Dai sighed. 'He's been like this since I picked him up. The police sergeant said he'd been like it since they picked him up, and the other man was the same, about as talkative as two stones, the two of them.' According to the police, the landlord of the Sylen Arms had called them to break up a fight and by the time they reached the pub, the two culprits were sitting in sullen silence by an upturned table and a broken chair, with swelling faces and no doubt the odd bruised rib. 'They'll likely get away with disorderly conduct although,' Dai hesitated, reluctant to tell his mother the worst of it, 'according to the landlord, Dad started it. This other man was talking to Dad when he just exploded.'

'Drunk there all my life. You'd think the bloody man could keep his mouth shut,' was the unexpected contribution from the back.

Gwen turned on him again. 'Like a pair of big kids. I can't believe you'd be such a fool. How much did you have for God's sake? ' It was obvious to all of them that Will was not drunk, which merely added to the mystery. 'Why, is what I want to know. Is anyone going to tell me?' Silence was the only response. 'And who was this other man anyway?' A sudden thought struck her. 'You been seeing his wife or something?'

That did draw a response from the back. 'Don't be so bloody daft, woman. You watch too much television you do. Apart from the fact I don't have the time, or the energy, don't you think he'd have been hitting me first?'

'I don't know what to make of it, I'm sure I don't.' Gwen's voice was losing the adrenalin anger and held a trace of tears.

'Then make nothing of it,' was Will's rough response.

There was no further comment until Dai and Helen were alone again. 'Do you think it was something to do with another woman?' she ventured.

Dai just laughed, 'No way. Now, if it was my grandfather...quite the ladies' man in his time, so I heard.'

'And who do you take after?' she asked, not quite joking.

'My mother,' he replied, reaching for her hand and squeezing it.

'What about the other man? Did you see him? Do you know who it is?'

Dai shook his head. 'The police wouldn't give me a name - in case I decided to take him on myself, I suppose. That's the world they work in. They did tell me that he was a stranger - the landlord said he'd never seen him before. I feel sorry for old Ken, he must have been fair worried about what my Dad was going to do to have shopped him like that.'

'You sound almost proud of him.'

'I can't say I want to pick him up from the cop-shop on a regular basis but I have to say I didn't think he had it in him, and if he's going to fight, I am glad to see he can hold his own.' *Men.* 'I hope you feel the same when it goes to court.'

'And when I think of all those times he told me fighting never solved anything, there is a certain satisfaction...'

'And if the court fines him?'

'It won't be much.'

Helen was deeply tempted to tell Dai about his mother's financial fears and involvement in the hearts scheme but she would not betray a trust, so she contented herself with saying, 'I can't believe you take it so lightly. It means a lot more than that to your Mum. We're talking about a criminal record.'

'I suppose so... but it's not as if he's a teacher...'

'Or a vet...'

'O.K., O.K. - I take your point. Which reminds me, we must sort out a wedding some time.'

'Who said I still want to marry into a violent and abusive family? Anyway, what reminds you?'

'You, nagging.' He ignored her sharp intake of insulted breath. 'He must have been really provoked, you know. I don't believe he lost it like that without good cause. If I can get him to say what really happened, if it does come to legal proceedings, that would get him off, surely.'

'Can you?'

'What, get him to say? Not tonight, but maybe tomorrow, or the next day, if I go about it the right way...'

A few days later, inspecting the mouths of their golden brown cows, Dai found the chance to ask his Dad what had happened.

'Do they look clear to you?'

'As beautiful as the day we chose them.' Dai stroked the broad muzzle, patched with cream, as liquid brown eyes stared trustingly into his. The same trusting stare had met the verdict of death he had doled out so often in Powys. 'We'll get through this - apart from that one case in Skewen and the odd outbreak in the south-east near Newport, it's not crossed the Powys border into the south-west. Keep your fingers crossed but I think Carmarthenshire's going to stay clear.' *This time around*, he thought, keeping to himself his fears that the cases still appearing in Powys and in the north of England would erupt into another epidemic in the autumn. 'Dad,' he tried again, 'tell me what happened.'

'I don't suppose it can do any harm now,' Will conceded, patting a cow's flanks as he sent her on her way. 'The short of it is, he knew I was a farmer - Ken said so - and he offered to sell me a diseased carcass.'

Dai knew what that meant. Will had been offered the chance to deliberately infect this herd, their investment, their pride and to claim the compensation which they both knew would be far more money than the herd would be worth for years, perhaps ever again, the way the market had gone. He would have been given enough money to retire on, security for the rest of his life for himself and Gwen, enough to pay Dai back for the money he'd invested. He would also have condemned Carmarthenshire - free so far - to foot and mouth; he'd have condemned his neighbours' stock to the slaughter-men; and he'd have condemned Dai to a repeat of his ordeal in Powys, with his own herd.

Dry-mouthed, Dai said, 'I'm surprised he's still alive.'

'I've put the word round, and let the Union know. He's gone back to Pembrokeshire sharpish and if he tries the same there, he'll regret it.'

'Why didn't you tell me? He should be arrested.'

'That's why, Dai fach.' Will smiled grimly. 'You're a vet, son. By the book, isn't it?' That was not what his father would have said if he'd heard the conversation with Helen, Dai thought ruefully, but his father did have a point. 'And suppose you filled in forms about what this man was doing. Where's the proof? My word against his is all. No, Dai, it wouldn't have worked. And if you didn't get what you wanted and you knew the man's name and all, you might finish what I started... if by the book didn't work...' Perhaps his Dad did know him, after all. 'No, this way, he's gone now and nothing you can do.'

Suddenly the full horror of it hit Dai. 'But what if someone else takes him up on it? Even someone next door here?'

'Trust me - I've put the word out and that will keep us safer than any policeman. He won't dare open his mouth and if he was daft enough to, and if some farmer was tempted, he would not dare take him up on it because everyone would know - that's the point of putting the word out. Anyone tried that malaki would be horsemeat, believe me. Now that's an end to it.'

'You might tell them all that if they press charges.'

'I might. Then again, I might not. How's the drainage around that cottage of yours?'

Anne and Helen were sitting in Neil's study, surrounded by his bookshelves and aura of academic discipline. Both were frowning in concentration.

'Hello... Shwmae, Helen adw i.'

'Shwmae, Anne adw i.'

'Where do you live... Ble ych chi'n byw, Helen?'

'I live in... dwy'n byw yn Mynydd Sylen. Ble ych chi'n byw, Anne?'

'Dwi'n byw yn Llanelli. Do you live in... Ych chi'n byw yn Llanelli, Helen?'

'No, I do not... Nac ydw, dwi ddim yn byw yn Llanelli, wi'n byw yn Mynydd Sylen. I don't get why it's sometimes wi, sometimes rwi, sometimes dwi - can't they just say I!' Helen sighed and carried on. 'Do you live in Cardiff... Ych chi'n byw yn Nghaerdydd, Anne? And don't ask me why Caerdydd turns into Nghaerdydd.'

During half an hour in Welsh establishing their names, their homes, their jobs and the composition of their families, chat about the weather seemed a highlight. When either of them was totally stuck, Anne would look up the section in the 'Teach Yourself Welsh' book that they were working through. It had started with a chance remark from Anne that as a languages teacher it would be a poor show if she didn't try and learn some Welsh before she went back to Alsace. Helen suddenly realized that she did know some Welsh, having absorbed snippets from the bilingual conversations that took place around her. She told Anne that she found it odd the way Dai's family would drift in and out of English. She had told him she didn't want them speaking English just for her when it must seem odd to them but he just looked puzzled and said, 'Were we speaking English?' As she listened to them, she became aware that the switches were natural to them, without them seeming to notice which language they spoke. Perhaps an English word or name, or the desire to include Helen, might trigger the switch from Welsh to English, and the need for a Welsh word might switch it back, but their world had two languages and they used both of them without thinking about it.

It was different in Alsace. Most people spoke the two formal languages of French and German but it was Alsacien that struck Anne as being closer to the status of Welsh, especially with the recent attempts to support and revive the language. Anne was not old enough to remember the days when Alsacien was a common home language and even her mother understood it rather than spoke it. Then of course there was English; love it or loathe it, the language had infiltrated everywhere and Anne was not the only Alsacien to speak it.

When Anne spoke to Helen about learning Welsh, the response was enthusiastic. Learning French had been a weekly routine between Helen and Neil and she associated this room with all the inevitable foolish mistakes as your tongue tripped over strange sounds and your memory failed you completely, so it seemed possible to make the same mistakes in Welsh in the same setting. She could laugh at herself as she tried the strange words of her lover's first language. She wanted to surprise him, even if it was only by understanding more of what was said, but she felt too shy to stumble into conversation with him.

The women's learning partnership was well matched. Although Anne found that she was quicker than Helen, it helped her too when she had to explain grammatical points from their daunting teach-yourself guide and Helen's biggest asset was her ear for the speech rhythms which had surrounded her for the last six years. A trip to Carmarthen allowed them to buy fruit and vegetables in Welsh, and a friendly market stall-holder taught them that tomatoes were 'afalau cariad', love apples, and that some words were rarely used now, like 'mavis' for strawberry, so that beans were 'bins' to most people. Their next unit of study would be 'Hobbies and Interests' which was a little closer to what Helen might want to say to Dai but she doubted that what she had in mind as a mutual interest would figure in the text. Still, it was interesting...

By tacit agreement, the language between bursts of Welsh was English. It was obvious that Helen found one foreign language at a time tiring enough, Anne realised, remembering her own exhaustion during the first few weeks in Wales. Now she found the switch from Welsh to English almost as relaxing as Helen did, so at least the professional aims of her exchange had been realised, whatever the personal outcomes. Mrs Phillips brought in the teatray at the agreed time.

'Has Helen heard your good news?' Anne prompted.

'I had a little bit of luck on the hearts,' Mrs Phillips beamed, 'three weeks ago. They've filled the next heart so I've won.' Her eyes shone. 'Twenty-four thousand pounds.'

'That's wonderful,' Helen replied but her smile seemed forced. 'I'm so pleased for you. What are you going to do with it all?'

'Put it in savings mostly but perhaps a little treat, you know?'

'I'm glad. I'm glad,' she repeated with more conviction, while Anne looked at her curiously.

'Are you going to join us for a cuppa?'

'I can't.' Mrs Phillips blushed. 'I'm meeting someone in town. I'll see you later, Anne.'

As the door closed, Anne smiled. 'She meets 'someone' very often these days.'

'I had noticed - I think it's sweet.'

'Have you joined in this hearts scheme?' Anne was following her own train of thought.

'No, no - to be honest I didn't trust it. Looks like I was wrong, thank goodness.'

'Me, too.' Anne shrugged, then registered the 'thank goodness'.

'I thought you weren't involved?'

'No, not me... I'm not supposed to tell anyone but Dai's Mum, Gwen, went into it. They've had such a hard time... first BSE, then foot and mouth. I don't know how they keep going through one crisis after another. And money's so tight. I'm sure Gwen wouldn't have risked putting her savings into hearts if she wasn't desperate.'

'You needn't worry - I've no-one to tell. I'm pleased for Mrs Phillips but I'm still not sure about the whole thing. I hope your mother-in-law will be all right.'

Helen let the definition of the relationship pass - after all, Gwen *was* her mother-in-law, sort of. Having let the basic fact slip, there was no harm in sharing her worry. 'The worst of it is that she's even borrowed the money from the bank to put into hearts, and every month that goes without her winning, will cost her an arm and a leg in interest.'

'But that's awful! What would make her do such a thing?'

'Electric bills.' Helen had given away enough private details. 'Speaking of which, I'd best be off to the supermarket. Dabochi'

'Dabo,' Anne replied and heard Helen repeating her Welsh good bye to Mrs Phillips, whose 'Hwyl' in return confused her completely. Why was it that whenever you learnt something in a new language, everyone who spoke it naturally, said something different?

An hour after Helen had said goodbye, so did Anne. She took the road out of town, passing quickly from rows of houses to fields and narrow lanes, bordered by hawthorn hedges. Trails of honeysuckle threaded through the thorns, scenting the air, and each bend opened up a different view, the reservoir glinting in the valley, but Anne was unable to appreciate the scenery. She was nervous of the Welsh lanes where each bend meant the risk of something coming towards her and the combination of high hedges and roadside ditches made it almost impossible to pull over.

Not that Alsace lacked narrow lanes and some of the mountain roads offered a death drop either side, but she was not used to the lack of visibility. Whose idea had it been to plant all these hedges? It just wasn't safe Anne fumed silently as she nerved herself before yet another blind bend, knowing the confident speeds at which locals took such corners - insane speeds as far as Anne was concerned. As she drew up by a farm entrance to check the name above the gate, a tractor tonned past her and she breathed silent thanks not to have passed that on the road.

Anne could see an open back door and hear the whir of an electric drill so she headed for the noise, able now to take in the view of lush hills and the full expanse of the reservoir filling the valley bottom. From here it was easier to imagine why it was called Swiss Valley but Anne still smiled at the local concept of mountains.

'Anyone home?' she called, knocking on the door. The drill came to natural pause and she called again.

'With you now.' The response was followed by the appearance of a curly-haired man in denim overalls.

'Sorry to bother you, but I'm trying to track down some relatives and it's just possible that they owned this house before you did...

'Yes?' Contrary to Anne's expectations, the man sounded interested. 'Like those TV programmes?' Anne looked blank. 'You know, House History and Find Your Family.' Anne nodded, none the wiser. 'You haven't got cameras with you, have you?' He looked around in an exaggerated way

'No indeed,' Anne hurried to reassure him, 'this will just be between you and me, very private.'

'Oh well. Anyway, we moved here, two years ago already - can't believe that - from Camberley...' Anne looked blank. 'Surrey,' he tried. Anne still looked blank. 'London,' he said, 'where we lived in a shoebox and look at what we've got now. Full-time job doing it up - I could show you what we've done around the place. You should see the new woodstove.'

'I can see you've put some work in... it's a pity I have so little time,' Anne smiled apologetically. 'Do you farm?'

'You must be joking. Just fancied a bit of land and you can't get a view like that in Camberley.'

'What about the people who sold it to you?'

'Middle-aged couple, kind face the lady had, lovely blue eyes... you saying they were relatives, you have a bit of the look of her about you... the eyes.' Her mother's eyes, so everyone told Anne.

'Now they *were* farmers - and enough to put you off the idea. They'd been through BSE and were very bitter, said there was no support for farmers in Wales and England was no better. They said there were grants going for farmers moving to Canada and that they'd rather be where they were appreciated and the farms were big enough to be viable. They sounded determined enough but as if they didn't believe in it any more - you know?'

'Did they have any children?'

The man sighed deeply. 'Don't talk to me about children. We get this fantastic place here and you'd think ours would be grateful? Not a chance. They hated Wales on principle before they even crossed the Severn Bridge and all they did was moan that they can't get takeaway pizza or walk to the video shop. They're coming round now but it's taken some time. I remember that when I asked your relatives if they had any children I got the impression they weren't too happy with parenthood either... there was a bit of a pause before they answered, as if it was a difficult question and I was feeling I'd put my foot in it - that's why I remember it so well - and then the lady said, 'Yes, one.' and then she sort of drew herself up tall and said something like 'A child is not always a blessing. Going to Canada will not be a problem.' And that's about all I can remember - sorry not to have been more helpful.'

'No, no, you have, thank you. I have a lot to think about.'

'Well if you ever want a look round, you just pop back. The wife's out at the moment and she might remember a bit more than I do."

'I'll leave you my phone number just in case.'

Two years too late. Anne negotiated the lanes once more, contemplating what few facts she had. It did sound like this could be her half-sister but Canada was a big country and she didn't even have a surname to go on. She didn't like the thought of telling her mother that the trail had gone cold but somewhere, deep down, she felt relieved. She had tried her best but she wouldn't have to meet this 'sister' - the best of both worlds, leaving her own, untroubled. And anyway, what good would it do this 'sister' to have *her* world turned upside down too? No, what would be, would be.

Conscience prompted her; and what about the daughter who is not a blessing, Sharon or Charlotte or whatever her name was? It didn't sound as if she had gone to Canada. How old would she be now? Late twenties, thirtyish, so she's hardly looking for a long-lost auntie or a long-lost grandmother... no, it seemed as if Anne had done all she could and her mother would at least have the comfort of knowing that her other daughter was alive and well, with a family of her own.

Helen found two emails waiting for her. 'Work before play' she told herself and clicked first on the one from the Voudoirs.

Bad news, I'm afraid. The bureaucrats have not accepted our application for artisanat status and inclusion in the Wool Fayre with your designer items. If we leave your name off the range and off the marketing at the Fayre and any stalls we work, there will be no problems - unofficially, I have been told that they will turn a blind eye to the designer being English. We have two months to remake some stock so we could do it. I don't need to tell you how useful this would be financially, and once customers come to the shop they would see your name up front, but I will understand if you do not accept these terms.

It has to be your decision on this but I need to know quickly as the Fayre is limited to a hundred artisans and our place is only held for another week for us to 'correct our application.'

I will try to work on people behind the scenes but I cannot say I am hopeful. I am so sorry, Helen.

Regards,

Amélie

Helen read it twice but nothing changed. She was being asked to give up being the designer on the designer label, to hide all her achievement. She might as well be back in a Wakefield factory, knitting up someone else's boring commercial pattern. And what for? For some French bureaucrat to maintain the national purity of a market! *Pah! I spit on your market!* Yet if she said no, it would be a big opportunity lost, not just for her but for the Voudoirs. Buyers from national stores would be trawling the quality markets for new lines and the selective nature of the Wool Fayre was one of its attractions. If Helen's designs caught a buyer's eye, business could really take off for all of them. Should she hold them back for the sake of her own artistic integrity? Was it just pride by another name? She needed time to think. The second email was from Neil and made her smile.

Sorry it's hard going for Dai - and for you. Fingers crossed that foot and mouth's coming to an end. Papers here present it as either a punishment on the English for poor farming methods (smug response) or a British plot against French farmers (paranoid nationalistic response)...

You said he felt like an executioner. Did you know that Saint-Saens, the composer, was the hereditary Executioner of France and spent all his life worrying in case he'd be asked to carry out his hereditary duty... he wasn't. Luc told me that.

Your Botanical Gardens idea sounds a real winner - good luck. Glad you've made friends with those dogs - not the sort you'd want as enemies.

You would love the baby Macaques - their hair is black and silk, only gradually turning brown. I've been helping Luc record births at the Centre, which are up on last year. There's no way of telling who's the father - bit of a free-for-all in the autumn mating - so we record the mother's number and note the family group. Females stay in the same group and keep much the same status as their mother; males change group, and work their way up by making the right friends and by flexing their muscles - much like the Welsh Assembly!

You'd think there would be no parental bonding between adult males and young, because of the lack of ownership, but it's the opposite. After the first few days, when the baby clings to its mother's chest sleeping and suckling, the rest of the family group take turns in touching the new arrival and they are allowed to babysit, always within suckling distance of the mother. This goes for males as well as females and - believe it or not - the young are deliberately used by adult males to defuse tension between them. You should see two adult males sitting face to face, hugging each other and clicking their teeth amicably at the baby between them. Can you imagine it with my sixteen-year-olds in school in Llanelli? When two of them start with 'What you looking at?' 'You want a smack in the teeth or what?' I could pass them the school baby and they would then coo at the little darling instead of pulverizing each other.

Seriously, I can think of hard youngsters who are wonderful with babies and small children - some of them have to be. I can also think of parents who could learn a lot from the Macaques. It's the way everyone looks out for the young, such a sense of community, that strikes me every time I watch them.

Update on storks next time.

Love

Neil

Helen smiled knowingly. The key to understanding Neil's emails these days seemed to lie in the one word 'Luc' and all that was not said. He sounded so happy. Monkeys indeed!

Alex curled up in a tight ball, pulled the duvet cover right over her head and willed herself to be asleep, to at least look asleep, so he would change his mind and the footsteps, which stopped at her bedroom door, would carry on to the double bedroom, to the double bed with the empty half where her mother ought to be.

It was happening more often.

Every time Alex saw her mother made up and glittering in a tight skirt and her high, block-heeled shoes, she knew it might happen again.

It didn't seem to matter what Alex wore during the day, his words were always the same, indelible smuts in her brain. She'd asked for it, she knew what she wanted, she was teasing him, she was a slut, she was his, if it stayed between them no-one would get hurt, she wouldn't want anyone to know how bad she was, what she got up to at night, she wouldn't want the social to take her away for being bad, she wouldn't want her mother to know how she was putting it about, she knew her mother's temper, she'd have no-one then, she was lucky having their special time and if she did it right she'd make him so happy.

He would thrust the words into her, inserting them beyond her resistance, insisting on acknowledgement through a nod, a whispered 'Yes'.

In the past she had tried with-holding that little act of complicity but he hit her, carelessly for once, so that the bruises showed finger-marks across her ribs, so that she could have been caught out by the social worker, by the strange woman with the dogs, if they'd seen.

Usually he took more care when he lost it, prodded, dug, left marks that looked less human. She didn't care afterwards about the hitting but while it happened it was too hard to hold back and it was that which made her cry afterwards, knowing she had said 'yes', that and knowing all she said 'yes' to. She was a dirty girl. He was right and she was his.

The footsteps paused long enough to make her hope. She held her breath. The handle turned and she breathed out in a long sigh, pretending sleep, the blood in her ears multiplying the steps across the room. She kept her eyes screwed tight while the duvet was pulled back. Another pause, then a sharp jerk on her hair and the instinctive 'Ow' and hand up to the sore spot, which were her undoing.

Alex left the dirty girl on the Outside and ran into The Place. She had to be quick to get in because she would need to build up the defences high tonight and then nothing would get in, not a finger, not a filthy word, not an AIDS virus. Trees, she summoned, grow taller. Around The Place Alex could feel the trees growing thicker, stronger, interlacing branches which dripped with cone fringes or with sprays of spring leaves. Stretching to the sky, her trees were unshakeable, rooted in a universe of her own making.

At a distance, she could feel the destroyer's rhythmic thumping against the outer ring of trees, brute force battering her impenetrable forest. She felt young trunks of those frontline trees gashed open, bleeding sticky resin in an endless painful flow, channelled through the bark down to pool on the earth, reflecting the canopy foliage and reinforcing the thickness of the forest.

Alex ran deeper into the heart of The Place into a tiny one-room cottage with a picture on a table by a cushion. Alex threw herself onto her knees on the cushion and stared at the picture, drawing strength from the blue eyes and serene face of her San Fairy Anne. 'Please,' she prayed, safe in The Place. Much later, curled on the cushion, she fell asleep in The Place and in her own bed.

Alex awoke to morning, hungry. She dealt with the sticky mess between her legs and went to school.

Chapter 11

Inhumanity took many forms and it seemed to Neil that all of them had taken place here, in a wooden stockade which commanded a view at cloud level across valley clefts to further peaks; here, in the only concentration camp built on French soil, le Struthof.

The day started with some light-hearted exploration of villages on the Route du Vin, famous for the frequent 'dégustation' invitations, the opportunities to stop at a 'cave' or two, or ten, and taste the fine white wines which Neil was learning to appreciate. The weather promised to support the region's claim to be the 'second driest in France' (after the south-east, near Perpignan) and, as always with Luc, there was something new to discover, so Neil was looking forward to the day. If he were honest with himself, Neil was living for his time with Luc and sunshine was merely a bonus.

Their first tourist stop was in Bergheim, despite Neil's protests. 'I've seen Bergheim - I bring Madame Grüber here every week because she likes the boulangerie on the square, I've seen the church, the medieval graveyard, the mural of the washerwomen on the purple medieval house, the German cemetry out of the village...' Neil counted off the list on his fingers. 'I can see Bergheim every time I look out of the window from Thannenkirch. On a really clear day I can even hear the Bergheim church bells floating up the mountain all the way to Thannenkirch. It's very pretty but I've seen it.'

'Done that, been there,' teased Luc. 'You sure your mother didn't have a fling with an American tourist?'

'My mother never had a fling in her life.'

'So, you who know Bergheim, you've seen Lagmi dropping his trousers then?'

'I might have,' Neil hedged.

'Was he in the usual place?'

'How would I know what's the usual place?'

'But you know Bergheim soooo well... where was he when you saw him then?' Luc was unrelenting.

'On the corner of the Square, by the café,' Neil hazarded.

'Miracle the gendarmes don't lock him up, isn't it?' Luc sparkled with mischief and Neil knew when to give in.

'This is all garbage isn't it. O.K. I haven't seen your Lucky or whatever his name is - I suppose it's a statue or something that I've missed.'

'Where do you usually park?'

'In the Square. We drive through the Arch,' Neil indicated the medieval stone gateway to the village, arching over their heads, 'go along the main street - if you can call it that - and turn left.'

'Which is why you've missed Lagmi.' Luc stopped between the two archways of the gateway and pointed to the grassy bank enclosed between them, to the left of the cobbled entrance to Bergheim. There was a floral display, presented with the care typical of the Alsacien villages where displays of trailing geraniums in window boxes competed with the parks department petunias, in all but the most wintry months.

'Pretty,' Neil pronounced with little enthusiasm. 'Botany not really my thing.'

'Look again and read the story, Mr Seen-everything.'

Neil read the little plaque which Luc brought to his attention, looked again and laughed. The floral arrangement created the symbolic Lagmi, a medieval criminal showing his feelings by revealing petalled buttocks in a defiant moony and a one-fingered gesture at those pursuing him. The law of the time offered Sanctuary within the town walls to anyone who made it that far, whatever he had done.

'I've taught plenty like him,' Neil observed.

'Thought you'd like him.'

'What if he went outside the walls again?'

Luc shrugged. 'You know the sorts of punishments around then. Cut their hands off for stealing, that sort of thing.'

'What if he carried on stealing or whatever, in Bergheim?'

'Don't know, never thought about it. Me, I just thought he had a nice body...' That glint was even more pronounced.

'Forget it. Nothing with flowers, I get hay fever.'

'No you don't.'

'I do now, it's just started.'

Somehow, although both men were aware of the harsh punishments suffered by medieval criminals, it was all too long ago to be anything other than stored knowledge, passing snippets of information. This was not the case with le Struthof.

Their route took them from the village of Schirmeck up through the forests, each hairpin opening up a view down the valley until they lost the villages along the bottom and gained a vista of peaks behind peaks, like paper cut-outs repeating into the distance. Signs announced the 'champs de fer', the battle-field, which raged across the forests, and Neil thought it one more such sign as he absent-mindedly read 'Le chambre du gaz', 'The gas chamber.' Nothing, not the information he'd read on the Internet, no films or literature had prepared him for the prosaic detail of horror. From the moment they followed that small white tourist sign and sat in the car beside what had once been a hotel annexe, the world made no sense. The hotel sign was clearly visible on the main building, across a narrow drive from the boarded up annexe, just as clearly signed 'Gas Chamber'.

'Do you still want to go?' Luc asked him quietly. He had made his pilgrimage in his student days but merely shook his head when Neil asked about the camp. Madame Grüber added nothing to her original suggestion that it would help him understand Alsace. From the Internet, Neil gained facts and read the witness statements of survivors, so he thought he knew what he was facing. He had been wrong, he knew nothing - which was why he said yes.

The camp itself was further along the road, the Gas Chamber having been situated at a discrete distance. Even the road had been built on the backs of the prisoners, who constructed their own route to hell, carrying materials right from the foot of the mountain up here to what had been a ski station near the village of Natzviller, at the most beautiful vantage point of the 'Hohwald', the High Forest. Like a cheap film set, the barbed wire fences enclosed a terraced compound containing barrack blocks, memorial plaques and a museum. Set against the arena of distant mountains, against the blue of the early summer sky, it could have been the holiday village it once was, but for the gallows noose left swinging, foreground on any photograph you might take. Neil was not taking snapshots.

In the open yard, the men and women would have assembled for the roll calls - one of which lasted eighteen hours in the bitter cold of winter - and for the public hangings. An officer would announce that there should be five less people by the next roll call and so it had to be, whether by suicide or by execution for an 'escape bid' when a guard would trip up a quarry worker then shoot him. There was no end to the petty acts of sadism within the greater horror.

Neil saw the crematorium and the room stacked with funeral urns, in which Germans were returned to their families - only Germans. The names of four women were recorded on a wall plaque, two English and two French parachutists who were executed, shot in the back of the neck in the purpose-built room, which sloped to a drain for the blood. According to an 'Avis', a Public Notice, displayed in the Museum, there was a reward of ten thousand francs for reporting the whereabouts of a parachutist to 'the authorities'. It would not have been as simple as holding your tongue. Failing to report a parachutist, or someone who carried out 'an act against the authorities', was itself treated as a criminal act and in such a case the 'Avis' also threatened 'the execution of all male relatives over seventeen, the imprisonment of all female relatives over seventeen and the placement in a corrective school of all relatives under seventeen.' The betrayed parachutist could have been Vernon from Llanelli, shot as a spy. The dangerous criminal could have been Mme Grüber, if she was caught taking bread to the soldiers in the woods, or - if someone acknowledged that she was under seventeen - an adult in her family paying for the sixteen-year-old's activities.

The camp executioner was given two bottles of eau-de-vie, a portion of sausage and two cigarettes for each job. After his three hundred and sixtieth execution, he lost his mind and was executed in his turn. Neil's light-hearted comment on Saens-Saens, in his email to Helen, stuck in his throat.

A corridor led away from the room with the silent furnace, past the execution room to a dormitory and a laboratory. Those selected for the latter were kept in the former, then taken as required to see the Doctor who used the porcelain operating table, finely cracked but still at the centre of the room, for medical experiments on human guinea pigs. When the Allies liberated Strasbourg on 23rd November 1944, they also reached le Struthof, taking its Kommandant by surprise so that every documentary detail was there for the world to read; objective medical records by a Professor from Strasbourg's Institute of Anatomy, detailing human reactions to slow death by gas, to implantation of leprosy or cancer cells, to surgical experiments.

No government had yet made such tortures illegal for non-military personnel but there were international laws on the treatment of soldiers captured in war-time. This did not protect those unlucky enough to be placed in le Struthof. Even a French General was termed 'a political prisoner' and therefore subject to the same regime as every other victim. At sixty-two, Monsieur le Général Frère died in le Struthof, officially of 'diphtheria', but - according to the Kommandant - actually of induced disease. Keeping him company were all those decreed by the 'Nacht und Nebel' edict to be undesirable to the Reich, all those who could be taken in the 'night and fog' of the law's name; political prisoners, 'ordinary' criminals - both French and German; conscientious objectors; Gypsies and other travellers; Jews. The multi-lingual population included a high representation of Russians, Poles and French colonials from Morocco and Algeria. There was final and total equality in the memorial graveyard, among the rows of crosses differentiated only on closer inspection, when Neil could see a star of David, or a name in Arabic.

Neil broke the silence. 'So many.'

'They say ten thousand died here and maybe forty thousand

passed through, to Auschwitz, Buchenwald, who knows.'

Neil shook his head. 'It's the way the killing was stepped up in those last months, when they knew the war was ending and they were losing. Why?'

Luc was wearing a formal suit and his hands were crossed in front of him, like a man in church. Neil had never known him subdued, never known him lost for an answer, but he said nothing.

'*Shema*,' Neil murmured.

'What's that?'

'Title of a poem. I think it's Hebrew or Yiddish and means something like '*Bear Witness*'

You who live secure
In your warm houses
Who return at evening to find
Hot food and friendly faces...
Consider that this has been:'

Primo Levi, the poet, survived Auschwitz...'

The excited chatter of a class of teenagers being shepherded up the steps to the cemetery jarred on Neil's senses and he could feel Luc tense. Their teacher's shushing merely changed the quality of the intrusion and although Neil could sympathise with the teacher's task, he could not forgive what seemed like a desecration of place.

'I can understand the idea of bringing them here but I don't think I could make it work...'

The teacher had adopted the stance of the public guide and his confident tones were ringing out in German, giving the official commentary on the dead. Two schoolgirls who were staring at Neil and Luc giggled, nudged each other, whispered behind their hands and called a friend to join their staring. Neil could feel the explosion building in Luc and was almost relieved when his lover reached out for his hand and took it firmly in his own. 'Let's go,' he said, still gripping Neil's hand in his own as he turned to walk past the teacher, past thirty adolescents and down the steps. Neil did not even think of dropping the hand that held his too tight, in pride and defiance, shaking with emotion. The commentary stopped and some of the youngsters sniggered. Luc stopped by the teacher.

'Tell them it was for this crime,' he held up their joined hands, 'that some men died here. Tell them that,' and he walked on down the steps, Neil at his side. Behind them the youngsters closed ranks again and the teacher's voice resumed its drone.

When they reached the car, Luc finally released Neil, who winced and shook his hand to circulate the blood again.

'Sorry.' Neil was relieved to see Luc smile ruefully and shake his head.

'No. I don't now how to say this but... I had forgotten. There was nothing in the displays and I was thinking of Madame Grüber, and that first love of hers and I forgot... it could have been us, couldn't it?'

'It *was* us. It *was* two men who loved each other and who were sent to a camp. It *was* young Madame Grüber, it *was* her young soldier with people calling him a spy and forgetting he was English - that's who all these people were - not those names of course but those are their stories, every one of them someone we know, every one of them treated like... like...' His gesture took in the compound and the beautiful, indifferent sweep of sky. 'We can cope with it when we think it was someone else. We should not be able to cope with it. We have to know it was us.'

There was a tacit understanding that there could be no sightseeing after such a visit and once more Neil was driving through forests which had echoed with gunfire and yet had also provided the only kind of sanctuary for Lagmi and his kind when the walls of Bergheim merely hosted an occupying army, when a man became Lagmi in an overnight decree, without knowing until the fisted knock came on his door.

'What's worst,' Luc's words were spoken so quietly Neil almost missed them, 'is knowing that they were us too, the Kommandant, the guards, the doctors who made people ill...'

'That's why the school trips.'

'So you went,' Madame Grüber prompted. Neil had returned straight to his Thannenkirch home, parting quietly from Luc with no need to explain.

'Yes.'

'I wanted you to see all the choices which never had to be made on your island, which are at the back of our lives, whether we talk about them or not.'

'You know what I have seen today. I feel I don't have the right to talk about it. What can I say?'

'None of us have the right, none of us who were not in that place, and most of them cannot speak now. If we don't let people know, even if the words are inadequate, we have failed in our duty, I think.'

'To bear witness... the same idea, I think. Vernon would not have been sent there, would he, but you might have been?'

'Vernon? Probably not if he was taken as a soldier, not a spy, but even then, the people in charge of what you saw today did not always play by the rules. I did not know any of this then. I just knew that people hushed their voices and were afraid when they referred to the place that our comrades in the Alliance were sent when they were caught. It was the fear of the bogeyman, the unknown, but the truth was even worse. As for me? At sixteen your heart beats fast, you don't think you will get caught, you want to be a hero.'

'You *were* heroes.'

'Perhaps. I have told you that it is sometimes better to watch the river flow. As you get older, you become less certain that you are doing good when you build your dams. If I had been older then, with little children, I do not know that I would have risked my life and theirs in such a way. I cannot judge my people who endured, who carried on their lives as best they could to keep Alsace herself for the time when she should come through yet another war. The Alliance took risks with other people's lives, not just their own. Hard choices, Neil, and we are living with them.'

'What I saw today should not be possible. Something should have been done.'

'I would be lying if I did not say I am proud of those, Alliance, French resistance, who accepted an equal fate with those others, the ones we were told were not human. But I would also be lying if I say I wish I had been with them, in le Struthof. I am not so brave.'

'No-one could be, if they knew...'

'Did you see that it was burned down in the seventies? The whole camp, all the documents lost, the museum destroyed and the site painted with filthy slogans. The shame of it filled the newspapers, broke the hearts of the survivors, who had eased their pain with building a memorial for the world to see.'

'I saw the news clippings. I wondered if it might have been an attempt to put the past behind, someone burning out the evidence, perhaps of evidence of someone in their own families who carried out...such things...'

Madame Grüber shook her head. 'The writing was the same old hate, still there. In our community, someone - among our friends, the shopkeeper, the schoolteacher, who knows? - someone would do it all again. That is the knowledge we live with. Do you believe in evil?'

A noose swung in Neil's mind, a silhouette against the mountains. 'Yes.'

Madame Grüber sighed. 'It is not the fault of the trees or the rocks that they were there and Alsace is herself - we must love her such as she is. There is no place on God's earth without a bloodstain and old blood makes for good stories. You look tired, you need to stretch your legs and work up an appetite for your dinner.'

It was good advice and Neil stretched his legs rather more than he had planned, striding along the waymarked paths, choosing the higher path at each fork, following the blue circle pegged on trees at regular intervals.

The path took him past a high wooden platform, a fire break or lookout he assumed, under sweet chestnut trees, where in the autumn he had gathered the glistening kernels and taken them back to Madame Grüber for roasting. Still climbing, it then curved round above the sprawling buildings known as Fox Farm.

Even on his local map, the farm was named in English, the legacy of its Canadian immigrant owner, who produced the highly prized silver fox furs worn by film stars in the nineteen-twenties. Once, this isolated farm above a tiny village had been the centre of European expertise in breeding foxes for the fur trade, selling its transatlantic knowledge to breeders in Germany, Romania, Czechoslovakia... Perhaps Helen should introduce fox farming to Brynglas. He smiled to himself. He had no difficulty imagining her nursing and stroking fox cubs; it was the next stage of farming he could not envisage her carrying out. Truly, there was no spot on God's earth without a bloodstain - and old stories.

At another fork Neil still felt the need to walk and again he chose the upward path, switching to the waymark of the yellow cross, which took him up vertically, challenging his breathing and his pounding heart. He paused to wipe the sweat from his forehead and fan air up his T-shirt, surprised at the heat from the late afternoon sunshine, then continued, reaching the 'Tranquil Zone' of the Taenchel Massif.

It was a relief when the ground levelled and he stopped to catch breath, his sweat cooling his skin to goose pimples. The forest was dense along the ridge, bisected by the Pagan wall, a sinuous dry stone mound half-buried in moss and snaking along the network of paths. Although a walker's paradise, the Taenchel was disorientating, narrow enough to cross and view valleys at opposite compass points, and broad enough to wander round the trees in circles, glimpsing shadowy rocks along half-formed tracks.

It was a world where the great rocks had names to match, the Titans, the Giants, the Three Tables, the Lizards - each a massive sculpture crafted by the ancient gods out of the mountain's pink sandstone. Neil looked up at what was surely a dragon's head in stone and felt the spinning of old worlds.

Light was fading as Neil retraced his steps past the rock formations and to the Pagan wall for a last look along the increasing gloom of the ridge. He touched the small rounded stones and wondered about their makers. Where there was a wall, there was a war. Blood again and old, old stories. It was hard to take the perspective of the mountains, to take the long view but up here it was possible, here where young lovers courted and soldiers killed each other for centuries, leaving as much trace as the rabbits and the deer. Neil was ready to go back down to where the people lived.

Madame Grüber was speaking on the phone in the hall as Neil walked past and whispered aside to him, 'It's Anne. Don't go away

- she wants a word with you when we're finished,' so Neil sat in the living room, unintentionally eavesdropping.

'French Canada perhaps?... No, you're right, not such good farming and she probably wouldn't have any French... Oh yes, I'm glad, so glad to know that she is there, somewhere and perhaps one day... You have done everything you could. I knew you would. You are so like your father, you understand. He would be very proud of you...

... You do whatever you think is best... no, no I won't mind if you stop looking. It must have taken up so much of your time and for you too, so many feelings...I can't believe that so much time has gone by... yes, definitely a grandmother, possibly a great grandma - no wonder I can't walk up the Taenchel any more... we will talk again... I'll put Neil on now and Anne - thank you, dear, for everything... Next Sunday? Yes, till then...'

Neil waited until he was called, his mind turning over possibilities. If Madame Grüber had only just found out that she was a grandmother, possibly a great grandmother, then Anne must have had a baby when she was a teenager or very young woman. If this was only just known to Madame Grüber then the baby must have been put up for adoption but then surely Madame Grüber would not have been so calm? How would she not have known about her daughter's pregnancy when the two of them seemed so close? He listened and responded to Anne's school stories with only half his mind.

'You haven't mentioned Alex. Are things better there?'

'She is no trouble, just not in school much and always so pale and tired, clothes in a state. I passed it on to Darren, the Head of Year, as you suggested, so I assume he's taking whatever action he should.'

'Yes, I'm sure he is.' Neil felt uneasy, knowing Darren.

'And there are so many... My current worry is Jason Donoghue. Do you remember him?'

'Do I just! Year ten... no, eleven now. Difficult to give him an oral grade - he only grunts in English and much the same in French. Smoker...'

'That sounds like him. He asked me if I could tell him how to train as a bodyguard... I told him French was a big help because the sort of person who needs a bodyguard can work all over he world.'

'Great idea to sell French to Year nine - I can see the options booklet now!'

'But he is serious and I need to... redirect him, gently... and his home is so bad, Neil - I can see why he wants to get away from there - what do you think?'

Anne was right, there were so many of them, and, as Head of Year, Neil had special responsibility for a hundred kids, worrying about the inter-relationship between their achievement, their attendance, their health, their home lives. Perhaps Darren was right to count sessions attended, check school grades and bollock the ones who weren't good at either, and to stop at that - it kept the job manageable. But it wasn't how Neil worked. His heart was full of le Struthof as he talked with Anne about the vulnerable, the victims and the bullies in the social microcosm called school.

'Your colleagues are not sure about the new unit,' he told her. The schools in Alsace had recently set up pilot schemes to integrate youngsters with special needs through separate units within their collèges, the secondary schools.

'They should try teaching here for a while! This is madness, this integration, what do you call it? Social inclusion?'

'You're really picking up the jargon...' Neil grinned at the thought of his new colleagues in Alsace facing the much wider range of pupils with difficulties likely to be in their class in a typical Welsh comprehensive school.

The doorbell rang while Neil was still talking and he watched Madame Grüber answer the door. A familiar shock of sleek black hair, passionate dark eyes and the sardonic twist of a smile hit his heart before his brain registered that it was Luc. There was a cursory polite greeting to Madame Grüber then Luc interrupted him, as always too exuberant to consider others.

'I went back to the monkeys, then I noticed you'd left this and it wasn't far so I thought I'd just drop it in. Must go,' and the dark dynamo at the heart of Neil's life handed over the wallet, put an arm round him, kissed him unambiguously and fully on the mouth, then left.

'Luc,' Neil explained, unnecessarily, to Madame Grüber and the phone receiver.

Helen pressed 'Send' decisively and it was done. She would not allow her collection to be shown in the Wool Fayre. Integrity or pride, whatever, she was the designer and her name would be attached to her work, whatever it cost. The answer to Amélie was no.

Excited barks alerted her to Dai's homecoming and she could sense straight away from the way the door closed, from the weight of his footsteps, from his quietness, before she even saw his face, that he was in deep - and not happy - thought. If this needed any confirmation, it was given by his first words, as he absent-mindedly accepted a cup of tea.

'Can we go to the comfy chairs, and talk.'

Foot and mouth, Helen thought. The police charge against his father. Anything, anything except us.

'I should have talked to you before but we really need to talk about money.'

Is that all? Thank God, thank God. 'Money? I'm getting more from France now, you know, and I can pay rent - I wanted to pay rent but you wouldn't let me.' In her relief, she wouldn't stop talking and he had to hold up a hand to stop her.

'Hey, hold on there, let me have my say first.' She clasped her hands in her lap. 'The simple truth is, I'm stretched beyond my limits. I know, like most people, you think a vet has money to burn and it's my fault I've shut you out. I'm used to being alone.'

'But you were married...'

'Doesn't stop you being alone. I've been the breadwinner and made my own decisions I suppose, at least the big ones. Well, first there's the house..'

She interrupted, 'And I should be earning more when...'

'Yes, well, perhaps we can look at *our* money when I've finished telling you about mine.' It was obvious to her that he didn't think her money would make any difference. Pin-money, he might call it. She fumed silently. 'I spent thousands doing it up,' *because she imagined it this way and he had hoped to win her back and see her in her dream cottage* - he didn't need to say it, 'and I'm paying Dad a rent instead of a mortgage, to buy the cottage from him - and you know it's an inflated price because I wanted to help out - and then I bought the cows, which he accepted because he thinks I'll take on the farm one day. Who knows, maybe I will... but that's not the issue at the moment. The short of it is, even with the extra I earnt from Powys' - *so that was why he put himself through so much* - 'I've spent my share from the house sale' - *his home with Karen* - 'and I'm keeping the herd going with no income to the farm. God knows what the two of them are living on themselves but they wouldn't take anything from me even if I offered. I'm going into overdraft but with me being a vet, the bank's good for it, and I just want you to know how things stand so that you don't think it's a falling off of love when I don't buy you the presents like I have been.' His hazel eyes held hers. 'I would buy you diamonds and pearls till you jangled from head to foot, if that was what you wanted.'

'You silly bugger.' Helen moved to the arm of his chair so she could hold him. 'So you bought a herd of cows instead...'

'Have you seen this year's calves!' Dai cheered up at the thought of the Salars.

'...and I love them.'

'Well, anyone would...'

'And we'll get through this foot and mouth, like we got through BSE, and our cows are going to make a fortune for us...'

'At least we don't pay vet's bills...'

'Just as well,' she teased , 'charge a bloody arm and leg, I've been told...'

'I've been stupid.'

'Yes,' she agreed. 'Now if you can look at me and see someone who's run her own business - yes, I know you're going to say 'and that went down the toilet' but it's doing very well now thank you and I've learnt from my mistakes, and from Amélie - she's a genius - if, as I say, you can just share for once, let's get all the bank statements out and go through both sets of income and outgoings...'

'You mean you'll show me yours if I show you mine?'

'No, I mean that we need to double enter our income against known expenditure and budget accordingly...'

'I love it when you talk dirty. If we mix up our money, we'll have to get married...'

'Maybe. Get off and get your bank statements.' *Bank overdraft*, Helen thought, *like his mother.* She had no intention of breaking Gwen's confidence but she was worried about the debt, which had certainly gone past a month with no sign of hearts winnings to pay it off. *Bank overdraft...* Perhaps that's why they called it 'hearts' she thought as hers sank, knowing that she had no need to gamble to find more money. Thinking time had run out and she knew what she had to say to Amélie. She swallowed, hard, tasting bile.

Gwen clutched her handbag tighter, standing, waiting in the hallway of a terraced house in Seaside, hearing raised voices through the closed door, which burst open, throwing out a huge woman in a frilled pink dress. Gwen squeezed back against the wall to allow the other woman out and was sickened by a gust of sweat, perfume and beer.

'Stan will see you now.' The young man who announced her looked about sixteen but towered over Gwen as he steered her through the door, a hand on her back.

Once more Gwen entered the room with its oak dining table and chairs, its three plates hanging on the wall, which had struck her as bare but friendlier than Lloyds when she came here in the first place to borrow £3,000 from Stan Walker, who was sitting at the table with bundles of notes and papers in front of him. She could see the strand brushed across his bald head before he looked up at her. She remembered how kind he had been, how understanding and he had asked none of the personal questions of the man in the bank. He just asked her to sign the form and given her the money. She had hoped that she would be able to repay him today but there it was, it could come out of the winnings which would surely reach her before the next month went by.

'Come to pay me back, Mrs Evans?' Stan smiled.

'Well, no actually, that is - not this time...'

The smile faded. 'Well that's a pity but you know the agreement, don't you...'

'Yes, that is... perhaps you could remind me...?'

Stan was brisk. '40% monthly on £2,000, that's £800 from you, Mrs Evans...'

She blanched. 'Are you sure? I don't remember it being so much.'

'If you are going to doubt me Mrs Evans, we're going to find it very difficult to do business together, but you can have a look at the contract, with my pleasure.'

The words danced in front of Mrs Evans' disbelieving eyes but here it was, her own signature to an agreement to pay this monstrous amount. 'I thought it was 40% a year...' she ventured.

'Well you were wrong, weren't you - you can see here, monthly,' he spelt the word out for her, 'M- O- N- T- H- L-Y, see?'

'But that's outrageous!'

He shrugged. 'That's business.' His eyes narrowed and he leaned forward across the table. 'You didn't find it too easy to get money somewhere else, did you?' He leaned back and swung on the chair, convivial again. 'But I know what it's like, don't ask questions, come up with the goods for you. You can't pay it, can you?'

'No.' There was the sort of pause in which Gwen could feel the flex of muscles in the attendant thug for so she was starting to think of him, as he stood there and loomed, sniffing.

Then Stan smiled. 'You're a nice lady and I think you can be trusted with that two thousand.'

'Thank you.' Gwen stammered in relief.

'So you only have to pay me £400 this month and what we'll do is, we'll put the extra £400 you owe me onto your loan, sort of an account you've got then, see? You can get £400 now can't you?'

'Yes, oh thank you.' She would have her winnings before next month's repayment and she'd still be so much in profit she could look back and laugh. 'So how much will I owe you next month.

'Let me see, don't want to cheat you now...' she laughed, a high, false sound, as he made a big play of using his calculator, 'I make that nine hundred and sixty pounds - not so bad is it?'

'No.' she was desperate to leave. 'I'll come back tomorrow with the £400.'

'Of course you will.' She could almost hear 'or else' in his voice and she could not get through the door quickly enough. She understood all too well why the woman in the pink frilly dress did not even notice her in the hallway.

It was only on the bus home that she realized that the sum he had quoted was only the interest on the amount she had borrowed and would not change her debt at all, which had now grown to £2,400 even if - as she must - she paid the £400 tomorrow. She could get that much out on her credit card. So how much would she have to pay Stan next month to clear her debt? She tried the sums in her head again and again but always came up with the staggering amount of about three thousand, four hundred - almost double what she had borrowed. That would be nothing, she comforted herself, not against winnings of twenty-four thousand pounds.

Chapter 12

'I'm warning you - get yourself a bloody fishing permit. Since Matthew got that job with the Water Board he's slicker than a duck's bum, so keen to get his score up, he'll run in a twelve-year-old, given half a chance.'

Jimmy had called in the Rugby Club for a sociable pint to slake his sunny-day thirst before a spot of fishing, and found a few of the boys there with the same idea.

'I haven't wasted money on a permit in twenty years and I'm not starting now,' he bragged.

'Well don't say you weren't told.'

'How's Charmaine?'

'Fine.' Jimmy took a long swig from his glass, sitting at the bar and barely glancing at the man who spoke. He'd been at school with Huw, who had kept his job at the Llanelli radiator plant and was dropping in for a pint at the end of his shift, before turning in for some sleep. He'd be back after his 'breakfast' at nine o'clock that night. He looked tired but the way a man does after a day's work, not the way a man does after yet another shamble through pointless, humiliating hours. Jimmy didn't need a man like Huw around him.

'As if you don't know, Huw. Leave him be.' The words - and their innuendo - were muttered low but Jimmy still caught them.

'What's that supposed to mean?' He turned to face the man who had asked after Charmaine. 'What you asking after my wife for anyway?'

'Just being friendly like. You're touchy, boy.'

Another mutter in the background. 'Not half as 'touchy' as Charmaine...' Nervous laughter rippled round the bar.

The barman reached across from behind the bar and put his hand on Jimmy's shoulder, half calming, half warning. 'There's no harm in them, Jimmy. Where you planning on fishing?'

Jimmy ignored him and shook off the hand, the warmth of a couple of pints adding to his righteous indignation. 'What you trying to say? You saying my wife's a slag? Well?' The other men's eyes slid off his, slippery as freshly caught trout. Jimmy twisted his wedding ring round and round till the skin reddened.

Huw was loud with fake warmth. 'Got it all wrong Jimmy. We're all heart here, give generously to charity.' He raised his voice to make sure all the men could hear him. 'And if there's a sex appeal going we know how to give don't we boys?' For emphasis he swung and jerked his hips in a thrusting movement which brought a mixture of jeers and nervous laughter from the watching men.

The barman was over the bar within seconds of Jimmy's clumsy lunge towards Huw but not before Huw responded in kind, causing a bloody nose and a sharp pain in the ribs. Huw suffered little more than some spilled beer and merely ducked the flailing fists, stepping backwards as the barman intervened. 'You, out.' Jimmy had no option but to leave, hustled to the door, angry spittle filling his mouth and preventing words. He heard Huw saying, 'What's he expect? Shouldn't think he can see his dick with a gut like that, never mind use it.' As the door closed behind him, his fishing gear thrown out with him, he shot impotent spit against the club wall, where it trickled like a teardrop down the white rendering.

He didn't hear the barman saying. 'And you, Huw. There was no call for that. What you and Charmaine do is your business but don't bring your private dirt to my club. There's more than Jimmy out of work and going under; there but for the grace of God lad, there but for the grace of God. Now go home.'

He didn't hear Huw, irritably leaving a half-drunk beer, giving his parting shot. 'You don't mind her 'working' here when it suits you. I'm going to get her out of this one way or another. I might just take a walk by the river and settle this once and for all.'

Jimmy just picked up his fishing gear and headed off to a spot he knew, just off the old railway track, well away from the risk of bailiffs, just in case that jumped-up Water Board kid was on the roam. If he were really lucky, he'd have a fight with a ten-pound sewin, the king of a Welsh river, and something to take home for tea. Odds on he'd at least get some eels and jelly them himself - Charmaine was too delicate for that. Not too delicate for other things though.

Alex sat on the flat stone which jutted into the river, supporting the railway arch. No trains had passed through in Alex's life-time, gone with the pits and the miners they serviced. It was a cycle path now, peopled at weekends by the families Alex regarded as if they were fairy tales brought to life.

There would be Daddy Bear, one or more Baby Bears, and Mummy Bear, with their respective too-big bike, too small bike and just-right bike but Alex never got the chance to steal into their house and try out their bikes for size. It was not a weekend, but a school day, and even if a cyclist came by - probably one of the lycra-clad, hunch-backed speeders - he would be above Alex's head and unable to see her. Weekday cyclists were usually a rare, faint whizzing - less troubling than the summer midges. Rooted in the river banks, the trees had grown hooked and complicated, old branches overhanging the water, looping and knotted in the richness of their growth. An unofficial path tracked the river's edge, through tangles of bramble already clustered with tiny white fruits, bullet-hard.

Alex could sit still for hours, especially when she thought she saw whiskers. She had seen water-rats before, their holes clearly visible along the opposite bank, but this seemed bigger. She was not wrong. A 'v' of ripples, approaching her from the shadows of a clump of trees, gave away broad nostrils, a flat head and the broad rudder of an otter, who rewarded his young observer by turning on his back and scratching lazily at his chest. A flicker of sunlight on the water, a twist of the sleek brown body and he was diving. She had to squint to make out the bubbles where he'd come up, yards further downstream.

'Bloody thing.' A stone accompanied the words hurled off the railway bridge, making Alex and the otter flinch. Her soul dived and swam for freedom, following the bubble trail that slowly cleared and left the water still, and her alone with a voice she recognised.

'Don't suppose there's any bloody fish left here now with that thing in the water.'

The heavy snapping of branches, sliding of boots and muttered swearwords told her he was coming down to the river but there was nowhere for her to go. She shrank back along the path but was trapped against the thicket behind. He would be mad at her for missing school and his 'discipline' hurt. He'd tell her mother too and then she'd have them both onto her.

It wouldn't be the first time her Mam had made her Dad 'sort her out' and then she'd had it twice over and the way her Mam would look at her, saying they were all the same kids today and what could you expect, which allowed her Dad, allowed him to do anything. Not quite anything here by the river bank - she thought at least she'd just get hit, for now. She felt in her mind for The Place, saw the way in, made ready.

'What are you doing here?' She said nothing. 'Well if that doesn't finish my sodding day. Why aren't you in school?'

He didn't like not being answered so she told him, keeping her head down. If she could only keep her head down. 'Didn't feel well.' It was no good saying her Mam knew, she'd only pay double later when the two of them got together. Not that they got together much these days.

'Doesn't look to me like you're home in bed and doesn't look to me like your Mam knows either. Looks to me like you're mitching. How you going to get a job if you don't go to school?'

'I do go to school, usually...' If silence was a mistake, speaking could be worse.

His punch told her she had made a mistake. She gasped and held her tummy. Never across the face where it showed.

'Cut the crap.' He was looking to hurt her, he was reeking of the need to hurt her, and she knew she could not get it right, at best she would survive again, go away in her mind.

She concentrated on The Place, seeing the way in, the tall trees she could close behind her, but his words sneaked in like plague rats. 'Think it's a nice place here, do you? Pretty with the river and everything. Think you'll find your San Fairy Anne here do you? Your Mam told me you still believe in that old story, like a little kid. Well there's no Father Christmas and there's no San Fairy Anne. Your Mam and I laugh at you, falling for that joke she played on you when you were too small to get it.'

He gave big phoney laughs, pretending to take big steps on the stones where Alex had been sitting, then jumping onto the path again. 'And there's no giants neither. San Fairy Anne - you know what that really means, don't you.'

His face was so close to hers she could smell his breath and see every hair of the stubble bursting up through the pores of his chin; she could not get away, she could only listen. 'S.F.A. sweet F.A.- get it? A dirty little girl knows what that stands for. 'San Fairy Anne, my arse, it stands for what you'll get in your life, same as your Dad, same as your slag of a mother, Sweet Fanny Adams, Sweet F-'

No longer caring that she would pay for it later, she pushed past him, summoning the forces of The Place to help her so she would not have to listen to his toilet words.

She had been so close to The Place and then he tricked her, trapped her with her own magic words - but she could get there still. She ran past him, up the side of the railway bridge, ignoring the grunts and shouts behind her, leaving the river bank and leaving that other Alex behind too, escaping into The Place where the trees enfolded her, rustling, soothing, blocking out a man struggling on a river bank.

Dai was weary after a call-out the night before and an afternoon on farm rounds, fending off the inevitable questions on Ministry proposals and movement restrictions. He drove past the small figure, hunched under a hedge beside the road, and would have continued on his way but for his sixth sense. It was the same sixth sense that made him a good vet, that told him whether an animal was physically ill or heart-sore and which let him get close enough to confirm his instincts. There was something wrong and he could not drive on, so he reversed at the first farm gate, turned and went back along the road to where the figure still sat, unmoving.

He approached cautiously, registering that it was a youngster and only too aware of modern attitudes to strangers. 'I'm a vet,' he offered, having found his profession to be one which - rightly or wrongly - inspired trust. 'I wondered if you were all right.'

The youth was soaked to the skin, enabling Dai to observe that it was a girl, and although her eyes were open, they were blank and unfocused. Drugs? he wondered. Mentally ill? Or just traumatized. He sighed. It had been a long day.

'Can I give you a lift home?' There was at last a flicker of emotion in the blue eyes but it looked like panic and Dai added hastily, 'I mean I could call someone at home, on my mobile, and they could come and get you.' He really didn't need accusations of kidnapping young girls... She unclasped the hands which had been wrapped around her knees as she huddled there against the hedge, and she pointed.

'He's there,' - the words were so quiet that Dai had to lean closer to hear her - 'in the river.'

Dai fetched his coat from his car and grabbed his medicine bag, more because he was uncertain about leaving it near the girl than because he thought vaccinations and worming tablets could be of any use. He didn't know what to do with her, or what she would do, but he couldn't just leave her here. He put his coat over her shoulders, covering the sodden T-shirt.

'I'll go to the river. If you want to sit in the car, it's open.' She made no response and Dai questioned his own sanity as he walked from the road up to the new cycle path, along there to the old railway arch and down to the river.

At first, he couldn't see anything unusual among the dappled reflections of the bridge itself and the trees, then he saw the man, lying at an awkward angle, face down in the river, his arm bobbing up and down with the small eddies of the current. There was something about the way the man lay which told Dai he was too late but he tried anyway, pulling the man round to try every resuscitation trick he knew, trying to jump-start the heart after clearing the airways and giving mouth to mouth.

He grew wetter himself in the fruitless attempt and he noticed the trickle of blood from cuts to the head, which were probably caused by the stone of the support pillar. Dai instinctively checked the stone and was pleased to see his theory confirmed by spots of blood on the stone. But if he'd fallen and hit his head on the stone, how had he ended up to the right of the stone, lying with his face in the water? He could have rolled of course. But then wouldn't he have been on his back? He was hardly going to do an acrobatic roly-poly full turn, while half- or fully-unconscious.

Stop playing detective, Dai told himself, suddenly aware that the police might like to know how he had found the body, which had now been dragged along the bank, turned prone and supine alternately, pumped from every angle and mauled by a veterinary surgeon. 'Bugger.' Dai used Helen's favourite word freely. 'Bugger, bugger, bugger.'

When he returned to the car, as wet as the girl herself, she was gone from the hedge like a wayside sprite. He was relieved to find her curled into the passenger seat of his car. 'I found him,' he said gently. 'It'll be all right.'

Why, he asked himself, did people always say that at times when it patently was not and would not be all right. 'Can I phone home?'

She shook her head violently, the panic back in her eyes, and he didn't even ask if he could take her home. 'I have to phone for the...' he was going to say 'police' but changed it 'ambulance but we can do that from my house.' There was no hurry now.

'And you can get dry and wait there till we can find...' who? Mother? Father? Who was the dead man and what was he to her? 'Till we can find someone for you.' She was looking at him warily. This was really not a good idea, taking a traumatized young girl - and he was sure now that it was trauma, not drugs - alone in his car, back to Helen. The reassuring thought struck him.

'My wife is there, she'll help you get dry, get you something to eat, a hot cup o tea...' He searched desperately for images that would convey safety and warmth to a child. 'And you can meet my dogs; there's a sheep-dog called Demi and a Jack Russell called Janie...' Surprisingly, she almost smiled as she interrupted him.

'And a giant grey dog, and a really nosey lady. I know your house.' That seemed to settle it for both of them and he'd worked out that little bit of the puzzle by the time he reached home and Helen.

'What's wrong?'

'I've got your young trespasser in the car. It seems your boy's a girl, and there's a much bigger problem...'

Dai's statement to the police was getting the response he had expected.

'So let me just check I've got this right. You carried the body to several different locations within a ten metre radius of its original position and,' the officer referred to her notebook, 'after pummelling the body and giving mouth to mouth, unsuccessfully, you abandoned the body where you last tried to revive it.' The two police officers shared a look of disbelief.

'I think you could safely say that the scene was disturbed before we arrived,' her partner commented.

'It was worth a try... I might have saved his life,' Dai commented, reasonably.

'If, as you say sir, he had lived, when I am sure your veterinary skills would have been invaluable. As it was, your dance with a wet corpse has not assisted us.'

'For God's sake - the man obviously slipped and fell. I told you about the blood on the stone and on his head.'

'Do we have a vacancy for a forensic pathologist?' She turned to her partner. 'I thought not. Television,' she told Dai sweetly, 'I blame television. Everyone thinks he can play detective. Now if you could just stick to the facts for me. About the young woman... so, you saw a girl, alone and,' again she checked her notes, ''traumatised' so you suggested she hop in your car while you had a quick look for a dead body - or rather a body with potential for resuscitation? Is that about right sir?' Dai held his head in his hands. Before he could speak she was adding, 'And you thought it would be a good idea to get her out of her clothes as soon as possible.'

'Wet clothes,' muttered Dai.

He was ignored as she turned again her partner. 'The clothes of course are now in the airing cupboard, having been handled by Ms Tanner, and the girl has cleaned up completely.' Another exchange of looks.

'She was wet through, cold, traumatized and I wouldn't let a lab rat stay in that condition, however much the police wanted to make notes about it.'

'Kind to animals,' she observed.

'Vet,' her partner commented. They both nodded. 'Don't I know you?'

Dai sighed in resignation. 'No, I don't think so,' he said hopefully.

'Yes, I do. Never forget a face - you came in to spring your Dad. Pub fight wasn't it? I remember now. Couple of farmers in a punch-up,' he told his partner.

She looked straight at Dai. 'Cruelty to animals, I expect.'

All in all, Dai got off lightly. Although they gave the impression that the death needed investigation before being declared an accident, they had certainly not treated Dai as if he were anything more than an idiot and pervert, from a criminal family.

From the moment Helen saw the bedraggled waif emerging, dazed, from Dai's car, her maternal instinct took over. Remembering the way the boy - girl, she corrected herself - had flinched and run from her when she had tried to check for cuts, Helen used words rather than touch to get the youngster into the house, out of wet clothes and, after some privacy in the bathroom, into a T-shirt and jeans of Helen's. The girl acquiesced mechanically.

'We can go into the sitting room and sit in the comfy chairs. One of my friends is here and she said she would just stay to see if we want her to get anything for you. She knows you aren't in a chatty mood. Is that all right?'

Helen took the shrug as indifference and was glad she had taken the time when the girl was in the bathroom to bring Anne quickly up to speed. The adrenalin was wearing off and Helen felt very unsure of what would happen next or what she could do. It would help to have some female company. 'Dai, the man who brought you home, the vet, has called the police to tell them there has been an accident and they're going to come here to talk to him.' She hesitated. 'They'll want to talk to you too.' Again the shrug.

Helen showed the girl into the sitting room, where Anne was flicking through a magazine.

'Alex!'

The girl's response was dutiful. 'Mademoiselle Grüber.' Helen looked questions at Anne.

'Alex is in my class. Or rather should have been in my class today.' Alex was shifting from foot to foot and glancing behind her towards the door, still blocked by Helen, and Anne added quickly, 'That doesn't matter, don't worry about school. I know something bad's happened and I just want to help.' The restless feet stilled.

'Have a seat... go on. I'll make us a cup of tea.' Helen left the room and Anne could hear the low marital murmurs of her and Dai, sharing their concerns. Alex sat on the edge of a chair, poised for flight, and Anne wondered what to say. She tried desperately to remember what had reassured her as a fourteen-year-old but the instant aroma of wood shavings only made her feel more inadequate.

'It'll be all right,' she said stupidly, 'we'll get you home to...' she tailed off, angry with herself for not knowing who this pupil of hers lived with. 'Mum and Dad,' was not the likeliest option. '... parents,' she finished lamely. If anything Alex withdrew further and

Anne went back to flicking through a magazine, in a fruitless attempt to defuse the tension. The fuss of Helen returning with tea things struck a false note in the silent sitting room like a karaoke in a graveyard but Anne was grateful nevertheless. She knew it wouldn't be right to ask Alex what had happened, especially before the police came, and yet how could anyone think or talk about anyone else? It would take more than a cup of tea to see this through.

Excited barking and Dai's orders in Welsh to 'quiet now'

announced the police car. The voices came indoors, then quietened again as the kitchen door was shut. Three dogs piled into the sitting room, the smallest, a Jack Russell, carrying a somewhat smelly red ball, enhanced by teeth marks and saliva.

'Janey,' Helen called and threw the ball across the room for an elegant retrieval by the terrier, with the sheepdog and the wolfhound tripping each other up in a more generalized excitement. The ball was back at Helen's feet, presented with single-minded doggy obsession.

Noting Alex's reactions, Anne picked up the ball when it rolled her way and she joined in the game. After suffering a couple of drooly retrievals, Anne held out the ball to Alex who gave a tiny experimental throw and found the ball returned to her feet. Janey immediately transferred her fixed gaze to Alex and the ball in her hand. The girl continued the repetitive game as tirelessly as the dog until the murmur from the kitchen turned to audible words as the kitchen door opened. Anne surreptitiously wiped her hands on the chair seat which, to judge by the hairy state of the cover, had served in this way before.

'I'm Police Constable Marion Coates and this is my partner Derrick Jones.' PC Coates spoke directly to Alex who carried on throwing the ball. 'We need to ask you a few questions.' Behind the police, Anne could see Dai through the open doorway, miming a cut throat, a gun to his head and other gestures suggesting his opinions of the police interviewing techniques. Contrary to Dai's insinuations, PC Coates spoke gently, sitting down and always treating Alex as the most important person in the room. 'You can take your time but it would help us to know what happened while it's fresh in your mind. Would you do that for us?' Alex shrugged and Coates took this as assent.

Anne was half-standing and caught Helen's eye. 'Should we leave?' she asked the policewoman.

'You are?'

'Her teacher - but I'm here because I'm a friend of Helen's...'

'Ah yes, Ms Tanner, whose partner found this young lady...' Anne warmed to her then, for not saying 'and the body', for considering the feelings of the young girl there in this cosy sitting room - in body - and who knew where in spirit.

Coates looked at her partner for confirmation. 'No, I think it's quite useful for someone to be here for her, especially if you're her teacher and know her.'

'Alex,' contributed Anne, 'Alex Simons.'

'...unless Alex wants me to call someone from home instead?' The word 'home' did get a reaction and Coates clearly read that as a 'no','... or if you don't want anyone else to stay here?' Alex shrugged and Anne sat down again, blushing at her own naïve notions of home being a comfort. 'Now Alex, you can call me Marion, and I'd like you to tell me in your own words what happened this afternoon.'

'I wasn't there.'

'Where was it, this place that you weren't there?'

'By the river. I was there at first and,' Alex's voice, already quiet, dropped, 'I saw the otter. Then I wasn't there.'

'And what do you think happened?'

'I don't know nothing.'

'You told Mr Evans that 'he was in the river'. Do you know who he is, Alex?'

'Yes.'

'Who is he, Alex? We need to know.'

'My father. He's my father.'

Anne heard her own intake of breath like a shout in the silent room but no-one was looking at her. She could see that Helen and Dai were as confused and full of pity as she was but there was nothing in Alex's face to suggest that the word 'father' meant any more than the word 'river'.

Nor was there any reaction from the police, who seemed interested only in whatever facts they could dig out.Through a painfully slow drawing out of monosyllabic responses, Marion still got little more than her address from Alex, who repeated that she wasn't there and that she didn't know nothing. Even when Marion told Alex that she was sorry, it was very bad news and her father was dead, Alex showed no emotion, repeating her mantra, 'I wasn't there. I don't know nothing.'

The questions were going round in circles, getting nowhere, until

PC Jones said, 'Enough Marion. Let's leave it there.'

It was Coates' turn to shrug but she accepted defeat. 'We're going to have to take you home and talk to...' she looked at Anne for help.

'Her mother. She lives with her mother... and father.'

Alex tensed again at the mention of home. 'We've got to talk to Mum but if you want to stay somewhere else for tonight we can talk to Mum...' Alex nodded violently,' but it would help if you told us why.' Silence. ' Lots of kids have rows with their parents...' No response. 'Or problems... you're never the only one with a problem you know, however bad it sounds...' no response. 'O.K. then, we'll take you home and have that talk with Mum.'

'I'm not going in no police car.'

Coates sighed and spoke to Anne. 'Perhaps you could come too - you're the closest connection we've got at the moment, given how she feels about going home.'

'But I don't know anything about... this. I'm just her teacher.' If only she had time to think, to find out what she was supposed to do. There must be some kind of professional guidelines...

'So you'll be there as her teacher... teacher will do fine.'

'We'll both go,' Helen declared. 'I'm not letting her go till I know she's all right.'

'No,' the policeman told her, 'Just the teacher will do. You drive?' he asked Anne.

'Yes.' She turned to the blankfaced girl. 'You can come in my car, Alex. I will come with you.' The shrug suggested that this was at least possible, if not what she wanted.

Dai caught Helen on her way out, following the procession of police, teacher, pupil. 'You're not going with Cruella de Vil and Attila the Hun?' Anne heard him hiss.

'I thought they were really nice, considerate with Alex.'

'Nice? I've put down dangerous dogs with nicer natures.'

'It's you, bringing out the Rottweiler in them.' She kissed him lightly, told him, 'I'm not wanted, I'm only seeing them off.' She turned back to Anne. ' Call me.'

Anne nodded, took a last look at the couple, arm in arm on the path, then she dived into the driver's seat, way out of her depth. In the rear view mirror she watched her friends recede as she followed the police car along the farm track.

Anne glanced at the figure beside her, hunched up, head down, hiding from the world. She still found the Llanelli accent difficult to understand and it took a minute before she understood the mumbled words sent her way.

'You're on the wrong side, you are.'

Anne laughed. 'This is a French car and in France, this is where the driver sits, because we drive on the right hand side of the road instead of the left.'

'Weird,' was the last word from the passenger seat.

It was only five minutes from Brynglas Fach to Alex's home, one of a cluster of older properties halfway down the hill towards the village. Square, grey, with rotting windowsills and damp trails evident down the walls, it detracted from its semi-detached partner, which had double-glazed upvc windows and a pot of geraniums on a table, visible through a lace curtained bay window.

Coates knew her patch well enough to go straight to the back door, knock, open it and shout through, 'Hello. Mrs Simons?'

Anne's first impression was of an eighteen-year-old, long legs in a short straight black skirt, orange skimpy top and bare midriff, eyes boldly lined in black, red lips outlined in vermilion. A closer look gave away an older face, hardened by the make-up and expression of petulant distrust. 'What now? Why me?' the face asked when she saw the police but then her gaze dropped to her daughter.

'You stupid cow, what have you done this time?'

Alex flinched and stepped back under the instinctive hand which Anne left hovering above the girl's shoulder, wanting to reassure, afraid of provoking the mother

The police officers worked their way efficiently into the house, casually standing between Alex and her mother.

'Does that mean she's often been in trouble?' Jones asked smoothly, giving away nothing yet as to why they were there, until he found out what he could.

'Ask the social,' was the bitter response. 'Mitching school, moody beyond at home. Lies about me and her Dad, always wanting attention with her little ways. Look at her, thirteen and can't be trusted. You know what they're like,' she appealed to the police,' I wouldn't be surprised if she was on something. Look at her eyes.' And it was true, Anne thought, the far-off glaze seemed otherworldly, perhaps drug-induced. 'And God knows we've tried. It's not like there's any excuse. I'm not a one parent family - she's always had the two of us and I've stuck with him, for her, even since he's gone to the dogs, no job, nothing...' She saw the dangers of following that tack too far in front of the police and continued, 'No, Jimmy and me have always taught her right and wrong. If we've been a bit strict sometimes, it was for her own good, and we've kept her away from the crap that live round here. If you ask me, you should be knocking on the door at 22, dealing in broad daylight.' She gestured at Anne. 'Who are they anyway? If they're social they're new to me.'

'This is Alex's teacher.'

'So,' Mrs Simons was satisfied, 'on the mitch again my girl. We'll see about that when your Dad gets home.'

'Social?' Jones picked up on the word and exchanged a look with Coates. 'Is there a social worker supports the family?'

'Told you, didn't I. Alex was in some bother and told the usual stories kids do, so yeah, we get a visit now and then. 'At risk' she is, or was, a year ago - bloody society at risk if you ask me, from all these teenagers no-one can control. Social worker says she's been better but I can't see it myself. Just when you think she's a human being she does something, or brings out some of her lies again.'

Anne could feel the blood rising, flushing her neck. Her brain raced trying to recall all she knew about this foreign system of 'at risk' children, which was not much more than the words themselves; what could they be 'at risk' of? She thought it was abuse, neglect, poverty... could it be for young criminals, as Alex's mother was suggesting? Why didn't she know? She felt stupid, she felt lost but above all, she felt angry. Why had no-one told her that this child was at risk? It wasn't as if she hadn't shown her concerns often enough... Darren, Neil... Why didn't she know about Alex's problems, whatever they were.

No doubt the mother had a point - Anne looked again at the

make-up, the clothes and heard the hard voice - but, she decided. But! This time she did put a deliberate hand on Alex's shoulder and was relieved to feel Alex tolerate it lying there, gently. Anne could feel the fragile angles of adolescent bones, like a bird's, against her open palm and she did not know how far she was supposed to go in her care for this, her pupil. How did the theory of 'in loco parentis' work when you were facing the child's real, and very hostile, parent? When the small tremors of Alex's fear ran directly into Anne's bloodstream?

'Why didn't you tell me?' Coates challenged Anne angrily. 'We should have called her social worker to be with Alex.'

'I didn't know.' Bitterly. She swallowed. 'I'm not high up enough to know.'

'Well you should have. Schools!' Jones could clearly have added more on the subject but Coates warned him, 'Not now,' flicking her head in the direction of Alex's mother, avid for ammunition. 'It's not really about Alex, Mrs Simons. We have something difficult to tell you...'

When they told her that her husband was dead, there was shock - Anne was sure of that - there were tears and choked breath but underlying all of that was something Anne could only later describe to Helen as a sense of relief. But then, how can you read someone else's emotions at such an announcement? The outburst took them all by surprise.

'It's you isn't it?' She hurled at her daughter. 'You've gone off your head this time and killed him.'

Jones intervened, 'As I said Mrs Simons, it looks like an accident, a tragic accident but still an accident. We just have to check on all the facts.'

'You don't know... the way they scheme in their little weasel brains... when you look at their eyes and there's no-one there... ' Anne didn't have to look at Alex to see the vacant stare that had been so odd, so different from the other twenty nine expressions around her when Alex had appeared in lessons. 'Them boys down the road, only sixteen weren't they, when they beat that man to death at Christmas? Started off by sticking the boot in and ended up killing him. That's how it happens, isn't it?' No-one could deny a crime which had shocked the valley almost as much as the sentence shocked the boys themselves.

'You know, don't you,' Mrs Simons was waggling an accusing finger at Alex and the hatred in her voice, however temporary it might be, poisoned the air. 'Go on then, tell them - who killed him? Who killed your Dad?'

The sound of her own heartbeat almost prevented Anne hearing the response from Alex's lowered head.

'San Fairy Anne.' The words were in defiance of her mother, triumphant.

Her mother laughed at the same time as Anne started in disbelief. How could this child respond in French, however badly pronounced, to such a question? It made no sense.

Alex turned to Anne. 'I knew you'd understand. Because it's magic words in French you see,' she explained to the police.

Anne gave the words their French pronunciation. 'Ça ne fait rien. Alex, why do you say it doesn't matter?' Alex looked blank.

'Told you. She's off her head. Some old story I told her from my childhood and she thinks there's this saintly Welsh fairy who's some kind of family bodyguard when you're in France. Well you're not in France and there is no bloody San Fairy Anne so you'll have to come up with a better story, girl.'

'I can see the 'San' and that it sounds like a name 'Fairy Anne' but why should you think it works in France,' Anne mused.

'This is not helping, Mrs Simons. I know you're upset right now and we will need to ask you some questions. I think it would be better if Alex stayed somewhere else for a bit to give you both some time to think things through. I need to phone your social worker but perhaps you could tell me if there's someone Alex could stay with... any relatives, like her Granny or someone?'

'No'

'Granny went to Canada two years ago,' Alex said wistfully. 'She and Mam didn't get on.'

'The police aren't interested in that now,' her mother cut her off, while Anne went numb. Oh no, not this one. It's a coincidence, just a coincidence...she told herself. Not this child, and not, please God, this mother. And yet her pulse quickened and she could almost see the sparks connecting her and Alex, for better or worse. One-way current, she reminded herself, the teacher.

'Neighbours?' Jones continued.

'No.'

'Can I have a word, er... Marion... in private?' asked Anne. While they spoke, in private, Jones took details of the social worker and sent Alex to collect belongings from her room. There was another of the silences which characterised the day and which made Anne wish for a small bouncy dog and a chewed red ball.

'Right then,' announced Coates, on their return, 'Can she stay overnight with you?' The briefest of glances checked Anne's bemused willingness, almost taking it as read. 'I think it would be best if Alex stays overnight at her teacher's house, till we get sorted. If that's all right with you, Mrs Simons and of course your social worker will visit Alex straight away and also come here to talk to you about arrangements for the future.' It was obvious to all of them that Mrs Simons had no real choice in the matter but she accepted the face-saving query.

'I suppose so.'

'And is it all right with you, Alex?' Anne spoke softly to the girl in the doorway, holding a tattered schoolbag with a dirty sweatshirt crumpled on the top, beneath a broken zip.

'I'm tired,' was the flat reply they all took for 'yes'.

Teachers don't do this, Anne thought, as she left the house with Alex, wondering quite what she was going to say to Neil's mother if she was less sure it was 'all right' than everyone else had assumed. *But the police had asked, so it must be all right for teachers do this. And if she was more than a teacher to Alex, her great aunt, then she wouldn't have to think any more about what teachers were allowed to feel.* She could hear Mrs Simons responding to police questioning.

'Yes there bloody is someone you should see. Some Pakki thumped him and threatened him a few weeks back. He came home in a right old state, bleeding and upset. If he's been fighting again it won't be him that started it. That Pakki said he'd get him and now he has.'

The conversation with Mrs Phillips proved to be easiest part of the day from the moment Anne introduced the weary girl and gave the official version of events. 'The police have asked if we can offer a place of safety, for the moment'.

Neil's mother was instant warmth, clucking 'Poor dab' and preparing vast quantities of food which Alex picked over and Anne tried to do justice to, before some television soap operas allowed each of them to follow their own thoughts in the comfort of the background noise.

Late, late, that night, Anne looked in on the child, who seemed to be asleep in the big spare bed. Ten steps would take Anne to the bedside and she could smooth the hair back from the girl's forehead, murmur something soothing... Too soon, she told herself reluctantly, far too soon. As Anne closed the bedroom door, the shadow crossed the bed and Alex curled up into a tight ball. Not asleep then, but afraid. Anne withdrew quietly.

Chapter 13

'So we've had a chat about money and done a sort out.' Helen glanced sideways at Gwen. It was a risk to open up about Dai's muddled banking as Gwen might take it as a hidden plea for being let off the rent for the cottage, or a way of saying they couldn't lend Gwen any money - just in case she asked for some. On the other hand, Helen thought it more likely that Gwen would open up herself, if Helen were open with her, and it wouldn't do any harm to let her know that Dai's financial organization was not perfect. 'I know you'll keep this to yourself and it helps to have someone to talk to,' Helen continued, 'and there is something I haven't told Dai, which I feel guilty about and I'm not sure now that I made the right decision in the first place. There was a chance of having a stall at a really important craft market in the Lot - the region where the Voudoirs have their shop, specializing in fabrics, including wool products...'

'But that's great...'

'Only there's a whole lot of laws about it being all-French produce and the authorities - whoever they are - won't accept my name on anything - and I didn't want my designs there without my name with them.'

'I can see they would want it to be French... it's like these local farmers' markets that they've set up once a month, to sell direct... good idea, it is... but we have the old French cheeses and wines and whatall sold here all the time, so they should do the same back. We always get the short-end in Wales however you look at it.' She paused, thought. 'Of course you were right to stand up to them.'

'I don't know.' Helen sighed. 'And then, just when I'd decided that, Dai talked to me about money, and we could do with what we can get to clear a little backlog, so I wrote to say go ahead. This market would have given good sales and a chance of hooking something bigger, maybe even a buyer from one of the city stores - you never know your luck. But by the time I made my mind up, Amélie had argued with some important people to try and get us in, with my name on everything, and now they won't have anything to do with her. I don't quite understand how it all works but craftspeople from all over France apply to show their goods and only a hundred are accepted. Because of me, Amélie has made herself unpopular and we've all lost out. I've stuffed everything.'

Mrs Evans squeezed Helen's arm. 'You only did what was right and that's what's wrong with the world today. If you do things properly, you get ripped off and treated like dirt. And when you really need a bit of money, no-one wants to give you any. How are things selling in the shop?'

'Good.' Helen brightened. 'Really good. They're knitting up the designs for Christmas now and I'm working on some ideas for the spring... I'll show you, after.'

'So you've got a bit of cash coming in then.'

'Yes, not loads but steady now.'

'Have you,' Gwen was hesitant, 'thought of putting some into hearts.'

Helen schooled her face and ducked the question, asking instead, 'Have you heard anything yet?' Gwen shook her head and Helen persevered, carefully. 'I was a bit annoyed that the bank just allowed Dai an overdraft on his account then made a lot of money on it, charging ridiculous interest without any warning and without giving Dai any advice on managing the outgoings - so much for your personal bank manager. But it sounded like you had a better experience...?'

'At least he got some money out of them,' Gwen said bitterly.

'I thought you said...'

'Helen, I've been a fool...' This time, Helen did not say,' Yes,' as she had with Gwen's son, but listened with increasing horror as Gwen told her about the contract with Stan Walker. Gwen was insistent that it would be sorted out when her hearts winnings came in, even if - at the worst - it were another month before this happened and Helen knew that, even if she and Dai could have raised such a vast sum, Gwen would not have accepted it from them. If there were a simple solution, Helen's racing brain could not see it. One thing she was even more certain about was that she would not join in the hearts scheme, not even to pass her money on to Gwen, which is what she told Anne when next they met.

To say things had not been going to plan for Anne would have underestimated the degree of emotional chaos which was the starting point, and how much worse it was now. She thought she knew enough about thirteen year-olds to have an idea of their practical needs and methods of non-communication, but even if she had not been in turmoil over the possible relationship, Alex's withdrawal from the world was beyond Anne's experience. The visit from the social worker, which Anne had thought would provide all the answers, instead left her feeling more alone than ever in her life before, carrying a burden of unbearable knowledge.

Sally Gordon was personable, friendly and harassed, recalling the details of Alex's case from amongst the many she had to deal with. She was accompanied by a police officer specially designated for child protection issues and they took a statement from Alex which consisted of 'Wasn't there, don't know nothing,' until Sally asked, 'You told the police that San Fairy Anne had killed your Dad. Why do you think San Fairy Anne killed him.'

'To save me.'

'What from, Alex?' and then, suddenly, the three women knew what the answer was going to be, and Anne didn't want to hear and she wanted so much to vomit that her stomach had hurt but she could not leave the child.

Alex started flailing her arms with the effort of speaking at all and then she was shouting, screaming in words blunt as bullets the thing that had been done to her, confessing her 'yes'. Anne suddenly understood Alex's repeated claim that she wasn't there; Anne herself was suddenly not there, suspending the words outside her own skin, saving herself. The two professionals, presumably immune to one more story of abuse, nodded silently during the outburst.

'What did San Fairy Anne do, Alex?'

'Dunno. I wasn't there.' Alex retreated, returned to her other world.

'Did you talk to your mother about your... problems?' Anne was indignant. They hadn't been Alex's 'problems'. There was nothing wrong with Alex - and everything wrong with the world around her, including a lack of care from her social worker and - how it hurt - the disinterest or impotence of her teachers. What exactly had Darren done with all those referrals she had passed on?

'Yeah... I tried. She slapped me for making stuff up, said I was a bit of a tart, reaching that age and she wasn't having any of that... told me to stop looking for attention, stop lying...' she trailed off and Anne tried not to imagine the conversation between mother and daughter, not being believed. Anne watched the representatives of authority closely; did they believe her? Did they see thirteen-year-olds making up such stories? Did they know the difference? Did you lose your sense of right and wrong if you lived in these sewers? There was no sign in their faces as they nodded and the policewoman made notes.

Suddenly Anne realized that Sally was speaking to her. 'We're very short of foster homes but will place Alex in Holgate House as soon as one of the girls there moves out - she's sixteen now and we've got her a flat. I don't think it's a good idea for Alex to move back with Mum until we've put in some family support sessions. Of course with Dad dead the situation has changed...'

Anne looked at this alien, lost for words. 'I'm Alex's aunt.' Great-aunt, and as yet only probably, but it was close enough to serve - Anne had already realized that a busy social worker was unlikely to check too closely or in the near future on her home's suitability, unless Mrs Simons objected. 'I would like her to stay with me.' The relief was palpable - a problem solved, for the moment, and living from one temporary solution to another seemed to Anne to be the best these two managed. What a job! Alex accepted the decision, showing no interest in her fate. After that one, vile outpouring, she showed no sign of caring what was said or done.

On the way out, the policewoman spoke to Anne. 'I'll contact you to arrange a video statement from her.'

Sally chipped in, 'If he was alive, we'd be pursuing a case of sexual assault, but with her word against the mother's it's likely that we'd fail - we'd have to get the child out by parental consent...'

'That's outrageous. You know she's telling the truth - you heard her.'

'Yes, she's telling the truth. I know it sounds hard but it's a pity she didn't disclose for the first time on camera - it was so clearly the truth. Next time it won't sound so emotional and then there would be room for doubt.' The policewoman concluded, 'Anyway, it's a death we're investigating, regardless of whether he was a nice man, and I don't think Alex is any use as a witness - at least the Coroner will understand why, if we need to use the statement at all, which we probably won't - to be honest, it does look like an accident - so unless we're going to consider Alex as a suspect' - they both laughed - 'then the only question is for Sally - what to do with Alex herself.'

'I will look after my niece,' Anne said coldly, her tongue curling round the new word, her new family.

'Don't get me wrong...' Sally informed her, 'I'm grateful for what you're doing but of course we need to check on what's best for Alex - and her mother has rights too... so we'll be in touch.'

Anne smiled, closed Neil's front door and smashed her hand against it so hard the bruise spread across her knuckle, not even starting to express the ache in her heart.

'Can I see her?' Elsë asked.

'I'm going to bring her home with me,' Anne promised, her stomach twisted at the way her mother's voice quavered, suddenly old. However, promising was one thing. She told herself a hundred times how much harder it was for Alex but Anne was raw from the invasion of her privacy necessary if she was to claim the girl as her niece. Suddenly she had to give her family details to the police, the social workers, to Neil's mother, to Helen...

'Are you sure?' Helen had asked.

Anne took the question on its easiest level and described her search. 'Alex and I looked at all the little bits of information that I have and then we went back to the births and marriages. Alex could tell me that her mother was called Charmaine...'

'So that fits with your Estate Agent's 'Sh... word, doesn't it?'

Anne acknowledged this.

'Just think... it could have been, Charlotte who was your niece and her baby your great-niece instead of...' Helen stopped, flustered and Anne read her face, *instead of...that woman... this strange girl...* Didn't she feel the same, when it first struck her as a possibility, on that police visit? When had this tearing need to protect the girl, to give her a place to heal, when had all this started and made Alex *her* Alex?

'And your niece, have you talked to her?' Helen persevered.

'We did meet, yes, at what the social services call 'a neutral venue' - we being Alex, me, her mother and Sally the social worker. I did explain to Charmaine that the registry records seemed to confirm that her mother, Marie, was my half-sister, and that my mother wanted me to find the other half of my family, and I was so pleased to have tracked them down, even at such a sad time.'

'How do you really feel about it all?'

There was a long silence. That was the hard question. 'It means a lot to my mother.'

'And you?'

'I have thought many times about not having a child of my own. But, as they say, the right man never came along.' And facing one of the wrong men, with Madame Anton, was something waiting for Anne in Alsace. Her year out was over and she was prepared to live with the changes it had brought, all of the changes. 'Now it seems that circumstances have given me a child and I feel responsible for her.' Anne knew the words were wrong but she had never been able to talk of such things. Why did she always sound so cold? For her the language of feelings would always be wood shavings or kugelhopf, home where her silences were understood. She knew no words for the storm that had broken inside her, the pain by proxy and a world suddenly full of dangers that she must fight on Alex's behalf. The lightest physical contact seared her with a longing to hug and 'kiss better', as her own mother had always done, but it would be a long time before she dared test the trust seeding slowly. 'This is not the child I imagined,' she ended lamely.

'It never is, love. Better and worse, but never what you expected,' Helen surprised her by saying. 'And you'll need all the luck in the world with this one. From what you say, home wasn't kind to her and she was like a whipped pup when I first met her.' Anne made no comment, having had to make just enough disparaging remarks about Charmaine and her husband to explain the need to rescue Alex.

'But that's the one you go for isn't it?' Helen laughed, then explained. ' When you choose a pup, it's the one in the corner, with its ears drooping, scared to come out but begging to be loved - that's the one you want to mother, isn't it. Well, pob luc.'

'Diolch, thanks.' Anne smiled weakly.

When Helen called on Anne, their conversation took place with Alex sitting in the room, silently pencilling circles in a book of wordsearches. Helen's eyes flicked to the girl, questioning and Anne's answer was meant for both of them. 'Alex is staying with me.' There was no flicker of response from Alex but Helen tried to make contact.

'Shouldn't you be at school?' she asked in a jolly tone.

'Me or Alex?' Anne responded lightly. If anything, Alex's head bent lower over its book. 'Now that I have bad company, I'm discovering the pleasures of mitching off, as they say round here.' No-one laughed. 'Seriously, the Head has been very understanding - I have taken some time off here and there - Neil's mother has an engagement today but mostly she has been at home with Alex, really kind, isn't she Alex?... And as for Alex, I have to say that I do not think there will be complaints at her missing a little more school - and in three weeks it is the end of term and the end of my year here. She needs time...' Anne wondered if eternity would be enough to heal the hurts Helen did not know about. Now Anne had learnt the term 'need to know' she was applying it herself; there was a lot no-one else needed to know, except possibly Mr Head of Year Neil Phillips, who had left her, Anne, out of what she had most definitely needed to know.

Anne continued, very matter of fact. 'Alex's mother was not interested in contacting Alex's grandmother - who is in Canada as we thought - nor was she interested in a new family. However, she accepted the proposal that Alex remain in my care, for now...'

'What will happen to Alex next?'

Anne wondered how it must feel to hear your fate discussed as if it were an episode of a TV soap, and was careful to include Alex. 'If Alex wants to,' she consulted the unresponsive head as if she were receiving and considering Alex's opinions, 'Maman - that is, Alex's great-grandma - and I would like her to live with us in Alsace, to make a fresh start.'

'But?'

There were so many 'buts' to consider 'but' Anne would not give in. 'That depends on what Alex's mother will allow, and also on the social services, which in its turn depends on what Alex says she wants...'

'And the police?'

'I think the police are happy now that they have their video interview - although perhaps happy is not the best word to describe your police...'

'I think it might depend on whether you want something from them - in which case you think they're wonderful - or whether they want something from you - in which case they're the enemy...'

'What if Alex's mother wants her back there?' Helen glanced again at the subject of debate.

'The social services are very keen on that,' Anne acknowledged with a grimace which expressed her disagreement. 'They have told me - and Alex - that her mother has rights and that it is important for families to stay together, and that they would support the two of them in making a family without Alex's father.' The pencil was totally still. 'Support! They have really given support for the last two years haven't they! But if Alex wants to come with me *I* will have to prove that *my* home is suitable and safe for her - it is too much! But we will get our way,' The pencil started moving again, 'if it is what Alex wants too. Is it, Alex?'

There was some frenetic activity from the pencil and then a quiet

'Dunno,' was heard and then, even softer, 'I'm not going back after what she said. I'm not a liar.'

'So, as long as I keep my temper in these endless meetings, it will be decided for me by the other things. I think Alex's mother has... many changes to her life, has to come to terms herself with her husband's death, cannot cope with Alex now... I think she trusts me enough to let Alex stay with me. I am going to talk to Neil about the social services. He is a Head of Year, he knows more about them and how they work.' *When I have given him a piece of my mind about everything he should have told me and didn't, then he can help...* 'Anyway how about you?'

'In a word, money. We were right about this hearts business,' Helen stated and shared her worries with Anne, uninhibited by the child in the corner as she described the financial hole Gwen had dug for herself. Unfortunately, Anne could see no solution either, other than reiterating the hope that another tier would subscribe to hearts, shifting the heartache to yet another - and even larger - tier of women, more victims.

On the doorstep, as they parted, Helen said, 'Alex's mother - coming to terms with changes? From what you said, a new man more like? Doesn't want Alex around to spoil things?'

'Probably. Replacement might have been lined up before husband's death, according to Sally. Did Dai say anything about what he thought happened, you know, when the man died?'

'He has talked about it. I think the police hurt his ego by ignoring all his deductions. He thinks the man fell and hit his head and then drowned because of falling with his face in the water, but then Dai's confused. He says the man was lying in the wrong place as if - but this is where he says he's only guessing and doesn't like to make too much of it - as if he'd rolled over twice. Only there's no slope and you wouldn't expect an unconscious - or semi-conscious - body to roll more than a half-turn. As if someone had pushed him... Oh, and he'd definitely been fighting - not just the cuts and whatever from the fall but bruises starting to colour up. But then, as the police told him, he's no pathologist.'

'Thank you. I just wondered... wanted to know what exactly Alex might have seen...'

Guptar Singh was complimenting his wife on her cooking, basking in the after-dinner glow induced by a thali with fresh chapatis, and by two outstanding school reports from his eldest children, when the police called to invite one of those very children to 'accompany them to the station to assist them with their enquiries.'

Grandfather Vijay helpfully commented in Punjabi that this was what you could expect from the best private school education Llanelli could offer; Guptar tucked stray hairs into his turban saying 'There must be some mistake'; Taj turned white and asked, 'What is this about?' and Asha cuffed her youngest son who could be heard saying 'Cool!'

'He is only seventeen!' Guptar protested.

'That's as maybe, Sir, but that doesn't mean he can't help us with our enquiries.'

'Enquiries? What does this mean, enquiries?' Guptar was as incensed as he was frightened at this invasion of the home in which the highest law was his word.

'I have the right to know what this is about,' Taj persisted, hoping desperately that it would have nothing to do with a certain political statement graffitoed on a twelve-foot wall during alcoholic experimentation, which he doubted would be acceptable to his father.

'You were involved in a fracas with a customer...' the policeman checked notes and gave a time and a date, 'and you were overheard threatening this gentleman. I believe it was Mr Singh senior who stopped you from carrying out your threats...'

'No, no, no, he did not hit this customer, he was merely ushering him from the shop because he was drunk and a little unpleasant, 'Guptar lied unconvincingly, showing his sincerity by smiling ceaselessly. 'Ushering, he was ushering, you understand...' Having found the word, he was reluctant to let it go.

'Dad! Shut up!' Taj was moved and embarrassed by his father's keenness to commit perjury on his behalf - whether or not it was necessary, or indeed horribly counter-productive. Ignoring his father's - and grandfather's outrage - he asked, 'What about this man?'

'He's dead.'

The chaos resolved itself into father and son being 'ushered' into the back of a police car, Guptar humiliated by a hand placed on his turban to encourage him to sit down, 'as if I can't get into a car without being pushed into it,' as he observed in Punjabi to his son, who replied 'What do you expect... the oldest game there is, pick on a 'Paki'...'. His father growled, 'I will not have this racist talk, you have no idea how lucky you are to live in such a place where you can express such views without being in prison for them.' 'It would be better if you spoke English,' drawled a voice from the front, 'then we won't think you were cooking a story all the way to the nick...'

'What were you just saying, father?' asked Taj sweetly in perfect public school English, 'about freedom?'

They sat in silence the rest of the way.

The interview consisted of terse questions from the police regarding the 'alleged assault' on Jimmy Wilkinson, and Taj's activities on the day of Jimmy's death. Father and son were interviewed separately so Taj was spared his father's mixture of truth and embroidery, with its inevitable contradictions. His own account of Jimmy's behaviour in the shop was received with scepticism, it seemed to him, as was his description of his own whereabouts on the day of Jimmy's death.

'So you were free, that is without a lesson, during that afternoon, and as part of your research for a speech you were in Llanelli Shopping Centre...'

'Yes.'

The policeman read back the notes, 'looking for homeless people and

Big Issue sellers?'

'Yes.'

'To interview them as research for a speech you are writing?'

'Yes.'

'And this can be corroborated by a lady with grey hair... sorry, a Caucasian lady with grey hair, who 'hangs out' with her dog in a doorway behind the bus station, and a Big Issue seller called Bob, also Caucasian and tall, with a big nose and black hair, whose patch is the precinct. Right so far?'

'Yes.'

'Bob. Any other name to go on?'

'No, just Bob. Homeless people lose their other names... there are so many reasons they drop out of a society that has failed them... and if they have no addresses so much is closed to them that they can't get jobs to get addresses... ' Taj was passionate in trying to communicate all that he had found out about the underworld of the street sleepers.

'All right, hold your horses, save your speech for whenever...Now about this Caucasian business. Are you trying to say something?'

'It is a factual description. Caucasian being a sub-group of Asian, meaning 'white' in popular English.'

'I know what Caucasian means, thank you.'

'The people I talked to that day are white. I think all homeless people are white but I have not yet carried out research in an area which is ethnically diverse enough to substantiate this theory.'

'Good God! Put the dictionary away again and let's just put the facts to you - as we Caucasians see them. You're not being charged at the present time - although you could have been over that rumpus in your shop - and we might need to talk to you again about the circumstances of Jimmy Wikinson's death, should these be established as suspicious in any way. Your alibis don't exactly look... how shall we say?... strong, especially as we have your Dad's word you were with him, whatever day we like to check up on.'

By choice, Taj and his father made their own way home from the police

station, and the argument was in full spate by the time they entered the front hallway where Ashta was hovering anxiously.

'Did it ever cross your tiny mind that I don't need defending because I've done nothing wrong!'

'It is better that we stick to our story, it is foolproof and you can get on with your schoolwork.'

'Foolproof? Dad, your story couldn't fool Mani at bedtime!'

Asha tried to intervene, 'Taj, don't talk to your father like that, there is wisdom in being older.'

'I wish!'

'You want to be a hotshot lawyer,' Guptar's voice was high with the anger he could afford to express, once more in the known territory of his home, 'you are still a boy, a boy who will be going to jail if I don't look out for you. It was you who jumped on that man, beating him and hinting all manner of bad things to him. Some law career - behind the bars on the wrong side!'

There was enough justification for this view of events to make Taj even angrier; nothing fuels a man's anger more than being, even slightly, in the wrong. 'This boy will not watch some - ' he used the most vulgar Punjabi term he could think of to describe Jimmy Wilkinson ' - insult my mother as he did. No man would!' he challenged.

Ashta drew her sari over her face, hiding from both the vulgar expression and the insult to Guptar.

'Go to your room, go now' Guptar roared.

'A punishment for a child!'

'And who is going to pay for you to go to law school? You *are* a child. Now go, get out of my sight, while I apologise to your mother for what she has suffered this evening.'

Taj went, restraining himself from slamming the bedroom door as he muttered from behind its safety, 'I am not a child!' He calmed himself by working on his speech for the Rotary Club Public Speaking Competition. It was such an honour to be chosen for the school's team, especially as the school had a reputation for winning not only the local heat but the regional one too, and - as he informed two imaginary policemen - usually with Asian team-members. He looked at the typed sheet:- 'Speaking for the Motion, that there is a rigid class system in Britain which creates and maintains homelessness, Tajinder Singh.' He lost himself in a diatribe against the vicious catch-22s of the social system as he saw it.

Neil had his first argument with Luc. At least he tried to argue with Luc, who was monumentally insensitive to any possibility of a problem...

'You outed me,' Neil accused him, pacing around Luc's Strasbourg flat, 'without asking what I thought or what I felt.'

'I kissed you. So what? What do you think's going to happen?'

'That's the whole point - I don't want to worry about what's going to happen, I don't want to wonder what people think, I do not want to be a public test case. Are you listening?'

Neil was incensed, watching Luc fuss around the kitchen, humming, as if changing his, Neil's, entire life was a mere matter of adding a little soupçon of whatever spice he'd pulled off his cupboard shelf.

'Not really. I think you need to storm a little, I need to hum a little and then,' Luc flashed the full force of his smile, 'perhaps we can make up?' The hopeful spark in those dark eyes drew a physical response from Neil that he could have done without during his righteous indignation and he had to turn his back and pace a bit to build up some more resentment.

'She hasn't said anything - which makes it worse - but I can see it in her eyes, it's different. It's like... oh I don't know... it's like your grandmother being disappointed in you.'

'Is your grandmother disappointed in you?' Luc asked with interest.

'I haven't got a grandmother. She died when I was a little boy.'

'That's a pity. My grandmother is splendidly disappointed in me. There would be so much less for her to tell her friends if she weren't. And as for the opportunities to explain to my parents what they did wrong in my upbringing - there is no end to the entertainment I provide.'

Neil realized he knew nothing of Luc's family and would have pursued the subject but now was no time to be distracted. 'It was wrong of you, Luc. People are not as open-minded as you pretend and you shouldn't make my decisions for me. I'm a teacher and it's more complicated for me.'

'Why, because you lust after the little boys you teach instead of after the little girls? This makes no sense.'

'They're not little, and I don't lust after any of the horrors, whatever their gender - nor do most of my colleagues, whatever their sexual orientation. Partly it's a trust thing, partly it's just not how it is - I don't fancy kids.'

Neil couldn't see the devilish twist to Luc's mouth. 'And school so inconvenient when you have wonderful English toilets for meeting men. I read it in the papers all the time and I think it's time we changed our French facilities - our urinals, half-doors, open to view, so difficult and impractical for romantic matters...'

'Wales, I live in Wales,' Neil corrected automatically, 'and if you think I hang around public toilets...' His indignation burst like a balloon on the pinprick of Luc's laughter.

'Isn't that what all gay men do?' Luc continued to tease. 'So serious, my friend Neil.'

'So irresponsible, my friend Luc.' When he'd stopped trying and changed the subject, Neil finally hit a nerve. 'Term finishes in three weeks. That's all I have left.'

'So soon. I thought we had longer.'

Neil couldn't hold back any longer and put an arm out to his lover. 'Let's make the most of it,' - he couldn't resist a final word - 'privately.'

Chapter 14

After suffering Michel's jocular comments about the superior attractions of monkeys, Neil was doubly conscientious in his work at the stork sanctuary. He missed a couple of weekends and in that time the young storks shot up, mewing like cats as they demanded their parents' regurgitated meals. Some of the adults he had observed during the year were now three years old and had been released, to find homes and, in the next year or two, mates. Whether they mated with companions from the Centre or returning wild migrants, the offspring would still have the urge to migrate, so the Centre kept a breeding population, to ensure the stork's future.

The French school term finished at the end of June and Neil was staying on for a last three weeks' holiday, until term finished in Wales. He sat on a bench in the July sunshine, oblivious to the passing families, whose children were as enthusiastic about the ducks on ornamental ponds as about the storks, perched on artificial nests in their netting havens.

The visitors' chatter mingled with the clapperboard sounds made by the mute adults clacking their beaks but Neil only looked up when a clumsy attempt at flight distracted him from his study of this summer's records. It hurt to watch the thwarted instinct and Neil often had to remember his mother's injunction that you had to be cruel to be kind. He returned to the reassurance of the statistics in front of him.

There were now more than two hundred and fifty breeding pairs in Alsace and he was reading the information gathered on this year's success stories. In September, these villages along the wine route had been mere names on a map but now he could visualize each of them as he read the magical names.

Three pairs in Ribeauvillé, which he first saw after walking through the forest, past the three medieval chateaux down the steep slope into the medieval heart, where the grey roof-scales of a conical tower pointed to the unmistakable straw-filled wheel and the bird sitting so still it seemed artificial, silhouetted against the autumnal blue sky.

No, Neil would not forget his first sighting of a stork in the wild. Small wonder that the stork was considered the lucky mascot of each village it claimed as home, bringer of new birth even to a village like Ostheim, razed to the ground in the battles over Colmar, and itself reborn. One pair, three offspring, at the top of a wall in Ostheim. One mixed pair, a stork from the Centre and a wild migrant, with one youngster, recorded nesting in a disused chimney in Eichhoffen.

Two pairs in Riquewihr, the medieval jewel in Alsace's crown, its cobbled main street and half-timbered houses in the characteristic blues, pinks and purples of the region, shops crammed with green-stemmed glassware and 'flute' shaped bottles, the scents of warm nougat and waffles, wrought iron inn and guild signs swinging from low gables. It was in Riquewihr that Neil discovered Uncle Hansi, the Alscacien illustrator whose folksy characters, the women in their headgear of huge black bows and the men in waistcoats and breeches, danced in endless mockery of the German soldiers who merely passed through their world. Riquewihr and all of the villages he had come to know would still be here when Neil left, in three weeks. He too was just passing through.

Another two pairs in Sélestat. A village name jumped out at Neil and he read the handwritten note again, incredulous. How could he not have noticed? Only a single stork but definitely on top of the church, there for the first time, and where there was one, another would come, perhaps next year. He must tell Madame Grüber.

'So there is a stork in Bergheim again, after all these years.'

'Only one,' Neil warned. 'Female, from the Centre and released this spring. She seems to have chosen a home now and she'll probably stay there through the winter. They don't find the cold a problem...'

'Not like me then... old bones,' Madame Grüber smiled. 'I used to laugh in the snow when I was young - and such snow we get up here. I remember tying boards to my shoes to walk in the snow to get bread.' Neil knew what it was like. He remembered his Alsace winter, snow dripping from fir trees, the Strasbourg market with every kind of tree decoration, bonbon and marzipaned cake - Christmas how you imagined it should be, when you were watching the

Llanelli rain on the park railings. Eighteen days left in Alsace.

'It's the lack of food in the winter - the insects, mice and what-have-you, hibernate - but people leave bits and pieces now - the storks get by, without migrating...'

'I'm like a Centre stork, aren't I. Alsace born and bred, and I have never left here...'

'Like the Bergheim stork you mean? But, if all goes well, she will greet a mate in the spring, who might be Centre born or who might be a wild one, full of tales of African adventures...and their offspring will fly free, risking the winter journeys and seeing the desert.'

'So I must feed on the stories of my migrant offspring?'

Neil smiled,' You've been so kind to this migrant...'

'I worry about you...'

'Now you do sound like my Granny.'

'We have not said anything... about Luc.'

'No.'

'It... Luc... this thing... does not seem good to me...'

His heart sank. What could he say? He knew - who better? - the forces of upbringing, religion, convention...

'But it does not seem bad to me either.'

'Is this you watching the river flow?'

'Perhaps. And perhaps this river is too quick for me, too different from what I know... as if the river is... shocking pink.'

'Against nature, you mean.'

'Perhaps. And perhaps it is the nature of this river to be shocking pink and for me to only watch, not understand.'

The phone rang. 'Anne,' was Madame Grüber's instinctive response.

'Perhaps the stork is bringing you good news.'

'Oh I hope so.' The words seemed rung from her heart and Neil wondered again about Anne and storks and babies. Neil left Madame Grüber in privacy, retreating to the bedroom he thought of as his... eighteen days. When he was called to the phone, he was shocked at the change in Anne's mother; for the first time she truly looked her age, the blue eyes rheumy with tears and her voice trembling. It could not have been the good news that she hoped for but he was unprepared for the blast of anger which hit him when Anne spoke.

'You could have told me! You said it was enough to tell Darren about Alex. He has been about as much use as the social services. You said Alex had a 'rough home background'. Was this the English gift for understatement? You must tell me now, Neil, everything you know about Alex, and nothing left out - you hear me?'

'O.K. O.K. but tell me first what's happened.' As Neil listened to the whole wonderful story of the search and sickening story of the finding, he blamed himself. If he hadn't been in Alsace, maybe he would have seen the child's need for help; it would not have been the first time a pupil disclosed abuse to him - and it would not have been the first time he felt helpless and frustrated by the social services.

If only he had told Anne everything he knew, she might have said a key word, been the one, the teacher Alex talked to. And then what? Would it have ended any differently? Alex might have been extricated from the mess earlier, not been there when her father died, but Anne wouldn't have known earlier that Alex was not just one more needy pupil and Alex would have been just another kid in foster care, breaking her heart over the punishment of losing her family.

If there had not been the family connection, which no one could have known, Neil still thought that he would have been wrong to pass on confidential information about a pupil. Inevitably, that was not the way Anne saw it. Nor had he, before he became a Head of Year.

'No. You are wrong! Even if I were not her aunt, as her teacher I should know that she has a social worker - can you imagine what a fool I felt in front of the police? I should know what her problems are - how else could I know what to see and listen to in class, how to help. What is the importance of her homework beside all... all...that! So, now you tell me everything you know.'

Neil sighed. 'The school referred Alex to the social services because we suspected physical abuse. There was suspicious bruising - the PE teacher spotted it in Year 7- and the social worker's visits picked up on money problems - father unemployed, drinking too much, nothing out of the ordinary - and a query over the money that was coming in.' Neil was only too conscious that he was talking to Charmaine's aunt, but Anne needed to know if she was going to help Alex. 'There were suggestions that Alex's mother might be supplementing the family's lack of income with occasional prostitution. It's not unknown,' he ended lamely.

'And the sexual abuse?' she challenged. 'Neil, I was there, I heard her.'

'No, we didn't know. There was never any disclosure in school. If she told the social worker, I didn't know about it... but then I wouldn't have. It would have been Darren from September... and, I hate to say but it's the truth... we can't always make a meeting and then we don't always get to know everything the other services know - health, social services, police...'

'It's a shambles.'

'There are so many of them, Anne...we do what we can.'

'Well you can do more than that now, for me and Alex, to make up for all the things you didn't say and that I should have known. How do I play this so she stays with me and comes to home to Maman? You know the way they work.'

Neil thought. His first instinct was to suggest that Anne applied for adoption, followed the procedures... he thought again. 'They're busy. Use all the things that drive you mad - they're slow, they're reeling from crisis to crisis with a high turnover of staff doing a horrific job. If something is not high profile, no parents complaining, no media hounding, no high risk of injury or death to someone on their list, then the status quo has its own laws... possession is nine-tenths of the law... if I were you, I'd play it really low key. If Alex's mother is fine with it, just bring her here and write a casual note to police and social services saying Alex is here on holiday. Let the holiday stretch... then fill in whatever forms you need...'

'Of course, a fait accompli... you are right and this is what we will do.'

'Be careful about her mother - if she kicks up a rumpus, the whole picture changes.'

'She won't.' Neil believed her, not surprised at all that Anne had coped all year with his most difficult classes. 'And - when you talk to Maman - I have only told her that Alex was hit by a bad father, who died in an accident, and that her mother does not get on with Alex so I am trying to bring her here. I don't think she needs to know the... detail.'

Neil saw again the drawn expression on Madame Grüber's face when she came off the phone. 'No,' he agreed. 'That is more than enough.'

Madame Grüber was standing at the window, looking down the valley and across the plain to Germany, but Neil suspected that what she saw was all in the past.

'She told you?'

'Yes.'

'When we went to the place in the woods, I told you about Vernon... I didn't tell you there was a baby, my Marie. I have never stopped wondering how she was, what she was doing now and when I talked to Anne, I hoped... When I was a girl there were always storks in the valley but the villagers up here said that storks would not bring babies up to Thannenkirch because it was too high. If you wanted a baby, you had to give a present to the witch who lived on the Taenchel, by the Rock of the Titans.

Of course no-one would ever own up to visiting the Rock, but I used to see the ribbons tied to the trees nearby and I used to see the little superstitious signs a woman made when a baby arrived...I don't know whether it's the witch or your solitary stork in

Bergheim, but this is a strange kind of miracle...'

'Anne didn't say anything about Marie, only about her daughter and grand-daughter; Alex the grand-daughter - your great-grand-daughter - was a pupil of mine.'

'Yes, it seems that I will have to think about Alex, very soon... but Anne doesn't know where Marie is. No, that's not quite true, Anne knows that Marie is in Canada but she doesn't know where. It's so strange to think of her as a grown-up, never mind as a farmer and a grandmother. I have let too much time go by...'

'Maybe you and Anne will be able to trace her - her daughter must have an address?'

'Maybe. Anne says they were not on good terms. I don't really understand why my...niece... is not coming here with her daughter... why these bad family relationships... and the husband dead in an accident...I wonder whether it is my fault, because of what I did or didn't do, so many years ago...'

Neil had never heard Madame Grüber sounding so confused and frail but he remembered his promise to Anne, and would not risk her being further hurt by understanding only too well. He took refuge in the line he'd used with countless adolescents, 'You make the best decision you can in a difficult situation - no-one can blame you for that.'

'And you Neil? Are you making the best decision that you can?'

He cleared his throat. 'I won't need an evening meal on Thursday - I'm going to a concert in Strasbourg, in the parc de Pourtalès.'

'With Luc?'

'With Luc.'

Anne took Neil's advice and paid a visit to Charmaine, who seemed to be the key to Alex's care although incapable of it herself. The social worker's attempt to get Anne to empathise with Charmaine, especially after what Neil had suggested about the family income, was as likely to succeed as asking a CND Protestor to celebrate the success of cruise missiles.

Every time Sally started, 'We need to consider so-and-so's point of view...' Anne responded, 'Why?', growing increasingly irritated with a system which seemed to her to consider everybody's 'interest' and protect nobody, least of all Alex. Whatever she thought of the situation, she knew that Neil was right and that if Charmaine accepted Anne's guardianship of Alex, it was probable that she could make it legal over time. That meant being nice to Charmaine...

Anne knocked firmly on the back door and was relieved to hear a voice yelling, 'Hang on a minute.' This was not a visit she would want to build up to, a second time. Charmaine appeared at the door, a little dishevelled but, Anne was relieved to note, less provocatively dressed. Her jeans and T-shirt still made Anne feel conscious of her own dress, cardigan and flat sandals as belonging to another world. She didn't mind belonging to a world different in culture from Charmaine's but it was the first time she had faced a difference of generation within her own family, with herself in the older generation.

'Oh it's you.' The mascara was smudged around Charmaine's eyes as if she had been crying.

'Who is it? Someone bothering you?' asked a masculine voice. A man of about Charmaine's age, also wearing jeans and tucking in a T-shirt , joined Charmaine and stood aggressively behind her, blocking entry.

''S'allright,' she told him. 'It's the auntie from France. You might as well come in.' The cigarette smoke still wafting from the stubs in the ashtray did not bother Anne, although after her year in Wales she noticed it in a way she would not have done previously. In her own collège, in the cafès and Winstübe, it was natural for people to smoke.

'Huw,' Charmaine indicated, jerking a thumb at her companion, who settled for an awkward pose standing in the middle of the room, half-threatening, half poised for flight. 'For Christ's sake, sit down, Huw - or go, if you're going.' He immediately sat.

'Alex is fine,' Anne started, as if someone had asked or cared, and when they both knew Alex was anything but fine.

'Good.'

'I know how hard things must be for you at the moment...'

'She's doing all right and she don't need nothing from you,' Huw contributed.

'S'allright Huw, she's not from the social...'

'Same difference, her sort...'

Anne persevered with an empathy which deserved an award from Sally. 'And thirteen is such a difficult age to put up with...' Surely, she thought, Charmaine would see the trowel she was laying it on with? But no, it seemed that someone so self-centred could be relied on to be...self-centred.

'It's been hard,' Charmaine agreed, lighting up. 'What with the police and the

social sniffing round, and the giros stopping - not that I ever saw much of that. He'd spent most of it before he even got home, the selfish git.' There was a pause to reflect on her dead husband. 'Anyway, accidents happen. That's what they've said, you know? 'Most likely a tragic accident'.'

'Yes, I know.' Anne had her own reasons for hoping the police - and the coroner - would stick with that verdict.

'But Huw's been a big help. We're going to get married.' She glared at Anne, defying her to comment.

'In a bit,' Huw added hastily.

'That's very nice,' seemed the safest response. 'And I suppose you'll want Alex to come and live with the two of you...' Anne looked straight at Huw, 'I think you're so brave taking Alex on, being a father to her... you must really think a lot of Charmaine to take on a thirteen-year-old... and especially that sort of thirteen-year-old... but I'm sure Charmaine has told you all about Alex... and she's coming on so well staying with me... I'm sure it will only be the first few months that will be a problem, a bit of settling in, that's all...' she left a pause, mentally crossing her fingers and hoping that she wasn't overplaying her hand. She counted to twenty then threw them the lifeline. 'I will miss her. I was hoping that she could come to France with me for a bit, meet her great Grandma...' Anne had to chew her lip not to smile at the way the other two brightened.

'I don't see any harm in that, meeting her relatives, a bit of a holiday like.' Then Charmaine's face clouded again. 'But what about the police and the social?'

Anne was all professional confidence. 'If you don't mind her coming with me, then I'll let them know where she is, and I don't see a problem.'

'No, I suppose with you being a teacher and all...'

I wish, thought Anne, *I wish it were as easy as that.* 'I don't suppose Charmaine has a passport?'

'I'll slip off down the Rugby Club while you're sorting out.' Huw was now as keen to slip off as he was earlier to stand behind Charmaine, who made no objection to him going and who was offering to fetch Alex's belongings from her bedroom. Anne made no comment on the collection of objects which Charmaine gathered into a black bin bag. A photo drew her attention and she rescued it from the bag.

'Your mother?' she guessed, recognizing the likeness both to Charmaine - in something about the mouth and chin - and to her own mother - those blue eyes.

'Yes and she's welcome to it. Don't know why she keeps a photo of that old bag. Fat lot her Granny ever did for any of us. Didn't like Jimmy from the moment I married him - in fairness, perhaps she was right there - and could have helped us out of a spot or two cash-wise but didn't - too tight.'

'Wasn't she finding it difficult, with her being a farmer and the way things have been with BSE and things...?'

Charmaine laughed. 'You don't want to believe all you read in the papers. Stacks of money the farmers round here have, and when times are hard all they do is bleat a bit - like their own sheep - and it's compensation, compensation all the way to the bank. Load of compensation Jimmy got when he was made redundant - naff-all.'

'And the story Alex is keen on, San Fairy Anne, was that from her Granny?'

'Used to tell me as a child... she said the soldiers told her, friends of her Dad who came round, talked about the war and old times. They weren't soldiers any more then of course but they still talked about the time when they were. Some of them had been in France and they used to laugh and say, 'Those are the magic words, Marie, just remember to say San Fairy Anne to the Frenchies' - no offence now but that's what they said to my Mam - and you'll get everyone smiling. And my Mam was only little and she had this picture in her head of this magical Saint - you know, San, from the Welsh - and with fairy blood too, and called Anne made it seem even more so and this Saint is everything good and wonderful who protects you and has magic powers - especially in France. And I told Alex the story when she was a little girl... her eyes used to light up and I'd tickle her...we had fun...'

There was a brief glimpse of a different Charmaine but the mouth turned down again, poisoning the moment. 'not like the lying bitch she is now, with her filthy mind. I wish I'd never told her the stupid story - it's almost like she believes in it. Load of mumbo, probably means 'piece of shit' in French - oh,' she suddenly realized and mockingly apologized, 'if it does, please do excuse me, I'm sure.'

'On the contrary; Alex is right. They *are* magic words in French.' Charmaine's expression was well worth the slight distortion of the truth and anyway, Anne thought, San Fairy Anne *had* worked magic for Alex and might still do so when they went home.

'Pint,' Huw ordered.

'Haven't seen you for a week or two,' the barman observed. 'Busy?'

'Mmm.'

'Bit of a business with Jimmy.'

'It is, but I'm not going to pretend I thought him anything other than a waste of space. You all know that so I'm not going to make up something pretty just because he's dead.'

'Just wondered, Huw... did you manage to catch up with him that day he went fishing... the day he died, wasn't it?'

'No. Changed my mind and went home. I thought to myself, leave him alone and he'd do himself more damage than anyone else could. Turns out I was right, wasn't I?'

'And how is Charmaine?'

'Better off than before. And I don't want loose talk in here about her. Things have changed. If she's back in here at all, it'll be with me, right?'

'I don't have a problem with that, Huw.'

'Nor me.'

Huw finished his pint in peace, fretting at the shape of the wedding ring in his pocket. He'd had a nasty moment when it had fallen out in a moment of passion with Charmaine and she'd wanted to know what he was up to, whether he'd got married without her or what. Good job one wedding ring looked much like another and she hadn't recognized it.

Good job he was a quick thinker and had said it was his father's ring and he'd been looking for the woman worth him wearing it for and he'd found her so would she marry him. Just as well his father - and mother - were dead. The wedding would have to be a bit quicker than he had planned but he supposed he'd go through with it now.

After all, she was a bit of all right was Charmaine and she'd been dragged down by her no-good husband for too long. Had stuck by him an' all, even putting up with what she had to at the club, to make ends meet. Well there'd be no need for that any more. Bit odd that he'd be wearing Jimmy's wedding ring when he married her but then - wasn't that why he'd taken it off the man? Couldn't bear the thought of him married to Charmaine, touching her... All for the best really.

Surprised by her own potential for duplicity and triumphant in her success, Anne was unable to furnish Neil's mother with a full account and constrained herself to relating the outcome of her visit. However positively Anne presented the planned 'holiday' to meet her great-Grandma and see Alsace, Alex would have to be stupid not to realize that her mother had rejected her, and this time not in the heat of an argument.

Increasingly, Anne was convinced that Alex was anything but stupid. There was a lack of education - not surprising, Anne thought ruefully, knowing the attendance record only too well; there was deep disturbance, another kind of absence - of the spirit; but Anne sensed a flicker of that spirit, a shimmer of fish in a forest pool where at first you saw nothing but reflected trees.

Or was she misled by the blue eyes she knew so well into recognizing a deeper kinship than they could ever have? She had to believe it was possible. She had to remember the policewoman saying she believed Alex, that you could tell when an abused youngster was telling the truth, and that whatever Alex saw - or did - on that river bank was part of a terrible personal history which would not magically disappear with the discovery of a new auntie.

If only San Fairy Anne had protected Alex sooner! Meanwhile Neil was half right about cats and bags; Anne had no intention of letting others know all she and Alex knew. If that were the only, unacknowledged bond between them, it was still a bond. What had Neil said? He told colleagues confidential information on a 'need to know' basis. Well no one else needed to know.

'You were lucky with your hearts win,' Anne searched for easier topics. 'Helen's mother-in-law didn't join in till a few weeks after you and there's no sign of her getting anything out of it. It's a bad time for her too with all the problems for farmers.'

Mrs Phillips stiffened slightly. 'I'm sure it'll come; she might just have to wait a bit longer that's all. She should get some more friends to come in on it then she'll get her money more quickly. Anyway, we all knew it was a gamble when we went into it. The whole point of a gamble is that you win some, lose some.'

'I wasn't meaning any criticism... quite the opposite. I admire your good business sense, going into it early when you had the best chance of winning, only betting what you could afford...' There was clearly no stopping Anne's diplomatic tactics; she wondered how her new-found skills would go down in language department meetings back at the collège. At this rate she could manipulate the best timetable for herself that she had ever had.

'Well I did talk it over with Ceri, and he knows about these things.' Mrs Phillips generously conceded the praise but was still evidently warmed by it.

'Getting advice in itself shows how astute you were but I feel so sorry for Mrs Evans. If only she had taken some advice... '

'Well she should just sit it out and, like I say, get some friends to join in.'

'You know how some women are not so good with their money

though, and it's not as if she has much - just between ourselves now - Helen would be furious if she knew I'd told you - she was so keen to help her husband out that she's borrowed money from one of these what-do-you-call-thems that charge crazy interest and never let go once they have their teeth into you.'

'Not loan sharks!'

'That's it. So she's being ripped off every month and nothing she can do about it except borrow more.'

'But that's terrible. Isn't it against the law?'

'I don't even know if it's against the law in France. Even if it is, people will be so desperate to borrow, they'll pass money over on the street.'

'She should just not pay.'

'She signed a contract which she thinks is legal, so she's stuck now. And her husband doesn't know about it - and the last thing she wants is for him or Dai to know. Neither of them has the money to sort it out and it would be the final humiliation for her in all this.'

'I can imagine exactly what it would be like telling your son you're in a money mess.' Her face was grim.

'I shouldn't have told you - there's no point more of us worrying about it.' Anne wondered exactly why she had told Neil's mother. Perhaps when she was keeping so much to herself it was a relief to betray someone else's small secret. Also, she genuinely couldn't think of how to help and there was the small hope that Mrs Phillips would have an idea.

'No indeed. If we worried about other people's gambling habits, we'd never sleep at nights.'

It was a very small hope.

'I can't sleep for thinking about it,' Mair told Ceri, in the candlelight of a dinner for two at their favourite restaurant in Swansea.

'You'd never run a business if you were sorry after every sharp deal you'd made.' Ceri laughed at her and shook his head. 'Too sweet, you are.'

'Yes but it's different when you know the person whose money you've taken and she can't afford it, Ceri. I keep thinking about that money sitting in my savings account, doing nothing except wait till I die and Neil will get it, when that poor woman is breaking her heart with worry. And I wonder,' her voice dropped, 'whether she'll do something stupid. People do sometimes, don't they, and I couldn't live with that you know.'

Ceri was still shaking his head. 'She's already done something stupid isn't it, in going to one of these vultures, and she wouldn't have been in this mess if she had talked to her husband. Call me old fashioned but I don't hold with all this women-acting-on-their-own business.'

'Nor me, you know that, but still... and she was trying to help her husband, a kind of surprise present for him and it would have been lovely if it worked out.'

'It still might and if not, it was her gamble. Strawberry pavlova?' It clearly gave him pleasure to predict her menu choices and she was far too fond of him to contradict him.

'You know me so well.'

'Passion fruit for me, please,' he told the waiter.

He shared a smile with Mair but she was not to be distracted for long. 'Even if it does, it's going to take too long Ceri - she has to pay this awful man every month. You know what I'm asking, don't you? And I know you're right about everything, it's just sometimes it's the Christian thing to do, isn't it?' She turned her most beseeching look on her companion with all the charm she could muster. He reached across the table, took both her hands in his.

'You know I can't refuse you anything when you look at me like that, you little schemer. What do you want me to do?'

'Well,' she said and made some tentative suggestions which he understood to be a three-line whip for immediate action - by him.

Chapter 15

Typical of his mother to send him old-fashioned handwritten letters, as well as phoning him, thought Neil. He felt a pang of guilt - she bravely described restaurant meals, theatre visits and concerts but although she hid it so well, she must be missing him terribly. He re-read the final page.

It has indeed been strange for me to have a young girl living in my house. Of course you know Alex. I thought it was short for Alexandra but no indeed, it seems to be the full name. It is such a boyish name to give a young lady, I am sure that it must have caused some difficulties for her and she is quite awkward in her dress sense. Anne has told me that Alex's home life has been troubled and it is quite the happy ending that they have found each other, don't you think? I bet Anne's mother can't wait to meet her young relative, although between you and me I think Anne is a little bemused at finding herself to be a great aunt. I suspect it would be easier for her if she was a mother herself but Anne is more of a career woman.

I cannot resist giving you a little hint of some exciting news. It is supposed to be a surprise when you come home, my dear, but I'm sure you've guessed that a relationship so important, so special, must lead to marriage, so you can expect to hear news of a wedding the moment you cross your home threshold again. I am so excited it is difficult for me not to tell you all the details but there! I haven't told you and please consider my lips are sealed on this matter until the official moment. It won't be long now until I hear all your stories in person and I can tell you all my news. I so hope you have made the most of your year adventuring and I will be able to put your memories alongside all that Anne has told me of Alsace. I can almost smell the wine!

All my love, dear, and see you soon.

Neil was amused by the intensity of his mother's excitement. He had known for some time that Helen and Dai were intending to make their commitment official and, although he was surprised that his friend didn't mention a wedding, it hardly struck him as a big news item. Women's fascination with weddings would always be a mystery to him, he thought indulgently.

He checked idly through Helen's last email in case he had missed something but, as just as he had remembered it, the only excitement was over the return of otters to the Llanelli estuary, recorded several times by observers at the Wildfowl and Wetland Centre. After his experience in tracking the Sanctuary otters re-introduced to the wild in Alsace, Neil was looking forward to further observations back home. He must tell Michel that he would be able to email him with comparative data. Perhaps the Penclacwydd Centre would be interested in developing academic links with Hunawihr. It was positive thinking like this which he needed, not worrying about how much he would miss the monkeys. His spirits lifted at the thought of a day - and night - with Luc, including the promised concert in the park.

When Neil reached Luc's Strasbourg flat, he found his friend unusually fretful. 'It's just a headache,' Luc responded to his concern, 'but I can't get rid of it. Why don't you go for a walk, I'll take an aspirin, lie down for a while and then I'll be fine.'

The weather felt heavy and unsettled as Neil followed the familiar paths across the medieval bridges of petit-France. He again wondered how Luc could afford to live in the Finkwiller quarter, so close to the half-timbered houses criss-crossing the river but then, everywhere in Strasbourg was near the river.

He had meant to ask Luc about his family and somehow never got round to it. He had meant to do so much and the time was running out. Fifteen days now. He stopped at the Pont du Corbeau, the Raven's Bridge, where - so Luc told him - the worst crimes were punished by their perpetrators being sewn into sacks and hurled into the icy river to drown. In classical tradition, the worst crimes were considered to be killing children or killing your father.

Lesser criminals were dangled in iron cages for the public to hurl both abuse and more concrete expressions of disgust at the sitting targets. Neil looked down at the swans, gliding towards the bank, and around at the cafés, jester-bright with tourists despite the threatening skies, and found it hard to imagine the old blood. He thought of Alex. How would it feel to throw rocks at her father, dangled in a cage over this river? To hear a soft thud and a groan as a stone hit its target? Or even watch him executed by drowning.

Neil walked along the Street of the 'Cordiers', the rope-makers to the Cathedral, where he ignored the grand entrance with its frieze of wise and foolish virgins, heading instead around the building to a side entrance, the clock portal. He was too late to catch the mid-day chimes of the famous astronomical clock, which actually took place at 12.30, when the full performance culminated in a procession of clockwork saints and the cockerel crowing three times, but he would watch the mechanical activities that accompanied the half-hour throughout the day.

A group of tourists gathered in front of the famous clock, waiting for the half- hour. Every couple of minutes the metred light ran out, the clock was in darkness and someone had to dash across to the slot machine, feed it two francs and rush back to watch the show. Presumably, if the light went out at the crucial moment you would see nothing, Neil thought.

While waiting, he was aware of American accents around him and he saw the emotion with which a man and his son discovered the plaque on the wall thanking the Americans for their liberation of Alsace in the Second World War. Perhaps this was as close as they would get to their own 'place in the woods' where, like Madame Grüber, they could remember someone who gave his life for... for whatever.

The clock started, with a chime struck by an angel, and there was a hush amongst the observers. The first time Neil watched the clock he benefited from Luc's direction, 'Watch Death now, sounding the hour, now the chariots of the gods for the days of the week...' Today it would be Jupiter for Thursday.

If you didn't know where to look, and when, you would miss all the little actions which made the clock a miracle of medieval invention. It was over so quickly the watchers sighed with disappointment. If they could have fed two francs into the meter to start the performance again, and again, then they would have done so. Then they might have caught one of the Four Ages of Man striking the second note and, at the last stroke, one of the angels in the gallery of lions turning an hourglass upside down.

Neil, more than a tourist and less than a local, had learned where to look. Luc also told him the less well-known fate of the medieval craftsman who built the clock. On finishing his masterpiece, he was blinded by the authorities to ensure that Strasbourg's clock was unique and in revenge he had carried out a 'repair' that prevented the clock working until it was renovated in 1838. Many guidebooks even referred to the clock as having been built in 1838 rather than acknowledge unsavoury details. Once again, thought Neil, history as old blood.

He left the Cathedral and continued along the Street of the 22nd November. He imagined Madame Grüber hearing that Strasbourg was liberated, hoping that her baby's father was safe somewhere; he imagined the soldiers spreading out in the mountains round Strasbourg, finding their worst fears confirmed in le Struthof. He could feel the layers of history in this most modern of cities, seat of the European Parliament and yet still bearing street names from old craft guilds such as the Tanners and the Lace-makers. He tallied off the names, adding them to the Alsace he was taking home with him, wondering if he would be able to describe even one word of it to his mother.

When he returned to the flat, Luc was still pale but more composed.

'It's eased a bit and I know what it is now. Have you heard the weather forecast?'

'No.' Since coming to France, Neil paid far less attention to the weather than was his habit in Wales where it was a daily topic of conversation and wonder. 'Why?'

'There are storms coming. I should have known.' He shook his head. 'Bad storms. There has been a suggestion of cancelling the concert tonight but the organizers are going ahead. Perhaps we should not go?'

Neil was bemused at his usually dauntless companion being so uncertain. 'Because it might rain? If I cancelled everything I'd planned in Wales, just because it might rain, I'd never go to anything at all.'

'But this is outdoors and the advice from weather forecasts is to stay indoors. If the storm breaks...'

'Is there any cover?'

'They'll have canvas up.'

'Well there you are then. We can't let a bit of weather spoil our evening. You promised me Cossack dancing and a chance to smash glasses and shout 'Oi Vey!''

Despite himself, Luc smiled. 'I think there is a little cultural misunderstanding here. I promised you a Yiddish folk group, simple rondels, a little gypsy violin perhaps...'

'Now who's got the culture wrong - if they're Yiddish, they aren't gypsies.'

'Pfff - gypsies came from Egypt, where they taught guitar to the Jews before these were driven out and led across the Red Sea, so Jews play gypsy violin...'

'That is an appalling treatment of history!'

'So long as I am right, why should we worry too much? Anyway, I think we should not go, Neil.'

'Please...'

'But if there is a storm...'

'I was a duck in a previous existence,' Neil insisted, 'I was born by an estuary, I live by an estuary, I get rained on all year round and I don't even notice it - trust me.'

Mellowed by good wine, a hearty pasta dish and Luc's company, Neil was in high spirits when they reached the parc de Pourtalès. He always felt he could be more open in a city - whether it was London or Strasbourg was all the same. He didn't mind if Luc reached for his hand sometimes or threw an arm around him. Living for the moment was what it was all about when you had fifteen days left together.

'This,' Luc gestured expansively, 'is a typical English park.'

Neil looked around at reddish gravel paths winding across vast lawns into woods; great grey plane trees with their distinctive peeling bark like half-stripped wallpaper; the brown and cream façade of a grand chateau, at least fourteen? sixteen? windows wide, all gables and curly cornices. 'No, it isn't. It's nothing like.'

'How would you know? You're Welsh.' Luc dismissed Neil's inferior knowledge.

'Plane trees are not English trees and we don't have buildings anything like that - it's frothier and the colours are different from any English stately home.'

'How many English stately homes have you been to?'

'One,' Neil admitted, 'but I've seen photos...'

'We French, we too can look at photos. And you are missing what is so English.'

Neil suspected he was going to be told.

'Tell me about the paths.'

Neil obediently looked at the path. 'They're red.'

'Irrelevant.'

'They're gravel.'

'Irrelevant.'

'I give up - you might as well tell me. Some spiteful god sent you to punish me for being a teacher.'

'It is good for you to get an education.'

'I know, it's what I came to France for.'

'Well you would have to, to get any real sort of an education. The paths, mon ami, are not straight,' he declared triumphantly.

'So?'

'Is there really no end to your ignorance. So they are not in the French style. Think of Versailles, Villandry, all the grand chateaux.'

'I don't know any of them,' Neil responded reasonably.

'Not even the photos?'

Neil could see that from a Franco-centric point if view, this could be considered unacceptable and he knew that, for Luc, the only viewpoint was Franco-centric. 'No,' he sighed and was grateful to get away with a withering look.

'The paths meander . The park gives the illusion of natural walks while of course being planned and planted. This is so English.'

'It is? I mean, it is,' Neil deepened his voice and agreed quickly.

'And also there are the so-English sculptures in the park, not your

Dianas and Apollos of the French style, but genuine pataphysical expressions. Look, I'll show you.'

Luc took Neil along a 'meandering path' to admire a statue made out of some kind of grey metal. It had a pointed 'face' with no features; two long ears, one flopped outwards at right angles to the other one sticking straight up; two 'arms' one looped in towards the 'waist' ; two 'legs', one sticking straight out in front, the other fixed to a wedged metal pedestal, as if in the middle of some mad goose-step; and the body, such as it was, formed a thin vertical stick linking legs and head.

Luc was looking worryingly awed. 'Such art. It is of course a hare or as you English would say, a rabbit, and yet at the same time it is not. It is called 'The Bowler' and the hare is in a classic stance for your English game of cricket. And the sculptor is English.'

'Of course! A rabbit playing cricket! I don't know how I could have been so slow!' If that rabbit moved to bowl its imaginary ball, it would fall flat on its face while the ball would arc vertically to land - in Neil's estimation - splat on the prone mammal's own back.

'You didn't recognise it?' Luc was disappointed in his cultural protégé.

'Well of course I could see the ears... and we do say 'hare' in English, you know.'

'No, the English say rabbit.' Neil opened his mouth to disagree but Luc closed the subject. 'You are Welsh. I am talking about the English.' Neil would never have thought he'd regret making a foreigner understand that Wales and England were different but it certainly had disadvantages.

'Those are my favourites.' Neil followed Luc along some more meandering paths until they were completely surrounded by trees. Neil could see nothing in the dwindling daylight although he looked where Luc's outstretched arm was pointing up into the trees. Neil kept looking and then suddenly he could distinguish the shape of a human figure clinging to the trunk, high above the path. There was the pleasure of discovery but he was still uncertain as to why anyone would want to create sculptures of tree-hugging humans.

'They're called 'Aborigines' and there are many of them, once you know where to look...the light is too bad. We'll come back another day.'

'You made up that word,' he accused Luc. 'That whatsit-physical word. I've heard of metaphysical...' *but please don't ask me to explain it or apply it to art*, he begged silently, realizing too late the dangers of the opening he had offered.

'So you have never heard of pataphysics, defined by a Frenchman of course, Jarry - as you should know. It is the science of imaginary solutions.'

'And you can tell me what the problem is, which is solved by a rabbit playing cricket?'

'The only important problem, the meaning of life - and as Jarry pointed out, its absurdity -which is expressed supremely well by 'The Bowler'. But there is also the deep link between the nature - all around us in the park and in the hare as an animal being - and the artificiality - also all round us in the park and in the human attributes and pose of the hare - of what is man-made, of thought itself. If you think about it...' Neil really, very much didn't want to think about it. He put his arm round the shorter man's shoulders.

'Luc, we don't want to miss the concert.'

And the concert was good. About a hundred people newspapers after the event reported one hundred and twenty - had braved the weather forecast and were giving the folk group all the encouragement they could want on this cool summer night, to play the old melodies which had survived across the world and across the centuries.

Gypsy violin,' Luc murmured, as they clicked their fingers, nodded their heads and stamped their feet to the traditional rhythms. The concert was good - until the storm struck. One minute everyone was humming along to a melody, the next torrents of rain hammered panic into a sodden crowd, who did not even have time to put up the hoods on the waterproofs which most had at least had the sense to bring with them.

There was a mass rush to the shelter of the marquee as a fistful of air punched people backwards into each other and onto the ground as they fought to get under cover. Neil felt assaulted by the winds which attacked from all angles through the beating rain, driven into his face, gusting round to whip his back.

He lost contact with Luc, yelled fruitlessly against the fury of the skies, 'The tent...' and he struggled towards the awning, part of the stampede, through the elbows in the ribs and the crushed feet, heedless.

All lights went out in the flashing war which seared the sky, blinding his dazzled eyes as Neil waited in total darkness, counting the fast heart-beats till the thunder, huddling with a wet nameless mass of others. He had hardly begun to count when the grumbling roar grew until he felt his heart banging with the final explosion as it burst directly above them.

So far Neil was only scared. He had never been in a storm like this, he had never known a storm could be like this but he was still expecting to endure and carry on with his life. So were all his companions.

The winds which forced them backwards as they walked were merely the hors d'oeuvres. The hairs on the back of Neil's neck lifted in ancient response to the forces around the parkland, shaking the canvas like tissue, howling for blood.

He could feel the wind whirling into a tornado, the cracks and creaking of broken trees joining the unidentified thumps of objects swirled into debris.

He would always say afterwards that he knew, just before it happened, that he felt the plane tree's anguish as its decades-old hold on life was ripped from the earth in one savage uprooting, its ear-piercing shriek as it fell. That was the worst.

He was conscious, crazy with confusion, blocked and battered by bits of tree and bits of people, all screaming unheard into the wildness of the tornado. Which moved on. As desperately as they tried to get under canvas, those who could move tried to get out of it, trampling each other in the grip of the oldest instinct, but also shouting their companion's names, mantras of love and fear.

'Luc,' Neil called, picking his way in the dark, not knowing if he was heading towards the outside or further into the crowd, stupidly saying, 'Sorry,' as he felt the strange shiftings underfoot which could have as easily been someone's fingers as twigs. He felt something sharp cut his cheek and brushed it with the back of his hand, which came away wet with blood and tears.

It was only then he realized that the tears were streaming down his cheeks as if they belonged to someone else. He felt nothing and yet still the tears came.

Several life-times later, Neil was stumbling around on the grass amid bits of broken trees when someone gently caught hold of him and made him sit on a fold-down stool, while amid flickering torches and headlights, the someone examined him.

He was vaguely aware of firemen and people in uniforms, paramedics, police and all their emergency vehicles. The noises in his head were slowly changing into sirens and speech. Suddenly Neil felt sore and cold. He started shivering, then shaking till his teeth chattered, despite the warmth of the blanket thrown round him.

'It's shock,' someone told him, 'but you will be fine. Not even any concussion, just some cuts and bruises. You are very very lucky.'

Luc. Neil could hear voices, people rushing around, stretchers being carried past him to the ambulances, sirens torturing the night as the vehicles sped off. It was the hushed voices which scared him, and the stretcher which went past, completely covered, a blanket over the face of whoever was lying there.

'I have to find my friend,' he tried to say but his numb mouth would not obey him.

'You'll be fine, just stay there for now,' he was reassured. *Luc.*

'Neil!' the shout erupted into his confused brain as a familiar face swam into view, Luc shaking off a paramedic who was trying to make him stop moving for a minute and then he felt the warmth of a hug which would have done a macaque justice.

'Are you all right?' Neil tried to ask but it was like being a stroke victim, his mouth drooping and shaking with nerves.

'You look like shit.' Luc hugged him again and again.

'Sit.' The paramedic caught up with Luc and snapped open a canvas stool.

A passing colleague commented, 'He looks all right to me - don't spend too long with that one.'

'See,' commented Luc.

Methodically the paramedic shone his torch on Luc's face, working down his body. 'And I've seen someone hit by a car run all the way down street before collapsing in a heap. Wonderful thing adrenalin but it wears off.' Luc winced. The paramedic moved the left arm again and Luc swayed forward on the stool, pushed the man away and was sick. 'I'm sorry,' he muttered.

'Broken,' Luc was informed, 'but not badly. Doctor will fix you up and the two of you will be taken home. Anyone there to look after you?'

'We're together, we'll take care of each other.' Luc was able to say.

'Then you need to check in at the hospital, but not today and not tomorrow, they'll have their hands full.'

'Many hurt?' Luc asked. The paramedic was already walking away, looking for a doctor.

'Easier to put it the other way,' was the grim response. 'You and your friend are as good as it gets. You don't know how lucky you've been.'

Then Luc started to cry and the two of them sat there, waiting for the doctor, alive.

Their love had never seemed deeper than when each held the other's battered body and bruised spirits into sleep that night. They watched their news story on television the next day and it seemed even less real when they saw the huge, uprooted tree crashed across the tatters which were once canvas; the meandering paths all blocked by fallen trees; and the smashed sculptures with only one surviving Aborigine clinging to a shattered trunk.

They heard that eleven people had died to date, twenty were in a critical condition and another fifty or so injured. 'To date,' Neil repeated. Thursday, 6th July was a date that would not be forgotten in Strasbourg. They heard that the winds were up to 150kph and, although the number meant nothing to them, they knew what winds like that felt like.

It took the police three hours to recover all the bodies from beneath the tree. 'We seemed to be there forever, wandering around in one of Dante's circles.' There were a hundred firefighters and thirty doctors, who set up a field hospital. 'Is that what my stool was!'

Rescuers needed to cut through soaking branches to reach those trapped underneath. The couple added all the statistics to their memories of chaos in the dark, to try and superimpose reason on panic and tears.

They told each other the story of losing one another, the tree crashing on them and of finding each other again, turning it into words so that they could control the pounding fears. They listened to the Mayor of Strasboug, Fabienne Keller, who visited the scene and said 'It was completely unforeseeable that the tree should be uprooted in this fashion.'

'He's worried we'll sue,' was Luc's cynical view. 'Ducking the blame before people have started thinking about blame, like all politicians.'

French Prime Minister Lionel Jospin expressed his condolences to the victims.

'We're national news.'

'International,' Neil corrected, having listened to his hysterical mother on a telephone, berating him for going out with storms forecast. 'And not us personally, Luc.'

'You underestimate my importance.'

'No-one,' was Neil's dry response, 'is ever likely to do that.'

Two days floated by in the timeless zone where Neil stayed at Luc's flat and they watched the news obsessively. Luc's style was cramped by his broken arm but he nevertheless insisted on cooking rather than face the insult to his stomach which he felt Neil would offer it. It was after eating too much on the third evening after the concert that Luc cleared his throat and said, 'Will you marry me?'

Neil thought he'd mis-heard. 'Sorry?'

'I have been waiting for the right time but there never is one. I'm asking you to marry me, to stay with me, to be my partner.' Awkwardly, with his one good arm, he reached into his pocket and pulled out a small jewellery box. With growing apprehension, Neil took the box.

'Open it.'

Neil stared open-mouthed at a plain gold wedding ring, indistinguishable from the one his mother wore. He thought of Helen, about to marry Dai. His face burned.

'Read it.' The inscription inside the ring read *pob Luc*. 'It is right, isn't it?'

'It's too much, Luc.'

'I love you.'

'Thank you. No, I mean it, thank you Luc, but I need to think.'

'And then you will realize what a sensible idea this is...'

'Do you always get what you want?' Neil asked, exasperated.

'It is so much better that way, I find.'

'Luc, I need to think. You must let me think.'

Their love-making that night combined the knowledge they had gained of each other's preferences with the high emotions of the preceding days and the tears which came so easily after the night of the concert, were never far away. For Neil, the night was special in the way only first and last times can be. Perhaps for Luc too there was a premonition of parting, or at least the knowledge that they had reached a crossroads.

Neil had to say the words the next day. He had to look at fire in Luc's eyes, the sharply etched angles of a much-loved face, the triangle of dark curls at the open neck of his shirt and he had to say the words to end it. 'I'm sorry Luc. I can't'

The fire was stilled, the shiny dark hair swung to one side as Luc turned away, presenting a graven profile to Neil. 'Can I ask why?'

There was a long silence while Neil searched for truthful words, when he didn't know or understand why, himself. It was like asking why the world was the way it was but that was no answer for Luc. There was no answer for Luc but he owed it to him to try.

'It's no lack of love, believe me.'

'Lack of courage then?'

'Perhaps. Perhaps it's because your trees are too tall, because your storms kill people...it's all too intense... I need to be ordinary again... I need to go home.'

'And because you can't explain me to your mother?'

'Perhaps... yes... perhaps that too. I told you, I'm no good as a role model, I'm just me.'

'I am happy with just you.'

'I can't, Luc.' Neil handed back the ring in its small red box but Luc put his hand behind his back and refused to take it.

'It is a present. You will keep it and perhaps you will not forget me.' Neil couldn't speak as he put the little box in his pocket. He gathered his clothes, his shaving toiletries from the bathroom they had shared, his books from the table.

'I'm so sorry, Luc.'

'It doesn't matter.'

Neil kissed him on both cheeks and said 'Au revoir.' They both knew they would not see each other again. When someone offered you a lifetime you could not turn him down and ask for two hours on Friday. Luc said nothing. Neil left.

'Is it for the best?' Madame Grüber asked. Neil assumed that his misery was written on his face for all to read.

'I don't know,' he admitted. 'But it's done now and I wouldn't insult Luc by telling him I've changed my mind, then change it back again and again - we've both had enough of whirlwinds.'

'I meant, is it for the best you going back home before you planned... I wasn't meaning to pry...'

'You couldn't pry. I have been so happy here.'

'This is your home now. You will always be welcome here.'

'I will think of you, and Anne and Alex...' *and Luc.*

'You will see them before I do.'

'Yes, Anne wants to stay till the end of term even though I'll be back there on Wednesday. She says we can finish the term together and she can hand over all the work while she sorts out a passport. She thinks she can get a proper passport, by going up to Newport to get it, rather than a visa. It might make it easier in the future.'

'I will miss you. What do you think of Alsace, now that you have lived as one of us for a year? Was it worth it?'

'I love it.' Neil blinked back the tears.

Chapter 16

Helen was also following a news story with added interest, her curiosity roused by her acquaintance with the victim's family and intimacy with the key witness.

'Listen,' she told the key witness himself and folding the newspaper over to read the article aloud more easily. 'Fisherman's mystery death. Police are still pursuing their enquiries...'

'Torturing people more like...'

'Into the death of thirty-four-year-old husband and father who was found...'

'By me...'

'By Alex actually if you think about what she said to you. I mean she told you he was there or so you told me. Anyway, stop interrupting. 'who was found by wonderfully attractive and intelligent local vet'...'

'Don't think so...'

'All right, 'who was found by the river, having apparently drowned while unconscious.' How could he have drowned if he was *by* the river? He was *in* the river,wasn't he?"

'I told you; his head was in the river, the rest of him wasn't, so I suppose technically he was in the river *and* by the river.'

'That's quibbling. And they shouldn't say he drowned...'

'Apparently...'

'Even 'apparently' - it'll put ideas into the jury's head...'

'Why should there be a jury? It was an accident.'

'But you said it was odd about him rolling. I mean, if he died from cracking his head open, then I don't suppose the rolling matters because he didn't drown then, did he?'

'No. Or is that, yes? What was the question again?'

'Just listen to this bit now... 'A post-mortem examination was carried out at Prince Philip Hospital by pathologist Dr Jane Cribbs'... I don't suppose we'll get to know the results of that.'

'Not till after the inquest, I shouldn't think.'

'Which will be when?'

'Months, I expect.'

'This is the bit... listen... 'The police are treating the death as suspicious and have interviewed a local Asian businessman regarding a fight in his shop between the deceased and his son...' '

'According to you, there weren't any other children. Unless they thought Alex was a boy, like you did.'

'No silly, not *his* son, *his* son - the shopkeeper's.'

'Well why doesn't it say so then?'

'Because it's a newspaper... anyway the next bit's good...'there is evidence that the deceased was involved in a fight before his death'...'

'I certainly didn't tell them that. I don't know where they get their information from - direct from the Gestapo I expect.'

'If you mean our respected constabulary, I very much doubt it.'

'Well all I'm saying is they shouldn't know that.'

'So it seems to suggest that this lad went after the man and coshed him then drowned him.'

'It doesn't suggest that at all!'

'It does if you read between the lines.'

'Well let's hope no-one else has your lurid imagination or it could be unpleasant for Mr Asian businessman.'

'But it doesn't give his name.'

'Shouldn't think his neighbours'd take long to have a good guess - they wouldn't worry too much if they guessed wrong either.'

'Last bit... his young widow was too distressed to comment on the circumstances of his death but said how grateful she was for her friend's support' - huh! You should hear Anne's version of *Mr* Friend's support - 'and that their teenage daughter was being looked after by a close relative.' That's one way of putting it!' There was a pause. 'Dai...'

'Mmmm?'

'Seriously now, there's something odd about Alex.'

'You told me, he's a girl, which means she doesn't dress tidy.'

'No, I mean it. If you'd heard the way her mother talked about her. I know the mother's no angel but something must have happened between them. I don't think Anne can see it, she's waited too long to take some long-lost child back to her mother... but I can't help wondering...you know when you found Alex and she was out of it but she'd obviously seen something or she couldn't have told you he was there, could she?'

'So?' Dai was cautious.

'So if she had one of these massive tempers, like her mother suggested she did, and argued with her father - I mean she was mitching wasn't she, so he'd have been angry with her and she might have answered back, and it all got worse - perhaps she pushed him so he fell...'

'And then rolled him into the river to make sure he died? And then sat and waited for me to find them?'

'Not exactly. I don't really see her murdering him, as such, just - you know- losing her temper and getting physical. I mean her mother told us there was quite a side to Alex. Perhaps you were wrong about the rolling being odd and he was just addled, half-conscious and rolled a bit, so that part was just an accident? Well, if you think about it, pushing him would be an accident too. So in a way, it was an accident but Alex might have done it.'

'And I suppose the fight marks were caused by Alex too?'

'That's it! I didn't think of that. I just hope Anne knows what she's taking on...I keep feeling there's something there we don't know about.'

'Perhaps,' he suggested gently , 'it's just you and I who don't know something - and don't need to.' He was giving her a very strange look and shaking his head.

'What?' she demanded.

'I've changed my mind. I can't marry you.'

'Good. I still haven't made up my mind. Why not?'

'You're turning into my grandfather. Before long you'll be going straight for any murder story in the local paper, saying 'Diw, Diw,

Diw and describing the full horrific details to anyone who'll listen.'

'I take that as a compliment. But you're a key witness and you should take it more seriously.'

'I do,' he protested, 'and you shouldn't be telling me all these stories and trying to influence me.'

'Can you be influenced?' she teased, in a husky voice, starting to unbutton her blouse. There was a gentle knock at the back door. 'Helen?' They both recognized the voice but Dai was first to respond.

'Mam - come on in!' He shrugged as Helen quickly rearranged her clothing and sat primly on the edge of a chair.

'I thought you were on surgery tonight,' Dai's mother said, clearly disappointed to find him there. 'I was hoping to talk to Helen about a... knitting pattern.'

'Urgent knitting pattern, is it?' Dai enquired. 'Urgent, private knitting pattern?'

Mrs Evans blushed, 'Women's things it is, Dai, of no interest to you...'

'What wouldn't be of interest to a man who spends half his working life with his arm up a cow's -'

'Dai!' both women cut him off.

'All right!' He turned ostentatiously to Helen. 'I thought I'd go up to the farm and have a chat with Dad.'

'Good idea,' said Helen, straight-faced. He kissed her, winked at his mother and left them to it.

Helen waited, knowing full well that Dai's mother was not going to talk to her about knitting patterns or medical complaints.

'It's that same old business, Helen. I don't quite know what to make of this and I wanted a second opinion.' 'This' was a letter, on official, headed police notepaper, which was passed over for Helen's inspection.

Dear Mrs Evans,

Dyfed Powys Police Force is currently investigating a scheme operating in the Llanelli area, known colloquially as 'hearts' and ostensibly managed by an organization entitled 'Women empowering women'. It has been brought to our attention that, as a subscriber to such a scheme, you would be able to help us with our enquiries.

The scheme appears to operate on a pyramid basis but through a process of women 'gifting' monies to other women, it evades some of the laws intended to protect consumers from unscrupulous trading, including pyramid selling, chain letters etc. There are however elements within the scheme which may not be legal, such as any profits taken by the self-styled organizers.

A subsidiary investigation is taking place into the alleged illegal money-lending activities of unregistered Llanelli residents, which has escalated as a consequence of the increased borrowing requirements of the least affluent sector of the ward, to enable participation in the 'hearts' scheme.

You are therefore invited to attend Llanelli Police Station on Monday 10th July at 10.00a.m. to assist with enquiries on both these matters. It is possible that certain monies outstanding from the scheme to which you subscribed could be confiscated and therefore within our jurisdiction to redistribute subsequent to your interview.

Yours sincerely,

D.I. Greaves

Mrs Evan was studying Helen's face closely while she read the letter twice. 'It's not just me, is it,' she observed with satisfaction.

''Bout as clear as mud,' Helen agreed, 'But I think there's a chance that neither the hearts nor the moneylending are legal, and that you just might get your money back.'

'That's what I thought but I didn't dare hope... still daren't - it only says 'might'. And I might still have to pay interest to that flesh-eater.'

'Not if it's not legal,' Helen mused. 'which means you've got to go to that interview and tell them all you know.'

'But what if I've broken the law by joining the hearts in the first place?'

'You've done nothing wrong,' Helen reassured her firmly, 'this could be really good news. I'll go with you if you like. I can tell them all the ways they tried to sell it to us in the first place.'

Mrs Evans brightened. 'Are you sure?'

'Positive.'

If he had heard the exchange, Ceri would have been very pleased by the outcome of a friendly conversation at the Rotary Club with his fellow Rotarian, Detective Inspector Greaves, although he might have been less impressed by the quality of police communication.

Huw had no difficulty understanding the policemen who were interviewing him; his problem was judging how much he should say. He had expected them to catch up with him as there were too many men watching the scuffle at the Rugby Club for it to stay quiet for long. He was perfectly willing to help the police with their enquiries but he felt it was for the best - his best - that certain actions remained between him and his conscience, which had needed a little laundering to reach its current pristine state.

'Why didn't you come forward before? You knew the man was dead.'

'I'm sorry, I should have but you know how it is - I didn't want to get involved. I knew it would look bad, me and him being at odds just before he died, and I didn't want to bring Charmaine into it.' There, that would take the wind out of their sails. They'd think they were one up on him if - as they would have - they'd found out about his relationship with Charmaine and were about to drop it on him. Did he imagine that little hesitation before the next question? He thought not.

'Charmaine... that would be Mrs Wilkinson, the wife of the deceased?'

'Yes, that's what the argument was about. He'd found out we were... seeing each other.'

'Seeing each other?,' one of the policemen sneered.

No-one was going to dirty the way he and Charmaine felt about each other. 'I'm going to marry her,' he told them. He still couldn't believe his luck in being with her at all, having her to himself. She was the best thing that ever happened to him and although he was a bit worried about the idea of marriage, if anyone was worth trying it with, she was. 'She's all right is Charmaine. She's never stood a chance with that bastard pulling her down.' Mistake, showing too much emotion, but how would any man feel in that situation? 'I know what you're thinking. Truth is, I didn't feel no sympathy for him and I still don't. He was nothing but bad luck to himself and everyone else and you can ask anyone. Couldn't hold a job down, hated anyone who could, nothing but one big chip on his shoulder and treating that beautiful wife of his like shit. Hit her sometimes you know but she'd never tell you - too proud. Well she'll be treated like a princess with me, like she deserves to be. But I never laid a finger on him after the Rugby Club.' *Not quite true, boy, but a necessary lie. No point digging yourself into a hole which you might not climb out of.*

Then the crucial question, the one he'd been waiting for. 'You were heard saying that you were going to follow Mr Wilkinson along the river bank that you'd 'settle this once and for all'. Did you? Did you follow him?'

When did you get charged? Huw wondered. Should he be asked this sort of question at all? Shouldn't he have a solicitor? People on the telly always seemed to know how to do this but he'd never been in a police station before, never been in trouble come to that. Oh what the hell. Get it over with and he could get back to Charmaine, help her clean up her life. Main thing was to have a steady wage coming in and he could provide that - like a real man. 'No,' he stated clearly. 'I thought about it, but everything I said was all hot air, evaporated in the daylight when I came out the Club door. What did I have to gain? I'd already beaten him in a fight so I didn't have nothing to prove. Charmaine was going to leave him and the way I see it that's her business - unless he come nasty with her then I'd have been in, believe me.'

'Oh we do, Mr Jones, we do. That's why we're a bit worried about all these bashes and bruises on his body, made by you?'

'I've already said we had a scuffle. Plenty there to tell you I hit him, caught him across the face and into the guts, I reckon. I can't remember what else - I was

out of it for a minute.'

'And you didn't follow him and while you were 'out of it' finish what you started?'

'No.'

'You don't mind us taking some samples for forensic?'

'No.' He would have left traces during the fight in the Club, they all knew that. They also all knew that there would be no way to pick out whether anything, DNA or clothes fragment, might have been left an hour or two later.

'So you know nothing about how Mr Wilkinson died?'

'No.'

The two policemen looked at each other and one sighed and nodded. The other spoke. 'We are not charging you, Mr Evans, although if Mr Wilkinson were alive he could have pressed charges for assault - I know you're going to say he started it but that would have been for the court to decide. Also, we're a bit disappointed that the barman of the Rugby Club is taking such a tolerant view of your behaviour...' *Good for him - that's worth a drink next time I'm in the Club*. 'And it seems you can confirm the origin of the fight marks on the body. Witness statements from the Club confirm that the blows struck by you tally with marks found on Mr Wilkinson so I don't see any reason to investigate any further. You'd better watch that temper of yours or we'll be seeing you again.'

'No need for it now.' Huw could feel the relief flushing up to his hairline and he had to get out before it showed too much.

'That will be all sir.'

'Thank you.' Huw counted the steps it took him to leave and lit a cigarette the moment he touched the footpath. He walked aimlessly for a few minutes. After all, his lie hurt no-one. And neither had he, so no point dwelling on it. He took another drag, inhaling deeply. Hard not to, though, knowing the man was dead and remembering what he had looked like.

Huw had walked likely bits of river, planning to tell Jimmy that Charmaine was leaving and to make sure she would be safe to get out. He didn't trust that wreck of a man not to hurt her so he wanted to frighten him, be at Charmaine's side to escort her out, safely. But when Huw caught up with Jimmy, he'd found him dead, his head bleeding as if that bastard had thought of the only way to spoil things for him and Charmaine, getting him into a right mess with the police - if not worse.

Huw couldn't help it. He'd sworn and kicked at the body which rolled over, the wedding ring glinting on Jimmy's finger as if it was a one finger at Huw. He didn't know what had come over him but he'd tugged at that ring till it came off and Jimmy rolled just a bit more till he was face down in the water. Huw just panicked and ran, then - what he should have done in the first place - he went straight home and slept, pretending he'd never been there until he almost believed it himself.

It seemed like a mad nightmare apart from the good news that Charmaine was free. It knocked Huw a bit to find out that somewhere near him on that river bank had been the weirdo daughter. He'd been scared she might have seen or heard something but if she had, she'd have said by now.

Maybe she did something herself, something bad... Best they both forgot it. He was certainly happy to. It was for the best, though, that she wouldn't be living with them. He didn't think he could cope with wondering what she was up to in her head, wondering what she knew, wondering if she'd come for him with her nails clawing and her mad eyes. Gave him the shivers. Still. All for the best and - his back straightened in pride - Charmaine to go home to.

'What time will Neil arrive?' Anne asked.

'Early afternoon on Thursday he said. He's going to stop overnight in Calais so as not to do the drive all in one go. Then he's getting the early morning ferry so it depends what the traffic's like from Dover, particularly the M25.' Mrs Phillips had memorized the details of a journey which meant nothing to her, so that she could imagine her son speeding home. She thought how wonderful it would be to see Neil again and to share her news with him. Then she would be able to tell everyone. She was a little shy about what people in chapel would think but, there we are, they would just have to accept it.

'I'll take Alex shopping in Swansea. She needs some clothes, and bits and pieces, and I think we'll have enough to do at home without a trip to town.' Anne was so thoughtful - but she was right, it would be easier to greet Neil without her visitors there, just her and Ceri. She must do some baking for the occasion - perhaps some bara brith or carrot cake. Ceri was particularly fond of her carrot cake. 'Well... if it fits in with you...'

'Helen phoned while you were out.'

'Any news?' Mair asked, innocently.

'Yes, actually. It seems there has been a police enquiry into the hearts scheme and into these money-lending sharks. The short of it is that Mrs Evans went to the police station and got all her money back.' Mair smiled, knowing exactly whose savings account the money came from and pleased that her little plan had worked so well. It wasn't likely that Mrs Evans would check on whether any of the other victims had been reimbursed - none of them would want to talk about the episode at all.

'Well that is good news isn't it?' she said smoothly. 'What will happen if the hearts scheme works out so that she wins?'

'I don't think that's likely now that the police are involved but I suppose she'd have to pay them back if that happens.'

'And that lender you told me about?'

'All the money,' Anne nodded. With any luck that might mean she would not have to chip in the interest too, Mair thought. If the police got - and returned - some money out of that disgusting character, so much the better for her little savings pot. She must get Ceri to find out. It was sweet of him, the way that he'd hung onto his own winnings to 'support her when she spent all of her own.' And she still had a profit of seven and a half thousand pounds as well as a clear conscience for rescuing Mrs Evans. She would feel much easier going to chapel this Sunday. 'According to Helen,' Anne continued, 'the police don't know if they can charge this Stan with anything but they've done worse than that.' 'Worse than charge him?'

'Oh yes - the Inland Revenue! There's no way this Stan was completing his tax forms in a tidy way so on the evidence that Mrs Evans and others have provided there is going to be a full investigation by the Inland Revenue. I've learnt ever so much about financial systems here - I thought the bureaucrats were fussy in France but Helen was telling me about your VAT and so on. I don't understand half of it but she told me that the Inland Revenue have powers beyond any other authority - they can search even your body.'

'I think that's the Customs dear. Anyway we don't really need to go into detail, do we. I'm very glad that these people will get what's coming to them. Would you like a cup of tea? Alex?' It was so easy to forget about Anne's silent shadow but after all, she was only thirteen and Anne really ought to remember what was appropriate in front of an innocent young girl. She would never have spoken in such a way in front of Neil at that age. She smiled again, thinking of Thursday. So much to tell him. She hugged herself with excitement as she boiled the kettle.

Neil found a parking space along the busy Llanelli road that was his home and was sitting in his once-prized car. When exactly did a new car cease to be new? It had happened without him noticing and he wondered if he could afford to buy a new one. Although it was July, he felt cool in his T-shirt. He skirted the town centre, still having to concentrate hard at roundabouts to go clockwise rather than French anti-clockwise.

He goggled like a tourist at the way the trees had grown along the landscaped dual carriageway but they were still small trees - and always would be. As the road curved up through the tumbling terraces, he kept feeling the urge to take off sunglasses, which he wasn't wearing.

All the colours were muted, mostly shades of grey, and he had grown used to the dazzle of cobalt blue and purple on half-timbered medieval houses. As he sat in the car, acclimatising, some sunlight flickered weakly through the clouds, silvering the pavement, and he felt a sudden longing to visit the marshes. He had missed the herons' deliberate walk upstream as they scanned for fish and bayoneted on sight. His stomach grumbled and he warmed to the thought of his mother's cooking and company, shaking off the shadows of mountains and tall trees. He smiled at the well-shined brass on the door knocker, went round to the back door, entered and yelled, 'Mam, I'm home,' a sense of 'hiraeth', roots, flooding over him as he was able to speak Welsh again face-to-face for the first time in a year.

Although she sounded like his mother, he did not recognise the woman who rushed into the kitchen, threw her arms round him and led him through to the living room. Her hair was different - brighter, shorter, straighter - and so were her clothes. She was talking non-stop and he couldn't take it all in but she was obviously pleased to see him home. An unknown man wearing a dark suit and a big smile rose from an armchair to shake Neil's hand.

'This is Ceri,' his mother beamed, switching to English.

'Ceri' put an arm around Neil's mother, who blushed and accepted the arm hugging her closer to the man's side.

'I've heard so much about you,' the stranger said,

'My mother does get carried away.'

'I think your mother is wonderful.' Neil was forced to watch another squeeze. 'And we've been bursting to tell you the news. We, your mother and I,' - what was wrong with the man that he couldn't stop smiling? 'want you to be the first to know that we are going to be married.'

'Yffarn darn!' Neil swore in Welsh, to his mother's horror and Ceri's smiling lack of comprehension.

'Neil!' His mother reprimanded him in Welsh for his language, then switched back to English, holding his eyes in her steady gaze as she said, 'I knew you would be happy for us.'

'I am,' he attempted, then with a mastery of understatement, 'I'm just a bit surprised.' He rallied. 'Congratulations. This is wonderful.' Did he sound sarcastic? He hurried on, 'I must just get the stuff out of the car and put it in my room, then I can relax...' Did he still have a room? Should he ask?

His mother was sharp. 'I'll help you. Ceri fach you pour us all a drink and we'll be back in two ticks.'

Nothing could shake that smile. Be fair Neil, he told himself, the man's pleased with himself. But what does it mean for me? Have I given up... all that... and my world ends anyway? And behind my back too, sneaking around while I was away.

'You are pleased for us, Neil?' his mother asked him when they were alone, with a hint of pleading - or was it a hint of a threat, implying 'If not, tough.' He had a feeling that this new woman was perfectly capable of saying 'Tough,' to her son.

'Yes of course.' What could he say? She was over eighteen after all. How old was she anyway? He worked it out - she must be nearly sixty, far too old for this sort of behaviour and certainly too old for clothes that were quite tight on her. He'd never thought of her as having a figure and would prefer to keep it that way. 'It was a bit of a surprise that's all.'

'Well it shouldn't have been. I've told you often enough that I was seeing Ceri and we'd been having such a good time.'

'I just thought you were friends,' Neil responded lamely, not daring to tell her that he'd assumed that Ceri was a woman. *Like Alex*, he thought, *one of those stupid names that could be anything!* Helen had even thought Alex was a boy when she saw her. No chance of that with Ceri - if Neil had caught a glimpse of that paunchy, bearded slimeball, he'd have certainly identified him as male! Listen to him - he caught himself - hardly the person to make politically incorrect comments about gender. Well he was fed up being sensitive.

'Well we are friends too of course but not like you and that French friend you made, Luc - we love each other and we want to get married.'

Neil opened his mouth but nothing came out. He had always thought that, deep down, his mother knew. Could she know and still talk that way? Was it possible she really didn't know?

'I even told you there was going to be a wedding. Really, Neil, I don't know where you keep that wonderful brain of yours when it comes to people. You don't listen.'

'I'm sorry. I had... other things on my mind. I thought you meant Helen and Dai.'

'Well that would be nice too, dear, but I'm sure Helen would tell you if she was getting married and anyway, I wouldn't have been that excited if it was someone else getting married would I?'

'No, I suppose not.' Neil ruefully remembered his dismissal of the excitement as 'typically feminine'. He wasn't doing very well in challenging gender stereotypes, was he.

By this time, his mother was sitting on his bed beside him, in the room that was unchanged since he left a year ago and which grew up around him from baby to adulthood. He could see the photograph of his father, standing proudly beside his mother, on his bedside table. Looking almost as young as in the photograph, his mother took his hand. 'I know.' She looked at the photograph. 'But I've been given a second chance, Neil. I can't bring your father back and Ceri is a good man. Give him a chance.' Neil couldn't speak, he just nodded. Her tone became more business-like. 'And we've talked about where we'll live.' Neil hoped she couldn't hear his heart hammering. He couldn't bear the two of them sweety-pie-ing around his childhood home and yet he didn't know where he would go. He said nothing. 'I told you he was a good man. He doesn't want my money, he says he has enough for both of us, and he wants me to go and live in his house in Swansea. I think a fresh start will help me too. Of course I'll take a few things of sentimental value but we can buy some little bits and pieces together.' That 'we' would take some getting used to. So the house would be sold. Neil knew he couldn't afford it, not on a teacher's salary. Not even if he were living with someone else, an employable monkey man for instance... but he had closed that door. 'Neil, you're doing it again! You didn't hear a word I said.'

'Sorry, it's a lot to take in... and I've driven a long way.'

'I said, we're going to sell you this house for one pound - if that's all right with you?'

'A pound?'

'A pound. If we just gave it to you there would be all kinds of fuss about the value of a gift in a year and then if - God forbid - we died within the next few years there would be more tax problems again. Ceri knows so much about these things.' Her pride was touching and yes, it was good to see those pink spots on his mother's cheeks. She had been making do for such a long time.

'Well couldn't I just live here - and it still belong to you? I could pay you rent?'

She shook her head, resolute. 'No, we want you to have the house, now, not wait till I'm dead.'

'What if,' he hesitated but he had to ask, 'things don't work out? This is your financial security.'

'Your generation,' she shook her head, 'no trust, no commitment. I sometimes think that's why you've not married - not willing to take the risk.' She smiled at him. 'But that's your affair. No, I've no worries that Ceri will run away with his secretary - he's retired.' She waited, then prompted, 'That's a joke, Neil.' He smiled, weakly. 'A marriage is just that for me, trust and sharing. So I'll take it that we can see a solicitor and sell the house to you?'

'A pound to buy it and two thousand for the solicitor?'

'I know but we need it done properly.'

'If you're sure that's what you want...'

'It is.'

'Then yes, I suppose so. I don't know. It's still going to be your house - you know that, don't you?'

'Thank you, cariad, but I don't need that. It's time for me to move on. No, I want you to make it yours. Move things about. You can even redecorate.' She squeezed his arm. 'We'd better go back down or Ceri will worry'

Neil braced himself to face the sherry like a man, for his mother's sake.

'I can't believe it!' Helen's exclamation while waving a newspaper drew cautious interest from Dai.

'Mmm?'

''The police have completed their investigation into the death of Jimmy Wilkinson and are satisfied that it was a tragic accident and that nobody else was involved. The pathologist's report indicated that although there was a blow to the head, the actual cause of death was drowning. If Mr Wilkinson had not rolled into the water, it is likely that he would have recovered from his fall.

This is the second death of an angler in the Gwendraeth Valley this year. Seventy-three-year-old grandfather of four Mr Iwan Stephens tripped over his landing net during the floods in March and was carried away by the swollen river. Anglers are being warned to check weather conditions carefully and organise their tackle with regard to health and safety. An Official for the Water Board, Mr Matthew James, commented that fishing without a permit is illegal and that monies raised keep local rivers healthy and stocked.' What's that got to do with anything?' Helen lowered the paper and turned her puzzled gaze on her partner.

'Not a lot but it's all useful publicity. It used to be there were more laws for moving fish than any other livestock but not since foot and mouth. You can't even cover your own cows with your own bull unless you get permission to move him from one field to another.'

'Thank you so much for that. This drowning business... you said he couldn't have moved on his own...'

'I must have been wrong.'

'So whoever moved him, murdered him.'

'Give it a rest! There was no-one - the police have closed it.'

'There's still the inquest.'

'Rubber stamping now.'

'Anyway, I didn't think you rated the police?'

'Well my mother certainly does, God knows why. She keeps saying they're wonderful.'

'Probably because they let her know your Dad's only likely to get a fine for his punch-up.'

'Retaliation under provocation, me and Dad prefer to call it.'

'I bet you do. Anyway, when did Mam get so friendly with the police?'

'Dunno.' *When she told them all about Hearts and about Stan* - Helen loved the thought of the Inland Revenue 'going in' - something which struck fear into her own heart as a self-employed businesswoman; when they gave her a cheque for three thousand, six hundred pounds, signed by the Chairman of the local Rotary Club - strange that, but Helen wasn't going to complain; when the Officer said 'Evans? Brynglas Farm? Any relation to Dafydd? Son, eh... interviewed regarding discovery of a dead person. Any relation to Will? Husband, eh, due up in front of the magistrates on an assault charge... bound to be a fine, from what he'd read of the case... quite a family'

Helen smiled, remembering her mother-in-law's shame at the questions. So this was what it was like to belong to a family 'known to the police.' She smiled at the much-loved dodgy character sprawled on the couch. 'Dunno,' she repeated.

Chapter 17

Late afternoon sunshine was shimmering on the Loughor estuary, turning sandbanks into liquid mirages, catching the green tints on the tufted head of a solitary lapwing. Neil adjusted his binoculars. 'Swans, this year's cygnets, three of them,' he murmured succinctly. He first met Helen four? five? years earlier in this very hide at the Wildfowl and Wetland Centre but there was no trace now of the awkward scanning which had marked her as a beginner.

'Where?' She was already focusing the telescope for a better view.

'Eleven o'clock. Heads bobbing up and down in one of the dips. Must be a rivulet.'

'Got them.' Neil took a closer look, identifying the adults as a Bewick pair. The three cygnets were the dirty grey plumage of adolescence, past the fluffy 'ugly duckling' stage but a way to go before they could arc white wings in classical pose.

It was pleasing to see the Centre attracting the wild swans back; easy enough to create a swannery, harder to convince the swans to come. He had found that in his work with wild otters but at least with swans there was an excellent chance of a pair returning each year and everyone knew swans mated for life.

He lost interest in the swans and sought his favourites, ignoring the u-bend of a cormorant's neck and the upended tails of mallards, until he found another large white bird, slighter and taller than a swan, with characteristic fish-stabbing beak - a little egret. When he and Helen first met, an egret had been a rare visitor and an occasion for celebration. Now they were so common that you might see as many as forty.

Neil still felt as if he were seeing an old friend each time he spotted the deliberate plod upstream and the halo of feathers disturbed by the estuary breeze. His target stopped preening and started its stilted walk into the main stream. Something wasn't right. It was too big. Neil followed it with his binoculars until he was rewarded with a profile view of an unmistakeable beak.

'Spoonbill,' he breathed, watching the large white heron supping fish from the surface with its spoon-shaped bill. 'Two o' clock.'

'Got it. I knew there'd been one around but you have to be lucky... Don't you just love the way it sieves the water like it's panning for gold.'

The solitary spoonbill stalked the marsh lagoons, formed in high tide. Beyond was the river Loughor, and, misty in the background, was the Gower village of Penclawdd, where local families still claimed rights to the rich cockle beds of the estuary. A line of cormorants fished the shore of the receding river. Neil lowered the binoculars and took in the shimmer of water and the muted colours of Penclawdd's row of cottages. It was always a source of wonder how there could be so much noise - the entertaining peal of a whistling duck, raucous laughter from the bigger birds and the bubbling call of a curlew - and yet create such a feeling of peace.

'The babies were so cute,' Helen observed as she brought two pepsis over to a table in the Centre's café.

Neil couldn't believe his ears. 'Babies? Cute? If you mean the cygnets they had reached a particularly ugly stage. You're not going broody or something are you?'

She gave him a sharp look but didn't rise to the comment. She passed him his drink and sat down heavily. 'Good to get the weight off my feet.'

Neil looked through the huge glass windows across the estuary. 'I've missed this.'

'You should have been here at dusk in the winter - five different kinds of owls. Too light now - the Centre closes before dusk.'

'Winter's always best here. More visitors on the marsh too.'

Helen agreed. 'Strange to see that one lapwing when there's usually hundreds in the winter. So what's it like to be home?'

'You know,' he ducked.

'It's going to be odd coming to your house and your Mum not being there.'

'Yes.' He gritted his teeth.

'I think you're so good about it all. I know it's great seeing her so happy and looking so young, but it means changes for you...'

He brushed it off lightly. 'I've got a life of my own.'

'You always have had. Time for a weekend in London?'

He wasn't in the mood for her teasing. 'Not for a while. I want to do some writing.'

'Poetry?'

'Perhaps. I've brought some stuff back from Alsace that I want to translate.'

'You seem a little... down. I know you've always said that side of your life wasn't important...' said with an emphasis on 'that', 'but I just wondered, if maybe Luc... I don't know if you'd found something different, special?'

'Luc?' He laughed. 'It was fun, it was all part of my year away but you move on. Who would want to be tied to one person. Speaking of different and special,' he mocked, 'how is the one and only?'

'The foot and mouth has been such a worry. We think' - Neil noted the comfortable 'we' of belonging to the Evans family - 'that the worst is over and it looks as if Carmarthenshire has escaped but we've still to wait for an all-clear. The disease is still breaking out in Powys though.'

'Will Dai be going back there?'

'No, thank God, they can cope on their own now. That's the last thing I want at the moment is him away for a month, upset and at risk of being killed by some loony demonstrator amok on a tractor. Did you see what happened to that young policeman?' Neil nodded, not because he had but because he wasn't interested. 'No chance of slaughter-houses or marts opening for a while though so the business is at a standstill.'

'I meant personally,' Neil interjected, to prevent more information about farmers and their problems. 'How are you and Dai working out?' The question had sounded friendlier in his head but she accepted it at face value.

'That's the thing - it would be great if it wasn't for the foot and mouth, and him being so busy. I've been so tired lately and all I seem to be doing is dusting, vacuuming, cleaning the bathroom and there's mould all along the window sills so that every time I spray them clean the condensations starts them off again and he just doesn't seem to see the work he leaves clothes where they land and the food has stuck to the dishes he's left when he eats at odd hours and I know he's a vet and he can't help it but if he tried to be just a bit more organised even not putting dirty clothes for washing the day after I've done a big load -'

The peace of the estuary was evaporating. 'I didn't mean the daily trivia...'

'It might seem like trivia to you but I'd just washed all the whites, had to bleach them first too - and you wouldn't believe some of the stains he gets into clothes in his job - and thought I'd finished the washing for the week when he adds this pile he'd left at work the day before -'

Neil exploded. 'For Christ's sake Helen. Do you think because I'm gay I'm interested in this stuff! That I want to listen to every detail of your cleaning rota? Why do you hang around me anyway? What are you? Some kind of fag-hag?'

Helen's mouth closed in a thin line, bright spots appeared in her cheeks and her neck flushed red. She stood up to leave and, still burning with his own frustrations, he escorted her to the car and dropped her in town where she could get a bus home. A tight-lipped 'Thank you,' as she got out of the car were the only words spoken between them.

Insensitive, trivial bitch, he told the swivel chair in his study, intellectual level of a four-year-old playing with dolls, 'cute babies'! Turning into a middle-aged whiner - fun? What would she know about fun! He deliberately selected Wagner's 'Tannhauser', letting the storm of music build up while he conducted it wildly, then he grabbed some paper and the collection of fables he had acquired in Alsace. He started to translate into English, with the idea of translating into Welsh too at some stage, while the orchestra crashed into the formalities celebrating Tannhauser's return to the sterility of his home court. Two kinds of love, and the choice between them, leading Tannhauser to exile from both. The strings shivered up the scales and he turned the music up louder; there was no-one else in the house to consider.

In olden times, he translated, *on a night when magical creatures crossed the valleys on invisible bridges, when terrified villagers stared into the freezing night at a thousand fireflies dancing amongst the rocks, when the Taenchel wept icy tears and the snow covered the last dead leaves of autumn, exposing the bare branches to the savage winds, a young hind sought shelter on the bleak mountainside.*

Exhausted and footsore, no shelter could she find in all the forest, not one tree which had kept its leaves. Unable to move one weary hoof further, she saw a carpet of moss at the foot of a fir tree, where she curled up close to the trunk, in a desperate attempt to escape the storm.

Much later, in a long white robe spangled with precious stones, her hair gleaming and her veil floating in the breeze, her magic wand in her hand, the Guardian of the Taenchel appeared. Moved by the sight of the little doe, curled at the foot of the fir, she asked 'Great tree, what took place here? Are you welcoming the homeless now?'

'I couldn't let her die of cold, my Lady, but it is hard to protect her with all of my leaves shed.'

Touched even more, the Guardian waved her wand and, in its magic spark, the fir was clothed from crown to root in green needles.

'You will keep your leaves always so that you may give shelter as and when you choose.'

The Guardian left.

In the spring she passed by again and found the fir tree bowed down, its branches weeping.

'Great tree, you seem unhappy. You are majestic, powerful and in leaf all year - what can be wrong?'

'In the spring-time all the trees leaf and I am just one among many, my Lady.'

'What do you wish?'

'Make me a different colour, more beautiful, if you would.'

With one wave of her magic wand the Guardian transformed all the green needles into sparkling gold and then she left.

Thieves came by. They could not believe their eyes when they saw the gold needles but they wasted no time ripping the tree bare and vanishing with their loot. Once more the fir was naked.

Came the summer, came the Guardian.

'What has happened? You are the only tree in the forest in such a state! At least the sun will keep you warm.'

'I was robbed. My Lady, please don't leave me like this. Dress me once more if you will, but this time in something no-one would want to steal.'

Once more the Guardian's light dressed the tree, this time in needles of sparkling glass, which caught the sun at every breath of the wind.

Came the Autumn, came the Guardian. What a disaster! The poor fir tree was trembling amidst piles of shattered glass. Spiteful gusts of wind blew off all the needles which were lying broken around the roots. Once more the tree was bare.

'My poor Tree. I can only give three wishes so this must be the last one, What do you wish?'

'My Lady, I promise to honour my standing, to protect the creatures of the forest and to live in harmony with my neighbours on God's own mountain, but I beg you, please give me back my green needles.'

From that day to this the fir trees of the Taenchel watch over the destiny of Humankind - and are evergreen.

It was only a children's tale, a storm and a year of three wishes. Neil took a wedding ring out of his pocket and spun it on the desk. He could wear it - on his right hand. He could put it on a chain and wear it round his neck. He spun it again then put it back in his pocket. Pob luc. He was facing the familiar view of occasional cars and pedestrians flashing across the greenery of Park Howard but all he could see was a flash of dark eyes and a toss of silky hair. 'Ça ne fait rien,' Luc had said, but it did matter, it mattered very much. He must phone Helen and apologise.

All the same, gays, one big chip on their shoulder, Helen generalised grumpily from a sample of one on a bad day, and felt much better. *Hormones - his, not hers!* A letter and an email were waiting for her when she arrived home and as soon as Helen saw her own handwriting, she knew it was the announcement of the bid winners for the Botanical Gardens wall-hanging. She made a cup of tea, sat down and looked at the envelope. Until she opened it, she could imagine that she had been successful. The email was from Amélie and she opened that first, hoping. In this euphoric state, she automatically logged on to check her email and double-clicked on the new arrival from Amélie, hoping .

Helen, I have good news. It is very complicated but the short version is that an artisan had to drop out of the Wool Fayre because of her mother's death. This left an opening because it is a Fayre of exactly one hundred approved artisans. The Board could only fill this place with someone who had completed all the necessary forms and met the required quality standards. It just so happened that I have been meeting with a gentleman who is on the Board, over the last month - I told you I would keep trying - and a little matter of his sister-in-law and an orchard proved to be most helpful, so that he immediately thought of us when there was a spare stall. I tried to convince him that there had been some over-enthusiasm in preserving the patriotic element of the market and that it was indeed forward-thinking to include a joint venture such as ours with your name up front but, despite us holding back on the orchard and some of Maman's excellent cuisine, I got nowhere. It was clearly beyond his powers to bend that particular set of rules and there was nothing he could do even if he agreed with me - and I believe him. He is an interesting man and I shall miss our little discussions. So my friend, I know how you will feel about the missing designer label but we know whose work will be on show and believe me, this will be the opportunity of a lifetime. Will you come out to help at the Fayre? We would love you to and it is your right to be there.

À bientôt.

Amélie

Be there as what, Helen wondered. If there were offers, or even compliments, they would all be for Amélie, while Helen collected the money and tidied the stall. *Selfish,* she shook herself, *Amélie is your partner, your friend, and this is good for business - and for your bank overdraft. Who knows what will come of it - a market tour of the south of France, a designer range for Galeries Lafayette...* a French designer range, she reminded herself, and the higher the company profile, the lower hers would be. She just wasn't meant to be lucky, so she might as well get the next kick in the teeth out of the way. She picked up the self-addressed envelope and indulged her dreams for a minute as she sat there, holding it.

She remembered every detail in the Celtic knot composed of rose petals metamorphosing into robin feathers and then again into sewin scales. In her imagination she had bought the yarns, designed and worked the fancy stitches, and now the dream was over. She looked at the envelope again, nursing her mug of tea. She delved into her purse for a coin, rejecting 5p and 10p pieces as too small, selecting a 2p piece as acceptable, and she tossed it, promising herself, 'Heads, I've won.' It was tails. Best of three, then. Tails, again.

She'd had enough and she ripped open the envelope to read a letter as confusing as any composed by the police. The words blurred as she skimmed, picking up 'delay...sorry... foot and mouth... final decision... three thousand pounds...resource budget... submit all receipts on the attached proforma... completion of work within one year from commission...'

When it finally sunk in that her submission had won the bid, that she was one of the three textile artists chosen to design a wall hanging for the National Botanical Gardens of Wales, the tears started. Somebody believed in her work, somebody trusted her with a national commission, somebody wanted her to knit for Wales. Thank you, somebody.

She looked back over the letter to put names to the 'somebody', re-reading how the bid had been selected, suddenly interested in how her work had been chosen and marvelling anew that complete strangers had pronounced her work good - better than good. And with her name on it, the English designer, a sour little voice told her. She ignored it and read the letter yet again.

She would think about her France another day. Sometimes, something went your way. Nothing could make up for the times in Helen's life when everything had gone wrong but Neil was right; you moved on. And there had been somebody who believed in her, who - as she had told Neil - drove her crazy with his scruffy habits, and who was due home.

Dai knew something was up from the slant of her head, cocked alert like the terrier's, reading his mood. It had been a long day and he hoped he wouldn't have to be tactful. He rubbed a dog's ears absent-mindedly and kissed Helen.

'Hard day?' she asked.

'The usual. You?'

'I've won it,' she announced, 'the Botanical Gardens bid.'

'I said you would.'

'Yes but I actually have. My design will be there, for everyone to see. And I get paid three thousand pounds.'

'Now that's useful. I've been talking to Dad about going organic...'

There was horror dawning in her eyes. 'You want to spend my money on manure and cabbages.'

'No,' he explained patiently, 'cows.'

'Oh,' she said sarcastically, 'cows. Well, that would be a change.'

'Not new cows.' he grinned at her. 'Once you find a cow that suits, I think you should stick with her. No, it's a matter of how we rear the cows...I want to break through this cycle where we prop up bad husbandry with pumping ever-more antibiotics into animals... I want to show how a good farmer can work with nature, work for a better future... and a bit of cash would come in useful to kick things off.'

'Never mind the cows for now. That's not the only news. 'She was still glowing with excitement. I haven't told you the best yet - 'the phone rang. 'Damn.' Helen picked up the receiver and launched straight into whoever was at the other end. 'You patronising git. If I wanted a fag, I'd find a sweety younger and prettier than you with better dress sense and an interest in make-up and housework. Just because you've had a year poncing around in France - yes, I did say poncing around - while the rest of us have been worried sick about our livelihoods and foot and mouth and not able to get out the house half the time. And I had such good news to tell you I even thought you might guess but now I'm going to tell Dai first so you can bugger off... And I was going to try out my Welsh on you but you don't deserve it... I resent that remark - I thought you were supposed to encourage people to speak foreign languages... what?... yes, I'll see you Tuesday, eleven o'clock, usual place.' She slammed the receiver down. Dai winced. 'Neil,' she explained, 'phoning to apologise.'

'Obviously. And you're going to tell me first,' he prompted.

'I've told you about the wall-hanging and I've told you about the stall in France... what makes you think there's more?' she asked suspiciously.

He grinned at her. 'Because you really ought to tell me you're pregnant.'

He reached out to hold her but she kept him at arms' length. 'You knew, didn't you? How? No, don't tell me, it's only going to include words like 'udders' and 'gestation' and I really don't want your professional view on my condition thank you very much.'

This time she allowed him to hold her and turn her around so he could gently clasp his hands across her belly. He nuzzled her neck. 'Told you we should have sorted out getting married.' He turned her to face him. 'Is it good, Helen? Is it what you want?'

She was clear-eyed as she met his gaze. 'Oh yes. And you? What do you want?'

He thought of the rose garden they planted together in memoriam, still blooming after all the damage caused by the young trespasser and from their own destructive rampage. You caused hurt and you repaired it, as best you could.

'I want to lay you down in a bed of roses,' he told her.

She sighed, suspicious. 'Which damn film is that from?'

'It's not from a film at all,' he replied, all innocent hurt at her implication that he couldn't speak for himself. One of his favourite rock stars could have testified for him that the line truly did not come from a film.

Nothing had changed. Parallel with Anne's route, the Vosges were silhouetted against the blue sky of summer and the familiar square outline of the chateau of Haut-Koenisborg was the reminder that she was near the turning off the dual carriageway through Bergheim and up the mountain, home. Everything had changed.

'The villages here are very old,' she told Alex, passive and tiny in the passenger seat. 'and those are our goldmines - the vineyards you see around you now. Can you see the bunches of grapes - small now but growing?'

Anne had forgotten just how rich her homeland was, glowing gold in the sunshine and, as they slowed on the smaller roads, fruit trees flaunted their stone-hard apples and cherries, and every building was frilly with flowers. The buildings themselves, confident in their history of burghers and old timbers, now shocked Anne with the frivolity of their deep purple, blue and pink paint-washes.

When Neil asked her what she thought of Llanelli, after a year there, she told him, 'Such friendly people, I love the river and the sea - so different from home and so many different types of countryside so close to your home but Neil - such poverty! Your Head seems so pleased about this European grant, Objective One money - but it is given because this is an area of great deprivation - in the context of all of Europe. This is terrible - and it is true, I have seen it. Can you imagine Alsace asking for such a grant?'

She was too polite to tell Neil how grey and ugly she thought the buildings were. In her first days in the area she visited a village, expecting a south Wales version of the cottages, floral displays and tourist events of Alsace. She found grey or off-white terraced and semi-detached houses in one long ribbon up a hill, with local children gathered in a bus-stop and, further up the hill, another group by a telephone box. She looked for a church, remembering how even the smallest village in Alsace had a church glowing with stained glass and steeped in the lives of local people who were celebrated by urns, photographs in ceramic frames and fresh flowers in the family plots of walled graveyards which they now inhabited. Instead, she found a bare, functional chapel and plain graves.

She called in the newsagent's but instead of advertisements for local craftsmen and events, there were badly-written offers of second-hand goods for sale. How the people who lived there kept up their spirits, she could not imagine. Her home village suffered all the problems of young people moving to the towns, and of diminishing off-season to a small group of permanent inhabitants, but it was always beautiful.

'Thannenkirch,' she told Alex, 'has two different stories about its name. Some people think that because 'Thann' means 'fir tree' in Alsacien dialect, that it is the place of fir trees, but all the oldest records are of this being Saint Anne's place. You have that in Wales too, don't you, like Saint David's - called after the Saint?'

'Llan,' Alex said reluctantly, 'like in Llanelli. 'Llan' means place and Elli was the saint so Llanelli means the place of Saint Elli. Did you know they got it wrong when they built the new shopping centre? Called it St Elli but they got Elli wrong - thought Elli was a man so they'd got the statue all wrong or whatever and when someone told them they had to make another one. Funny isn't it. Our R.E. teacher told us.'

That was the longest speech Alex ever made. Anne wondered how she had spent a year there and yet it took an uneducated thirteen-year-old to tell her such a basic fact about Llanelli. Perhaps there was more to learn than she had thought. 'Yes, it's funny. Perhaps that makes Elli everyone's saint, men and women?'

'Men don't need saints.'

'Why not?'

'They just don't.'

So many closed subjects and Anne had no idea whether she should bulldoze every opening and rip apart the surface or whether to leave the wounds to heal. Who knew what poison was being sealed into that young mind?

'Saint Anne is my name saint, which means I celebrate the day of Saint Anne as sort of a birthday. Saint's days are our special days.'

'When is it?'

'July the twenty-sixth.'

'Tomorrow!'

'Yes. Perhaps we'll have a little party.'

'Will I have a saint's day?'

'We will have to see if there is a day for Saint Alex...'

'So I might not have one.'

'But you do have a special saint, don't you...' Anne could sense the stiffening of the body beside her. This was personal territory. She persevered. 'San Fairy Anne, it's the same for you as for me and Thannenkirch. We can share our saint.' She carried on, treading lightly. 'Kirch means 'church' so the theory is that St Anne slid together over time to become 'Thanne' and joined up with 'kirch'. You will find our language in Alsace mixes the French and the German. All those French lessons will come in handy.'

There was no response to her attempt at teasing. Alex returned to silently staring out of the window. In truth, Alex's lack of French seemed to be the least of her - or Anne's - problems.

As Anne rounded the bend to see the wooden sign of St Anne that heralded the village, she forgot Alex for a moment of what she had learnt was called 'hiraeth'. She forgot the weariness of the journey and she could not wait to throw open her bedroom windows, to breathe in the forests and to sleep in the float of bells and the hoot of owls, not a car in earshot.

Her mother was sitting at the front of the house, on the wooden bench amongst the flowers, waiting as peacefully as if she had waited all year, since her second daughter had left her - or fifty-seven years, since she had parted with her first child. She turned towards them as Anne approached her with Alex in tow but didn't stand until the first touch of Anne's hand, helping her to stand without seeming to support her, as mother and daughter embraced.

Anne moved to let her mother see the waif whom she had spirited across the channel, sprung from the prison of police formalities, of social service paperwork, of that house in which she grew up. She had not known how to prepare Alex for this moment so she hadn't tried. She had not even known how to prepare herself and she couldn't begin to imagine her mother's thoughts. She had at least tried to prepare her mother for the sullen reality of this disturbed adolescent.

Disbelieving, Anne watched the deep shadows chased across Alex's face like clouds across the mountain, her blue eyes sparkling and her face glowing for the first time with the beauty of the woman she could become. She was staring at Anne's mother with a look of dawning, hopeful recognition. 'San Fairy Anne,' she gulped and let herself be folded into the arms of the old woman who reached to her.

'Ça ne fait rien,' agreed Anne's mother, unable to say more as she held the child. Anne looked away.

'Anne,' her mother insisted on her inclusion, 'it is what Vernon always said. It is a miracle.'

Understanding nothing of the quick French, Alex remained in the circle of her great-grandmother's arms. It was not for Anne to untangle the chain of chance remarks which echoed from past to present. 'Yes,' she said simply, 'it is a miracle.' And like most miracles, it was going to require a lot of love, a lot of work and a lot of readjustments.

'Let her go,' Anne's mother told her, 'she will be safe in the forest.' Anne opened her mouth to protest but her mother added, 'We always were and it is her turn. Besides, it is you I need to talk to. I have missed you, my dear.'

'The forest will have an easier job if I give a few practical instructions.' Anne made sure that Alex would be able to find her way back and then let her go. Would she have been able to stop the girl going if they disagreed? Alex had been so passive until now that Anne had not considered the possibility of disagreement. She sighed.

'I know,' her mother observed, 'it has been so hard for you and now it is going to be hard for both of us. But it will be worth it.' She put her hand under Anne's chin and tilted it up. 'I am so very proud of you. Now, tell me everything about Neil's life. Do they really have no woodpiles and no cuisine?'

Anne smiled. This was going to take some time.

Alex was in The Place. She went off the path, climbing all the time, and was sitting at the base of the tallest tree she had ever seen in her life, which was shaped like an umbrella with its huge bare trunk and crown of some kind of needles at the top. The sun was making her drowsy and if she wanted to, she could shut her eyes and sleep.

She shut her eyes and she could feel a whisper of warm breeze stirring the leaves, promising her she would be safe. She opened her eyes again but it had not vanished. She had summoned these trees to grow and here they were, living, beyond her control now.

She had made all these paths to take her to the heart of The Place and here they were, neatly marked with symbols on trees so she could do as Anne had told her and find her way back to... Thannenkirch. The Place was not just in her head; it was out here, even when her eyes were open. That meant that there was one world and only one Alex. The other world, the one which had hurt the other Alex, had been taken over by The Place.

Always, at the heart of The Place, had been the San Fairy Anne. As soon as Alex saw the old lady on the bench, looking a bit like her grandmother, looking at her with so much love and concern, she had known. Of course it was a bit strange that her teacher had brought her here but then that was how magic worked, wasn't it? There was always a way that it looked possible, to the people who didn't believe in it, who wanted some practical scientific explanation, like your teacher really being your auntie and not a fairy godmother or whatever.

Alex lay on her back, squinting in the direction away from the sun, at treetops and mountains behind them in the distance. She could feel the tiniest tickle on her ankle progressing to her knee, then changing direction, crossing the vast landscape of her other knee and down to vanish into the grass. Another ant crossed the wrist on which she was resting her head and she lay still, listening to the grass part for its small residents. There was a quick knocking on wood and a flash of a spotted bird. Water bubbled, quick and shallow, somewhere nearby.

The last time she had heard the water sounds had been the day she saw the otter, the day that other Alex had let San Fairy Anne kill that man, the one who'd taken over her father's body, possessed him like in the films. He shouldn't have said those dirty things, not by the river where the magic was so strong.

Alex had jerked away from him, slipping past him, hearing him fall behind her. She had known it was San Fairy Anne, pushing him, and she had not turned to look. It was too late to save her real father, he had been taken over completely by that man and was beyond rescue. She had found somewhere to sit, to shut her eyes and escape into The Place, but she could still hear noises outside and a man swearing.

It must have been that man as he fought the San Fairy Anne but his voice sounded different and there had been thumpings and a splash and footsteps thudding away as if her father's ghost had run off. She was protected so no ghost could have found her but still she'd felt The Place shaking with the effort of hiding her.

She heard a voice telling her to stay still and she had not moved, not even opened her eyes until the other man, the vet, asked her what was the matter. She knew that man would be dead, she hadn't needed to look. She knew it would be finished this time and that San Fairy Anne had killed for her. It was her fault that her father had died along with the thing that had taken him over. Perhaps the thing had been taking over the other Alex too, those times she didn't like to think about.

A sharp yap, coming from a spaniel, alerted her to the walkers on the path but they didn't look up as they carried on walking, and Alex relaxed. It was strange to share The Place with people but she knew she was safe now. All she had to do was to follow the cream sandwich - a white bar between two red ones - marked on the trees and they would lead her to the heart of The Place, where - as always - she would find San Fairy Anne, whom she now must call Mamie. She would go... home... in a bit.

She closed her eyes. This time it was not a tickle so much as the tiniest weight imaginable, on her stomach. She peeped through one eye and was rewarded by a glimpse of a small butterfly, brown like a leaf and then dazzling blue each time it opened its wings. Her red Tshirt turned her into a flower and she shut her eyes again, opening her petals to the sun, breathing gently so as not to disturb the butterfly, breathing so gently that she fell deeply and blissfully asleep.

If you liked my book, please help other readers find it by writing a review

Thank you.

For news, offers and a FREE ebook of 'One Sixth of a Gill', please visit www.jeangill.com and sign up for my newsletter. This collection of shorts was a finalist in the Wishing Shelf and SpASpa Awards

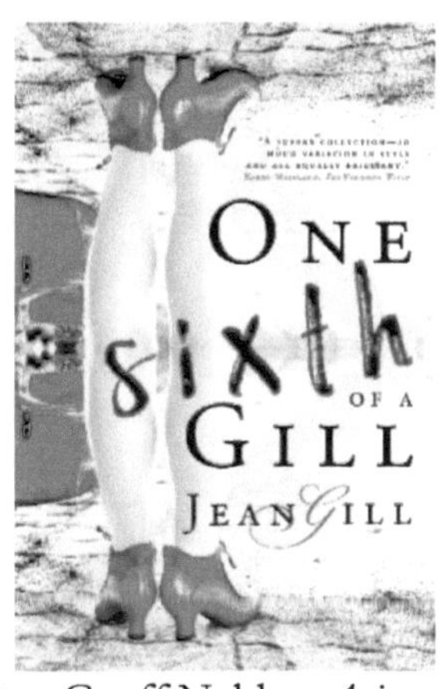

A book with 'Wow' factor - Geoff Nelder, *Aria*
A fantastic array of wonderful prose, from bee-keeping to Top Tips on Dogs! A FINALIST and highly recommended - The Wishing Shelf Awards

Five-minute reads. Meet people you will never forget: the night photographer, the gynaecologist's wife, the rescue dog. Dip into whatever suits your mood, from comedy to murders; from fantastic stories to blog posts, by way of love poetry.

Fully illustrated by the author; Jean Gill's original photographs are as thought-provoking as her writing. An out of body experience for adventurous readers. Or, of course, you can 'Live Safe'.

Not for you
the blind alley on a dark night,
wolf-lope pacing you step for step
as shadows flare on the walls.

About the Author

I'm a Welsh writer and photographer living in the south of France with a big white dog, a scruffy black dog, a Nikon D750 and a man. I taught English in Wales for many years and my claim to fame is that I was the first woman to be a secondary headteacher in Carmarthenshire. I'm mother or stepmother to five children so life has been pretty hectic.

I've published all kinds of books, both with conventional publishers and self-published. You'll find everything under my name from prize-winning poetry and novels, military history, translated books on dog training, to a cookery book on goat cheese. My work with top dog-trainer Michel Hasbrouck has taken me deep into the world of dogs with problems, and inspired one of my novels. With Scottish parents, an English birthplace and French residence, I can usually support the winning team on most sporting occasions.

MORE BOOKS BY JEAN GILL

Recommendations, if you would like to read another book by Jean Gill:

If you want to read more about my life in France, try *How Blue is my Valley*. Humorous travel/autobiography about my first year living in Provence and how it compared with Wales. Amazon uk No1 bestseller in 2013.

'Laugh out loud in many places... such a vivid picture of fields of lavender, sunflowers and olive trees that you could almost be there with her.' **Living France Magazine**

The true scents of Provence?

Lavender, thyme and septic tank.

How can you resist a village called Dieulefit, `God created it', the village 'where everyone belongs'. Discover the real Provence in good company.

If you are a dog-lover, try *Someone to Look Up To.* Based on true stories. It's a dog's life in the south of France. From puppyhood, Sirius the Pyrenean Mountain Dog has been trying to understand his humans and train them with kindness...

How this led to divorce he has no idea. More misunderstandings take Sirius to Death Row in an animal shelter, as a so-called dangerous dog learning survival tricks from the other inmates. During the twilight barking, he is shocked to hear his brother's voice but the bitter-sweet reunion is short-lived. Doggedly, Sirius keeps the faith.

One day, his human will come.

If you like biographies and true war stories, try *Faithful through Hard Times.*

'A most unusual military history book. There are few military non-combatant accounts of life in the Second World War, fewer still from an Other Rank. Based on words and feelings recorded at the time it is probably unique.' - Don Marshall, Military History Enthusiast

This is not a WW2 memoir. It is a riveting reconstruction from an eye-witness account written at the time in a secret diary, a diary too dangerous to show anyone and too precious to destroy.

The true story of four years, 3 million bombs, one small island out-facing the might of the German and Italian airforces - and one young Scotsman who didn't want to be there.

If you like Young Adult that works for adults too; if you're left-handed or know a leftie, try *On the Other Hand*

A mix of gripping story with fascinating facts on left-handedness. Everyone should think left-handed - or so fourteen-year-old Jamie thought when she tied her hand behind her back for a day-long protest in school, against persecution of left-handers over the centuries. Her best friend Ryan publicised their cause with a new series of articles in the school magazine but just when their campaign is going well, Ryan's Mum drags him off from Wales to live in America. There he faces bullying at its most deadly and Jamie has to live from one email to the next to know whether her friend is coping. Teachers' Resource materials available free from jeangill.com

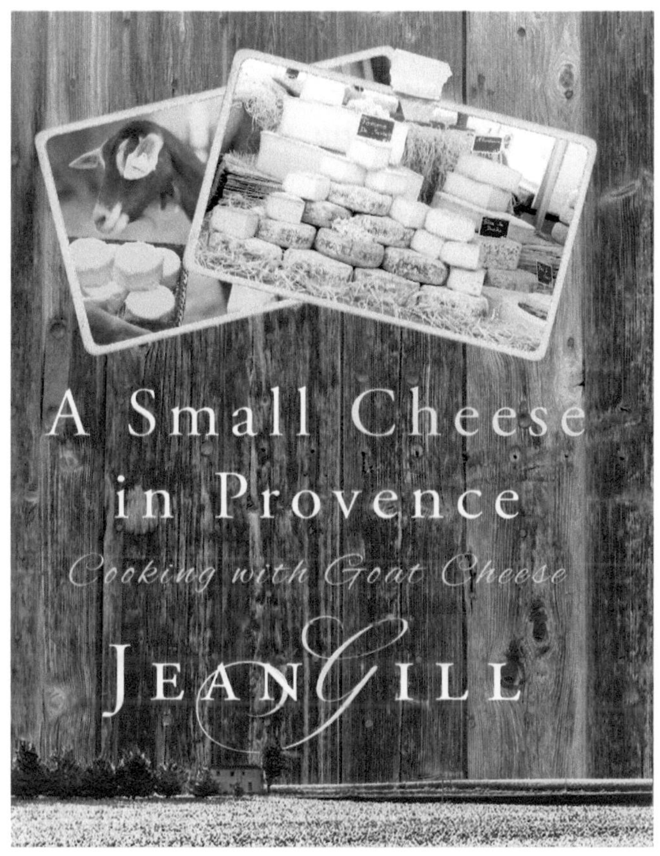

If you like food and France, try *A Small Cheese in Provence*

Provençal food for the brain as well as the table. Cheese information, recipes, stories and quotations in French, Occitan and English, with beautiful full colour photographs throughout. A must for cheese-loving Francophiles, who will discover the Picodon 'a small cheese in Provence' that even travelled into space on an Apollo mission.

The Troubadours Quartet

Winner of The Global Ebook Award for Best Historical Fiction

Book 1 'Song at Dawn'

1150: Provence

On the run from abuse, Estela wakes in a ditch with only her lute, her amazing voice, and a dagger hidden in her underskirt. Her talent finds a patron in Aliénor of Aquitaine and more than a music tutor in the Queen's finest troubadour and Commander of the Guard, Dragonetz los Pros.

Weary of war, Dragonetz uses Jewish money and Moorish expertise to build that most modern of inventions, a papermill, arousing the wrath of the Church. Their enemies gather, ready to light the political and religious powder-keg of medieval Narbonne.

Set in the period following the Second Crusade, Jean Gill's spellbinding romantic thrillers evoke medieval France with breathtaking accuracy. The characters leap off the page and include amazing women like Eleanor of Aquitaine and Ermengarda of Narbonne, who shaped history in battles and in bedchambers.

Chapter 1

She woke with a throbbing headache, cramp in her legs and a curious sensation of warmth along her back. The warmth moved against her as she stretched her stiff limbs along the constraints of the ditch. She took her time before opening her eyes, heavy with too little sleep. The sun was already two hours high in the sky and she was waking to painful proof that her choice of sleeping quarters had been forced.

'I am still alive. I am here. I am no-one,' she whispered. She remembered that she had a plan but the girl who made that plan was dead. Had to be dead and stay dead. So who was she now? She needed a name.

A groan beside her attracted her attention. The strange warmth along her back, with accompanying thick white fur and the smell of damp wool, was easily identified. The girl pushed against a solid mass of giant dog, which shifted enough to let her get herself out of the ditch, where they had curved together into the sides. She recognized him well enough even though she had no idea when he had joined her in the dirt. A regular scrounger at table with the other curs, all named 'Out of my way' or worse. You couldn't mistake this one though, one of the mountain dogs bred to guard the sheep, his own coat shaggy white with brindled parts on his back and ears. Only he wouldn't stay with the flock, whatever anyone tried with him. He'd visit the fields happily enough but at the first opportunity he'd be back at the chateau. Perhaps he thought she was heading out to check on the sheep and that he'd tag along to see what he was missing.

'Useless dog,' she gave a feeble kick in his general direction. 'Can't even do one simple job. They say you're too fond of people to stay in the field with the sheep. Well, I've got news for you about people, you big stupid bastard of a useless dog. Nobody wants you.' She felt tears pricking and smeared them across her cheeks with an impatient, muddy hand. 'And if you've broken this, you'll really feel my boot.' She knelt on the edge of the ditch to retrieve an object completely hidden in a swathe of brocade.

She had counted on having the night to get away but by now there would be a search on. If Gilles had done a good job, they would find her bloody remnants well before there was any risk of them finding her living, angry self. If he had hidden the clues too well, they might keep searching until they really did find her. And if the false trail was found but too obvious, then there would be no let-up, ever. And she would never see Gilles again. She shivered, although the day was already promising the spring warmth typical of the south. She would never see Gilles again anyway, she told herself. He knew the risks as well as she did. And if it had to be done, then she was her mother's daughter and would never - 'Never!' she said aloud - forget that, whoever tried to make her. She was no longer a child but sixteen summers.

All around her, the sun was casting long shadows on the bare vineyards, buds showing on the pruned vine-stumps but no leaves yet. Like rows of wizened cats tortured on wires, the gnarled stumps bided their time. How morbid she had become these last months! Too long a winter and spent in company who considered torture-methods an amusing topic of conversation. Better to look forward. In a matter of weeks, the vines would start to green, and in another two months, the spectacular summer growth would shoot upwards and outwards but for now, all was still wintry grey.

There was no shelter in the April vineyards and the road stretched forward to Narbonne and back towards Carcassonne, pitted with the holes gouged by the severe winter of 1149. Along this road east-west, and the Via Domitia north-south, flowed the life-blood of the region, the trade and treaties, the marriage-parties and the armies, the hired escorts sent by the Viscomtesse de Narbonne and the murderers they were protection against. The girl knew all this and could list fifty fates worse than death, which were not only possible but a likely outcome of a night in a ditch. What she had forgotten was that as soon as she stood up in this open landscape, in daylight, she could see for miles - and be seen.

She looked back towards Carcassonne and chewed her lip. It was already too late. The most important reason why she should not have slept in a ditch beside the road came back to her along with the growing clatter of a large party of horse and, from the sound of it, wagons. The waking and walking was likely to be even more dangerous than the sleeping and it was upon her already.

The girl stood up straight, brushed down her muddy skirts and clutched her brocade parcel to her breast. She knew that following her instinct to run would serve for nothing against the wild mercenaries or, at best, suspicious merchants, who were surely heading towards her. She was lucky to have passed a tranquil night - or so the night now seemed compared with the bleak prospect in front of her. What a fool to rush from one danger straight into another, forgetting the basic rules of survival on the open road. To run now would make her prey so she searched desperately for another option. In her common habit, bedraggled and dirty, she was as invisible as she could hope to be. No thief would look twice at her, nor think she had a purse to cut, far less a ransom waiting at home. No reason to bother her.

What she could not disguise was that, common or not, she was young, female and alone, and the consequences of that had been beaten into her when she was five years old and followed a cat into the forest. Not, of course, that anything bad happened in the forest, where she had lost sight of the cat but instead seen a rabbit's white scut vanishing behind a tree, as she tried to tell her father when he found her. His hard hand cut off her words, to teach her obedience for her own good, punctuated with a graphic description of the horrors she had escaped.

All that had not happened in the dappled light and crackling twigs beneath the canopy of leaves and green needles, visited her nightmares instead, with gashed faces and shuddering laughter as she ran and hid, always discovered. Until now, she *had* obeyed, and it had not been for her own good. Fool that she had been. But no more. Now she would run and hide, and not be discovered.

She drew herself up straight and tall. No, bad idea. Instead, she slumped, as ordinary as she could make herself, and felt through the slit in her dress, just below her right hip, for her other option should a quick tongue fail her. The handle fitted snugly into her hand and her fingers closed round it, reassured. The dagger was safe in its sheath, neatly attached to her under-shift with the calico ties she had laboriously sewn into the fabric in secret candle-light. She had full confidence in its blade, knowing well the meticulous care her brother gave his weapons. As to her capacity to use it, let the occasion be judge. And after that, God would be, one way or another.

By now, the oncoming chink of harness and thud of hooves was so loud that she could hardly hear the low growl beside her. The dog was on his feet, facing the danger. He threw back his head and gave the deep bark of his kind against the wolf. The girl crossed herself and the first horse came into sight.

Dragonetz considered their progress. They had been seven days on the road since Poitiers, and many had objected to the undignified haste. Such a procession of litters, wagons and horse inevitably travelled slowly but they had kept overnight stops as simple as possible, resting at the Abbey and with loyal vassals, strengthening the ties. Apart from Toulouse of course, where Aliénor had insisted on a 'courtesy visit', her smile as polite as a dog baring its teeth. It had taken all his diplomacy to talk her out of instructing her herald to announce 'Comtesse de Toulouse' among her many titles and she had found a thousand other ways to throw her embroidered glove in the young Comte's face.

It was no easy matter to be in the service of Aliénor, Queen of France, but he would say this for her; it was never dull. The Lord be thanked that she had decided to insult Toulouse by the brevity of her stay or he could not answer for the casualties that would have ensued. Two more days of travel should see them in Narbonne and safe with Ermengarda and then he could relax his guard to the usual twenty-four hour check on every movement near Aliénor.

He was aware of the bustle behind him, wheels stopping, voices raised, and he slowed his horse almost to a standstill, anticipating the imperious voice beside him. Aliénor had tired of the litter and, mounted on her favourite palfrey, reined in beside him. He inclined his head. 'My Lady.' Queen of France she might be but like all born in Aquitaine, he had sworn fealty to Aquitaine and its Duchesse, and France came second.

'Amuse me,' Aliénor instructed her companion, her pearl ear-rings spinning. The Queen's idea of dressing down for travelling might have included one less bracelet, a touch less rouge on her exquisitely painted face, and a switch of jeweled circlet, but there was little other compromise. The fur edging her dress could have been traded for a mercenary army. And that was exactly as it should be, she would have told him, had he questioned the wisdom of flaunting her status on the open road. She might have been spoiled as a child but she had been taught that a Lord of Aquitaine commanded respect as much through display and largesse as through a mailed fist, and she had learned the lesson well. In Aquitaine, she was adored. France, however, was a different country and they did things differently there.

'Once,' he began, 'there was a beautiful lady with red-gold hair, riding a white palfrey between Carcassonne and Narbonne, unaware of the danger lurking on the road ahead…'

She laughed. The pearls on her circlet gleamed and the matching ear-rings danced. Some red-gold hair escaped its net and coils under her veil. Everything about Aliénor was impatient for action. 'We have travelled more dangerous roads than this, my friend.' She was referring to their trek two years earlier, when they took the cross and the road to Damascus, the road paved with good intentions and finishing as surely in hell as anything either of them had ever known. A Crusade started in all enthusiasm and finished in shame. Each of them had good reason to bury what they had shared and he said nothing.

She rallied. 'Wouldn't you love to deal with monsters, dragons and ogres instead of Toulouse and his wet-nurses?' Her smile clouded over again. 'Or the Frankish vultures, flapping their Christian piety over me. Do you know how Paris seems to me? Black, white and grey, the northern skies, the drab clothes, the drab minds. All the colour is being leeched out of my life, month by month and I cannot continue like this.'

'You must, my Lady. It is your birthright and your birth curse. You know this.'

'I cannot exercise my birthright when I am relegated to embroidery and garden design. It is insufferable.'

'Power does not always shout its presence, my Lady, and each of the two hundred armed men behind you on this road represent a thousand more ready to die at your command. Every word you speak has the weight of those men.'

'Tell that to my husband, the Monk!' was the bitter reply. Her companion knew better than to reply to treason, especially when it came from a wife's mouth. 'Oh to be free of Sackcloth and Ashes, to hear a lute without seeing a pursed mouth or hearing that bony friar Clairvaux invoke God's punishment on the ways of Satan.'

'Clairvaux,' her companion mused, 'Bernard of Clairvaux, now what was that story about him? No, I mustn't say, not to a lady.'

'But you must, my wicked friend, that's exactly what I need, gossip. The more scurrilous the better.'

'Scurrilous gossip? About the saintly Clairvaux? How could that be possible? Anyway it's an old tale so you'll have heard it before,' he teased.

'I want to hear it again,' she ordered.

'As my Lady commands. But don't blame me if you have nightmares.'

'I already have nightmares. And Clairvaux is the least of it, curse his skinny, goose-pimpled arse.'

'You've stolen the best of my tale, my Lady, for it does indeed concern his skinny, goose-pimpled arse.'

'Tell anyway.'

'Once -'

She cut him off. 'No troubadour tricks. No romancing the rogue. He doesn't deserve it.'

'So then, even Bernard was once a young man and his body was supple, muscled, toned, bronzed and -'

'For shame!'

'You prefer I leave out some of the detail of a young man's body? I've only just started.'

'The only toned bit of that man's body is his knees, for he is always on them, and it was ever so, whatever age he was. No, I shall have no description of him as a beautiful young man. Next part of the story, if you will.'

'I have to mention one part of the young man's anatomy, my Lady, for therein lies the story and the problem, from Bernard's point of view. He had stopped at an Inn and was served by a beautiful young serving girl, skin transparent as lace, hair golden as -'

'Yes, yes, a pretty girl. On!'

'- and poor Bernard found that part of his anatomy preferred to follow its own will rather than God's. Horrified at this inappropriate rectitude in the only situation where he would rather have been less rigid, he raced out the Inn as one possessed by a Demon, tore off his clothes and jumped into the freezing water of the village fountain, extinguishing all rebellious behaviour from his shivering, goose-pimpled body. And so ended the one and only moment when Bernard of Clairvaux wondered what a warm body would be like against his own. From then on, his body was ruled by icy regime.'

'It's not true.' Aliénor was rueful. 'He never took his clothes off.'

'My Lady, how can you doubt my word?'

'Your word as my Knight or your word as a troubadour, teller of outrageous tales?'

'The latter, my Lady,' he concurred sighing. 'But don't you think it makes a satisfying portrait - the shivering, naked monk in the fountain?'

'To the life,' she agreed. 'But I am no Bernard of Clairvaux and there are times, I too wonder what it would be like to hold a warm body against my own.' If this were an invitation, he gave no sign of taking it as such and she returned to the more entertaining subject. 'And did you hear the other one, how he ran into the street shouting that someone was trying to rob him -'

'- and it was some sinner after his virginity!'

'Must have been a blind, desperate sinner!' Aliénor called over her shoulder to the four Ladies-in-waiting keeping a discreet distance. 'Ladies, come join us. We are engaged in character destruction and the more the merrier.' As the other horses were jostled near enough to take turn-about beside the Queen, her companion's attention shifted to the road ahead, where a slight movement stabilized into an unmistakably human figure.

'Sire?' the alert came from one of his men up front.

No longer teasing, he ordered, 'My lady, you must fall back with your women. Keep to the middle. No-one sane walks this road alone and there is likely a trap ahead.' He had already moved ahead, throwing orders behind him as he caught up with his hand-picked vanguard. He glanced over his shoulder, satisfied that Aliénor was already invisible in the middle of a thick shield of armoured men.

Swords out, reins tight in one hand, they advanced on the lone figure standing at the roadside, which seemed to get smaller as they grew nearer.

'It's a woman, Sire!' his man exclaimed.

'Be on guard, Danton, a woman can have a band of cut-throats on hand as easily as a man,' but there was as much chance of hiding men in the open vineyards around them as behind a molehill. He sheathed his sword, and a signal passed back along the line in a wave of relief.

The Commander reined in beside a girl who stood stock-still, a great hound at her side, growling menaces. The entire procession ground to a halt behind its leader and Danton jumped out the saddle, sword unsheathed, eyes on the dog.

'No!' came instinctively from the girl, who stepped forward, interposing a reckless arm between Danton's approaching sword and the growling dog. Her other arm clutched some sort of large bundle close to her chest.

'No,' agreed the Commander, looking fixedly at the girl. 'Danton, I think the whelp would benefit from some space while we decide whether to slit its throat or not.' Danton backed off but kept his sword ready. It was obvious to all there that his leader was not only referring to the dog. 'You see,' he said gently, 'we can't be sure that you won't run across the fields, then get ahead of us and prepare your bandit-friends to slit our throats and steal our valuables. And that just wouldn't do.'

The girl looked at him, astonished. 'But I'm on my own!' Topaz eyes, like those of the hunting leopards in Alexandria, green shadows and muddy depths, sparks where there should have been fear. Topaz eyes and black hair, silky as the tents of the Moorish armies. Olive skin like a slave girl but smooth, unpitted, ripe. Her clothes spoke of the servant but the fire in her eyes did not.

Even more gently, he told her, 'We just can't take the risk. And so that gives us two choices.

www.ingramcontent.com/pod-product-compliance
Ingram Content Group UK Ltd.
Pitfield, Milton Keynes, MK11 3LW, UK
UKHW042004190726
13854UKWH00005B/2155

9 791096 459001